MERRY CHRISTMAS, Baby!

MAUREEN CHILD ANNIE O'NEIL CATHY McDAVID

MILLS & BOON

MERRY CHRISTMAS, BABY! © 2024 by Harlequin Books S.A.

MAID UNDER THE MISTLETOE
© 2016 by Maureen Child   First Published 2016
Australian Copyright 2016   Third Australian Paperback Edition 2024
New Zealand Copyright 2016   ISBN 978 1 038 93927 2

Annie O'Neil is acknowledged as the author of this work
CHRISTMAS WITH THE SINGLE DAD DOC
© 2022 by Harlequin Enterprises ULC   First Published 2022
Australian Copyright 2022   Second Australian Paperback Edition 2024
New Zealand Copyright 2022   ISBN 978 1 038 93927 2

A SECRET CHRISTMAS WISH
© 2021 by Cathy McDavid   First Published 2021
Australian Copyright 2021   Second Australian Paperback Edition 2024
New Zealand Copyright 2021   ISBN 978 1 038 93927 2

Published by
Mills & Boon
An imprint of Harlequin Enterprises (Australia) Pty Limited
(ABN 47 001 180 918), a subsidiary of HarperCollins
Publishers Australia Pty Limited (ABN 36 009 913 517)
Level 19, 201 Elizabeth Street
SYDNEY NSW 2000
AUSTRALIA

MIX
Paper | Supporting
responsible forestry
FSC
www.fsc.org   FSC® C001695

® and ™ (apart from those relating to FSC®) are trademarks of Harlequin Enterprises (Australia) Pty Limited or its corporate affiliates. Trademarks indicated with ® are registered in Australia, New Zealand and in other countries. Contact admin_legal@Harlequin.ca for details.

Printed and bound in Australia by McPherson's Printing Group

CONTENTS

Maid Under The Mistletoe

Maureen Child

Maureen Child writes for the Harlequin Desire line and can't imagine a better job. A seven-time finalist for a prestigious Romance Writers of America RITA® Award, Maureen is an author of more than one hundred romance novels. Her books regularly appear on bestseller lists and have won several awards, including a Prism Award, a National Readers' Choice Award, a Colorado Romance Writers Award of Excellence and a Golden Quill Award. She is a native Californian but has recently moved to the mountains of Utah.

Books by Maureen Child

The Fiancée Caper
After Hours with Her Ex
Triple the Fun
Double the Trouble
The Baby Inheritance
Maid Under the Mistletoe

Pregnant by the Boss

Having Her Boss's Baby
A Baby for the Boss
Snowbound with the Boss

Visit her Author Profile page at
millsandboon.com.au,
or maureenchild.com, for more titles.

Dear Reader,

I love Christmas books—reading them *and* writing them. This time of year, I buy every holiday-themed book I can and treat myself to a romance marathon. So when the idea for *Maid Under the Mistletoe* popped into my head, I couldn't have been more pleased.

Sam Henry is a world-famous painter whose world crashed down around him a few years ago. In response to the tragedy, he's turned his back on what he loves most—his work and his family.

Joy Curran is a woman who always sees the bright side of any given situation. She's the mother of Holly, a precocious five-year-old girl who, like her mother, naturally assumes that everyone loves Christmas as much as they do.

When these three people come together, it's an eye-opener for Sam and a lesson in patience for Joy.

I really do love this book and had so much fun writing it. I hope you love it, too—and in this holiday season, I wish you much joy, whichever holiday you're celebrating!

Happy reading!

Maureen Child

To all the moms who are out there
right now, making magic

CHAPTER ONE

SAM HENRY HATED DECEMBER.

The days were too short, making the nights seem an eternity. It was cold and dark—and then there was the incessant Christmas badgering. Lights, trees, carols and an ever-increasing barrage of commercials urging you to shop, spend, buy. And every reminder of the holiday season ate at the edges of his soul and heart like drops of acid.

He scowled at the roaring fire in the hearth, slapped one hand on the mantel and rubbed his fingers over the polished edge of the wood. With his gaze locked on the flames, he told himself that if he could, he'd wipe the month of December from the calendar.

"You can't stick your head in the snow and pretend Christmas isn't happening."

Sam flicked a glance at the woman in the open doorway. His housekeeper/cook/nag, Kaye Porter, stood there glaring at him through narrowed blue eyes. Hands at her wide hips, her gray-streaked black hair pulled back into a single thick braid that hung down over one shoulder, she shook her head. "There's not enough snow to do it anyway, and whether you like it or not, Christmas is coming."

"I don't and it's only coming if I acknowledge it," Sam told her.

"Well, you're going to have to pay attention because I'm out of here tomorrow."

"I'll give you a raise if you cancel your trip," he said, willing to bargain to avoid the hassle of losing the woman who ran his house so he didn't have to.

A short bark of laughter shot from her throat. "Not a chance. My friend Ruthie and I do this every year, as you well know. We've got our rooms booked and there's no way we're canceling."

He'd known that—he just hadn't wanted to think about it. Another reason to hate December. Every year, Kaye and Ruthie took a month-long vacation. A cruise to the Bahamas, then a stay at a splashy beachside hotel, followed by another cruise home. Kaye liked to say it was her therapy to get her through the rest of the year living with a crank like himself.

"If you love Christmas so much, why do you run to a beach every year?"

She sighed heavily. "Christmas is everywhere, you know. Even in hot, sandy places! We buy little trees, decorate them for our rooms. And the hotel lights up all the palm trees..." She sighed again, but this time, it was with delight. "It's gorgeous."

"Fine." He pushed away from the hearth, tucked both hands into the pockets of his jeans and stared at her. Every year he tried to talk her out of leaving and every year he lost. Surrendering to the inevitable, he asked, "You need a ride to the airport?"

A small smile curved her mouth at the offer. "No, but thanks. Ruthie's going to pick me up at the crack of dawn tomorrow. She'll leave her car there so when we come back we don't have to worry about taking one of those damn shuttles."

"Okay then." He took a breath and muttered, "Have a great time."

"The enthusiasm in that suggestion is just one of the reasons I need this trip." One dark eyebrow lifted. "You worry me, Sam. All locked away on this mountain hardly talking to anyone but me—"

She kept going, but Sam tuned out. He'd heard it all before. Kaye was determined to see him "start living" again. Didn't seem to matter that he had no interest in that. While she talked, he glanced around the main room of what Kaye liked to call his personal prison.

It was a log home, the wood the color of warm honey, with lots of glass to spotlight the view that was breathtaking from every room. Pine forest surrounded the house, and a wide, private lake stretched out beyond a narrow slice of beach. He had a huge garage and several outbuildings, including a custom-designed workshop where Sam wished he was right at that moment.

This house, this *sanctuary*, was just what he'd been looking for when he'd come to Idaho five years ago. It was isolated, with a small town—Franklin—just fifteen minutes away when he needed supplies. A big city, with the airport and all manner of other distractions, was just an hour from there, not that he ever went. What he needed, he had Kaye pick up in Franklin and only rarely went to town himself.

The whole point of moving here had been to find quiet. Peace. *Solitude*. Hell, he could go weeks and never talk to anyone but Kaye. Thoughts of her brought him back to the conversation at hand.

"...Anyway," she was saying, "my friend Joy will be here about ten tomorrow morning to fill in for me while I'm gone."

He nodded. At least Kaye had done what she always did, arranged for one of her friends to come and stay for the month she'd be gone. Sam wouldn't have to worry about cooking, cleaning or pretty much anything but keeping his distance from whatever busybody she'd found this year.

He folded his arms over his chest. "I'm not going to catch this one rifling through my desk, right?"

Kaye winced. "I will admit that having Betty come last year was a bad idea…"

"Yeah," he agreed. She'd seemed nice enough, but the woman had poked her head into everything she could find. Within a week, Sam had sent her home and had spent the following three weeks eating grilled cheese sandwiches, canned soup and frozen pizza. "I'd say so."

"She's the curious sort."

"She's nosy."

"Yes, well." Kaye cleared her throat. "That was my mistake, I know. But my friend Joy isn't a snoop. I think you'll like her."

"Not necessary," he assured her. He didn't want to like Joy. Hell, he didn't want to *talk* to her if he could avoid it.

"Of course not." Kaye shook her head again and gave him the kind of look teachers used to reserve for the kid acting up in class. "Wouldn't want to be human or anything. Might set a nasty precedent."

"Kaye…"

The woman had worked for him since he'd moved to Idaho five years ago. And since then, she'd muscled her way much deeper into his life than he'd planned on allowing. Not only did she take care of the house, but she looked after *him* despite the fact that he didn't want her to. But Kaye was a force of nature, and it seemed her friends were a lot like her.

"Never mind. Anyway, to what I was saying, Joy already knows that you're cranky and want to be left alone—"

He frowned at her. "Thanks."

"Am I wrong?" When he didn't answer, she nodded. "She's a good cook and runs her own business on the internet."

"You told me all of this already," he pointed out. Though she hadn't said what *kind* of business the amazing Joy ran. Still, how many different things could a woman in her fifties or sixties do online? Give knitting lessons? Run a babysitting service? Dog sitting? Hell, his own mother sold handmade dresses online, so there was just no telling.

"I know, I know." Kaye waved away his interruption. "She'll stay out of your way because she needs this time here. The contractor says they won't have the fire damage at her house repaired until January, so being able to stay and work here was a godsend."

"You told me this, too," he reminded her. In fact, he'd heard more than enough about Joy the Wonder Friend. According to Kaye, she was smart, clever, a hard worker, had a wonderful sense of humor and did apparently everything just short of walking on water. "But how did the fire in her house start again? Is she a closet arsonist? A terrible cook who set fire to the stove?"

"Of course not!" Kaye sniffed audibly and stiffened as if someone had shoved a pole down the back of her sweatshirt. "I told you, there was a short in the wiring. The house she's renting is just ancient and something was bound to go at some point. The owner of the house is having all the wiring redone, though, so it should be safe now."

"I'm relieved to hear it," he said. And relieved he didn't have to worry that Kaye's friend was so old she'd forgotten to turn off an oven or something.

"I'm only trying to tell you—" she broke off to give him a small smile of understanding "—like I do every year, that you'll survive the month of December just like you do every year."

He ground his teeth together at the flash of sympathy that stirred and then vanished from her eyes. This was the problem with people getting to know too much about him. They felt as if they had the right to offer comfort where none was wanted—or needed. Sam liked Kaye fine, but there were parts of his life that were closed off. For a reason.

He'd get through the holidays his way. Which meant ignoring the forced cheer and the never-ending lineup of "feel good" holiday-themed movies where the hard-hearted hero does a turnaround and opens himself to love and the spirit of Christmas.

Hearts should never be open. Left them too vulnerable to being shattered.

And he'd never set himself up for that kind of pain again.

Early the following day Kaye was off on her vacation, and a few hours later Sam was swamped by the empty silence. He reminded himself that it was how he liked his life best. No one bothering him. No one talking at him. One of the reasons he and Kaye got along so well was that she respected his need to be left the hell alone. So now that he was by himself in the big house, why did he feel an itch along his spine?

"It's December," he muttered aloud. That was enough to explain the sense of discomfort that clung to him.

Hell, every year, this one damn month made life damn near unlivable. He pushed a hand through his hair, then scraped that hand across the stubble on his jaw. He couldn't settle. Hadn't even spent any time out in his workshop, and usually being out there eased his mind and kept him too busy to think about—

He put the brakes on that thought fast because he couldn't risk opening doors that were better off sealed shut.

Scowling, he stared out the front window at the cold, dark day. The steel-gray clouds hung low enough that it looked as though they were actually skimming across the tops of the pines. The lake, in summer a brilliant sapphire blue, stretched out in front of him like a sheet of frozen pewter. The whole damn world seemed bleak and bitter, which only fed into what he felt every damn minute.

Memories rose up in the back of his mind, but he squelched them flat, as he always did. He'd worked too hard for too damn long to get beyond his past, to live and breathe—and hell, *survive*—to lose it all now. He'd beaten back his demons, and damned if he'd release them long enough to take a bite out of him now.

Resolve set firmly, Sam frowned again when an old blue four-door sedan barreled along his drive, kicking up gravel as it came to a stop in front of the house. For a second, he thought it must be Kaye's friend Joy arriving. Then the driver stepped out of the car and that thought went out the window.

The driver was too young, for one thing. Every other friend Kaye had enlisted to help out had been her age or older. This woman was in her late twenties, he figured, gaze locked on her as she turned her face to stare up at the house. One look at her and Sam felt a punch of lust that stole his breath. Everything in him fisted tightly as he continued to watch her. He couldn't take his eyes off her as she stood on the drive studying his house. Hell, she was like a ray of sunlight in the gray.

Her short curly hair was bright blond and flew about her face in the sharp wind that slapped rosy color into her cheeks. Her blue eyes swept the exterior of the house even as she moved around the car to the rear passenger side. Her black jeans hugged long legs, and her hiking boots looked scarred and well-worn. The cardinal-red parka she wore over a cream-colored sweater was a burst of color in a black-and-white world.

She was beautiful and moved with a kind of easy grace that made a man's gaze follow her every movement. And even while he admitted that silently, Sam resented it. He wasn't interested in women. Didn't want to feel what she was making him feel. What he had to do was find out why the hell she was there and get her gone as fast as possible.

She had to be lost. His drive wasn't that easy to find—purposely. He rarely got visitors, and those were mainly his family when he couldn't stave off his parents or sister any longer.

Well, if she'd lost her way, he'd go out and give her directions to town, and then she'd be gone and he could get back to—whatever.

"Damn." The single word slipped from his throat as she opened the car's back door and a little girl jumped out. The eager anticipation stamped on the child's face was like a dagger to the heart for Sam. He took a breath that fought its way into his chest and forced himself to look away from the kid.

He didn't do kids. Not for a long time now. Their voices. Their laughter. They were too small. Too vulnerable.

Too breakable.

What felt like darkness opened up in the center of his chest. Turning his back on the window, he left the room and headed for the front door. The faster he got rid of the gorgeous woman and her child, the better.

"It's a fairy castle, Mommy!"

Joy Curran glanced at the rearview mirror and smiled at the excitement shining on her daughter's face. At five years old, Holly was crazy about princesses, fairies and everyday magic she seemed to find wherever she looked.

Still smiling, Joy shifted her gaze from her daughter to the big house in front of her. Through the windshield, she scanned the front of the place and had to agree with Holly on this one. It did look like a castle.

Two stories, it spread across the land, pine trees spearing up all around it like sentries prepared to stand in defense. The smooth, glassy logs were the color of warm honey, and the wide, tall windows gave glimpses of the interior. A wraparound porch held chairs and gliders that invited visitors to sit and get comfortable. The house faced a private lake where a long dock jutted out into the water that was frozen over for winter. There was a wide deck studded with furniture draped in tarps for winter and a brick fire pit.

It would probably take her a half hour to look at everything, and it was way too cold to simply sit in her car and take it all in. So instead, she turned the engine off, then walked around to get Holly out of her car seat. While the little girl jumped up and down in excitement, pigtails flying, Joy grabbed her purse and headed for the front door. The cold wrapped itself around them and Joy shivered. There hadn't been much snow so far this winter, but the cold sliced right down to the bone. All around her, the pines were green but the grass was brown, dotted with shrinking patches of snow. Holly kept hoping to make snow angels and snowmen, but so far, Mother Nature wasn't cooperating.

The palatial house looked as if it had grown right out of the woods surrounding it. The place was gorgeous, but a little intimidating. And from everything she'd heard, so was the man who lived here. Oh, Kaye was crazy about him, but then Kaye took in stray dogs, cats, wounded birds and any lonely soul she happened across. But there was plenty of speculation about Sam Henry in town.

Joy knew he used to be a painter, and she'd actually seen a few of his paintings online. Judging by the art he created, she would have guessed him to be warm, optimistic and, well, *nice*. According to Kaye, though, the man was quiet, reclusive to the point of being a hermit, and she thought he was lonely at the bottom of it. But to Joy's way of thinking, if you didn't want to be lonely, you got out and met people. Heck, it was so rare to see Sam Henry in town, spotting him was the equivalent of a Bigfoot sighting. She'd caught only the occasional rare glimpse of the man herself.

But none of that mattered at the moment, Joy told herself. She and Holly needed a place to stay for the month, and this housesitting/cooking/cleaning job had turned up at just the right time. Taking Holly's hand, she headed for the front door, the little girl skipping alongside her, chattering about princesses and castles the whole way.

For just a second, Joy envied her little girl's simpler outlook on life. For Holly, this was an adventure in a magical castle. For Joy, it was moving into a big, secluded house with a secretive and, according to Kaye, cranky man. Okay, now she was making it sound like she was living in a Gothic novel. Kaye lived here year-round, right? And had for years. Surely Joy could survive a month. Determined now to get off on the right foot, she plastered a smile on her face, climbed up to the wide front porch and knocked on the double doors.

She was still smiling a moment later when the door was

thrown open and she looked up into a pair of suspicious brown eyes. An instant snap of attraction slapped at Joy, surprising her with its force. His black hair was long, hitting past the collar of his dark red shirt, and the thick mass lifted slightly as another cold wind trickled past. His jaws were shadowed by whiskers and his mouth was a grim straight line. He was tall, with broad shoulders, narrow hips and long legs currently encased in worn, faded denim that stacked on the tops of a pair of weathered brown cowboy boots.

If it wasn't for the narrowed eyes and the grim expression on his face, he would have been the star of any number of Joy's personal fantasies. Then he spoke and the already tattered remnants of said fantasy drifted away.

"This is private property," he said in a voice that was more of a growl. "If you're looking for town, go back to the main road and turn left. Stay on the road and you'll get there in about twenty minutes."

Well, this was starting off well.

"Thanks," she said, desperately trying to hang on to the smile curving her mouth as well as her optimistic attitude. "But I'm not lost. I've just come from town."

If anything, his frown deepened. "Then why're you here?"

"Nice to meet you, too," Joy said, half tugging Holly behind her. Not that she was afraid of him—but why subject her little girl to a man who looked like he'd rather slam the door in their faces than let them in?

"I repeat," he said, "who are you?"

"I'm Joy. Kaye's friend?" It came out as a question though she hadn't meant it as one.

"You're kidding." His eyes went wide as his gaze swept her up and down in a fast yet thorough examination.

She didn't know whether to be flattered or insulted. But when his features remained stiff and cold, she went for insulted.

"Is there a problem?" she asked. "Kaye told me you'd be expecting me and—"

"You're not old."

She blinked at him. "Thank you for noticing, though I've got to say, if Kaye ever hears you call her 'old,' it won't be pretty."

"That's not—" He stopped and started again. "I was expecting a woman Kaye's age," he continued. "Not someone like you. Or," he added with a brief glance at Holly, "a child."

Why hadn't Kaye told him about Holly? For a split second, Joy worried over that and wondered if he'd try to back out of their deal now. But an instant later she assured herself that no matter what happened, she was going to hold him to his word. She needed to be here and she wasn't about to leave.

She took a breath and ignored the cool chill in his eyes. "Well, that's a lovely welcome, thanks. Look, it's cold out here. If you don't mind, I'd like to come in and get settled."

He shook his head, opened his mouth to speak, but Holly cut him off.

"Are you the prince?" She stepped out from behind her mother, tipped her head back and studied him.

"The what?"

Joy tensed. She didn't want to stop Holly from talking— wasn't entirely sure she *could*—but she was more than willing to intervene if the quietly hostile man said something she didn't like.

"The prince," Holly repeated, the tiny lisp that defined her voice tugging at Joy's heart. "Princes live in castles."

Joy caught the barest glimmer of a smile brush across his face before it was gone again. Somehow, though, that ghost of real emotion made her feel better.

"No," he said and his voice was softer than it had been. "I'm not a prince."

Joy could have said something to that, and judging by the glance he shot her, he half expected her to. But irritating him further wasn't going to get her and Holly into the house and out of the cold.

"But he looks like a prince, doesn't he, Mommy?"

A prince with a lousy attitude. A dark prince, maybe.

"Sure, honey," she said with a smile for the little girl shifting from foot to foot in her eagerness to get inside the "castle."

Turning back to the man who still stood like an immovable object in the doorway, Joy said reasonably, "Look, I'm sorry we aren't what you were expecting. But here we are. Kaye told you about the fire at our house, right?"

"The firemen came and let me sit in the big truck with the lights going and it was really bright and blinking."

"Is that right?" That vanishing smile of his came and went again in a blink.

"And it smelled really bad," Holly put in, tugging her hand free so she could pinch her own nose.

"It did," Joy agreed, running one hand over the back of Holly's head. "And," she continued, "it did enough damage that we can't stay there while they're fixing it—" She broke off and said, "Can we finish this inside? It's cold out here."

For a second, she wasn't sure he'd agree, but then he nodded, moved back and opened the wide, heavy door. Heat rushed forward to greet them, and Joy nearly sighed in pleasure. She gave a quick look around at the entry hall. The gleaming, honey-colored logs shone in the overhead light. The entry floor was made up of huge square tiles in mottled earth tones. Probably way easier to clean up melting snow from tile floors instead of wood, she told herself and let her gaze quickly move over what she could see of the rest of the house.

It seemed even bigger on the inside, which was hard to believe, and with the lights on against the dark of winter, the whole place practically glowed. A long hallway led off to the back of the house, and on the right was a stairway leading to the second floor. Near the front door, there was a handmade coat tree boasting a half-dozen brass hooks and a padded bench attached.

Shrugging out of her parka, Joy hung it on one of the hooks, then turned and pulled Holly's jacket off as well, hanging it alongside hers. The warmth of the house surrounded her and all

Joy could think was, she really wanted to stay. She and Holly needed a place and this house with its soft glow was…welcoming, in spite of its owner.

She glanced at the man watching her, and one look told her that he really wanted her gone. But she wasn't going to allow that.

The house was gigantic, plenty of room for her and Holly to live and still stay out of Sam Henry's way. There was enough land around the house so that her little girl could play. One man to cook and clean for, which would leave her plenty of time to work on her laptop. And oh, if he made them leave, she and her daughter would end up staying in a hotel in town for a month. Just the thought of trying to keep a five-year-old happy when she was trapped in a small, single room for weeks made Joy tired.

"Okay, we're inside," he said. "Let's talk."

"Right. It's a beautiful house." She walked past him, forcing the man to follow her as she walked to the first doorway and peeked in. A great room—that really lived up to the name.

Floor-to-ceiling windows provided a sweeping view of the frozen lake, a wide lawn and a battalion of pines that looked to be scraping the underside of the low-hanging gray clouds. There was a massive hearth on one wall, where a wood fire burned merrily. A big-screen TV took up most of another wall, and there were brown leather couches and chairs sprinkled around the room, sitting on brightly colored area rugs. Handcrafted wood tables held lamps and books, with more books tucked onto shelves lining yet another wall.

"I love reading, too, and what a terrific spot for it," Joy said, watching Holly as the girl wandered the room, then headed straight to the windows where she peered out, both hands flat against the glass.

"Yeah, it works for me." He came up beside her, crossed his arms over his chest and said, "Anyway…"

"You won't even know we're here," Joy spoke up quickly.

"And it'll be a pleasure to take care of this place. Kaye loves working here, so I'm sure Holly and I will be just as happy."

"Yeah, but—"

She ignored his frown and the interruption. On a roll, she had no intention of stopping. "I'm going to take a look around. You don't have to worry about giving me a tour. I'll find my own way—"

"About that—"

Irritation flashed across his features and Joy almost felt sorry for him. Not sorry enough to stop, though. "What time do you want dinner tonight?"

Before he could answer, she said, "How about six? If that works for you, we'll keep it that way for the month. Otherwise, we can change it."

"I didn't agree—"

"Kaye said Holly and I should use her suite of rooms off the kitchen, so we'll just go get settled in and you can get back to what you were doing when we got here." A bright smile on her face, she called, "Holly, come with me now." She looked at him. "Once I've got our things put away, I'll look through your supplies and get dinner started, if it's all right with you." *And even if it isn't*, she added silently.

"Talking too fast to be interrupted doesn't mean this is settled," he told her flatly.

The grim slash of his mouth matched the iciness in his tone. But Joy wasn't going to give up easily. "There's nothing to settle. We agreed to be here for the month and that's what we're going to do."

He shook his head. "I don't think this is going to work out."

"You can't know that, and I think you're wrong," she said, stiffening her spine as she faced him down. She needed this job. This place. For one month. And she wouldn't let him take it from her. Keeping her voice low so Holly wouldn't overhear, she said, "I'm holding you to the deal we made."

"*We* didn't make a deal."

"You did with Kaye."

"Kaye's not here."

"Which is why we are." *One point to me.* Joy grinned and met his gaze, deliberately glaring right into those shuttered brown eyes of his.

"Are there fairies in the woods?" Holly wondered aloud.

"I don't know, honey," Joy said.

"No," Sam told her.

Holly's face fell and Joy gave him a stony glare. He could be as nasty and unfriendly with her as he wanted to be. But he wouldn't be mean to her daughter. "He means he's never seen any fairies, sweetie."

"Oh." The little girl's smile lit up her face. "Me either. But maybe I can sometime, Mommy says."

With a single look, Joy silently dared the man to pop her daughter's balloon again. But he didn't.

"Then you'll have to look harder, won't you?" he said instead, then lifted his gaze to Joy's. With what looked like regret glittering in his eyes, he added, "You'll have a whole month to look for them."

CHAPTER TWO

A FEW HOURS in the workshop didn't improve Sam's mood. Not a big surprise. How the hell could he clear his mind when it was full of images of Joy Curran and her daughter?

As her name floated through his mind *again*, Sam deliberately pushed it away, though he knew damn well she'd be sliding back in. Slowly, methodically, he ran the hand sander across the top of the table he was currently building. The satin feel of the wood beneath his hands fed the artist inside him as nothing else could.

It had been six years since he'd picked up a paintbrush, faced a blank canvas and brought the images in his mind to life. And even now, that loss tore at him and his fingers wanted to curl around a slim wand of walnut and surround himself with the familiar scents of turpentine and linseed oil. He wouldn't— but the desire was always there, humming through his blood, through his dreams.

But though he couldn't paint, he also couldn't simply sit in the big house staring out windows, either.

So he'd turned his need for creativity, for creation, toward the woodworking that had always been a hobby. In this workshop, he built tables, chairs, small whimsical backyard lawn ornaments, and lost himself in the doing. He didn't have to think. Didn't have to remember.

Yet, today, his mind continuously drifted from the project at hand to the main house, where the woman was. It had been a long time since he'd had an attractive woman around for longer than an evening. And the prospect of Joy being in his house for the next month didn't make Sam happy. But damned if he could think of a way out of it. Sure, he could toss her and the girl out, but then what?

Memories of last December when he'd been on his own and damn near starved to death rushed into his brain. He didn't want to repeat that, but could he stand having a kid around all the time?

That thought brought him up short. He dropped the block sander onto the table, turned and looked out the nearest window to the house. The lights in the kitchen were on and he caught a quick glimpse of Joy moving through the room. Joy. Even her name went against everything he'd become. She was too much, he thought. Too beautiful. Too cheerful. Too tempting.

Well, hell. Recognizing the temptation she represented was only half the issue. Resisting her and what she made him want was the other half. She'd be right there, in his house, for a month. And he was still feeling that buzz of desire that had pumped into him from the moment he first saw her getting out of her car. He didn't want that buzz but couldn't ignore it, either.

When his cell phone rang, he dug it out of his pocket and looked at the screen. His mother. "Perfect. This day just keeps getting better."

Sam thought about not answering it, but he knew that Catherine Henry wouldn't be put off for long. She'd simply keep calling until he answered. Might as well get it over with.

"Hi, Mom."

"There's my favorite son," she said.

"Your *only* son," he pointed out.

"Hence the favorite," his mother countered. "You didn't want to answer, did you?"

He smiled to himself. The woman was practically psychic. Leaning one hip against the workbench, he said, "I did, though, didn't I?"

"Only because you knew I'd harangue you."

He rolled his eyes and started sanding again, slowly, carefully moving along the grain. "What's up, Mom?"

"Kaye texted me to say she was off on her trip," his mother said. "And I wanted to see if Joy and Holly arrived all right."

He stopped, dropped the sander and stared out at the house where the woman and her daughter were busily taking over. "You knew?"

"Well, of course I knew," Catherine said with a laugh. "Kaye keeps me up to date on what's happening there since my favorite son tends to be a hermit and uncommunicative."

He took a deep breath and told himself that temper would be wasted on his mother. It would roll right on by, so there was no point in it. "You should have warned me."

"About what? Joy? Kaye tells me she's wonderful."

"About her daughter," he ground out, reminding himself to keep it calm and cool. He felt a sting of betrayal because his mother should have understood how having a child around would affect him.

There was a long pause before his mother said, "Honey, you can't avoid all children for the rest of your life."

He flinched at the direct hit. "I didn't say I was."

"Sweetie, you didn't have to. I know it's hard, but Holly isn't Eli."

He winced at the sound of the name he never allowed himself to so much as think. His hand tightened around the phone as if it were a lifeline. "I know that."

"Good." Her voice was brisk again, with that clipped tone that told him she was arranging everything in her mind. "Now that that's settled, you be nice. Kaye and I think you and Joy will get along very well."

He went completely still. "Is that right?"

"Joy's very independent and according to Kaye, she's friendly, outgoing—just what you need, sweetie. Someone to wake you up again."

Sam smelled a setup. Every instinct he possessed jumped up and shouted a warning even though it was too late to avoid what was already happening. Scraping one hand down his face, he shook his head and told himself he should have been expecting this. For years now, his mother had been nagging at him to move on. To accept the pain and to pick up the threads of his life.

She wanted him happy, and he understood that. What *she* didn't understand was that he'd already lost his shot at happiness. "I'm not interested, Mom."

"Sure you are, you just don't know it," his mother said in her crisp, no-nonsense tone. "And it's not like I've booked a church or expect you to sweep Joy off her feet, for heaven's sake. But would it kill you to be nice? Honestly, sweetie, you've become a hermit, and that's just not healthy."

Sam sighed heavily as his anger drained away. He didn't like knowing that his family was worried about him. The last few years had been hard. On everyone. And he knew they'd all feel better about him if he could just pick up the threads of his life and get back to some sort of "normal." But a magical wave of his hands wasn't going to accomplish that.

The best he could do was try to convince his mother to leave him be. To let him deal with his own past in his own way. The chances of that, though, were slim. That was the burden of family. When you tried to keep them at bay for their own sake, they simply refused to go. Evidence: she and Kaye trying to play matchmaker.

But just because they thought they were setting him up with Joy didn't mean he had to go along. Which he wouldn't. Sure, he remembered that instant attraction he'd felt for Joy. That slam of heat, lust, that let him know he was alive even when he hated to acknowledge it. But it didn't change anything. He didn't want another woman in his life. Not even one with hair like sunlight and eyes the color of a summer sky.

And he for damn sure didn't want another child in his life.

What he had to do, then, was to make it through December, then let his world settle back into place. When nothing happened between him and Joy, his mother and Kaye would have to give up on the whole Cupid thing. A relief for all of them.

"Sam?" His mother's voice prompted a reaction from him. "Have you slipped into a coma? Do I need to call someone?"

He laughed in spite of everything then told himself to focus. When dealing with Catherine Henry, a smart man paid attention. "No. I'm here."

"Well, good. I wondered." Another long pause before she said, "Just do me a favor, honey, and don't scare Joy off. If she's willing to put up with you for a month, she must really need the job."

Insulting, but true. Wryly, he said, "Thanks, Mom."

"You know what I mean." Laughing a little, she added, "That didn't come out right, but still. Hermits are *not* attractive, Sam. They grow their beards and stop taking showers and mutter under their breath all the time."

"Unbelievable," he muttered, then caught himself and sighed.

"It's already started," his mother said. "But seriously. People in those mountains are going to start telling their kids scary stories about the weird man who never leaves his house."

"I'm not weird," he argued. And he didn't have a beard. Just whiskers he hadn't felt like shaving in a few days. As far as muttering went, that usually happened only when his mother called.

"Not yet, but if things don't change, it's coming."

Scowling now, he turned away from the view of the house and stared unseeing at the wall opposite him. "Mom, you mean well. I know that."

"I do, sweetie, and you've got to—"

He cut her off, because really, it was the only way. "I'm already doing what I have to do, Mom. I've had enough change in my life already, thanks."

Then she was quiet for a few seconds as if she was remembering the pain of that major change. "I know. Sweetie, I know. I just don't want you to lose the rest of your life, okay?"

Sam wondered if it was all mothers or just his who refused to see the truth when it was right in front of them. He had nothing left to lose. How the hell could he have a life when he'd already lost everything that mattered? Was he supposed to forget? To pretend none of it had happened? How could he when every empty day reminded him of what was missing?

But saying any of that to his mother was a waste of time. She wouldn't get it. Couldn't possibly understand what it cost him every morning just to open his eyes and move through the day. They tried, he told himself. His whole family tried to be there for him, but the bottom line was, he was alone in this. Always would be.

And that thought told Sam he'd reached the end of his patience. "Okay, look, Mom, good talking to you, but I've got a project to finish."

"All right then. Just, think about what I said, okay?"

Hard not to when she said it every time she talked to him.

"Sure." A moment later he hung up and stuffed the phone back into his pocket. He shouldn't have answered it. Should have turned the damn thing off and forced her to leave a message. Then he wouldn't feel twisted up inside over things that could never be put right. It was better his way. Better to bury those memories, that pain, so deeply that they couldn't nibble away at him every waking moment.

A glance at the clock on the wall told him it was six and time for the dinner Joy had promised. Well, he was in no mood for company. He came and went when he liked and just because his temporary housekeeper made dinner didn't mean he had to show up. He scowled, then deliberately, he picked up the sander again and turned his focus to the wood. Sanding over the last coat of stain and varnish was meticulous work. He could laser in on the task at hand and hope it would be enough to ease the tension rippling through him.

It was late by the time he finally forced himself to stop working for the day. Darkness was absolute as he closed up the shop and headed for the house. He paused in the cold to glance up at the cloud-covered sky and wondered when the snow would start. Then he shifted his gaze to the house where a single light burned softly against the dark. He'd avoided the house until he was sure the woman and her daughter would be locked away in Kaye's rooms. For a second, he felt a sting of guilt for blowing off whatever dinner it was she'd made. Then again, he hadn't asked her to cook, had he? Hell, he hadn't even wanted her to stay. Yet somehow, she was.

Tomorrow, he told himself, he'd deal with her and lay out a few rules. If she was going to stay then she had to understand that it was the *house* she was supposed to take care of. Not him. Except for cooking—which he would eat whenever he damn well pleased—he didn't want to see her. For now, he wanted a shower and a sandwich. He was prepared for a can of soup and some grilled cheese.

Later, Sam told himself he should have known better. He opened the kitchen door and stopped in the doorway. Joy was sitting at the table with a glass of wine in front of her and turned her head to look at him when he walked in. "You're late."

That niggle of guilt popped up again and was just as quickly squashed. He closed and locked the door behind him. "I don't punch a clock."

"I don't expect you to. But when we say dinner's at six, it'd be nice if you showed up." She shrugged. "Maybe it's just me, but most people would call that 'polite.'"

The light over the stove was the only illumination and in the dimness, he saw her eyes, locked on him, the soft blond curls falling about her face. Most women he knew would have been furious with him for missing a dinner after he'd agreed to be there. But she wasn't angry, and that made him feel the twinge of guilt even deeper than he might have otherwise. But at the bottom of it, he didn't answer to her and it was just as well she learned that early on.

"Yeah," he said, "I got involved with a project and forgot the time." A polite lie that would go down better than admitting *I was avoiding you.* "Don't worry about it. I'll fix myself something."

"No you won't." She got up and walked to the oven. "I've kept it on warm. Why don't you wash up and have dinner?"

He wanted to say no. But damned if whatever she'd made didn't smell amazing. His stomach overruled his head and Sam surrendered. He washed his hands at the sink then sat down opposite her spot at the table.

"Did you want a glass of your wine?" she asked. "It's really good."

One eyebrow lifted. Wryly, he said, "Glad you approve."

"Oh, I like wine," she said, disregarding his tone. "Nothing better than ending your day with a glass and just relaxing before bed."

Bed. Not a word he should be thinking about when she was so close and looking so…edible. "Yeah. I'll get a beer."

"I'll get it," she said, as she set a plate of pasta in a thick red meat sauce in front of him.

The scent of it wafted to him and Sam nearly groaned. "What is that?"

"Baked mostaccioli with mozzarella and parmesan in my grandmother's meat sauce." She opened the fridge, grabbed a beer then walked back to the table. Handing it to him, she sat down, picked up her wineglass and had a sip.

"It smells great," he said grudgingly.

"Tastes even better," she assured him. Drawing one knee up, she propped her foot on her chair and looked at him. "Just so you know, I won't be waiting on you every night. I mean getting you a beer and stuff."

He snorted. "I'll make a note."

Then Sam took a bite and sighed. Whatever else Joy Curran was, the woman could *cook*. Whatever they had to talk about could wait, he thought, while he concentrated on the unexpected prize of a really great meal. So he said nothing else for a few bites, but finally sat back, took a drink of his beer and looked at her.

"Good?"

"Oh, yeah," he said. "Great."

She smiled and her face just—lit up. Sam's breath caught in his chest as he looked at her. That flash of something hot, something staggering, hit him again and he desperately tried to fight it off. Even while that strong buzz swept through him, remnants of the phone call with his mother rose up in his mind and he wondered if Joy had been in on whatever his mother and Kaye had cooking between them.

Made sense, didn't it? Young, pretty woman. Single mother. Why not try to find a rich husband?

Speculatively, he looked at her and saw sharp blue eyes without the slightest hint of guile. So maybe she wasn't in on it. He'd reserve judgment. For now. But whether she was or not, he had to set down some rules. If they were going to be living together for the next month, better that they both knew where they stood.

And, as he took another bite of her spectacular pasta, he admitted that he was going to let her stay—if only for the sake of his stomach.

"Okay," he said in between bites, "you can stay for the month."

She grinned at him and took another sip of her wine to celebrate. "That's great, thanks. Although, I wasn't really going to leave."

Amused, he picked up his beer. "Is that right?"

"It is." She nodded sharply. "You should know that I'm pretty stubborn when I want something, and I really wanted to stay here for the month."

He leaned back in his chair. The pale wash of the stove light reached across the room to spill across her, making that blond hair shine and her eyes gleam with amusement and determination. The house was quiet, and the darkness crouched just outside the window made the light and warmth inside seem almost intimate. Not a word he wanted to think about at the moment.

"Can you imagine trying to keep a five-year-old entertained in a tiny hotel room for a month?" She shivered and shook her head. "Besides being a living nightmare for me, it wouldn't be fair to Holly. Kids need room to run. Play."

He remembered. A succession of images flashed across his mind before he could stop them. As if the memories had been crouched in a corner, just waiting for the chance to escape, he saw pictures of another child. Running. Laughing. Brown eyes shining as he looked over his shoulder and—

Sam's grip on the beer bottle tightened until a part of him wondered why it didn't simply shatter in his hand. The images in his mind blurred, as if fingers of fog were reaching for them, dragging them back into the past where they belonged. Taking a slow, deep breath, he lifted the beer for a sip and swallowed the pain with it.

"Besides," she continued while he was still being dogged by memories, "this kitchen is amazing." Shaking her head, she looked around the massive room, and he knew what she was seeing. Pale oak cabinets, dark blue granite counters with flecks of what looked like abalone shells in them. Stainless steel appliances and sink and an island big enough to float to Ireland on. And the only things Sam ever really used on his own were the double-wide fridge and the microwave.

"Cooking in here was a treat. There's so much space." Joy took another sip of wine. "Our house is so tiny, the kitchen just a smudge on the floor plan. Holly and I can't be in there together without knocking each other down. Plus there's the ancient plumbing and the cabinet doors that don't close all the way…but it's just a rental. One of these days, we'll get our own house. Nothing like this one of course, but a little bigger with a terrific kitchen and a table like this one where Holly can sit and do her homework while I make dinner—"

Briskly, he got back to business. It was either that or let her go far enough to sketch out her dream kitchen. "Okay, I get it. You need to be here, and for food like this, I'm willing to go along." She laughed shortly.

He paid zero attention to the musical sound of that laugh or how it made her eyes sparkle in the low light. "So here's the deal. You can stay the month like we agreed."

"But?" she asked. "I hear a *but* in there."

"But." He nodded at her. "We steer clear of each other and you keep your daughter out of my way."

Her eyebrows arched. "Not a fan of kids, are you?"

"Not for a long time."

"Holly won't bother you," she said, lifting her wineglass for another sip.

"All right. Good. Then we'll get along fine." He finished off the pasta, savoring that last bite before taking one more pull on his beer. "You cook and clean. I spend most of my days out in the workshop, so we probably won't see much of each other anyway."

She studied him for several long seconds before a small smile curved her mouth and a tiny dimple appeared in her right cheek. "You're sort of mysterious, aren't you?"

Once again, she'd caught him off guard. And why did she look so pleased when he'd basically told her he didn't want her kid around and didn't particularly want to spend any time with *her*, either?

"No mystery. I just like my privacy is all."

"Privacy's one thing," she mused, tipping her head to one side to study him. "Hiding out's another."

"Who says I'm hiding?"

"Kaye."

He rolled his eyes. Kaye talked to his mother. To Joy. Who the hell *wasn't* she talking to? "Kaye doesn't know everything."

"She comes close, though," Joy said. "She worries about you. For the record, she says you're lonely, but private. Nice, but shut down."

He shifted in the chair, suddenly uncomfortable with the way she was watching him. As if she could look inside him and dig out all of his secrets.

"She wouldn't tell me why you've locked yourself away up here on the mountain—"

"That's something," he muttered, then remembered his mother's warning about hermits and muttering. Scowling, he took another drink of his beer.

"People do wonder, though," she mused. "Why you keep to yourself so much. Why you almost never go into town. I mean, it's beautiful here, but don't you miss talking to people?"

"Not a bit," he told her, hoping that statement would get her to back off.

"I really would."

"Big surprise," he muttered and then inwardly winced. Hell, he'd talked more in the last ten minutes than he had in the last year. Still, for some reason, he felt the need to defend himself and the way he lived. "I have Kaye to talk to if I desperately need conversation—which I don't. And I do get into town now and then." Practically never, though, he thought.

Hell, why should he go into Franklin and put up with being stared at and whispered over when he could order whatever he wanted online and have it shipped overnight? If nothing else, the twenty-first century was perfect for a man who wanted to be left the hell alone.

"Yeah, that doesn't happen often," she was saying. "There was actually a pool in town last summer—people were taking bets on if you'd come in at all before fall."

Stunned, he stared at her. "They were betting on me?"

"You're surprised?" Joy laughed and the sound of it filled the kitchen. "It's a tiny mountain town with not a lot going on, except for the flood of tourists. Of course they're going to place bets on the local hermit."

"I'm starting to resent that word." Sam hadn't really considered that he might be the subject of so much speculation, and he didn't much care for it. What was he supposed to do now? Go into town more often? Or less?

"Oh," she said, waving one hand at him, "don't look so grumpy about it. If it makes you feel better, when you came into Franklin and picked up those new tools at the hardware store, at the end of August, Jim Bowers won nearly two hundred dollars."

"Good for him," Sam muttered, not sure how he felt about all of this. He'd moved to this small mountain town for the solitude. For the fact that no one would give a damn about him. And after five years here, he found out the town was paying close enough attention to him to actually lay money on his comings and goings. Shaking his head, he asked only, "Who's Jim Bowers?"

"He and his wife own the bakery."

"There's a bakery in Franklin?"

She sighed, shaking her head slowly. "It's so sad that you didn't know that."

A short laugh shot from his throat, surprising them both.

"You should do that more often," she said quietly.

"What?"

"Smile. Laugh. Lose the etched-in-stone-grumble expression."

"Do you have an opinion on everything?" he asked.

"Don't you?" she countered.

Yeah, he did. And his considered opinion on this particular situation was that he might have made a mistake in letting Joy and her daughter stay here for the next month.

But damned if he could regret it at the moment.

CHAPTER THREE

BY THE FOLLOWING MORNING, Joy had decided the man needed to be pushed into getting outside himself. Sitting in the kitchen with him the night before had been interesting and more revealing than he would have liked, she was sure. Though he had a gruff, cold exterior, Joy had seen enough in his eyes to convince her that the real man was hidden somewhere beneath that hard shell he carried around with him.

She had known he'd been trying to avoid seeing her again by staying late in his workshop. Which was why she'd been waiting for him in the kitchen. Joy had always believed that it was better to face a problem head-on rather than dance around it and hope it would get better. So she'd been prepared to argue and bargain with him to make sure she and Holly could stay for the month.

And she'd known the moment he tasted her baked mostaccioli that arguments would not be necessary. He might not want her there, but her cooking had won him over. Clearly, he didn't like it, but he'd put up with her for a month if it meant he wouldn't starve. Joy could live with that.

What she might not be able to live with was her body's response to being near him. She hadn't expected that. Hadn't felt anything remotely like awareness since splitting with Holly's father before the little girl was born. And she wasn't looking for it now. She had a good life, a growing business and a daughter who made her heart sing. Who could ask for more than that?

But the man…intrigued her. She could admit, at least to herself, that sitting with him in the shadow-filled night had made her feel things she'd be better off forgetting. It wasn't her fault, of course. Just look at the man. Tall, dark and crabby. What woman wouldn't have a few fantasies about a man who looked like he did? Okay, normally she wouldn't enjoy the surly attitude—God knew she'd had enough "bad boys" in her life. But the shadows of old pain in his eyes told Joy that Sam hadn't always been so closed off.

So there was interest even when she knew there shouldn't be. His cold detachment was annoying, but the haunted look in his eyes drew her in. Made her want to comfort. Care. Dangerous feelings to have.

"Mommy, is it gonna snow today?"

Grateful for that sweet voice pulling her out of her circling thoughts, Joy walked to the kitchen table, bent down and kissed the top of her daughter's head.

"I don't think so, baby. Eat your pancakes now. And then we'll take a walk down to the lake."

"And skate?" Holly's eyes went bright with excitement at the idea. She forked up a bite of pancake and chewed quickly, eager now to get outside.

"We'll see if the lake's frozen enough, all right?" She'd brought their ice skates along since she'd known about the lake. And though she was no future competitor, Holly loved skating almost as much as she loved fairy princesses.

Humming, Holly nodded to herself and kept eating, pausing now and then for a sip of her milk. Her heels thumped against the chair rungs and sounded like a steady heartbeat in the quiet morning. Her little girl couldn't have been contained in a hotel room for a month. She had enough energy for three healthy kids and needed the room to run and play.

This house, this place, with its wide yard and homey warmth, was just what she needed. Simple as that. As for what Sam Henry made Joy feel? That would remain her own little secret.

"Hi, Sam!" Holly called out. "Mommy made pancakes. We're cellbrating."

"Celebrating," Joy corrected automatically, before she turned to look at the man standing in the open doorway. And darn it, she felt that buzz of awareness again the minute her gaze hit his. So tall, she thought with approval. He wore faded jeans and the scarred boots again, but today he wore a long-sleeved green thermal shirt with a gray flannel shirt over it. His too-long hair framed his face, and his eyes still carried the secrets that she'd seen in them the night before. They stared at each other as the seconds ticked past, and Joy wondered what he was thinking.

Probably trying to figure out the best way to get her and Holly to leave, she thought.

Well, that wasn't going to happen. She turned to the coffee-maker and poured him a cup. "Black?"

He accepted it. "How'd you guess?"

She smiled. "You look like the no-frills kind of man to me. Just can't imagine you ordering a half-caf, vanilla bean cap-puccino."

He snorted, but took a long drink and sighed at the rush of caffeine in his system. Joy could appreciate that, since she usually got up a half hour before Holly just so she could have the time to enjoy that first, blissful cup of coffee.

"What're you celebrating?" he asked.

Joy flushed a little. "Staying here in the 'castle.'"

Holly's heels continued to thump as she hummed her way through breakfast. "We're having pancakes and then we're going skating on the lake and—"

"I said we'll see," Joy reminded her.

"Stay away from the lake."

Joy looked at him. His voice was low, brusque, and his tone brooked no argument. All trace of amusement was gone from eyes that looked as deep and dark as the night itself. "What?"

"The lake," he said, making an obvious effort to soften the hard note in his voice. "It's not solid enough. Too dangerous for either of you to be on it."

"Are you sure?" Joy asked, glancing out the kitchen window at the frigid world beyond the glass. Sure, it hadn't snowed much so far, but it had been below freezing every night for the last couple of weeks, so the lake should be frozen over completely by now.

"No point in taking the chance, is there? If it stays this cold, maybe you could try it in a week or two..."

Well, she thought, at least he'd accepted that she and Holly would still be there in two weeks. That was a step in the right direction, anyway. His gaze fixed on hers, deliberately avoiding looking at Holly, though the little girl was practically vibrating with barely concealed excitement. In his eyes, Joy saw real worry and a shadow of something darker, something older.

"Okay," she said, going with her instinct to ease whatever it was that was driving him. Reaching out, she laid one hand on his forearm and felt the tension gripping him before he slowly, deliberately pulled away. "Okay. No skating today."

"Moooommmmmyyyyy..."

How her daughter managed to put ten or more syllables into a single word was beyond her.

"We'll skate another day, okay, sweetie? How about today we take a walk in the forest and look for pinecones?" She kept her gaze locked on Sam's, so she actually saw relief flash across his eyes. What was it in his past that had him still tied into knots?

"Can we paint 'em for Christmas?"

"Sure we can, baby. We'll go after we clean the kitchen, so eat up." Then to Sam, she said, "How about some pancakes?"

"No, thanks." He turned to go.

"One cup of coffee and that's it?"

He looked back at her. "You're here to take care of the house. Not me."

"Not true. I'm also here to cook. For you." She smiled a little. "You should try the pancakes. They're really good, even if I do say so myself."

"Mommy makes the *best* pancakes," Holly tossed in.

"I'm sure she does," he said, still not looking at the girl.

Joy frowned and wondered why he disliked kids so much, but she didn't ask.

"Look, while you're here, don't worry about breakfast for me. I don't usually bother and if I change my mind I can take care of it myself."

"You're a very stubborn man, aren't you?"

He took another sip of coffee. "I've got a project to finish and I'm going out to get started on it."

"Well, you can at least take a muffin." Joy walked to the counter and picked a muffin—one of the batch she'd made just an hour ago—out of a ceramic blue bowl.

He sighed. "If I do, will you let me go?"

"If I do, will you come back?"

"I live here."

Joy smiled again and handed it over to him. "Then you are released. Go. Fly free."

His mouth twitched and he shook his head. "People think I'm weird."

"I don't." She said it quickly and wasn't sure why she had until she saw a quick gleam of pleasure in his eyes.

"Be sure to tell Kaye," he said, and left, still shaking his head.

"'Bye, Sam!" Holly's voice followed him and Joy was pretty sure he quickened his steps as if trying to outrun it.

Three hours later, Sam was still wishing he'd eaten those damn pancakes. He remembered the scent of them in the air, and his stomach rumbled in complaint. Pouring another cup of coffee from his workshop pot, he stared down at the small pile of blueberry muffin crumbs and wished he had another one. Damn it.

Wasn't it enough that Joy's face kept surfacing in his mind? Did she have to be such a good cook, too? And who asked her to make him breakfast? Kaye never did. Usually he made do with coffee and a power bar of some kind, and that was fine. Always had been anyway. But now he still had the lingering taste of that muffin in his mouth, and his stomach was still whining over missing out on pancakes.

But to eat them, he'd have had to take a seat at the table beside a chattering little girl. And all that sunshine and sweet innocence was just too much for Sam to take. He took a gulp of hot coffee and let the blistering liquid burn its way to the pit of his sadly empty stomach. And as hungry as he was, at least he'd completed his project. He leaned back against the workbench, crossed his feet at the ankles, stared at the finished table and gave himself a silent pat on the back.

In the overhead shop light, the wood gleamed and shone like a mirror in the sun. Every slender grain of the wood was displayed beautifully under the fresh coat of varnish, and the finish was smooth as glass. The thick pedestal was gnarled and twisted, yet it, too, had been methodically sanded until all the rough edges were gone as if they'd never been.

Taking a deadfall tree limb and turning it into the graceful pedestal of a table had taken some time, but it had been worth it. The piece was truly one of a kind, and he knew the people he'd made it for would approve. It was satisfying, seeing something in your head and creating it in the physical world. He used to do that with paint and canvas, bringing imaginary places to life, making them real.

Sam frowned at the memories, because remembering the passion he'd had for painting, the rush of starting something new and pushing himself to make it all perfect, was something he couldn't know now. Maybe he never would again. And that thought opened up a black pit at the bottom of his soul. But there was nothing he could do about it. Nothing that could ease that need, that bone-deep craving.

At least he had this, he told himself. Woodworking had given him, if not completion, then satisfaction. It filled his days and helped to ease the pain of missing the passion that had once driven his life. But then, he thought, once upon a time, his entire world had been different. The shame was, he hadn't really appreciated what he'd had while he had it. At least, he told himself, not enough to keep it.

He was still leaning against the workbench, studying the table, when a soft voice with a slight lisp asked, "Is it a fairy table?"

He swiveled his head to the child in the doorway. Her blond hair was in pigtails, she wore blue jeans, tiny pink-and-white sneakers with princesses stamped all over them and a pink parka that made her look impossibly small.

He went completely still even while his heart raced, and his mind searched for a way out of there. Her appearance, on top of old memories that continued to dog him, hit him so hard he could barely take a breath. Sam looked into blue eyes the exact shade of her mother's and told himself that it was damned cowardly to be spooked by a kid. He had his reasons, but it was lowering to admit, even to himself, that his first instinct when faced with a child was to bolt.

Since she was still watching him, waiting for an answer, Sam took another sip of coffee in the hopes of steadying himself. "No. It's just a table."

"It looks like a tree." Moving warily, she edged a little farther into the workshop and let the door close behind her, shutting out the cold.

"It used to be," he said shortly.

"Did you make it?"

"Yes." She was looking up at him with those big blue eyes, and Sam was still trying to breathe. But his "issues" weren't her fault. He was being an ass, and even he could tell. He had no reason to be so short with the girl. How was she supposed to know that he didn't do kids anymore?

"Can I touch it?" she asked, giving him a winsome smile that made Sam wonder if females were *born* knowing how to do it.

"No," he said again and once more, he heard the sharp brusqueness in his tone and winced.

"Are you crabby?" She tilted her head to one side and looked up at him in all seriousness.

"What?"

Gloomy sunlight spilled through the windows that allowed views of the pines, the lake and the leaden sky that loomed threateningly over it all. The little girl, much like her mother, looked like a ray of sunlight in the gray, and he suddenly wished that she were anywhere but there. Her innocence, her easy smile and curiosity were too hard to take. Yet, her fearlessness at facing down an irritable man made her, to Sam's mind, braver than him.

"Mommy says when I'm crabby I need a nap." She nodded solemnly. "Maybe you need a nap, too."

Sam sighed. Also, like her mother, a bad mood wasn't going to chase her off. Accepting the inevitable, that he wouldn't be able to get rid of her by giving her one-word, bit-off answers, he said, "I don't need a nap, I'm just busy."

She walked into the workshop, less tentative now. Clearly oblivious to the fact that he didn't want her there, she wandered the shop, looking over the benches with tools, the stacks of reclaimed wood and the three tree trunks he had lined up along a wall. He should tell her to go back to the house. Wasn't it part of their bargain that the girl wouldn't bother him?

Hell.

"You don't look busy."

"Well, I am."

"Doing what?"

Sam sighed. Irritating, but that was a good question. Now that he'd finished the table, he needed to start something else. It wasn't only his hands he needed to keep busy. It was his mind. If he wasn't focusing on *something*, his thoughts would invariably track over to memories. Of another child who'd also had unending questions and bright, curious eyes. Sam cut that thought off and turned his attention to the tiny girl still exploring his workshop. Why hadn't he told her to leave? Why hadn't he taken her back to the house and told Joy to keep her away from him? Hell, why was he just standing there like a glowering statue?

"What's this do?"

The slight lisp brought a reluctant smile even as he moved toward her. She'd stopped in front of a vise that probably looked both interesting and scary to a kid.

"It's a wood vise," he said. "It holds a piece of wood steady so I can work on it."

She chewed her bottom lip and thought about it for a minute. "Like if I put my doll between my knees so I can brush her hair."

"Yeah," he said grudgingly. Smart kid. "It's sort of like that. Shouldn't you be with your mom?"

"She's cleaning and she said I could play in the yard if I stayed in the yard so I am but I wish it would snow and we could make angels and snowballs and a big snowman and—"

Amazed, Sam could only stare in awe as the little girl talked without seeming to breathe. Thoughts and words tumbled out of her in a rush that tangled together and yet somehow made sense.

Desperate now to stop the flood of high-pitched sounds, he asked, "Shouldn't you be in school?"

She laughed and shook her head so hard her pigtails flew back and forth across her eyes. "I go to pre-K cuz I'm too little for Big-K cuz my birthday comes too late cuz it's the day after Christmas and I can probably get a puppy if I ask Santa and Mommy's gonna get me a fairy doll for my birthday cuz Christmas is for the puppy and he'll be all white like a snowball and he'll play with me and lick me like Lizzie's puppy does when I get to play there and—"

So…instead of halting the rush of words and noise, he'd simply given her more to talk about. Sam took another long gulp of his coffee and hoped the caffeine would give him enough clarity to follow the kid's twisty thought patterns.

She picked up a scrap piece of wood and turned it over in her tiny hands.

"What can we make out of this?" she asked, holding it up to him, an interested gleam in her eye and an eager smile on her face.

Well, hell. He had nothing else to work on. It wasn't as though he was being drawn to the kid or anything. All he was doing was killing time. Keeping busy. Frowning to himself, Sam took the piece of wood from her and said, "If you're staying, take your jacket off and put it over there."

Her smile widened, her eyes sparkled and she hurried to do just what he told her. Shaking his head, Sam asked himself what he was doing. He should be dragging her back to the house. Telling her mother to keep the kid away from him. Instead, he was getting deeper.

"I wanna make a fairy house!"

He winced a little at the high pitch of that tiny voice and told himself that this didn't matter. He could back off again later.

Joy looked through the window of Sam's workshop and watched her daughter work alongside the man who had insisted he wanted nothing to do with her. Her heart filled when Holly turned a wide, delighted smile on the man. Then a twinge of guilt pinged inside her. Her little girl was happy and well-adjusted, but she was lacking a male role model in her life. God knew her father hadn't been interested in the job.

She'd told herself at the time that Holly would be better off without him than with a man who clearly didn't want to be a father. Yet here was another man who had claimed to want nothing to do with kids—her daughter in particular—and instead of complaining about her presence, he was working with her. Showing the little girl how to build...*something*. And Holly was loving it.

The little girl knelt on a stool at the workbench, following Sam's orders, and though she couldn't see what they were working on from her vantage point, Joy didn't think it mattered. Her daughter's happiness was evident, and whether he knew it or not, after only one day around Holly, Sam was opening up. She wondered what kind of man that opening would release.

The wind whipped past her, bringing the scent of snow, and Joy shivered deeper into her parka before walking into the warmth of the shop. With the blast of cold air announcing her presence, both Sam and Holly turned to look at her. One of them grinned. One of them scowled.

Of course.

"Mommy! Come and see, come and see!"

There was no invitation in Sam's eyes, but Joy ignored that and went to them anyway.

"It's a fairy house!" Holly squealed it, and Joy couldn't help but laugh. Everything these days was fairy. Fairy princesses. Fairy houses.

"We're gonna put it outside and the fairies can come and live in it and I can watch from the windows."

"That's a great idea."

"Sam says if I get too close to the fairies I'll scare 'em away," Holly continued, with an earnest look on her face. "But I wouldn't. I would be really quiet and they wouldn't see me or anything..."

"Sam says?" she repeated to the man standing there pretending he was somewhere else.

"Yeah," he muttered, rubbing the back of his neck. "If she watches through the window, she won't be out in the forest or—I don't know."

He was embarrassed. She could see it. And for some reason, knowing that touched her heart. The man who didn't want a child anywhere near him just spent two hours helping a little girl build a house for fairies. There was so much more to him than the face he showed to the world. And the more Joy discovered, the more she wanted to know.

Oh, boy.

"It's beautiful, baby." And it was. Small, but sturdy, it was made from mismatched pieces of wood and the roof was scalloped by layering what looked like Popsicle sticks.

"I glued it and everything, but Sam helped and he says I can put stuff in it for the fairies like cookies and stuff that they'll like and I can watch them…"

He shrugged. "She wanted to make something. I had some scrap wood. That's all."

"Thank you."

Impatience flashed across his face. "Not a big deal. And not going to be happening all the time, either," he added as a warning.

"Got it," Joy said, nodding. If he wanted to cling to that grumpy, don't-like-people attitude, she wouldn't fight him on it. Especially since she now knew it was all a front.

Joy took a moment to look around the big room. Plenty of windows would let in sunlight should the clouds ever drift away. A wide, concrete floor, scrupulously swept clean. Every kind of tool imaginable hung on the pegboards that covered most of two walls. There were stacks of lumber, most of it looking ragged and old—reclaimed wood—and there were deadfall tree trunks waiting for who knew what to be done to them.

Then she spotted the table and was amazed she hadn't noticed it immediately. Walking toward it, she sighed with pleasure as she examined it carefully, from the shining surface to the twisted tree limb base. "This is gorgeous," she whispered and whipped her head around to look at him. "You made this?"

He scowled again. Seemed to be his go-to expression. "Yeah."

"It's amazing, really."

"It's also still wet, so be careful. The varnish has to cure for a couple of days yet."

"I'm not touching."

"I didn't either, Mommy, did I, Sam?"

"Almost but not quite," he said.

Joy's fingers itched to stroke that smooth, sleek tabletop, so she curled her hands into fists to resist the urge. "I've seen some of your things in the gallery in town, and I loved them, too, by the way. But this." She shook her head and felt a real tug of possessiveness. "This I love."

"Thanks."

She thought the shadows in his eyes lightened a bit, but a second later, they were back so she couldn't be sure. "What are you working on next?"

"Like mother like daughter," he muttered.

"Curious?" she asked. "You bet. What are you going to do with those tree trunks?" The smallest of them was three feet around and two feet high.

"Work on them when I get a minute to myself." That leave-me-alone tone was back, and Joy decided not to push her luck any further. She'd gotten more than a few words out of him today and maybe they'd reached his limit.

"He's not mad, Mommy, he's just crabby."

Joy laughed.

Holly patted Sam's arm. "You could sing to him like you sing to me when I'm crabby and need a nap."

The look on Sam's face was priceless. Like he was torn between laughter and shouting and couldn't decide which way to go.

"What's that old saying?" Joy asked. "Out of the mouths of babes…"

Sam rolled his eyes and frowned. "That's it. Everybody out."

Still laughing, Joy said, "Come on, Holly, let's have some lunch. I made soup. Seemed like a good, cold day for it."

"You *made* soup?" he asked.

"Uh-huh. Beef and barley." She helped Holly get her jacket on, then zipped it closed against the cold wind. "Oh, and I made some beer bread, too."

"You made bread." He said it with a tinge of disbelief, and Joy couldn't blame him. Kaye didn't really believe in baking from scratch. Said it seemed like a waste when someone went to all the trouble to bake for her and package the bread in those nice plastic bags.

"Just beer bread. It's quick. Anyway," she said with a grin, "if you want lunch after your nap, I'll leave it on the stove for you."

"Funny."

Still smiling to herself, Joy took Holly's hand and led her out of the shop. She felt him watching her as they left and told herself that the heat swamping her was caused by her parka. And even she didn't believe it.

CHAPTER FOUR

LATE AT NIGHT, the big house was quiet, but not scary at all.

That thought made Joy smile to herself. She had assumed that a place this huge, with so many windows opening out onto darkness, would feel sort of like a horror movie. *Intrepid heroine wandering the halls of spooky house, alone, with nothing but a flashlight—until the battery dies.*

She shook her head and laughed at her own imagination. Instead of scary, the house felt like a safe haven against the night outside. Maybe it was the warmth of the honey-toned logs or maybe it was something else entirely. But one thing she was sure of was that she already loved it. Big, but not imposing, it was a happy house. Or would be if its owner wasn't frowning constantly.

But he'd smiled with Holly, Joy reminded herself as she headed down the long hallway toward the great room. He might have wished to be anywhere else, but he had been patient and kind to her little girl, and for Joy, nothing could have touched her more.

Her steps were quiet, her thoughts less so. She hadn't seen much of Sam since leaving him in the workshop. He'd deliberately kept his distance and Joy hadn't pushed. He'd had dinner, alone, in the dining room, then he'd disappeared again, barricading himself in the great room. She hadn't bothered him, had given him his space, and even now wouldn't be sneaking around his house if she didn't need something to read.

Holly was long since tucked in and Joy simply couldn't concentrate on the television, so she wanted to lose herself in a book. Keep her brain too busy to think about Sam. Wondering what his secrets were. Wondering what it would be like to kiss him. Wondering what the heck she was doing.

She threw a glance at the staircase and the upper floor, where the bedrooms were—where *Sam* was—and told herself to not think about it. Joy had spent the day cleaning the upstairs, though she had to admit that the man was so tidy, there wasn't much to straighten up.

But vacuuming and dusting gave her the chance to see where he slept, how he lived. His bedroom was huge, offering a wide view of the lake and the army of pine trees that surrounded it. His bed was big enough for a family of four to sleep comfortably, and the room was decorated in soothing shades of slate blue and forest green. The attached bath had had her sighing in imagined pleasure.

A sea of pale green marble, from the floors to the counters, to the gigantic shower and the soaker whirlpool tub that sat in front of a bay window with a view of the treetops. He lived well, but so solitarily it broke her heart. There were no pieces of *him* in the room. No photos, no art on the wall, nothing to point to this being his *home*. As beautiful as it all was, it was still impersonal, as if even after living there for five years he hadn't left his own impression on the place.

He made her curious. Gorgeous recluse with a sexuality that made her want to drool whenever he was nearby. Of course, the logical explanation for her zip of reaction every time she saw the man was her self-imposed Man Fast. It had been so long since she'd been on a date, been kissed…heck, been *touched*, that her body was clearly having a breakdown. A shame that she seemed to be enjoying it so much.

Sighing a little, she turned, slipped into the great room, then came to a dead stop. Sam sat in one of the leather chairs in front of the stone fireplace, where flames danced across wood and tossed flickering shadows around the room.

Joy thought about leaving before he saw her. Yes, cowardly, but understandable, considering where her imaginings had been only a second or two ago. But even as she considered sneaking out, Sam turned his head and pinned her with a long, steady look.

"What do you need?"

Not exactly friendly, but not a snarl, either. Progress? She'd take it.

"A book." With little choice, Joy walked into the room and took a quick look around. This room was gorgeous during the day, but at night, with flickering shadows floating around... amazing. Really, was there anything prettier than firelight? When she shifted her gaze back to him, she realized the glow from the fire shining in his dark brown eyes was nearly hypnotic. Which was a silly thought to have, so she pushed it away fast. "Would you mind if I borrow a book? TV is just so boring and—"

He held up one hand to cut her off. "Help yourself."

"Ever gracious," she said with a quick grin. When he didn't return it, she said, "Okay, thanks."

She walked closer, surreptitiously sliding her gaze over him. His booted feet were crossed at the ankle, propped on the stone edge of the hearth. He was staring into the fire as if looking for something. The flickering light danced across his features, and she recognized the scowl that she was beginning to think was etched into his bones. "Everything okay?"

"Fine." He didn't look at her. Never took his gaze from the wavering flames.

"Okay. You've got a lot of books." She looked through a short stack of hardbacks on the table closest to him. A mix of mysteries, sci-fi and thrillers, mostly. Her favorites, too.

"Yeah. Pick one."

"I'm looking," she assured him, but didn't hurry as he clearly wanted her to. Funny, but the gruffer and shorter he became, the more intrigued she was.

Joy had seen him with Holly. She knew there were smiles inside him and a softness under the cold, hard facade. Yet he seemed determined to shut everyone out.

"Ew," she said as she quickly set one book aside. "Don't like horror. Too scary. I can't even watch scary movies. I get too involved."

"Yeah."

She smiled to herself at the one-word answer. He hadn't told her to get out, so she'd just keep talking and see what happened. "I tried, once. Went to the movies with a friend and got so scared and so tense I had to go sit in the lobby for a half hour."

She caught him give her a quick look. Interest. It was a start.

"I didn't go back into the theater until I convinced an usher to tell me who else died so I could relax."

He snorted.

Joy smiled, but didn't let him see it. "So I finally went back in to sit with my friend, and even though I knew how it would end, I still kept my hands over my eyes through the rest of the movie."

"Uh-huh."

"But," she said, moving over to the next stack of books, "that doesn't mean I'm just a romantic comedy kind of girl. I like adventure movies, too. Where lots of things blow up."

"Is that right?"

Just a murmur, but he wasn't ignoring her.

"And the Avengers movies? Love those. But maybe it's just Robert Downey Jr. I like." She paused. "What about you? Do you like those movies?"

"Haven't seen them."

"Seriously?" She picked up a mystery she'd never read but instead of leaving with the book, she sat down in the chair beside his. "I think you're the first person I've ever met who hasn't seen those movies."

He spared her one long look. "I don't get out much."

"And isn't that a shame?"

"If I thought so," he told her, "I'd go out more."

Joy laughed at the logic. "Okay, you're right. Still. Heard of DVDs? Netflix?"

"You're just going to keep talking, aren't you?"

"Probably." She settled into her chair as if getting comfy for a long visit.

He shook his head and shifted his gaze back to the fire as if that little discouragement would send her on her way.

"But back to movies," she said, leaning toward him over the arm of her chair. "This time of year I like all the Christmas ones. The gushier the better."

"Gushy."

It wasn't a question, but she answered anyway. "You know, the happy cry ones. Heck, I even tear up when the Grinch's heart grows at the end of that little cartoon." She sighed. "But to be fair, I've been known to get teary at a heart-tugging commercial at Christmastime."

"Yeah, I don't do Christmas."

"I noticed," she said, tipping her head to one side to study him. If anything, his features had tightened, his eyes had grown darker. Just the mention of the holiday had been enough to close him up tight. And still, she couldn't resist trying to reach him.

"When we're at home," she said, "Holly and I put up the Christmas decorations the day after Thanksgiving. You have to have a little restraint, don't you think? I mean this year, I actually saw Christmas wreaths for sale in *September*. That's going a little far for me and I love Christmas."

He swiveled a look at her. "If you don't mind, I don't really feel like talking."

"Oh, you don't have to. I like talking."

"No kidding."

She smiled and thought she saw a flicker of a response in his eyes, but if she had, it wasn't much of one because it faded away fast. "You can't get to know people unless you talk to them."

He scraped one hand across his face. "Yeah, maybe I don't want to get to know people."

"I think you do, you just don't want to want it."

"What?"

"I saw you today with Holly."

He shifted in his chair and frowned into the fire. "A one-time thing."

"So you said," Joy agreed, getting more comfortable in the chair, letting him know she wasn't going anywhere. "But I have to tell you how excited Holly was. She couldn't stop talking about the fairy house she built with you." A smile curved Joy's mouth. "She fell asleep in the middle of telling me about the fairy family that will move into it."

Surprisingly, the frown on his face deepened, as if hearing that he'd given a child happiness made him angry.

"It was a small thing, but it meant a lot to her. And to me. I wanted you to know that."

"Fine. You told me."

Outside, the wind kicked up, sliding beneath the eaves of the house with a sighing moan that sounded otherworldly. She glanced toward the front window at the night beyond, then turned back to the man with darkness in his eyes. She wondered what he was thinking, what he was seeing as he stared into the flames. Leaning toward him, she locked her hands around her up-drawn knees and said, "That wide front window is a perfect place for a Christmas tree, you know. The glass would reflect all the lights…"

His gaze shot to hers. "I already told you, I don't do Christmas."

"Sure, I get it," she said, though she really didn't. "But if you don't want to, Holly and I will take care of decorating and—"

He stood up, grabbed a fireplace poker and determinedly

stabbed at the logs, causing sparks to fly and sizzle on their wild flight up the chimney. When he was finished, he turned a cold look on her and said, "No tree. No decorations. No Christmas."

"Wow. Speak of the Grinch."

He blew out a breath and glared at her, but it just didn't work. It was too late for him to try to convince her that he was an ogre or something. Joy had seen him with Holly. His patience. His kindness. Even though he hadn't wanted to be around the girl, he'd given her the gift of his time. Joy'd had a glimpse of the man behind the mask now and wouldn't be fooled again. Crabby? Yes. Mean? No.

"You're not here to celebrate the holidays," he reminded her in a voice just short of a growl. "You're here to take care of the house."

"I know. But, if you change your mind, I'm an excellent multitasker." She got to her feet and held on to the book she'd chosen from the stack. Staring up into his eyes, she said, "I'll do my job, but just so you know? You don't scare me, Sam, so you might as well quit trying so hard."

Every night, she came to the great room. Every night, Sam told himself not to be there. And every night, he was sitting by the fire, waiting for her.

Not like he was talking to her. But apparently *nothing* stopped *her* from talking. Not even his seeming disinterest in her presence. He'd heard about her business, about the house fire that had brought her to his place and about every moment of Holly's life up until this point. Her voice in the dark was both frustrating and seductive. Firelight created a cocoon of shadows and light, making it seem as if the two of them were alone in the world. Sam's days stretched out interminably, but the nights with Joy flew past, ending long before he wanted them to.

And that was an irritation, as well. Sam had been here for five years and in that time he hadn't wanted company. Hadn't wanted anyone around. Hell, he put up with Kaye because the woman kept his house running and meals on the table—but she also kept her distance. Usually. Now, here he was, sitting in the dark, waiting, *hoping* Joy would show up in the great room and shatter the solitude he'd fought so hard for.

But the days were different. During the day, Joy stayed out of his way and made sure her daughter did the same. They were like ghosts in the house. Once in a while, he would catch a little girl's laughter, quickly silenced. Everything was clean, sheets on his bed changed, meals appeared in the dining room, but Joy herself was not to be seen. How she managed it, he wasn't sure.

Why it bothered him was even more of a mystery.

Hell, he hadn't wanted them to stay in the first place. Yet now that he wasn't being bothered, wasn't seeing either of them, he found himself always on guard. Expecting one or both of them to jump out from behind a door every time he walked through a room. Which was stupid, but kept him on edge. Something he didn't like.

Hell, he hadn't even managed to get started on his next project yet because thoughts of Joy and Holly kept him from concentrating on anything else. Today, he had the place to himself because Joy and Holly had gone into Franklin. He knew that because there'd been a sticky note on the table beside his blueberry muffin and travel mug of coffee that Joy routinely left out in the dining room every morning.

Strange. The first morning they were here, it was *him* avoiding having breakfast with them. Now, it seemed that Joy was perfectly happy shuffling him off without even seeing him. Why that bothered him, Sam didn't even ask himself. There was no damn answer anyway.

So now, instead of working, he found himself glancing out the window repeatedly, watching for Joy's beat-up car to pull into the drive. All right, fine, it wasn't a broken-down heap, but her car was too old and, he thought, too unreliable for driving in the kind of snow they could get this high up the mountain. Frowning, he noted the fitful flurries of snowflakes drifting from the sky. Hardly a storm, more like the skies were teasing them with just enough snow to make things cold and slick.

So naturally, Sam's mind went to the road into town and the possible ice patches that dotted it. If Joy hit one of them, lost control of the car...his hands fisted. He should have driven them. But he hadn't really known they were going anywhere until it was too late. And that was because he wasn't spending any time with her except for those late-night sessions in the library.

Maybe if he'd opened his mouth the night before, she might have told him about this trip into town and he could have offered to drive them. Or at the very least, she could have driven his truck. Then he wouldn't be standing here wondering if her damn car had spun out.

Why the hell was he watching? Why did he care if she was safe or not? Why did he even bother to ask himself why? He knew damn well that his own past was feeding the sense of disquiet that clung to him. So despite resenting his own need to do it, he stayed where he was, watching. Waiting.

Which was why he was in place to see Ken Taylor when he arrived. Taylor and his wife, Emma, ran the gallery/gift shop in Franklin that mostly catered to tourists who came up the mountain for snow skiing in winter and boating on the lake in summer. Their shop, Crafty, sold local artisans' work—everything from paintings to jewelry to candles to the hand-made furniture and decor that Sam made.

Grateful for the distraction, Sam shrugged into his black leather jacket and headed out of the workshop into the cold bite of the wind and swirl of snowflakes. Tugging the collar up around his neck, Sam squinted into the wind and walked over to meet the man as he climbed out of his truck.

"Hey, Sam." Ken held out one hand and Sam shook it.

"Thanks for coming out to get the table," Sam said. "Appreciate it."

"Hey, you keep building them, I'll drive up the mountain to pick them up." Ken grinned. About forty, he had pulled his black hair into a ponytail at the base of his neck. He wore a heavy brown coat over a flannel shirt, blue jeans and black work boots. He opened the gate at the back of his truck, then grinned at Sam. "One of these times, though, you should come into town yourself so you can see the reactions of the people who buy your stuff." Shaking his head, he mused, "I mean, they all but applaud when we bring in new stock."

"Good to know," Sam said. It was odd, he thought, that he'd taken what had once been a hobby—woodworking—and turned it into an outlet for the creativity that had been choked off years ago. He liked knowing that his work was appreciated.

Once upon a time, he'd been lauded in magazines and newspapers. Reporters had badgered him for interviews, and one or two of his paintings actually hung in European palaces. He'd been the darling of the art world, and he'd enjoyed it all. He'd poured his heart and soul into his work and drank in the adulation as his due. Sam had so loved his work, he'd buried himself in it to the detriment of everything else. His life outside the art world had drifted past without him even realizing it.

Sam hadn't paid attention to what should have been most important, and before he could learn his lesson and make changes, he'd lost it and all he had left was the art. The paintings. The name he'd carved for himself. Left alone, it was only when he had been broken that he realized how empty it all was. How much he'd sacrificed for the glory.

So he wasn't interested in applause. Not anymore.

"No thanks," he said, forcing a smile in spite of his dark thoughts. He couldn't explain why he didn't want to meet prospective customers, why he didn't care about hearing praise, so he said, "I figure being the hermit on the mountain probably adds to the mystique. Why ruin that by showing up in town?"

Ken looked at him, as if he were trying to figure him out, but a second later, shook his head. "Up to you, man. But anytime you change your mind, Emma would love to have you as the star of our next Meet the Artist night."

Sam laughed shortly. "Well, that sounds hideous."

Ken laughed, too. "I'll admit that it really is. Emma drives me nuts planning the snacks to get from Nibbles, putting out press releases, and the last time, she even bought some radio ads in Boise..." He trailed off and sighed. "And the artist managed to insult almost everyone in town. Don't understand these artsy types, but I'm happy enough to sell their stuff." He stopped, winced. "No offense."

"None taken," Sam assured him. "Believe me." He'd known plenty of the kind of artists Ken was describing. Those who so believed in their own press no one could stand to be around them.

"But, Emma loves doing it, of course, and I have to give it to her, we do big business on those nights."

Imagining being in the center of a crowd hungering to be close to an artist, to ask him questions, hang on everything he said, talk about the "art"... It all gave Sam cold chills and he realized just how far he'd come from the man he'd once been. "Yeah, like I said, awful."

"I even have to wear a suit. What's up with that?" Ken shook his head glumly and followed after Sam when he headed for the workshop door. "The only thing I like about it is the food, really. Nibbles has so many great things. My favorite's those tiny grilled cheese sandwiches. I can eat a dozen of 'em and still come back for more..."

Sam was hardly listening. He'd done so many of those "artist meets the public" nights years ago that he had zero interest in hearing about them now. His life, his *world*, had changed so much since then, he couldn't even imagine being a part of that scene anymore.

Ken was still talking. "Speaking of food, I saw Joy and Holly at the restaurant as I was leaving town."

Sam turned to look at him.

Ken shrugged. "Deb Casey and her husband, Sean, own Nibbles, and Deb and Joy are tight. She was probably in there visiting since they haven't seen each other in a while. How's it going with the two of them living here?"

"It's fine." What the hell else could he say? That Joy was driving him crazy? That he missed Holly coming into the workshop? That as much as he didn't want them there, he didn't want them gone even more? Made him sound like a lunatic. Hell, maybe he was.

Sam walked up to the table and drew off the heavy tarp he'd had protecting the finished table. Watery gray light washed through the windows and seemed to make the tabletop shine.

"Whoa." Ken's voice went soft and awe-filled. "Man, you've got some kind of talent. This piece is amazing. We're going to have customers outbidding each other trying to get it." He bent down, examined the twisted, gnarled branch pedestal, then stood again to admire the flash of the wood grain beneath the layers of varnish. "Dude, you could be in an art gallery with this kind of work."

Sam stiffened. He'd been in enough art galleries for a lifetime, he thought, and had no desire to do it again. That life had ultimately brought him nothing but pain, and it was best left buried in the past.

"Your shop works for me," he finally said.

Ken glanced at him. The steady look in his eyes told Sam that he was wondering about him. But that was nothing new. Everyone in the town of Franklin had no doubt been wondering about him since he first arrived and holed up in this house on the mountain. He had no answers to give any of them, because the man he used to be was a man even Sam didn't know anymore. And that's just the way he liked it.

"Well, maybe one day you'll explain to me what's behind you hiding out up here." Ken gave him a slap on the back. "Until then, though, I'd be a fool to complain when you're creating things like this for me to sell—and I'm no fool."

Sam liked Ken. The man was the closest thing to a friend Sam had had in years. And still, he couldn't bring himself to tell Ken about the past. About the mess he'd made of his life before finding this house on the mountain. So Sam concentrated instead on securing a tarp over the table and making sure it was tied down against the wind and dampness of the snow and rain. Ken helped him cover that with another tarp, wrapping this one all the way down and under the foot of the pedestal. Double protection since Sam really hated the idea of having the finish on the table ruined before it even made it into the shop. It took both of them to carry the table to the truck and secure it with bungee cords in the bed. Once it was done, Sam stuffed his hands into the pockets of his jacket and nodded to Ken as the man climbed behind the wheel.

"Y'know, I'm going to say this—just like I do every time I come out here—even knowing you'll say 'no, thanks.'"

Sam gave him a half smile, because he was ready for what was coming next. How could he not be? As Ken said, he made the suggestion every time he was here.

"Why don't you come into town some night?" the other man asked, forearm braced on the car door. "We'll get a couple beers, tell some lies…"

"No, thanks," Sam said and almost laughed at the knowing smile creasing Ken's face. If, for the first time, he was almost tempted to take the man up on it, he'd keep that to himself.

"Yeah, that's what I thought." Ken nodded and gave him a rueful smile. "But if you change your mind…"

"I'll let you know. Thanks for coming out to pick up the table."

"I'll let you know as soon as we sell it."

"I trust you," Sam said.

"Yeah, I wish that was true," Ken told him with another long, thoughtful look.

"It is."

"About the work, sure, I get that," Ken said. "But I want you to know, you can trust me beyond that, too. Whether you actually do or not."

Sam had known Ken and Emma for four years, and if he was looking for friendships, he couldn't do any better and he knew it. But getting close to people—be it Ken or Joy—meant allowing them close enough to know about his past. And the fewer people who knew, the less pity he had to deal with. So he'd be alone.

"Appreciate it." He slapped the side of the truck and took a step back.

"I'll see you, then."

Ken drove off and when the roar of his engine died away, Sam was left in the cold with only the sigh of the wind through the trees for company. Just the way he liked it.

Right?

CHAPTER FIVE

"OH, GOD, look at her with that puppy," Joy said on a sigh.

Her heart filled and ached as she watched Holly laughing at the black Lab puppy jumping at her legs. How could one little girl mean so much? Joy wondered.

When she'd first found herself pregnant, Joy remembered the rush of pleasure, excitement that she'd felt. It hadn't mattered to her that she was single and not exactly financially stable. All she'd been able to think was, she would finally have her own family. Her child.

Joy had been living in Boise back then, starting up her virtual assistant business and working with several of the small businesses in town. One of those was Mike's Bikes, a custom motorcycle shop owned by Mike Davis.

Mike was charming, handsome and had the whole bad-boy thing going for him, and Joy fell hard and fast. Swept off her feet, she gave herself up to her first real love affair and thought it would be forever. It lasted until the day she told Mike she was pregnant, expecting to see the same happiness in him that she was feeling. Mike, though, had no interest in being anyone's father—or husband, if it came to that. He told her they were through. She was a good time for a while, but the good time was over. He signed a paper relinquishing all future rights to the child he'd created and Joy walked away.

When she was a kid, she'd come to Franklin with a foster family for a long weekend in the woods and she'd never forgotten it. So when she needed a fresh start for her and her baby, Joy had come here, to this tiny mountain town. And here is where she'd made friends, built her family and, at long last, had finally felt as though she belonged.

And of all the things she'd been gifted with since moving here, Deb Casey, her best friend, was at the top of the list.

Deb Casey walked to Joy and looked out the window at the two little girls rolling around on the winter brown grass with a fat black puppy. Their laughter and the puppy's yips of excitement brought a quick smile. "She's as crazy about that puppy as my Lizzie."

"I know." Joy sighed a little and leaned on her friend's kitchen counter. "Holly's telling everyone she's getting a puppy of her own for Christmas."

"A white one," Deb supplied.

Rolling her eyes, Joy shook her head. "I've even been into Boise looking for a white puppy, and no one has any. I guess I'm going to have to start preparing her for the fact that Santa can't always bring you what you want."

"Oh, I hate that." Deb turned back to the wide kitchen island and the tray of tiny brownies she was finishing off with swirls of white chocolate icing. "You've still got a few weeks till Christmas. You might find one."

"I'll keep looking, sure. But," Joy said, resigned, "she might have to wait."

"Because kids wait so well," Deb said with a snort of laughter.

"You're not helping."

"Have a brownie. That's the kind of help you need."

"Sold." Joy leaned in and grabbed one of the tiny brownies that was no more than two bites of chocolate heaven.

The brownies, along with miniature lemon meringue pies,

tiny chocolate chip cookies and miniscule Napoleons, would be filling the glass cases at Nibbles by this afternoon. The restaurant had been open for only a couple of years, but it had been a hit from the first day. Who wouldn't love going for lunch where you could try four or five different types of sandwiches—none of them bigger than a bite or two? Gourmet flavors, a fun atmosphere and desserts that could bring a grown woman to tears of joy, Nibbles had it all.

"Oh, God, this should be illegal," Joy said around a mouthful of amazing brownie.

"Ah, then I couldn't sell them." Deb swirled white chocolate on a few more of the brownies. "So, how's it going up there with the Old Man of the Mountain?"

"He's not old."

"No kidding." Deb grinned. "I saw him sneaking into the gallery last summer, and I couldn't believe it. It was like catching a glimpse of a unicorn. A gorgeous unicorn, I've got to say."

Joy took another brownie and bit into it. *Gorgeous* covered it. Of course, there was also *intriguing, desirable, fascinating*, and as yummy as this brownie. "Yeah, he is."

"Still." Deb looked up at Joy. "Could he be more antisocial? I mean, I get why and all, but aren't you going nuts up there with no one to talk to?"

"I talk to him," Joy argued.

"Yes, but does he talk back?"

"Not really, though in his defense, I do talk a lot." Joy shrugged. "Maybe it's hard for him to get a word in."

"Not that hard for me."

"We're women. Nothing's that hard for us."

"Okay, granted." Deb smiled, put the frosting back down and planted both hands on the counter. "But what's really going on with you? I notice you're awful quick to defend him. Your protective streak is coming out."

That was the only problem with a best friend, Joy thought. Sometimes they saw too much. Deb knew that Joy hadn't dated anyone in years. That she hadn't had any interest in sparking a relationship—since her last one had ended so memorably. So of course she would pick up on the fact that Joy was suddenly very interested in one particular man.

"It's nothing."

"Sure," Deb said with a snort of derision. "I believe that."

"Fine, it's *something*," Joy admitted. "I'm not sure what, though."

"But he's so not the kind of guy I would expect you to be interested in. He's so—cold."

Oh, there was plenty of heat inside Sam Henry. He just kept it all tamped down. Maybe that's what drew her to him, Joy thought. The mystery of him. Most men were fairly transparent, but Sam had hidden depths that practically demanded she unearth them. She couldn't get the image of the shadows in his eyes out of her mind. She wanted to know why he was so shut down. Wanted to know how to open him up.

Smiling now, she said, "Holly keeps telling me he's not mean, he's just crabby."

Deb laughed. "Is he?"

"Oh, definitely. But I don't know why."

"I might."

"What?"

Deb sighed heavily. "Okay, I admit that when you went to stay up there, I was a little worried that maybe he was some crazed weirdo with a closet full of women's bones or something."

"I keep telling you, stop watching those horror movies."

Deb grinned. "Can't. Love 'em." She picked up the frosting bag as if she needed to be doing something while she told the story. "Anyway, I spent a lot of time online, researching the local hermit and—"

"What?" And why hadn't Joy done the same thing? Well, she knew why. It had felt like a major intrusion on his privacy. She'd wanted to get him to actually *tell* her about himself. Yet here she was now, ready to pump Deb for the information she herself hadn't wanted to look for.

"You know he used to be a painter."

"Yes, that much I knew." Joy took a seat at one of the counter stools and kept her gaze fixed on Deb's blue eyes.

"He was famous. I mean *famous*." She paused for emphasis. "Then about five years ago, he just stopped painting entirely. Walked away from his career and the fame and fortune and moved to the mountains to hide out."

"You're not telling me anything I didn't know so far."

"I'm getting there." Sighing, Deb said softly, "His wife and three-year-old son died in a car wreck five years ago."

Joy felt as though she'd been punched in the stomach. The air left her lungs as sympathetic pain tore at her. Tears welled in her eyes as she tried to imagine that kind of hell. That kind of devastation. "Oh, my God."

"Yeah, I know," Deb said with a wince. Laying down the pastry bag, she added, "When I found out, I felt so bad for him."

Joy did, too. She couldn't even conceive the level of pain Sam had experienced. Even the thought of such a loss was shattering. Remembering the darkness in his eyes, Joy's heart hurt for him and ached to somehow ease the grief that even five years later still held him in a tight fist. Now at least she could understand a little better why he'd closed himself off from the world.

He'd hidden himself away on a mountaintop to escape the pain that was stalking him. She saw it in his eyes every time she looked at him. Those shadows that were a part of him were really just reflections of the pain that was in his heart. Of *course* he was still feeling the soul-crushing pain of losing his family. God, just the thought of losing Holly was enough to bring her to her knees.

Instinctively, she moved to Deb's kitchen window and looked out at two little girls playing with a puppy. Her gaze locked on her daughter, Joy had to blink a sheen of tears from her eyes.

So small. So innocent. To have that...*magic* winked out like a blown-out match? She couldn't imagine it. Didn't want to try.

"God, this explains so much," she whispered.

Deb walked to her side. "It does. But Joy, before you start riding to the rescue, think about it. It's been five years since he lost his family, and as far as I know, he's never talked about it. I don't think anyone in town even knows about his past."

"Probably not," she said, "unless they took the time to do an internet search on him."

Deb winced again. "Maybe I shouldn't have. Sort of feels like intruding on his privacy, now that I know."

"No, I'm glad you did. Glad you told me," Joy said, with a firm shake of her head. "I just wish I'd thought of doing it myself. Heck, I'm on the internet all the time, just working."

"That's why it didn't occur to you," Deb told her. "The internet is work for you. For the rest of us, it's a vast pool of unsubstantiated information."

She had a point. "Well, then I'm glad I came by today to get your updates for your website."

As a virtual assistant, Joy designed and managed websites for most of the shops in town, plus the medical clinic, plus she worked for a few mystery authors who lived all over the country. It was the perfect job for her, since she was very good at computer programming and it allowed her to work at home and be with Holly instead of sending the little girl out to day care.

But, because she spent so much time online for her job, she rarely took the time to browse sites for fun. Which was why it hadn't even occurred to her to look up Sam Henry.

Heart heavy, Joy looked through the window and watched as Holly fell back onto the dry grass, laughing as the puppy lunged up to lavish kisses on her face. Holly. God, Joy thought, now she knew why Sam had demanded she keep her daughter away from him. Seeing another child so close to the age of his lost son must be like a knife to the heart.

And yet...she remembered how kind he'd been with Holly

in the workshop that first day. How he'd helped her, how Holly had helped *him.*

Sam hadn't thrown Holly out. He'd spent time with her. Made her feel important and gave her the satisfaction of building something. He had closed himself off, true, but there was clearly a part of him looking for a way out.

She just had to help him find it.

Except for her nightly monologues in the great room, Joy had been giving him the space he claimed to want. But now she thought maybe it wasn't space he needed…but less of it. He'd been alone too long, she thought. He'd wrapped himself up in his pain and had been that way so long now, it probably felt normal to him. So, Joy told herself, if he wouldn't go into the world, then the world would just have to go to him.

"You're a born nurturer," Deb whispered, shaking her head.

Joy looked at her.

"I can see it on your face. You're going to try to 'save' him."

"I didn't say that."

"Oh, honey," Deb said, "you didn't have to."

"It's annoying to be read so easily."

"Only because I love you." Deb smiled. "But Joy, before you jump feetfirst into this, maybe you should consider that Sam might not *want* to be saved."

She was sure Deb was right. He didn't want to come out of the darkness. It had become his world. His, in a weird way, comfort zone. That didn't make it right.

"Even if he doesn't want it," Joy murmured, "he needs it."

"What *exactly* are you thinking?" Deb asked.

Too many things, Joy realized. Protecting Holly, reaching Sam, preparing for Christmas, keeping up with all of the holiday work she had to do for her clients… Oh, whom was she kidding? At the moment, Sam was uppermost in her mind. She was going to drag him back into the land of the living, and she had the distinct feeling he was going to put up a fight.

"I'm thinking that maybe I'm in way over my head."

Deb sighed a little. "How deep is the pool?"

"Pretty deep," Joy mused, thinking about her reaction to him, the late-night talks in the great room where it was just the two of them and the haunted look in his eyes that pulled at her.

Deb bumped her hip against Joy's. "I see that look in your eyes. You're already attached."

She was. Pointless to deny it, especially to Deb of all people, since she could read Joy so easily.

"Yes," she said and heard the worry in her own voice, "but like I said, it's pretty deep waters."

"I'm not worried," Deb told her with a grin. "You're a good swimmer."

That night, things were different.

When Sam came to dinner in the dining room, Joy and Holly were already seated, waiting for him. Since every other night, the two of them were in the kitchen, he looked thrown for a second. She gave him a smile even as Holly called out, "Hi, Sam!"

If anything, he looked warier than just a moment before. "What's this?"

"It's called a communal meal," Joy told him, serving up a bowl of stew with dumplings. She set the bowl down at his usual seat, poured them both a glass of wine, then checked to make sure Holly was settled beside her.

"Mommy made dumplings. They're really good," the little girl said.

"I'm sure." Reluctantly, he took a seat then looked at Joy. "This is not part of our agreement."

He looked, she thought, as if he were cornered. Well, good, because he was. Dragging him out of the darkness was going to be a step-by-step journey—and it started now.

"Actually…" she told him, spooning up a bite of her own stew, then sighing dramatically at the taste. Okay, yes she was a good cook, but she was putting it on for his benefit. And it was working. She saw him glance at the steaming bowl in front of his chair, even though he hadn't taken a bite yet. "...our agreement was that I clean and cook. We never agreed to not eat together."

"It was implied," he said tightly.

"Huh." She tipped her head to one side and studied the ceiling briefly as if looking for an answer there. "I didn't get that implication at all. But why don't you eat your dinner and we can talk about it."

"It's good, Sam," Holly said again, reaching for her glass of milk.

He took a breath and exhaled on a sigh. "Fine. But this doesn't mean anything."

"Of course not," Joy said, hiding the smile blossoming inside her. "You're still the crabby man we all know. No worries about your reputation."

His lips twitched as he tasted the stew. She waited for his reaction and didn't have to wait long. "It's good."

"Told ya!" Holly's voice was a crow of pleasure.

"Yeah," he said, flicking the girl an amused glance. "You did."

Joy saw that quick look and smiled inside at the warmth of it.

"When we went to town today I played with Lizzie's puppy," Holly said, taking another bite and wolfing it down so she could keep talking. "He licked me in the face again and I laughed and Lizzie and me ran and he chased us and he made Lizzie fall but she didn't cry..."

Joy smiled at her daughter, loving how the girl could launch into a conversation that didn't need a partner, commas or periods. She was so thrilled by life, so eager to experience everything, just watching her made Joy's life better in every possible way. From the corner of her eye, she stole a look at Sam and saw the flicker of pain in his eyes. It had to be hard for him to listen to a child's laughter and have to grieve for the loss of his own child. But he couldn't avoid children forever. He'd end up a miserable old man, and that would be a waste, she told herself.

"And when I get my puppy, Lizzie can come and play with

it, too, and it will chase us and mine will be white cuz Lizzie's is black and it would be fun to have puppies like that..."

"She's really counting on that puppy," Joy murmured.

"So?" Sam dipped into his stew steadily as if he was hurrying to finish so he could escape the dining room—and their company.

Deliberately, Joy refilled his bowl over his complaints.

"So, there aren't any white puppies to be had," she whispered, her own voice covered by the rattle of Holly's excited chatter.

"Santa's going to bring him, remember, Mommy?" Holly asked, proving that her hearing was not affected by the rush of words tumbling from her own mouth.

"That's right, baby," Joy said with a wince at Sam's smirk. "But you know, sometimes Santa can't bring everything you want—"

"If you're not a good girl," Holly said, nodding sharply. "But I am a good girl, right, Mommy?"

"Right, baby." She was really stuck now. Joy was going to have to go into Boise and look for a puppy or she was going to have a heartbroken daughter on Christmas morning, and that she couldn't allow.

Too many of Joy's childhood Christmases had been empty, lonely. She never wanted Holly to feel the kind of disappointment Joy had known all too often.

"I told Lizzie about the fairy house we made, Sam, and she said she has fairies at her house, but I don't think so cuz you need lots of trees for fairies and there's not any at Lizzie's..."

"The kid never shuts up," Sam said, awe in his voice.

"She's excited." Joy shrugged. "Christmas is coming."

His features froze over and Joy could have kicked herself. Sure, she planned on waking him up to life, but she couldn't just toss him into the middle of a fire, could she? She had to ease him closer to the warmth a little at a time.

"Yeah."

"I know you said no decorations or—"

His gaze snapped to hers, cold. Hard. "That's right."

"In the great room," she continued as if he hadn't said a word, as if she hadn't gotten a quick chill from the ice in his eyes, "but Holly and I are here for the whole month and a little girl needs Christmas. So we'll keep the decorations to a minimum."

His mouth worked as if he wanted to argue and couldn't find a way to do it without being a complete jerk. "Fine."

She reached out and gave his forearm a quick pat. Even with removing her hand almost instantly, that swift buzz of something amazing tingled her fingers. Joy took a breath, smiled and said, "Don't worry, we won't be too happy around you, either. Wouldn't want you upset by the holiday spirit."

He shot her a wry look. "Thanks."

"No problem." Joy grinned at him. "You have to be careful or you could catch some stray laugh and maybe even try to join in only to have your face break."

Holly laughed. "Mommy, that's silly. Faces can't break, can they, Sam?"

His brown eyes were lit with suppressed laughter, and Joy considered that a win for her. "You're right, Holly. Faces can't break."

"Just freeze?" Joy asked, her lips curving.

"Yeah. I'm good at freezing," he said, gaze meeting hers in a steady stare.

"That's cuz it's cold," Holly said, then added, "Can I be done now, Mommy?"

Joy tore her gaze from his long enough to check that her daughter had eaten most of her dinner. "Yes, sweetie. Why don't you go get the pinecones we found today and put them on the kitchen counter? We'll paint them after I clean up."

"Okay!" The little girl scooted off the chair, ran around the table and stopped beside Sam. "You wanna paint with me? We got glitter, too, to put on the pinecones and we get to use glue to stick it."

Joy watched him, saw his eyes soften, then saw him take a

deliberate, emotional step back. Her heart hurt, remembering what she now knew about his past. And with the sound of her daughter's high-pitched, excited voice ringing in the room, Joy wondered again how he'd survived such a tremendous loss. But even as she thought it, Joy realized that he was like a survivor of a disaster.

He'd lived through it but he wasn't *living*. He was still existing in that half world of shock and pain, and it looked to her as though he'd been there so long he didn't have a clue how to get out. And that's where Joy came in. She wouldn't leave him in the dark. Couldn't watch him let his life slide past.

"No, thanks." Sam gave the little girl a tight smile. "You go ahead. I've got some things I've got to do."

Well, at least he didn't say anything about hating Christmas. "Go ahead, sweetie. I'll be there in a few minutes."

"Okay, Mommy. 'Bye, Sam!" Holly waved, turned and raced toward the kitchen, eager to get started on those pinecones.

When they were alone again, Joy looked at the man opposite her and smiled. "Thanks for not popping her Christmas balloon."

He scowled at her and pushed his empty bowl to one side. "I'm not a monster."

"No," she said, thoughtfully. "You're not."

He ignored that. "Look, I agreed to you and Holly doing Christmas stuff in your part of the house. Just don't try to drag me into it. Deal?"

She held out one hand and left it there until he took it in his and gave it a firm shake. Of course, she had no intention of keeping to that "deal." Instead, she was going to wake him up whether he liked it or not. By the time she was finished, Joy assured herself, he'd be roasting chestnuts in the fireplace and stringing lights on a Christmas tree.

His eyes met hers and in those dark depths she saw...everything. A tingling buzz shot up her arm and ricocheted around in the center of her chest like a Ping-Pong ball in a box. Her heartbeat quickened and her mouth went dry. Those eyes of his gazed into hers, and Joy took a breath and held it. Finally, he let go of her hand and took a single step back as if to keep a measure of safe distance between them.

"Well," she said when she was sure her voice would work again, "I'm going to straighten out the kitchen then paint pinecones with my daughter."

"Right." He scrubbed one hand across his face. "I'll be in the great room."

She stood up, gathered the bowls together and said, "Earlier today, Holly and I made some Christmas cookies. I'll bring you a few with your coffee."

"Not necessary—"

She held up one hand. "You can call them winter cookies if it makes you feel better."

He choked off a laugh, shook his head and started out of the room. Before he left, he turned to look back at her. "You don't stop, do you?"

"Nope." He took another step and paused when she asked, "The real question is, do you want me to?"

He didn't speak, just gave her a long look out of thoughtful, chocolate-brown eyes, then left the room. Joy smiled to herself, because that nonanswer told her everything she wanted to know.

CHAPTER SIX

SAM USED TO hate the night.

The quiet. The feeling of being alone in the world. The seemingly endless hours of darkness. It had given him too much time to think. To remember. To torture himself with what-might-have-beens. He couldn't sleep because memories became dreams that jolted him awake—or worse, lulled him into believing the last several years had never really happened. Then waking up became the misery, and so the cycle went.

Until nearly a week ago. Until Joy.

He had a fire blazing in the hearth as he waited for her. Night was now something he looked forward to. Being with her, hearing her voice, her laughter, had become the best part of his days. He enjoyed her quick mind, and her sense of humor—even when it was directed at him. He liked hearing her talk about what was happening in town, even though he didn't know any of the people she told him about. He liked seeing her with her daughter, watching the love between them, even though it was like a knife to his heart.

Sam hadn't expected this, hadn't thought he wanted it. He rubbed his palms together, remembering the flash of heat that enveloped him when he'd taken her hand to seal their latest deal. He could see the flash in her eyes that told him she'd felt the same damn thing. And with the desire gripping him, guilt speared through Sam, as well. Everything he'd lost swam in his mind, reminding him that *feeling*, *wanting*, was a steep and slippery road to loss.

He stared into the fire, listened to the hiss and snap of flame on wood, and for the first time in years, he *tried* to bring those long-abandoned memories to the surface. Watching the play of light and shadow, the dance of flames, Sam fought to draw his dead wife's face into his mind. But the memory was indistinct, as if a fog had settled between them, making it almost impossible for him to remember just the exact shade of her brown eyes. The way her mouth curved in a smile. The fall of her hair and the set of her jaw when she was angry.

It was all...hazy, and as he battled to remember Dani, it was Joy's face that swam to the surface of his mind. The sound of *her* laughter. The scent of her. And he wanted to know the taste of her. What the hell was happening to him and why was he allowing it? Sam told himself to leave. To not be there when Joy came into the room. But as much as he knew he should, he also knew he wouldn't.

"I brought more cookies."

He turned in his chair to look at her, and even from across the room, he felt that now-familiar punch of awareness. Of heat. And he knew it was too late to leave.

At her smile, one eyebrow lifted and he asked, "More reindeer and Santas?"

That smile widened until it sparkled in her eyes. She walked toward him, carrying a tray that held the plate of cookies and two glasses of golden wine.

"This time we have snowmen and wreaths and—" she paused "—*winter* trees."

He shook his head and sighed. It seemed she was determined to shove Christmas down his throat whether he liked it or not. "You're relentless."

Why did he like that about her?

"That's been said before," she told him and took her usual seat in the chair beside his. Setting the tray down on the table between them, she took a cookie then lifted her glass for a sip of wine.

"Really. Cookies and wine."

"Separately, they're both good," she said, waving her cookie at the plate, challenging him to join her. "Together, they're amazing."

The cookies were good, Sam thought, reaching out to pick one up and bite in. All he'd had to do was close his eyes so he wasn't faced with iced, sprinkled Santas and they were just cookies. "Good."

"Thanks." She sat back in the chair. "That wasn't so hard, was it?"

"What?"

"Talking to me." She folded her legs up beneath her, took another sip of her wine and continued. "We've been sitting in this room together for five nights now and usually, the only voice I hear is my own."

He frowned, took the wine and drank. Gave him an excuse for not addressing that remark. Of course, it was true, but that wasn't the point. He hadn't asked her to join him every night, had he? When she only looked at him, waiting, he finally said, "Didn't seem to bother you any."

"Oh, I don't mind talking to myself—"

"No kidding."

She grinned. "But it's more fun talking to other people."

Sam told himself not to notice how her hair shined golden in the firelight. How her eyes gleamed and her mouth curved as if she were always caught on the verge of a smile. His gaze dropped to the plain blue shirt she wore and how the buttons pulled across her chest. Her jeans were faded and soft, clinging to her legs as she curled up and got comfortable. Red polish decorated her toes. Why that gave him a quick, hot jolt, he couldn't have said.

Everything in him wanted to pull her out of that chair, wrap his arms around her and take her tantalizing mouth in a kiss that would sear both of them. And *why*, he asked himself, did he suddenly feel like a cheating husband? Because since Dani, no other woman had pulled at him like this. And even as he wanted Joy, he hated that he wanted her. The cookie turned to chalk in his mouth and he took a sip of wine to wash it down.

"Okay, someone just had a dark thought," she mused.

"Stay out of my head," Sam said, slanting her a look.

Feeling desire didn't mean that he welcomed it. Life had been—not easier—but more clear before Joy walked into his house. He'd known who he was then. A widower. A father without a child. And he'd wrapped himself up in memories designed to keep him separate from a world he wasn't interested in anyway.

Yet now, after less than a week, he could feel those layers of insulation peeling away and he wasn't sure how to stop it or even if he wanted to. The shredding of his cloak of invisibility was painful and still he couldn't stop it.

Dinner with Joy and Holly had tripped him up, too, and he had a feeling she'd known it would. If he'd been smart, he would have walked out of the room as soon as he'd seen them at the table. But one look into Joy's and Holly's eyes had ended that idea before it could begin. So instead of having his solitary meal, he'd been part of a unit—and for a few minutes, he'd enjoyed it. Listening to Holly's excited chatter, sharing knowing looks with Joy. Then, of course, he remembered that Joy and Holly weren't *his*. And that was what he had to keep in mind.

Taking another drink of the icy wine, he shifted his gaze to the fire. Safer to look into the flames than to stare at the deep blue of her eyes. "Yeah," he said, finally responding to her last statement, "I don't really talk to people anymore."

"No kidding." She threw his earlier words back at him, and Sam nodded at the jab.

"Kaye tends to steer clear of me most of the time."

"Kaye doesn't like talking to people, either," Joy said, laughing. "You two are a match made in heaven."

"There's a thought," he muttered.

She laughed again, and the sound of it filled every empty corner of the room. It was both balm and torture to hear it, to know he *wanted* to hear it. How was it possible that she'd made such an impact on him in such a short time? He hadn't even noticed her worming her way past his defenses until it was impossible to block her.

"So," she asked suddenly, pulling him from his thoughts, "any idea where I can find a puppy?"

"No," he said shortly, then decided there was no reason to bark at her because he was having trouble dealing with her. He looked at her. "I don't know people around here."

"See, you should," she said, tipping her head to one side to look at him. "You've lived here five years, Sam."

"I didn't move here for friends." He came to the mountains to find the peace that still eluded him.

"Doesn't mean you can't make some." Sighing, she turned her head to the flames. "If you did know people, you could help me on the puppy situation." Shaking her head, she added, "I've got her princess dolls and a fairy princess dress and the other small things she asked for. The puppy worries me."

He didn't want to think about children's Christmas dreams. Sam remembered another child dictating letters to Santa and waking to the splendor of Christmas morning. And through the pain he also recalled how he and his wife had worked to make those dreams come true for their little boy. So, though he hated it, he said, "You could get her a stuffed puppy with a note that Santa will bring her the real thing as soon as the puppy's ready for a new home."

She tipped her head to one side and studied him, a wide smile on her face. God, when she smiled, her eyes shone and something inside him fisted into knots.

"A note from Santa himself? That's a good idea. I think Holly would love that he's going to make a special trip just for her." Clearly getting into it, she continued, "I could make up a certificate or something. You know—" she deepened her voice for dramatic effect "—*this is to certify that Holly Curran will be receiving a puppy from Santa as soon as the puppy is ready for a home.*" Wrinkling her brow, she added thoughtfully, "Maybe I could draw a Christmas border on the paper and we could frame it for her—you know, with Santa's signature—and hang it in her bedroom. It could become an heirloom, something she passes down to her kids."

He shrugged, as if it meant nothing, but in his head, he could see Holly's excitement at a special visit from Santa *after* Christmas. But once December was done, he wouldn't be seeing Joy or Holly again, so he wouldn't know how the Santa promise went, would he? Frowning to himself, he tried to ignore the ripple of regret that swept through him.

"Okay, I am not responsible for your latest frown."

"What?" He turned his head to look at her again.

She laughed shortly. "Nothing. So, what'd you work on today?"

"Seriously?" Usually she just launched into a monologue.

"Well, you're actually speaking tonight," she said with a shrug, "so I thought I'd ask a question that wasn't rhetorical."

"Right." Shaking his head, he said, "I'm starting a new project."

"Another table?"

"No."

"Talking," she acknowledged, "but still far from chatty."

"Men are not chatty."

"Some men you can't shut up," she argued. "If it's not a table you're working on, what is it?"

"Haven't decided yet."

"You know, in theory, a job like that sounds wonderful." She took a sip of wine. "But I do better with a schedule all laid out in front of me. I like knowing that website updates are due on Monday and newsletters have to go out on Tuesday, like that."

"I don't like schedules."

She watched him carefully, and his internal radar went on alert. When a woman got that particular look in her eye—curiosity—it never ended well for a man.

"Well," she said softly, "if you haven't decided on a project yet, you could give me some help with the Santa certificate."

"What do you mean?" He heard the wariness in his own voice.

"I mean, you could draw Christmassy things around the borders, make it look beautiful." She paused and when she spoke again, the words came so softly they were almost lost in the hiss and snap of the fire in front of them. "You used to paint."

And in spite of those flames less than three feet from him, Sam went cold right down to the bone. "I used to."

She nodded. "I saw some of your paintings online. They were beautiful."

He took a long drink of wine, hoping to ease the hard knot lodged in his throat. It didn't help. She'd looked him up online. Seen his paintings. Had she seen the rest, as well? Newspaper articles on the accident? Pictures of his dead wife and son? Pictures of him at their funeral, desperate, grieving, throwing a punch at a photographer? God he hated that private pain was treated as public entertainment.

"That was a long time ago," he spoke and silently congratulated himself on squeezing the words from a dry, tight throat.

"Almost six years."

He snapped a hard look at her. "Yeah. I *know*. What is it you're looking for here? Digging for information? Pointless. The world already knows the whole story."

"Talking," she told him. "Not digging."

"Well," he said, pushing to his feet, "I'm done talking."

"Big surprise," Joy said, shaking her head slowly.

"What's that supposed to mean?" Damn it, had he really just

been thinking that spending time with her was a good thing? He looked down into those summer-blue eyes and saw irritation sparking there. Well, what the hell did *she* have to be mad about? It wasn't *her* life being picked over.

"It means, I knew you wouldn't want to talk about any of this."

"Yet, you brought it up anyway." Hell, Kaye knew the whole story about Sam's life and the tragedy he'd survived, but at least she never threw it at him. "What the hell? Did some reporter call you asking for a behind-the-scenes exclusive? Haven't they done enough articles on me yet? Or maybe you want to write a tell-all book, is that it?"

"Wow." That irritation in her eyes sparked from mild to barely suppressed fury in an instant. "You really think I would do that? To you? I would never sell out a friend."

"Oh," he snapped, refusing to be moved by the statement, "we're friends now?"

"We could be, if you would stop looking at everyone around you like a potential enemy."

"I told you I didn't come here for friends," he reminded her. Damn it, the fire was heating the air. That had to be why breathing was so hard. Why his chest felt tight.

"You've made that clear." Joy took a breath that he couldn't seem to manage, and he watched as the fury in her eyes softened to a glimmer. "Look, I only said something because it seemed ridiculous to pretend I didn't know who you were."

He rubbed the heel of his hand at the center of his chest, trying to ease the ball of ice lodged there. "Fine. Don't pretend. Just ignore it."

"What good will that do?" She set her wine down on the table and stood up to face him. "I'm sorry but—"

"Don't. God, don't say you're sorry. I've had more than enough of that, thanks. I don't want your sympathy." He pushed one hand through his hair and felt the heat of the fire on his back.

This place had been his refuge. He'd buried his past back east and come here to get away from not only the press, but also the constant barrage of memories assaulting him at every familiar scene. He'd left his family because their pity had been thick enough to choke him. He'd left *himself* behind when he came to the mountains. The man he'd once been. The man who'd been so wrapped up in creating beauty that he hadn't noticed the beauty in his own life until it had been snatched away.

"Well, you've got it anyway," Joy told him and reached out to lay one hand on his forearm.

Her touch fired everything in him, heat erupting with a rush that jolted his body to life in a way he hadn't experienced in too many long, empty years. And he resented the hell out of it.

He pulled away from her, and his voice dripped ice as he said, "Whatever it is you're after, you should know I don't want another woman in my life. Another child. Another loss."

Her gaze never left his, and those big blue pools of sympathy and irritation threatened to drown him.

"Everybody loses, Sam," she said quietly. "Houses, jobs, people they love. You can't insulate yourself from that. Protect yourself from pain. It's how you respond to the losses you experience that defines who you are."

He sneered at her. She had no idea. "And you don't like how I responded? Is that it? Well, get in line."

"Loss doesn't go away just because you're hiding from it."

Darkness beyond the windows seemed to creep closer, as if it were finding a way to slip right inside him. This room with its bright wood and soft lights and fire-lit shadows felt as if it were the last stand against the dark, and the light was losing.

Sam took a deep breath, looked down at her and said tightly, "You don't know what you're talking about."

Her head tipped to one side and blond curls fell against her neck. "You think you're the only one with pain?"

Of course not. But his own was too deep, too ingrained to allow him to give a flying damn what someone else might be suffering. "Just drop it. I'm done with this."

"Oh no. This you don't get to ignore. You think I don't know loss?" She moved in closer, tipped her head back and sent a steely-blue stare into his eyes. "My parents died when I was eight. I grew up in foster homes because I wasn't young enough or cute enough to be adopted."

"Damn it, Joy—" He'd seen pain reflected in his own eyes often enough to recognize the ghosts of it in hers. And he felt like the bastard he was for practically insisting that she dredge up her own past to do battle with his.

"As a foster kid I was never 'real' in any of the families I lived with. Always the outsider. Never fitting in. I didn't have friends, either, so I went out and made some."

"Good for you."

"Not finished. I had to build everything I have for myself *by* myself. I wanted to belong. I wanted family, you know?"

He started to speak, but she held up one hand for silence, and damned if it didn't work on him. He couldn't take his eyes off her as he watched her dip into the past to defend her present.

"I met Holly's father when I was designing his website. He was exciting and he loved me, and I thought it was forever—it lasted until I told him about Holly."

And though Sam felt bad, hearing it, watching it, knowing she'd had a tough time of it, he couldn't help but ask, "Yeah? Did he die? Did he take Holly away from you, so that you knew you'd never see her again?"

She huffed out a breath. "No, but—"

"Then you don't know," Sam interrupted, not caring now if he sounded like an unfeeling jerk. He wouldn't feel bad for the child she'd once been. *She* was the one who had dragged the ugly past into the present. "You can't possibly *know*, and I'm not going to stand here defending myself and my choices to you."

"Great," she said, nodding sharply as her temper once again rose to meet his. "So you'll just keep hiding yourself away until the rest of your life slides past?"

Sam snapped, throwing both hands high. "Why the hell do you care if I do?"

"Because I *saw* you with Holly," Joy said, moving in on him again, flavoring every breath he took with the scent of summer flowers that clung to her. "I saw your kindness. She needed that. Needs a male role model in her life and—"

"Oh, stop. Role models. For God's sake, I'm no one's father figure."

"Really?" She jammed both hands on her hips. "Better to shut yourself down? Pretend you're alone on a rock somewhere?"

"For me, yeah."

"You're lying."

"You don't know me."

"You'd like to think so," Joy said. "But you're not that hard to read, Sam."

Sam shook his head. "You're here to run the house, not psychoanalyze me."

"Multitasker, remember?" She smiled and he resented her for it. Resented knowing that he wanted her in spite of the tempers spiking between them. Hell, maybe *because* of it. He hated knowing that maybe she had a point. He really hated realizing that whatever secrets he thought he'd been keeping were no more private than the closest computer with an internet connection.

And man, it bugged him that she could go from anger to smiles in a blink.

"This isn't analysis, Sam." She met his gaze coolly, steadily, firelight dancing in her eyes. "It's called conversation."

"It's called my *family*," he said tightly, watching the reflection of flame and shadow in the blue of her eyes.

"I know. And—"

"Don't say you're sorry."

"I have to," she said simply. "And I am."

"Great. Thanks." God he wanted to get out of there. She was too close to him. He could smell her shampoo and the scent of flowers—Jasmine? Lilies?—fired a bolt of desire through him.

"But that's not all I am," she continued. "I'm also a little furious at you."

"Yeah? Right back at you."

"Good," she said, surprising him. "If you're angry at least you're *feeling* something." She moved in closer, kept her gaze locked with his and said, "If you love making furniture and working with wood, great. You're really good at it."

He nodded, hardly listening, his gaze shifting to the open doorway across the room. It—and the chance of escape—seemed miles away.

"But you shouldn't stop painting," she added fiercely. "The worlds you created were beautiful. Magical."

That magic was gone now, and it was better that way, he assured himself. But Sam couldn't remember a time when anyone had talked to him like this. Forcing him to remember. To face the darkness. To face himself. One reason he'd moved so far from his parents, his sister, was that they had been so careful. So cautious in everything they'd said as if they were all walking a tightrope, afraid to make the wrong move, say the wrong thing.

Their...*caution* had been like knives, jabbing at him constantly. Creating tiny nicks that festered and ached with every passing minute. So he'd moved here, where no one knew him. Where no one would offer sympathy he didn't want or advice he wouldn't take. He'd never counted on Joy.

"Why?" she asked. "Why would you give that up?"

It had been personal. So deeply personal he'd never talked about it with anyone, and he wasn't about to start now. Chest tight, mouth dry, he looked at her and said, "I'm not talking about this with you."

With anyone.

He took a step or two away from her, then spun back and around to glare down at her. In spite of the quick burst of fury inside him, sizzling around and between them, she didn't seem the least bit intimidated. Another thing to admire about her, damn it. She was sure of herself even when she was wrong.

"I already told you, Sam. You don't scare me."

"That's a damn shame," he muttered, trying not to remember that his mother had warned him about lonely old recluses muttering to themselves. He turned from her again, and this time she reached out and grabbed his arm as he moved away from her.

"Just stop," she demanded. "Stop and talk to me."

He glanced down at her hand on his arm and tried not to relish the heat sliding from her body into his. Tried not to notice that every cell inside him was waking up with a jolt. "Already told you I'm not talking about this."

"Then don't. Just stay. Talk to me." She took a deep breath, gave his arm a squeeze, then let him go. "Look, I didn't mean to bring any of this up tonight."

"Then why the hell did you?" He felt the loss of her touch and wanted it back.

"I don't like lying."

Scowling now, he asked, "What's that got to do with anything?"

Joy folded both arms in front of her and unconsciously lifted them until his gaze couldn't keep from admiring the pull of her shirt and the curve of those breasts. He shook his head and attempted to focus when she started talking again.

"I found out today about your family and not saying something would have felt like I was lying to you."

Convoluted, but in a weird way, she made sense. He wasn't much for lies, either, except for the ones he told his mother every time he assured her that he was fine. And truth be told, he would have been fine with Joy pretending she knew nothing about his past. But it was too late now for pretense.

"Okay, great. Conscience clear. Now let's move on." He started walking again and this time, when Joy tugged on his arm to get him to stop, he whirled around to face her.

Her blue eyes went wide, her mouth opened and he pulled her into him. It was instinct, pure, raw instinct, that had him grabbing her close. He speared his fingers through those blond curls,

pulled her head back and kissed her with all the pent-up frustration, desire and, yeah, even temper that was clawing at him.

Surprised, it took her only a second or two to react. Joy
wrapped her arms around his waist and moved in even closer.
Sam's head exploded at the first, incredible taste of her. And
then he wanted more. A groan slid from her throat, and that
sound fed the flames enveloping him. God, he'd had no idea
what kissing her would do to him. He'd been thinking about
this for days, and having her in his arms made him want the
feel of her skin beneath his hands. The heat of her body surrounding his.

All he could think was to get her clothes off her. To cup her
breasts, to take each of her nipples into his mouth and listen to
the whimpering sounds of pleasure she would make as he took
her. He wanted to look down into blue eyes and watch them go
blind with passion. He wanted to feel her hands sliding across
his skin, holding him tightly to her.

His kiss deepened farther, his tongue tangling with hers in
a frenzied dance of desire that pumped through him with the
force and rush of a wildfire screaming across the hillsides.

Joy clung to him, letting him know in the most primal way
that she felt the same. That her own needs and desires were
pushing at her. He took her deeper, held her tighter and spun
her around toward the closest couch. Heart pounding, breath
slamming in and out of his lungs, he kept his mouth fused to
hers as he laid her down on the wide, soft cushions and followed after, keeping her close to his side. She arched up, back
bowing as he ran one hand up and down the length of her. All
he could think about was touching her skin, feeling the heat
of her. He flipped the button of her jeans open, pulled down
the zipper, then slid his hand down, across her abdomen, feeling her shiver with every inch of flesh he claimed. His fingers
slipped beneath the band of her panties and she lifted her hips
as he moved to cup her heat.

She gasped, tore her mouth from his and clutched at his

shoulders when he stroked her for the first time. He loved the feel of her—slick, wet, hot. His body tightened painfully as he stared into her eyes. His mind fuzzed out and his body ached. He touched her, again and again, stroking, pushing into her heat, caressing her inside and out, driving them both to the edge of insanity.

"Sam—" She breathed his name and that soft, whispered sound rattled him.

When had she become so important? When had touching her become imperative? He took her mouth, tangling his tongue with hers, taking the taste of her deep inside him as he felt her body coil tighter with the need swamping her. She rocked into his hand, her hips pumping as he pushed her higher, faster. He pulled his head back, wanting, needing to see her eyes glaze with passion when the orgasm hit her.

He wasn't disappointed. She jolted in his arms when his thumb stroked across that one small nub of sensation at the heart of her. Everything she was feeling flashed through her eyes, across her features. He was caught up, unable to tear his gaze from hers. Joy Curran was a surprise to him on so many levels, he felt as though he'd never really learn them all. And at the moment, he didn't have to. Right now, he wanted only to hold her as she shattered.

She called his name again and he clutched her to him as her body trembled and shivered in his grasp. Her climax rolled on and on, leaving her breathless and Sam more needy than ever.

His body ached to join hers. His heart pounded in a fast gallop that left him damn near shaking with the want clawing at him.

"Sam," she whispered, reaching up to cup his face with her palms. "Sam, I need—"

He knew just what she needed because he needed it too. He shifted, pulled his hand free of her body and thought only about stripping them both out of their clothes.

In one small, rational corner of his mind, Sam admitted to

himself that he'd never known anything like this before. This pulsing, blinding, overpowering sense of need and pleasure and craving to be part of a woman. To be locked inside her body and lose himself in her. Never.

Not even with Dani.

That thought broke him. He pulled back abruptly and stared down at Joy like a blind man seeing the light for the first time. Both exhilarated and terrified. A bucket full of ice water dumped on his head wouldn't have shocked him more.

He fought for breath, for balance, but there wasn't any to be had. His own mind was shouting at him, telling him he was a bastard for feeling more for Joy than he had for his wife. Telling him to deny it, even to himself. To bury these new emotions and go back to feeling nothing. It was safer.

"That's it," he said, shaking his head, rolling off the couch, then taking a step, then another, away from her. "I can't do this."

"Sure you can," Joy assured him, a confused half smile on her face as her breath came in short, hard gasps. She pushed herself up to her elbows on the couch. Her hair was a wild tumble of curls and her jeans still lay open, invitingly. "You were doing great."

"I *won't* do this." His eyes narrowed on her. "Not again."

"Sam, we should talk—"

He actually laughed, though to him it sounded harsh, strained as it scraped against his throat. "Talking doesn't solve everything and it won't solve this. I'm going out to the workshop."

Joy watched him go, her lips still buzzing from that kiss. Her heart still pounding like a bass drum. She might even have gone after him if her legs weren't trembling so badly she was forced to drop into the closest chair.

What the hell had just happened?

And how could she make it happen again?

CHAPTER SEVEN

JOY DIDN'T SEE Sam at all the next morning, and maybe that was just as well.

She'd lain awake most of the night, reliving the whole scene, though she could admit to herself she spent more time reliving the kiss and the feel of his amazingly talented fingers on her body than the argument that had prompted it. Even now, though, she cringed a little remembering how she'd thrown the truth of his past at him out of nowhere. Honestly, what had she been thinking, just blurting out the fact that she knew about his family? She hadn't been thinking at all—that was the problem.

She'd stared into those amazing eyes of his and had seen him shuttered away, closing himself off, and it had just made her so angry, she'd confronted him without considering what it might do to the tenuous relationship they already had.

In Kaye's two-bedroom suite off the kitchen, there had been quiet in Joy's room and innocent dreams in Holly's. The house seemed to sigh with a cold wind that whipped through the pines and rattled glass panes. And Joy hadn't been able to shut off her brain. Or her body. But once she'd gotten past the buzz running rampant through her veins, all she'd been able to think about was the look in his eyes when she'd brought up his lost family.

Lying there in the dark, she'd assured herself that once she'd said the words, opened a door into his past, there'd been no going back. She could still see the shock in his eyes when she'd brought it up, and a twinge of guilt wrapped itself around her heart. But it was no match for the ribbon of anger that was there as well.

Not only had he walked away from his talent, but he'd shut himself off from life. From any kind of future or happiness. Why? His suffering wouldn't bring them back. Wouldn't restore the family he'd lost.

"Mommy, are you all done now?"

Joy came out of her thoughts and looked at her daughter, beside her at the kitchen table. Behind them, the outside world was gray and the pines bent nearly in half from that wind sweeping in off the lake. Still no snow and Joy was beginning to think they wouldn't have a white Christmas after all.

But for now, in the golden lamplight, she looked at Holly, doing her alphabet and numbers on her electronic tablet. The little girl was squirming in her seat, clearly ready to be done with the whole sit-down-and-work thing.

"Not yet, baby," Joy said, and knew that if her brain hadn't been filled with images of Sam, she'd have been finished with the website update a half hour ago. But no, all she could think of was the firelight in his eyes. The taste of his mouth. The feel of his hard body pressed to hers. And the slick glide of his fingers.

Oh, boy.

"Almost, honey," she said, clearing her throat and focusing again on the comments section of her client's website. For some reason people who read books felt it was okay to go on the author's website and list the many ways the author could have made the book better. Even when they loved it, they managed to sneak in a couple of jabs. It was part of Joy's job to remove the comments that went above and beyond a review and deep into the realm of harsh criticism.

"Mommy," Holly said, her heels kicking against the rungs of the kitchen chair, "when can we gooooooo?"

A one-syllable word now six syllables.

"As soon as I'm finished, sweetie," Joy promised, focusing on her laptop screen rather than the never-ending loop of her time with Sam. Once the comment section was cleaned up, Joy posted her client's holiday letter to her fans, then closed up the site and opened the next one.

Another holiday letter to post and a few pictures the author had taken at the latest writers' conference she'd attended.

"How much longer, though?" Holly asked, just a touch of a wheedling whine in her voice. "If we don't go soon all the Christmas trees will be *gone*."

Drama, thy name is Holly, Joy thought with a smile. Reaching out, she gave one of the girl's pigtails a tug. "Promise, there will be lots of trees when we get into town. But remember, we're getting a little one this year, okay?" Because of the Grinch and his aversion to all things festive.

"I know! It's like a fairy tree cuz it's tiny and can go on a table to put in our room cuz Sam doesn't like Christmas." Her head tipped to one side. "How come he doesn't, Mommy? Everybody likes presents."

"I don't know, baby." She wasn't about to try to explain Sam's penchant for burying himself in a loveless, emotionless well. "You should ask him sometime."

"I'll ask him now!" She scrambled off her chair and Joy thought about calling her back as she raced to get her jacket. But why should she? Joy had already seen Sam with Holly. He was kind. Patient. And she knew darn well that even if the man was furious with *her*, he wouldn't take it out on Holly.

And maybe it would be good for him to be faced with all that cheerful optimism. All that innocence shining around her girl.

In seconds, Holly was back, dancing in place on the toes of her pink princess sneakers. Joy zipped up the jacket, pulled up Holly's hood and tied it at the neck. Then she took a moment to just look at the little girl who was really the light of her life.

Love welled up inside her, thick and rich, and she heard Sam's voice in her mind again.

Did he take Holly away from you, so that you knew you'd never see her again?

That thought had Joy grabbing her daughter and pulling her in close for a tight hug that had Holly wriggling for freedom. He was right, she couldn't really *know* what he'd survived. She didn't even want to imagine it.

"You're squishing me, Mommy!"

"Sorry, baby." She swallowed the knot in her throat and gave her girl a smile. "You go ahead and play with Sam. I'll come get you when it's time to go. As soon as I finish doing the updates on this website. Promise."

"Okay!" Holly turned to go and stopped when Joy spoke up again.

"No wandering off, Holly. Right to the workshop."

"Can't I look at my fairy house Sam helped me make? There might be fairies there now."

Boy, she was really going to miss this imaginative age when Holly grew out of it. But, though the fairy house wasn't exactly *inside* the woods, it was close enough that a little girl might be tempted to walk in more deeply and then end up getting lost. So, no. "We'll look later."

"Okay, 'bye!" And she was gone like a tiny pink hurricane.

Joy glanced out the window and watched her daughter bullet across the lawn to the workshop and then slip inside the doors. Smiling to herself, she thought she'd give a lot to see Sam's reaction to his visitor.

"Hi, Sam! Mommy said I could come play with you!"

She didn't catch him completely by surprise. Thankfully, Sam had spotted the girl running across the yard and had had time to toss a heavy beige tarp over his latest project. Although why he'd started on it was beyond him. A whim that had come on him two days ago, he'd thrown himself into it late last night when he'd left Joy in the great room.

Guilt had pushed him away from her, and it was guilt that had kept him working half the night. Memories crowded his brain, but it was thoughts of Joy herself that kept him on edge. That kiss. The heavy sigh of her breath as she molded herself to him. The eager response and matching need that had thrown him harder than he'd expected.

Shaking his head, he grumbled, "Don't have time to play." He turned to his workbench to find *something* to do.

"I can help you like I did with the fairy house. I want to see if there are fairies there but Mommy said I couldn't go by myself. Do you want to go with me? Cuz we can be busy outside, too, can't we?" She walked farther into the room and, as if she had radar, moved straight to the tarp draped across his project. "What's this?"

"Mine," he said and winced at the sharpness of his tone. But the girl, just like her mother, was impossible to deflate. She simply turned that bright smile of hers on him and said, "It's a secret, right? I like secrets. I can tell you one. It's about Lizzie's mommy going to have another baby. She thinks Lizzie doesn't know but Lizzie heard her mommy tell her daddy that she passed the test."

Too much information coming too quickly. He'd already learned about the wonderful Lizzie and her puppy. And this latest news blast might come under the heading of TMI.

"I wanted a sister, too," Holly said and walked right up to his workbench, climbing onto the stool she'd used the last time she was there. "But Mommy says I have to have a puppy instead and that's all right cuz babies cry a lot and a puppy doesn't..."

"Why don't we go check the fairy house?" Sam said, interrupting the flow before his head exploded. Getting her out of the shop seemed the best way to keep her from asking about the tarp again. It wasn't as if he *wanted* to go look for fairies in the freezing-cold woods.

"Oh, boy!" She squirmed off the stool, then grabbed his hand with her much smaller one.

Just for a second, Sam felt a sharp tug at the edges of his heart, and it was painful. Holly was older than Eli had been, he told himself, and she was a girl—so completely different children. But he couldn't help wondering what Eli would have been like at Holly's age. Or as he would be now at almost nine. But Eli would always be three years old. Just finding himself. Just becoming more of a boy than a baby and never a chance to be more.

"Let's go, Sam!" Holly pulled on his hand and leaned forward as if she could drag him behind her if she just tried hard enough.

He folded his fingers around hers and let her lead him from the shop into the cold. And he listened to her talk, heard again about puppies and fairies and princesses, and told himself that maybe this was his punishment. Being lulled into affection for a child who wasn't his. A child who would disappear from his life in a few short weeks.

And he wasn't completely stupid, he told himself. He could see through Joy's machinations. She wanted to wake him up, she'd said. To drag him back into the land of the living, and clearly, she was allowing her daughter to be part of that program.

"There it is!" Holly's excitement ratcheted up another level, and Sam thought the girl's voice hit a pitch that only dogs should have been able to hear. But her absolute pleasure in the smallest things was hard to ignore, damn it.

She let go of his hand and ran the last few steps to the fairy house on her own. Bending down, she inspected every window and even opened the tiny door to look inside. And Sam was drawn to the girl's absolute faith that she would see *something*. Even disappointment didn't jar the thrill in her eyes. "I don't see them," she said, turning her head to look at him.

"Maybe they're out having a picnic," he said, surprising himself by playing into the game. "Or shopping."

"Like Mommy and me are gonna do," Holly said, jumping

up and down as if she simply couldn't hold back the excitement any more. "We're gonna get a Christmas tree today."

He felt a hitch in the center of his chest, but he didn't say anything.

"We're getting a little one this time to put in our room cuz you don't like Christmas. How come you don't like Christmas, Sam?"

"I...it's complicated." He hunched deeper into his black leather jacket and stuffed both hands into the pockets.

"Compulcated?"

"Complicated," he corrected, wondering how the hell he'd gotten into this conversation with a five-year-old.

"Why?"

"Because it's about a lot of things all at once," he said, hoping to God she'd leave it there. He should have known better.

Her tiny brow furrowed as she thought about it. Finally, though, she shrugged and said, "Okay. Do you think fairies go buy Christmas trees? Will there be lights in their little house? Can I see 'em?"

So grateful to have left the Christmas thing behind, he said, "Maybe if you look really hard one night you'll see some."

"I can look *really* hard, see?" Her eyes squinted and her mouth puckered up, showing him just how strong her looking power was.

"That's pretty hard." The wind gave a great gust and about knocked Holly right off her feet. He reached out, steadied her, then said, "You should go on back to the house with your mom."

"But we're not done looking." She grabbed his hand again, and this time, it was more comforting than unsettling. Pulling on him, she wandered over to one side of the fairy house, where the pine needles lay thick as carpet on the ground. "Could we make another fairy house and put it right here, by this big tree? That's like a Christmas tree, right? Maybe the fairies would put lights on it, too."

He was scrambling now. He'd never meant to get so involved.

Not with the child. Not with her mother. But Holly's sweetness and Joy's…*everything*…kept sucking him in. Now he was making fairy houses and secret projects and freezing his ass off looking for invisible creatures.

"Sure," he said, in an attempt to get the girl moving toward the house. "We can build another one. In a day or two. Maybe."

"Okay, tomorrow we can do it and put it by the tree and the fairies will have a Christmas house to be all nice and warm. Can we put blankets and stuff in there, too?"

Tomorrow. Just like her mother, Holly heard only what she wanted to hear and completely disregarded everything else. He glanced at the house and somehow wasn't surprised to see Joy in the kitchen window, watching them. Across the yard, their gazes met and heat lit up the line of tension linking them.

All he could think of was the taste of her. The feel of her. The gnawing realization that he was going to have her. There was no mistaking the pulse-pounding sensations linking them. No pretending that it wasn't there. Guilt still chewing at him, he knew that even that wouldn't be enough to keep him from her.

And when she lifted one hand and laid it palm flat on the window glass, it was as if she was touching him. Feeling what he was feeling and acknowledging that she, too, knew the inevitable was headed right at them.

The trunk was filled with grocery bags, the backseat held a Charlie Brown Christmas tree on one side and Holly on the other, and now, Joy was at her house for the boxes of decorations they would need.

"Our house is tiny, huh, Mommy?"

After Sam's house, *anything* would look tiny, but in this case especially. "Sure is, baby," she said, "but it's ours."

She noted Buddy Hall's shop van in the driveway and hurriedly got Holly out of the car and hustling toward the house. Funny, she'd never really noticed before that they didn't have many trees on their street, Joy thought. But spending the last week or so at Sam's house—surrounded by the woods and a view of the lake—she couldn't help thinking that her street looked a little bare. But it wasn't Sam's house that intrigued her. It was the man himself. Instantly, she thought of the look he'd given her just that morning. Even from across the wide yard, she'd felt the power of that stare, and her blood had buzzed in reaction. Even now, her stomach jumped with nerves and expectation. She and Sam weren't finished. Not by a long shot. There was more coming. She just wasn't sure what or when. But she couldn't wait.

"Stay with me, sweetie," Joy said as they walked into the house together.

"Okay. Can I have a baby sister?"

Joy stopped dead on the threshold and looked down at her. "What? Where did that come from?"

"Lizzie's getting a new sister. It's a secret but she is and I want one, too."

Deb was pregnant? Why hadn't she told? And how the heck did Holly know before Joy did? Shaking her head, she told herself they were all excellent questions that would have to be answered later. For now, she wanted to check on the progress of the house repairs.

"Buddy?" she called out.

"Back here." The deep voice came from the kitchen, so Joy kept a grip on Holly and headed that way.

Along the way, her mind kept up a constant comparison between her own tiny rental and the splendor of Sam's place. The hallway alone was a fraction of the length of his. The living room was so small that if four people were in there at the same time, they'd be in sin. The kitchen, she thought sadly, walking into the room, looked about as big as the island in Sam's kitchen. Its sad cabinets needed paint and really just needed to be torn down and replaced, but since she was just a renter, it wasn't up to her. And the house might be small and a little on the shabby side, but it was her home. The one she'd made for her and Holly, so there was affection along with the exasperation.

"How's it going, Buddy?" she asked.

"Not bad." He stood up, all five feet four inches of him, with his barrel chest and broader stomach. A gray fringe of hair haloed his head, and his bright blue eyes sparkled with good humor. "Just sent Buddy Junior down to the hardware store. Thought while I was here we could fix the hinges on some of these cabinets. Some of 'em hang so crooked they're making me dizzy."

Delighted, Joy said, "Thank you, Buddy. That's going the extra mile."

"Not a problem." He pushed up the sleeves of his flannel shirt, took a step back and looked at the gaping hole where a light switch used to be. "Got the wiring all replaced and brought up to code out in the living room, but I'm checking the rest, as well. You've got some fraying in here and a hot wire somebody left uncapped in the smaller bedroom—"

Holly's bedroom, Joy thought and felt a pang of worry. God, if the fire had started in her daughter's room in the middle of the night, maybe they wouldn't have noticed in time. Maybe smoke inhalation would have knocked them out and kept them out until—

"No worries," Buddy said, looking right at her. "No point in thinking about what-ifs, either," he added as if he could look at her and read her thoughts. And he probably could. "By the time this job's done I guarantee all the wiring. You and the little one there will be safe as houses."

"What's a safe house?" Holly asked.

Buddy winked at her. "This one, soon's I'm done."

"Thank you, Buddy. I really appreciate it." But maybe, Joy told herself, it was time to find a new house for her and her daughter. Something newer. Safer. Still, that was a thought for later on, so she put it aside for now.

"I know you do and we're getting it done as fast as we can."

He gave his own work a long look. "The way it's looking, you could be back home before Christmas."

Back home. Away from Sam. Away from what she was beginning to feel for him. Probably best, she told herself, though right at the moment, she didn't quite believe it. As irritating as the man could be, he was so much more. And that more was drawing her in.

"Appreciate that, too," Joy said. "We're just here to pick up some Christmas decorations, then we'll get out of your hair."

He grinned and scrubbed one hand across the top of his bald head. "You'd have quite the time getting *in* my hair. You two doing all right up the mountain?"

"Yes." Everyone in town was curious about Sam, she thought. Didn't he see that if he spent more time talking to people they'd be less inclined to talk about him and wonder? "It's been great. Sam helped Holly build a fairy house."

"Is that right?"

"It's pretty and in the woods and I'm going to bring some of my dolls to put in it to keep the fairies company and Sam's gonna help me make another one, too. He's really nice. Just crabby sometimes."

"Out of the mouths of babes," Joy murmured with a smile. "Well, we've got to run. Trees to decorate, cookies to bake."

"You go ahead then," Buddy said, already turning back to his task. Then over his shoulder he called out, "You be sure to tell Sam Henry my wife, Cora, loves that rocking chair he made. She bought it at Crafty and now I can't hardly get her out of it."

Joy smiled. "I'll tell him."

Then with Holly rummaging through her toys, Joy bundled up everything Christmas. A few minutes later, they were back in the car, and she was thinking about the crabby man who made her want things she shouldn't.

Of course, she had to stop by Deb's first, because hello, *news*. "Why didn't you tell me you're pregnant?"

Deb's eyes went wide and when her jaw dropped she popped a mini apple pie into it. "How did you know?"

"Lizzie told Holly, Holly told me."

"Lizzie—" Deb sighed and shook her head. "You think your kids don't notice what's going on. Boy, I'm going to have to get better at the secret thing."

"Why a secret?" Joy picked up a tiny brownie and told herself the calories didn't count since it was so small. Drawing it out into two bites, she waited.

"You know we lost one a couple of years ago," Deb said, keeping her voice low as there were customers in the main room, separated from them only by the swinging door between the kitchen and the store's front.

"Yeah." Joy reached out and gave her friend a sympathetic pat on the arm.

"Well, this time we didn't want to tell anyone until we're at least three months. You know?" She sighed again and gave a rueful smile. "But now that Lizzie's spreading the word…"

"Bag open, cat out," Joy said, grinning. "This is fabulous. I'm happy for you."

"Thanks. Me, too."

"Of course, now Holly wants a baby, too."

Deb gave her a sly look. "You could do something about that, you know."

"Right. Because I'm such a great single mom I should do it again."

"You are and it wouldn't kill you," Deb told her, "but I was thinking more along the lines of gorgeous hermit slash painter slash craftsman."

"Yeah, I don't think so." Of course, she immediately thought of that kiss and the tension that had been coiled in her middle all day. Briefly, her brain skipped to hazy images of her and Sam and Holly living in that big beautiful house together. With a couple more babies running around and a life filled with hot kisses, warm laughter and lots of love.

But fantasies weren't real life, and she'd learned long ago to concentrate on what was real. Otherwise, building dreams on boggy ground could crush your heart. Yes, she cared about Sam. But he'd made it clear he wasn't interested beyond stoking whatever blaze was burning between them. And yet, she thought, brain still racing, he was so good with Holly. And Joy's little girl was blossoming, having a man like Sam pay attention to her. Spend time with her.

Okay, her mind warned sternly, *dial it back now, Joy. No point in setting yourself up for that crush.*

"You say no, but your eyes are saying yum." Deb filled a tray with apple pies no bigger than silver dollars, laying them all out on paper doilies that made them look like loosely wrapped presents.

"Yum is easy—it's what comes after that's hard."

"Since when are you afraid of hard work?"

"I'm not, but—" Not the same thing, she told herself, as working to make a living, to build a life. This was bringing a man out of the shadows, and what if once he was out he didn't want her anyway? No, that way lay pain and misery, and why should she set herself up for that?

"You're alone, he's alone, match made in heaven."

"Alone isn't a good enough reason for anyone, Deb." She stopped, snatched another brownie and asked, "When did this get to be about me instead of you?"

"Since I hate seeing my best friend—a completely wonderful human being—all by herself."

"I'm not alone. I have Holly."

"And I love her, too, but it's not the same and you know it."

Slumping, Joy leaned one hip against the counter and nibbled at her second brownie. "No, it's not. And okay, fine—I'm...intrigued by Sam."

"Intrigued is good. Sex is better."

Sadly, she admitted, "I wouldn't know."

"Yeah, that would be my point."

"It's not that easy," Joy said wistfully. Then she glanced out the window at the house across the yard where Holly and Lizzie were probably driving Sean Casey insane about now. "I mean, he's—and I'm—"

"Something happened."

Her gaze snapped to Deb's. "Just a kiss."

"Yay. And?"

"And," Joy admitted, "then he got a little more involved and completely melted my underwear."

"Wow." Deb gave a sigh and fluttered one hand over her heart.

"Yeah. We were arguing and we were both furious and he kissed me and—" she slapped her hands together "—boom."

"Oh, boom is good."

"It's great, but it doesn't solve anything."

"Honey," Deb asked with a shake of her head, "who cares?"

Joy laughed. Honestly, Deb was really good for her. "Okay, I'm heading back to the house. Even when it's this cold outside, I shouldn't be leaving the groceries in the car this long."

"Fine, but I'm going to want to hear more about this 'boom.'"

"Yeah," Joy said, "me, too. So are the girls still on for the sleepover?"

"Are you kidding? Lizzie's been planning this for days. Popcorn, princess movies and s'mores cooked over the fireplace."

Ordinarily, Holly would be too young for a sleepover, but Joy knew Deb was as crazy protective as she was. "Okay, then I'll bring her to your house Saturday afternoon."

"Don't forget to pray for me," Deb said with a smile. "Two five-year-olds for a night filled with squeals…"

"You bet."

"And take that box of brownies with you. Sweeten up your hermit and maybe there'll be more 'boom.'"

"I don't know about that, but I will definitely take the brownies." When she left the warm kitchen, she paused on the back porch and tipped her face up to the gray sky. As she stood there, snow drifted lazily down and kissed her heated cheeks with ice.

Maybe it would be enough to cool her off, she told herself, crossing the yard to Deb's house to collect Holly and head home. But even as she thought it, Joy realized that nothing was going to cool her off as long as her mind was filled with thoughts of Sam.

CHAPTER EIGHT

ONCE IT STARTED SNOWING, it just kept coming. As if an invisible hand had pulled a zipper on the gray, threatening clouds, they spilled down heavy white flakes for days. The woods looked magical, and every day, Holly insisted on checking the fairy houses—there were now two—to see if she could catch a glimpse of the tiny people living in them. Every day there was disappointment, but her faith never wavered.

Sam had to admire that even as his once-cold heart warmed with affection for the girl. She was getting to him every bit as much as her mother was. In different ways, of course, but the result was the same. He was opening up, and damned if it wasn't painful as all hell. Every time that ice around his heart cracked a little more, and with it came the pain that reminded him why the ice had been there in the first place.

He was on dangerous ground, and there didn't seem to be a way to back off. Coming out of the shadows could blind a man if he wasn't careful. And that was one thing Sam definitely was.

Once upon a time, things had been different. *He* had been different. He'd gone through life thinking nothing could go wrong. Though at the time, everywhere he turned, things went his way so he couldn't really be blamed for figuring it would always be like that.

His talent had pushed him higher in the art world than he'd ever believed possible, but it was his own ego that had convinced him to believe every accolade given. He'd thought of himself as blessed. As *chosen* for greatness. And looking back now, he could almost laugh at the deluded man he'd been.

Almost. Because when he'd finally had his ass handed to him, it had knocked the world out from under his feet. Feeling bulletproof only made recovering from a crash that much harder. And he couldn't even really say he'd recovered. He'd just marched on, getting by, getting through. What happened to his family wasn't something you ever got *over*. The most you could do was keep putting one foot in front of the other and hope that eventually you got somewhere.

Of course, he'd gotten *here*. To this mountain with the beautiful home he shared with a housekeeper he paid to be there. To solitude that sometimes felt like a noose around his neck. To cutting ties to his family because he couldn't bear their grief as well as his own.

He gulped down a swallow of hot coffee and relished the burn. He stared out the shop window at the relentless snow and listened to the otherworldly quiet that those millions of falling flakes brought. In the quiet, his mind turned to the last few days. To Joy. The tension between them was strung as tight as barbed wire and felt just as lethal. Every night at dinner, he sat at the table with her and her daughter and pretended his insides weren't churning. Every night, he avoided meeting up with Joy in the great room by locking himself in the shop to work on what was under that tarp. And finally, he lay awake in his bed wishing to hell she was lying next to him.

He was a man torn by too many things. Too twisted around on the road he'd been walking for so long to know which way to head next. So he stayed put. In the shop. Alone.

Across the yard the kitchen light sliced into the dimness of the gray morning when Holly jerked the door open and stepped outside. He watched her and wasn't disappointed by her shriek of excitement. The little girl turned back to the house, shouted something to her mother and waited, bouncing on her toes until Joy joined her at the door. Holly pointed across the yard toward the trees and, with a wide grin on her face, raced down the steps and across the snow-covered ground.

Her pink jacket and pink boots were like hope in the gray, and Sam smiled to himself, wondering when he'd fallen for the kid. When putting up with her had become caring for her. When he'd loosened up enough to make a tiny dream come true.

Sam was already outside when Holly raced toward him in a wild flurry of exhilaration. He smiled at the shine in her eyes, at the grin that lit up her little face like a sunbeam. Then she threw herself at him, hugging his legs, throwing her head back to look up at him.

"Sam! Sam! Did you see?" Her words tumbled over each other in the rush to share her news. She grabbed his hand and tugged, her pink gloves warm against his fingers. "Come on! Come on! You have to see! They came! They came! I knew they would. I knew it and now they're here!"

Snow fell all around them, dusting Holly's jacket hood and swirling around Joy as she waited, her gaze fixed on his. And suddenly, all he could see were those blue eyes of hers, filled with emotion. A long, fraught moment passed between them before Holly's insistence shattered it. "Look, Sam. Look!"

She tugged him down on the ground beside her, then threw her arms around his neck and held on tight. Practically vibrating with excitement, Holly gave him a loud, smacking kiss on the cheek, then pulled back and looked at him with wonder in her eyes. "They came, Sam. They're living in our houses!"

Still reeling from that freely given hug and burst of affection, Sam stood up on unsteady legs. Smiling down at the little girl as she crawled around the front of the houses, peering into windows that shone with tiny Christmas lights, he felt another chunk of ice drop away from his heart. In the gray of the day, those bright specks of blue, green, red and yellow glittered like magic. Which was, he told himself, what Holly saw as she searched in vain to catch a glimpse of the fairies themselves.

He glanced at Joy again and she was smiling, a soft, knowing curve of her mouth that gleamed in her eyes, as well. There was something else in her gaze, too—beyond warmth, even beyond heat, and he wondered about it while Holly spun long, intricate stories about the fairies who lived in the tiny houses in the woods.

"You didn't have to do this," Joy said for the tenth time in a half hour.

"I'm gonna have popcorn with Lizzie and watch the princess movie," Holly called out from the backseat.

"Good for you," Sam said with a quick glance into the rearview mirror. Holly was looking out the side window, watching the snow and making her plans. He looked briefly to Joy. "How else were you going to get into town?"

"I could have called Deb, asked her or Sean to come and pick up Holly."

"Right, or we could do it the easy way and have me drive you both in." Sam kept his gaze on the road. The snow was falling, not really heavy yet, but determined. It was already piling up on the side of the road, and he didn't even want to think about Joy and Holly, alone in a car, maneuvering through the storm that would probably get worse. A few minutes later, he pulled up outside the Casey house and was completely stunned when, sprung from her car seat, Holly leaned over and kissed his cheek. "'Bye, Sam!"

It was the second time he'd been on the receiving end of a simple, cheerfully given slice of affection that day, and again, Sam was touched more deeply than he wanted to admit. Shaken, he watched Joy walk Holly to her friend's house and waited until she came back, alone, and slid into the car beside him.

"She hardly paused long enough to say goodbye to me." Joy laughed a little. "She's been excited by the sleepover for days, but now the fairy houses are the big story." She clicked her seat belt into place, then turned to face him. "She was telling Lizzie all about the lights in the woods and promising that you and she will make Lizzie a fairy house, too."

"Great," he said, shaking his head as he backed out of the driveway. He wasn't sure how he'd been sucked into the middle of Joy's and Holly's lives, but here he was, and he had to admit—though he didn't like to—that he was *enjoying* it. Honestly, it worried him a little just how much he enjoyed it.

He liked hearing them in his house. Liked Holly popping in and out of the workshop, sharing dinner with them at the big dining room table. He even actually liked building magical houses for invisible beings. "More fairies."

"It's your own fault," she said, reaching out to lay one hand on his arm. "What you did was—it meant a lot. To Holly. To *me*."

The warmth of her touch seeped down into his bones and quickly spread throughout his body. Something else he liked. That jolt of heat when Joy was near. The constant ache of need that seemed to always be with him these days. He hadn't wanted a woman like this in years. He swallowed hard against the demand clawing at him and turned for the center of town and the road back to the house.

"We're not in a hurry, are we?" she asked.

Sam stopped at a red light and looked at her warily. "Why?"

"Because, it's early, but we could stay in town for a while. Have dinner at the steak house…"

She gave him a smile designed to bring a man to his knees. And it was working.

"You want to go out to dinner?" he asked.

"Well," she said, shrugging. "It's early, but that won't kill us."

He frowned and threw a glance out the windshield at the swirls of white drifting down from a leaden sky. "Still snowing. We should get up the mountain while we still can."

She laughed and God, he loved the sound of it—even if it was directed at him and his lame attempt to get out of town.

"It's not a blizzard, Sam. An hour won't hurt either of us."

"Easy for you to say," Sam muttered darkly. "You *like* talking to people." The sound of her laughter filled the truck and eased his irritation as he headed toward the restaurant.

Everybody in town had to be in the steak house, and Joy thought it was a good thing. She knew a lot of people in Franklin and she made sure to introduce Sam to most of them. Sure, it didn't make for a relaxing dinner—she could actually *see* him tightening up—but it felt good to watch people greet him. To tell him how much they loved the woodworking he did. And the more uncomfortable he got with the praise, the more Joy relished it.

He'd been too long in his comfort zone of solitude. He'd made himself an island, and swimming to the mainland would be exhausting. But it would so be worth the trip.

"I've never owned anything as beautiful as that bowl you made," Elinor Cummings gushed, laying one hand on Sam's shoulder in benediction. She was in her fifties, with graying black hair that had been ruthlessly sprayed into submission.

"Thanks." He shot Joy a look that promised payback in the very near future. She wasn't worried. Like an injured animal, Sam would snarl and growl at anyone who came too close. But he wouldn't bite.

"I love what you did with the bowl. The rough outside, looks as though you just picked it up off the forest floor—" Elinor continued.

"I did," Sam said, clearly hoping to cut her off, but pasting a polite, if strained, smile on his face.

"—and the inside looks like a jewel," she continued, undeterred from lavishing him with praise. "All of those lovely colors in the grain of that wood, all so polished, and it just gleams in the light." She planted one hand against her chest and gave a sigh. "It's simply lovely. Two sides of life," she mused, "that's what it says to me, two sides, the hard and the good, the sad and the glad. It's lovely. Just lovely."

"All right now, Ellie," her husband said, with an understanding wink for Sam and Joy, "let's let the man eat. Good to meet you, Sam."

Sam nodded, then reached for the beer in front of him and took a long pull. The Cummingses had been just the last in a long stream of people who'd stopped by their table to greet Joy and meet Sam. Every damn one of them had given him a look that said *Ah, the hermit. That's what he looks like!*

And then had come the speculative glances, as they wondered whether Sam and Joy were a couple, and that irritated him, as well. This was what happened when you met people. They started poking their noses into your life and pretty soon, that life was open season to anyone with a sense of curiosity. As the last of the strangers went back to their own tables, he glared at Joy.

"You're enjoying this, aren't you?"

In the light of the candle at their table, her eyes sparkled as she grinned. "I could try to deny it, but why bother? Yes, I am. It's good to see you actually forced to talk to people. And Elinor clearly loves your work. Isn't it nice to hear compliments?"

"It's a bowl." He sighed. "Nothing deep or meaningful to the design. Just a bowl. People always want to analyze, interpret what the artist meant. Sometimes a bowl is just a bowl."

She laughed and shook her head. "You can't fool me. I've seen your stuff in Crafty. Nothing about what you make is 'just' anything. People love your work, and if you gave them half a chance, they'd like you, too."

"And I want that because..."

"Because it's better than being a recluse." Joy leaned forward, bracing her elbows on the table. "Honestly, Sam, you can't stay on the mountain by yourself forever."

He hated admitting even to himself that she was right. Hell, he'd talked more, listened more, in the last couple of weeks than he had in years. His house wasn't empty. Wasn't filled with the careful quiet he normally knew. Kaye generally left him to his own devices, so he was essentially alone, even when his house-keeper was there. Joy and Holly had pushed their way into the center of his life and had shown him just how barren it had been.

But when they left, his life would slide back onto its original course and the silence would seem even deeper. And God, he didn't like the thought of that.

Sam frowned. "Why are we really here?"

"To eat that amazing steak, for one," Joy said, sipping at her wine. Interesting, she thought, how his facial expressions gave hints to what he was thinking. And even more interesting how fast a smile from him could dissolve into the more familiar scowl. She'd have given a lot in that moment to know exactly what was running through his mind.

"And for another?"

"To show you how nice the people of Franklin are. To prove to you that you can meet people without turning into a pillar of salt…" She sat back, sipped at her wine again and kept her voice lighter than she felt. "Admit it. You had a good time."

"The steak was good," he said grudgingly, but she saw a flash of a smile that appeared and disappeared in a heartbeat.

"And the company."

His gaze fixed on hers. "You already know I like the company."

"I do," she said and felt a swirl of nerves flutter into life in the pit of her belly. Why was it this man who could make her feel things she'd never felt before? Life would have been so much easier if she'd found some nice, uncomplicated guy to fall for. But then she wouldn't be able to look into those golden-brown eyes of his, would she? "But you had a good time talking to other people, too. It just makes you uncomfortable hearing compliments."

"Think you know me, don't you?"

"Yep," she said, smiling at him in spite of the spark of irritation in his eyes. Just as Holly had once said, *he's not mean, he's just crabby.* He didn't fool her anymore. Even when he was angry, it didn't last. Even when she ambushed him with knowledge of his past, he didn't cling to the fury that had erupted inside him. Even when he didn't want to spend time with a child, he went out of his way to make her dreams come true.

Joy's heart ached with all she was feeling, and she wondered if he could see it in her eyes.

The room was crowded. The log walls were smoke-stained from years of exposure to the wood fireplace that even now boasted a roaring blaze. People sat at round tables and a few leather booths along one wall while the wall facing Main Street was floor-to-ceiling windows, displaying the winter scene unfolding outside. Tonight, the music pumping through the speakers overhead was classical, something weepy with strings and piano. And sitting across the table from her, looking like he'd rather be anywhere else but there, was the man who held her heart.

Stupid? Maybe. But there was no going back for Joy now. She'd been stumbling over him a little every day, of course. His kindness to Holly. His company in the dead of night when the house sat quiet around them. His kiss. The way his eyes flared with heat and more whenever he looked at her. His reluctant participation in the "family" dinners in the dining room. All of those things had been drawing her in, making her fall.

But today, she'd simply taken the final plunge.

He must have gone into town on his own and bought those silly little fairy lights. Then he'd sneaked out into the freezing cold late at night when he wouldn't be seen. And he'd decorated those tiny houses because her little girl had believed. He'd given Holly that. Magic.

Sam had sparked her imagination, protected her dreams and her fantasies. Joy had watched her baby girl throw herself into the arms of the man she trusted, loved, and through a sheen of tears had seen Sam hold Holly as tenderly as if she'd been made of glass. And in that one incredible moment, Joy told herself, he'd completely won her heart. Whether he wanted it or not was a different question.

She, Joy thought, was toast.

He could pretend to be aloof, crabby, disinterested all he wanted now, and she wouldn't believe it. He'd given her daughter a gift beyond price and she would always love him for that.

"What?" he asked, frowning a little harder. "What is it?"

She shook her head. "Nothing."

The frown came back instantly. "Makes a man nervous when a woman gets that thoughtful look in her eyes."

"Nervous is good, though I doubt," she said quietly, "that you ever have to worry about nerves."

"You might be surprised," he murmured, then said more firmly, "Let's go before the storm settles in and we're stuck down here."

Right then, Joy couldn't think of anywhere she'd rather be than back in that amazing house, alone with Sam. She looked him dead in the eye and said softly, "Good idea."

The ride up the mountain seemed to take forever, or maybe it was simply because Joy felt so on edge it was as if her skin was one size too tight. Every inch of her buzzed with anticipation because she knew what she wanted and knew she was done waiting. The tension between them had been building for days now, and tonight, she wanted to finally release it. To revel in being with a man she loved—even if she couldn't tell him how she felt.

At the house, they left the car in the garage and walked through the connecting door into the mudroom, where they hung their jackets on hooks before heading into the kitchen. Joy hit a switch on the wall, and the soft lights above the table blinked into life. Most of the room was still dark, and that was just as she wanted it. When she turned to Sam, she went up on her toes, cupped his face in her palms and kissed him, putting everything she was feeling into it.

Her heartbeat jumped into a frantic rhythm, her stomach

swirled with excitement and the ache that had been building inside her for days began to pulse. It took only a second for Sam to react. To have his arms come around her. He lifted her off her feet, and she wrapped herself around him like a ribbon around a present.

As if he'd only been awaiting her signal, he took her with a desperation that told Joy he wanted her as much as she wanted him. She *felt* the hunger pumping off him in thick waves and gave herself up to it, letting it feed her own until a raging storm overtook them both. His mouth covered hers, his tongue demanding entry. She gave way and sighed in growing need as he groaned and kissed her harder, deeper.

His hands, those talented, strong hands, dropped to her bottom. He turned her around so fast her stomach did a wild spin, then he slammed her up against the back door. Joy hardly felt it. She'd never experienced anything like what swept over her in those few frantic moments. Every inch of her body was alive with sensations. Her skin was buzzing, her blood boiling, and her mind was a tangled, hazy mass of thoughts that pretty much went, *yes, harder, now, be inside me.*

Her fingers scraped through his hair, held his head to hers. Every breath came strangled, harsh, and she didn't care. All she wanted, all she needed, was the taste of him filling her. The feel of his hands holding her. Then, when she became light-headed, she thought, okay, maybe air, too.

She broke the kiss, letting her head drop back as she gasped for breath. Staring up at the dimly lit ceiling, she concentrated solely on the feel of Sam's mouth at her throat, latching on to the pulse point at the base of her neck. He tasted, he nibbled, he licked, and she sighed heavily.

"Oh, boy. That feels really…" She gasped again. *"Good."*

With his mouth against her throat, he smiled. "You taste good, too."

"Thanks." She chuckled and the sound bubbled up into the room. "Always good to hear."

"I've wanted my hands on you for days." He lifted his head and waited for her to look at him. His eyes were alight with a fire that seemed to be sweeping both of them along in an inferno. "I tried to keep my distance, but it's been killing me."

"Me, too," she said, holding him a little tighter. "I've been dreaming about you."

One corner of his mouth lifted. "Yeah? Well, time to wake up." He let her slide down the length of his body until she was on her feet again. "Let's go."

"Where?"

"Upstairs, where the beds are." He started pulling her. "After waiting this long, we're not doing this on the kitchen floor."

Right about then, Joy thought, the floor looked pretty good. Or the granite island. Or just the stupid wall she'd been up against a second ago. Especially since her knees felt like rubber and she wasn't sure she'd make it all the way up those stairs. Then she realized they didn't have to.

"Yeah, but my bed's quicker." She gave a tug, too, then grinned when he looked at her in admiration.

"Good thinking. I do like a smart woman." He scooped her up again, this time cradling her in his arms, and headed for Kaye's suite.

"Well, I always wanted to be swept off my feet." Really, her poor, foolish heart was stuttering at being carried off to bed. The romance of it tugged at everything inside her. He stepped into the darkened suite, and she hit the light switch for the living area as he passed it.

Instantly, the tiny, misshapen Christmas tree burst into electric life. Softly glowing lights burned steadily all around the room, but it was the silly tree that had center stage.

"What the—" He stopped, his grip on her tightening, and let his gaze sweep around the room. So Joy looked, too, admiring all she and Holly had done to their temporary home. Sam hadn't wanted the holidays leaking out into the main house, so they'd gone overboard here, in their corner of it. Christmas lights lined the doorways and were draped across the walls like garland. The tiny tree stood on a table and was practically bowed under the weight of the ornaments, popped corn and strings of lights adorning it.

After a long minute or two, he shook his head. "That tree is sad."

"It is not," she argued, spearing it with a critical eye. "It's loved." She looked past the tree in the window to the night outside and the fairy lights just visible through the swirls of snow, and her heart dissolved all over again. Cupping his cheek in her palm, she turned his face to hers. "You lit up Holly's world today with those strings of lights."

He scowled but there wasn't much punch to it. "I hated seeing her check for signs every day and not getting any. But she never stopped believing."

Her heart actually filled up and spilled over into her chest. How could she *not* love a man who'd given life to her baby's imagination?

"I put 'em on a timer," Sam said, "so they'll go off and on at different times and Holly will have something to watch for."

Shaking her head, she looked into his eyes and whispered, "I don't have the words for what I'm feeling right now."

"Then we're lucky. No words required."

He kissed her again and Joy surrendered to the fire. She forgot about everything else but the taste of him, the feel of him. She wanted to stroke her hands all over his leanly muscled body, feel the warm slide of flesh to flesh. Lifting her face, she nibbled at his throat and smiled when she heard him groan tightly.

She hardly noticed when he carried her through the main room and dropped her onto her bed. *Wild*, was all she could think. Wild for him, for his touch, for his taste. She'd been alone for so long, having this man, *the* man with her, was almost more than she could stand.

He felt the same, because in a few short seconds, they were both naked, clothes flying around the room as they tore at them until there was nothing separating them. The quilt on the bed felt cool beneath her, but he was there, sliding on top of her, to bring the heat.

"Been wanting to peel you out of those sweaters you wear for days now," he murmured, trailing kisses up from her belly to just below her breasts.

"Been wanting you to do it," she assured him and ran the flat of her hands over his shoulders in long, sensuous strokes.

His hands moved over her, following every line, every curve. She gasped when he dipped his head to take first one hard nipple then the other into his mouth. Damp heat fractured something inside her as his teeth, tongue, lips teased at her sensitive skin. She was writhing mindlessly, chasing the need, when he dipped one hand to her center and cupped her heat completely.

Joy's mind simply splintered from the myriad sensations slamming into her system all at once. She hadn't felt this way in...ever. He shifted, kissing her mouth, tangling his tongue with hers as those oh-so-talented fingers dipped inside her heat. She lifted her hips into his touch and held his head to hers as they kissed, as they took and gave and then did it all again. Their breath mingled, their hearts pounded in a wild tandem that raced faster and faster as they tasted, explored, discovered.

It was like being caught in a hurricane. There was no safe place to hide, even if she'd wanted to. And she didn't. She wanted the storm, more than she'd ever wanted anything in her life. Demand, need, hands reaching, mouths seeking. Hushed words flew back and forth between them, whispers, breathless sighs. Heat ratcheted up in the tiny bedroom as outside, the snow fell, draping the world in icy white.

Sam's hand at her core drove her higher, faster. A small ripple of release caught her and had Joy calling his name as she shivered, shuddered in response. But she'd barely recovered from that tiny explosion before he pushed her again. His fingers danced over her body, inside and out, caressing, stroking until she thought she'd lose what was left of her mind if he didn't get inside her. Now.

Whimpering, Joy didn't care. All she could think of was the release she wanted more than her next breath. "Be inside me," she told him, voice breaking on every word as air struggled in and out of her lungs.

"Now," he agreed in a strained whisper.

Shadows filled the room, light from the snow, reflections of the lights in the living area. He took her mouth again in a frenzied kiss that stole her breath and gave her his. She arched into him as he moved over her, parting her thighs and sliding into her with one long thrust.

Joy gasped, her head tipping back into the pillow, her hips lifting to welcome him, to take him deeper. His hands held her hips, his fingers digging into her skin as he drove into her again and again. She locked her legs around his hips, pulling him tighter to her, rocking with him, following the frenzied rhythm he set.

The storm claimed them. Hunger roared up into the room and overtook them both. There was nothing in the world but that need and the race to completion. Their bodies moved together, skin to skin, breath to breath. They raced to the edge of the cliff together, and together they took the leap, locked in each other's arms.

"I think I'm blind."

Sam pushed off her and rolled to one side. "Open your eyes."

"Oh. Right." She looked at him and Sam felt the solid punch of her gaze slam into him. His body was still humming, his blood still pounding in his ears. He'd just had the most intense experience of his life and he wanted her again. Now.

He stroked one hand down her body, following the curve of breast to belly to hip. She shivered and he smiled. He couldn't touch her enough. The feel of her was addictive. How could his craving for her be as sharp now as it had been before? He should be relaxed. Instead, he felt more fired up. The need building inside him was sharper now because he *knew* what he'd been missing. Knew what it was to be inside her, to feel her wrapped around him, holding him tight. To look into her eyes and watch passion burst like fireworks on the Fourth.

It felt as if cold, iron bands were tightening around his chest. Danger. He knew it. He knew that feeling anything for Joy was a one-way trip to disaster, pain and misery. Yet it seemed that he didn't have any choice about that.

"Well." She blew out a breath and gave him a smile that had his body going rock hard again. "That was amazing. But I'm suddenly so thirsty I could drink a gallon of water."

"I'll get some," he told her, "as soon as I'm sure my legs will hold me."

"Isn't that a nice thing to say? There's no hurry," she said, turning into him, snuggling close. She buried her face in the curve of his neck and gave a sigh. "Here's good."

"Here's great." He rolled onto his back, pulling her over with him until she lay sprawled across his chest. Her blond curls tumbled around her face and her eyes sparkled in the dim light. "You caught me by surprise with that kiss."

She folded her arms on his chest and grinned down at him. "Well, then, you have an excellent reaction time."

"Not complaining." He hadn't been prepared for that kiss, and it had pushed him right over the edge of the control he'd been clinging to for days. Wincing a little, he thought he should have taken his time with her. To slowly drive them both to the breaking point. Instead, he'd been hit by an unstoppable force and hadn't been able to withstand it. They'd rushed together so quickly he hadn't—Sam went completely still as reality came crashing down on him, obliterating the buzz of satisfaction as if it had never been.

"What is it? Sam?"

He looked up into her eyes and called himself every kind of name he could think of. How could he have been so stupid? So careless? It was too late now, he told himself grimly. Too late to do anything but worry. "Joy, the downside to things happening by surprise is you're not prepared for it."

She smiled. "I'd say you were plenty prepared."

He rolled again, flopping her over onto the mattress and leaning over her, staring her in the eyes. "I'm trying to tell you that I hope to hell you're on birth control because I wasn't suited up."

CHAPTER NINE

SAM WATCHED HER AS, for a second or two, she just stared at him as if she were trying to make sense of a foreign language. And since he was staring into those clear blue eyes of hers, he *saw* the shift of emotions when what he'd said finally sunk in.

And even then, the uppermost thought in his mind was her scent and how it clung to her skin and seeped into his bones. Every breath he drew pulled her inside him, until summer flowers filled every corner of his heart, his soul.

What the hell was wrong with him? *Focus.* He'd led them both into a risky situation, and he had to keep his mind on what could, potentially, be facing them. It had been a long time since he'd been with anyone, sure. But it was Joy herself who had blown all thought, all reason, right out of his head with that one surprise kiss in the kitchen. After that, all he'd been able to think about was getting her naked. To finally have her under him, over him. He'd lost control for the first time in his life, and even though the consequences could be steep, he couldn't really regret any of it.

"Oh. Well." Joy lifted one hand and pushed his hair back from his face. Her touch sent a fresh new jolt of need blasting through him, and he had to grit his teeth in the effort to hold on to what was left of the tattered threads of his control.

"Are you," he asked, voice tight, "on birth control?"

"No."

One word. One simple word that hit the pit of his stomach like a ball of ice. "Okay. Look. This is my fault, Joy. I shouldn't have…"

"Fault? If you're looking to place blame here, you're on your own," she said, sliding her fingers through his hair. "This isn't on you alone, so don't look like you're about to be blindfolded and stood up against a wall in front of a firing squad."

He frowned and wondered when he'd become so easy to read.

"You weren't alone in this room, Sam," she said. "This is on me as much as you. We got…carried away—"

He snorted. "Yeah, you could say that."

"—and we didn't think. We weren't prepared," she finished as if he hadn't interrupted her.

He laughed shortly but there was no humor behind it. This had to be the damnedest after-sex conversation he'd ever had. He should have known that Joy wouldn't react as he would have expected her to. No recriminations, no gnashing of teeth, just simple acceptance for what couldn't be changed.

Still. "That's the thing," he said with a shake of his head. "I thought I was. Prepared, I mean. When I went into town to get those damn fairy lights, I also bought condoms."

She drew her head back and grinned down at him. "You're kidding. Really?"

"Yes, really. They're upstairs. In my room."

She laughed and shook her head. "That's perfect. Well, in your defense, you did try to get me upstairs…"

"True." But they probably wouldn't have made it, as hot as they'd both been. Most likely, they'd have stopped and had at each other right there on the stairs anyway.

"And I love that you bought condoms," she said, planting a soft kiss on his mouth. "I love that you wanted me as much as I wanted you."

"No question about that," he admitted, though the rest of this situation was settling in like rain clouds over an outdoor party.

"But you realize that now everyone in Franklin knows you bought them."

"What?"

"Oh, yes," she said, nodding sagely. "By now, word has spread all over town and everyone is speculating about just what's going on up here."

"Perfect." Small-town life, he told himself, knowing she was right. He hadn't thought about it. Hadn't considered that by buying condoms at the local pharmacy he was also feeding fuel to the gossip. It had been so long since he'd been part of a community that he hadn't given it a thought, but now he remembered the speculative gleam in the cashier's eye. The smile on the face of the customer behind him in line. "Damn."

"We're the talk of the town," Joy assured him, still smiling. "I've always wanted to be gossiped about."

All of that aside for the moment, Sam couldn't understand how she could be so damned amused by any of this. All he could feel was the bright flash of panic hovering on the edges of his mind. By being careless, he might have created a child. He'd lost a child already. Lost his son. How could he make another and not have his heart ripped out of his chest?

"Forget what people are saying, Joy," he said, and his tone, if nothing else, erased her smile. "Look, whatever happens—"

"You can get that unnerved look off your face," she said softly. "I'm a big girl, Sam. I can take care of myself. You don't owe me anything, and I don't need you to worry about me or what might happen."

"I'll decide what I owe, Joy," he told her. It didn't matter what she said, Sam told himself. He would worry anyway. He laid one hand on her belly and let it lay there, imagining what might already be happening deep within her.

"Sam." She cupped his face in her hands and waited until he

looked into her eyes. "Stop thinking. Can we just enjoy what we shared? Leave it at that?"

His heartbeat thundered in his chest. Just her touch was enough to push him into forgetting everything but her. Everything but this moment. He wanted her even more than he had before and didn't know how that was possible. She was staring up at him with those wide blue eyes of hers, and Sam thought he could lose himself in those depths. Maybe she was right. At least for now, for this moment, maybe it was better if they stopped thinking, worrying, wondering. Because these moments were all they had. All they would ever have.

He wasn't going to risk loss again. He wouldn't put his soul up as a hostage to fate, by falling in love, having another family that the gods could snatch from him. A future for them was out of the question. But they had tonight, didn't they?

"Come with me," he said, rolling off the bed and taking her hand to pull her up with him.

"What? Why? Where?"

"My room. Where the condoms live." He kept pulling her after him and she half ran to keep up. "We can stop and get water—or wine—on the way up."

"Wine. Condoms." She tugged him to a stop, then plastered herself against him until he felt every single inch of her body pressed along his. Then she stepped back. "Now, that kind of thinking is a good thing. I like your plan. Just let me get my robe."

Amazing woman. She could be wild and uninhibited in bed but quailed about walking naked through an empty house.

"You don't need a robe. We're the only ones here. There are no neighbors for five miles in any direction, so no one can look in the windows."

"It's cold so I still want it," she said, lifting one hand to cup his cheek.

For a second, everything stopped for Sam. He just stared at her. In the soft light, her skin looked like fine porcelain. Her hair was a tumbled mass of gold and her eyes were as clear and blue as the lake. Her seductively sly smile curved a mouth that was made to be kissed. If he were still an artist, Sam thought, he'd want to paint her like this. Just as she was now.

That knowing half smile on her face, one arm lifted toward him, with the soft glow of Christmas lights behind her. She looked, he thought, like a pagan goddess, a woman born to be touched, adored, and that's how he would paint her. If he still painted, which he didn't. And why didn't he?

Because he'd lost the woman he'd once loved. A woman who had looked at him as Joy did now. A woman who had given him a son and then taken him with her when she left.

Pain grabbed his heart and squeezed.

Instantly, she reacted. "Sam? What is it?"

"I want you," he said, moving in on her, backing her into the wall, looking down into her eyes.

"I know, I feel the same way."

He nodded, swallowed hard, then forced the words out because they had to be said. Even if she pulled away from him right now, they had to be said. "But if you're thinking there's a future here for us, don't. I'm not that guy. Not anymore."

"Sam—" Her hands slid up and down his arms, and he was grateful for the heat she kindled inside him. "I didn't ask you for anything."

"I don't want to hurt you, Joy." Yet he knew he would. She was the kind of woman who would spin dreams for herself, her daughter. She would think about futures. As a mother, she had to. As a former father, he couldn't. Not again. Just the thought of it sharpened the pain in his heart. If he was smart, he'd end this with Joy right now.

But apparently, he had no sense at all.

She gave him another smile and went up on her toes to kiss him gently. "I told you. You don't have to worry about me, Sam. I know what I'm doing."

He wished that were true. But there would be time enough

later for regrets, for second-guessing decisions made in the night. For now, there was Joy.

A few days later, Joy was upstairs, looking out Sam's bedroom window at the workshop below. Holly was out there with Sam right now, probably working on more fairy houses. Since the first two were now filled with fairy families, Holly was determined to put up a housing development at the foot of the woods.

Her smile was wistful as she turned away and looked at the big bed with the forest green comforter and mountain of pillows. She hadn't been with Sam up here since that first night. He came to her now, in Kaye's room, where they made love with quiet sighs and soft whispers so they wouldn't wake Holly in the next room. And after hours wrapped together, Sam left her bed early in the morning so the little girl wouldn't guess what was happening.

It felt secret and sad and wonderful all at the same time. Joy was in love and couldn't tell him because she knew he didn't want to hear it. She might be pregnant and knew he wouldn't want to hear that, either. Every morning when he left her, she felt him go just a bit further away. And one day soon, she knew, he wouldn't come back. He was distancing himself from her, holding back emotionally so that when she left at the end of the month he wouldn't miss her.

Why couldn't he see that he didn't *have* to miss her? It was almost impossible to believe she'd known Sam for less than three weeks. He was so embedded in her heart, in her life, she felt as if she'd known him forever. As if they'd been meant to meet, to find each other. To be together. If only Sam could see that as clearly as Joy did.

The house phone rang and she answered without looking at the caller ID. "Henry residence."

"Joy? Oh, it's so nice to finally talk to you!" A female voice, happy.

"Thanks," she said, carrying the phone back to the window so she could look outside. "Who is this?"

"God, how stupid of me," the woman said with a delighted laugh. "I'm Catherine Henry, Sam's mother."

Whoa. A wave of embarrassment swept over her. Joy was standing in Sam's bedroom, beside the bed where they'd had sex, and talking to his mother. Could this be any more awkward? "Hello. Um, Sam's out in the workshop."

"Oh, I know," she said and Joy could almost see her waving one hand to dismiss that information. "I just talked to him and your adorable daughter, Holly."

"You did?" Confused, she stared down at the workshop and watched as Sam and Holly walked out through the snow covering the ground. Sam was carrying the latest fairy house and Holly, no surprise, was chattering a mile a minute. Joy's heart ached with pleasure and sorrow.

"Holly tells me that she and Sam are making houses for fairies and that my son isn't as crabby as he used to be."

"Oh, for—" Joy closed her eyes briefly. "I'm so sorry—"

"Don't be silly. He *is* crabby," Catherine told her. "But he certainly seemed less so around your little girl."

"He's wonderful with her."

There was a pause and then a sniffle as if the woman was fighting tears. "I'm so glad. I've hoped for a long time to see my son wake up again. Find happiness again. It sounds to me like he is."

"Oh," Joy spoke up quickly, shaking her head as if Sam's mother could see her denial, "Mrs. Henry—"

"Catherine."

"Fine. Catherine, please don't make more of this than there is. Sam doesn't want—"

"Maybe not," she interrupted. "But he needs. So much. He's a good man, Joy. He's just been lost."

"I know," Joy answered on a sigh, resting her hand on the ice-cold windowpane as she watched the man she loved and her daughter kneeling together in the snow. "But what if he doesn't want to be found?"

Another long pause and Catherine said, "Kaye's told me so much about you, Joy. She thinks very highly of you, and just speaking to your daughter tells me that you're a wonderful mother."

"I hope so," she said, her gaze fixed on Sam.

"Look, I don't know how you feel, but if you don't mind my saying, I can hear a lot in your voice when you speak of Sam."

"Catherine—" If she couldn't tell Sam how she felt she certainly couldn't tell his *mother*.

"You don't have to say anything, dear. Just please. Do me a favor and don't give up on him."

"I don't want to." Joy could admit that much. "I…care about him."

"I'm so glad." The next pause was a short one. "After the holidays I'm going to come and visit Sam. I hope we can meet then."

"I'd like that," Joy said and meant it. She just hoped that she would still be seeing Sam by then.

When the phone call ended a moment later, she hung up the phone and walked back to the window to watch the two people in the world she loved most.

"Will more fairies move in and put up some more lights like the other ones did?" Holly asked, kneeling in the snow to peek through the windows of the tiny houses.

"We'll have to wait and see, I guess," Sam told her, setting the new house down on a flat rock slightly above the others.

"I bet they do because now they have friends here and—"

Sam smiled to himself as the little girl took off on another long, rambling monologue. He was going to miss spending time with Holly. As much as he'd fought against it in the beginning, the little girl had wormed her way into his heart—just like her mother had. In his own defense, Sam figured there weren't many people who could have ignored a five-year-old with as much charm as this one. Even the cold didn't diminish her energy level. If anything, he thought, it pumped her up. Her little cheeks were rosy, her eyes, so much like her mother's, sparkled.

"Do fairies have Christmas trees?"

"What?"

"Like Mommy and me got a tiny little tree because you don't like Christmas, but maybe if you had a great big tree you'd like Christmas more, Sam."

He slid a glance at her. He'd caught on to Holly's maneuvers. She was giving him that sly smile that he guessed females were born knowing how to deliver.

"You want a big Christmas tree," he said.

"I like our little one, but I like big ones, too, and we could make it really pretty with candy canes and we could make popcorn and put it on, too, and I think you'd like it."

"I probably would," he admitted. Hell, just because he was against Christmas didn't mean a five-year-old had to put up with a sad little tree tucked away in her room. "Why don't you go get your mom and we'll cut down a tree."

Her eyes went wide. "Cut it down ourselves? In the woods?"

"You bet. You can help." As long as he had his hands over hers on the hatchet, showing her how to do it without risking her safety. Around them, the pines rustled in the wind and sounded like sighs. The sky was heavy and gray and looked ready to spill another foot or two of snow any minute. "You can pick out the tree—as long as it's not a giant," he added with a smile.

She studied him thoughtfully for so long, he had to wonder what she was thinking. Nothing could have prepared him, though, for what she finally said. "You're a good daddy."

He sat back on his heels to look at her, stunned into silence. Snow was seeping into the legs of his jeans, but he paid no attention. "What?"

"You're a good daddy," she said again and moved up to lay one hand on his cheek. "You help me with stuff and you show me things and I know you used to have a little boy but he had to go to heaven with his mommy and that's what makes you crabby."

Air caught in his chest. Couldn't exhale or inhale. All he could do was watch the child watching him.

How did she know about Eli? Had her mother told her? Or had she simply overheard other adults talking about him? Kids, he knew, picked up on more than the grown-ups around them ever noticed. As Holly watched him, she looked so serious. So solemn, his heart broke a little.

"But if you want," she went on, her perpetually high-pitched, fast-paced voice softening, "I could be your little girl and you could be *my* daddy and then you wouldn't be crabby or lonely anymore."

His heart stopped. He felt it take one hard beat and then clutch. Her eyes were filled with a mixture of sadness and hope, and that steady gaze scorched him. This little girl was offering all the love a five-year-old held and hoping he'd take it. But how could he? How could he love a child again and risk losing that child? But wasn't he going to lose her anyway? Because of his own fears and the nightmares that had never really left him?

Sam had been so careful, for years, to stay isolated, to protect his heart, to keep his distance from the world at large. And now there was a tiny girl who had pierced through his defenses, showing him just how vulnerable he really was.

She was still looking at him, still waiting, trusting that he would want her. Love her.

He did. He already loved her, and that wasn't something he could admit. Not to himself. Not to the child who needed him. Sam had never thought of himself as a coward, but damned if he didn't feel like one now. How could he give her what she needed when the very thought of loving and losing could bring him to his knees?

He stood up, grabbed her and pulled her in for a tight hug, and her little arms went around his neck and clung as if her life depended on it. There at the edge of the woods with fairy magic shining in the gray, he was humbled by a little girl, shattered by the love freely offered.

"Do you want to be my daddy, Sam?" she whispered.

How to get out of this without hurting her? Without ripping his own heart out of his chest? Setting her down again, he crouched in front of her and met those serious blue eyes. "I'm proud you would ask me, Holly," he said, knowing just how special that request had been. "But this is pretty important, so I think you should talk to your mom about this first, okay?"

Not a no, not a yes. He didn't want to hurt her, but he couldn't give her what she wanted, either. Joy knew her daughter best. She would know how to let her down without crushing that very tender heart. And Joy knew—because he'd told her—that there was no future for them. What surprised him, though, was how much he wished things were different—that he could have told that little girl he would be her daddy and take care of her and love her. But he couldn't do it. Wouldn't do it.

"Okay, Sam." Holly grinned and her eyes lit up. "I'll go ask her right now, okay? And then we can show her the new fairy house and then we can get our big tree and maybe have hot chocolate and—" She took off at a dead run, still talking, still planning.

He turned to look at the house and saw Joy in the bedroom window, watching them. Would he always see her there, he wondered? Would he walk through his empty house and catch the faint scent of summer flowers? Would he sit in the great room at night and wait for her to come in and sit beside him? Smile at him? Would he spend the rest of his life reaching across the bed for her?

A few weeks ago, his life was insular, quiet, filled with the shadows of memories and the ghosts he carried with him everywhere. Now there would be *more* ghosts. The only difference being, he would have *chosen* to lose Joy and Holly.

That thought settled in, and he didn't like it. Still looking up at Joy, Sam asked himself if maybe he was wrong to pass up this opportunity. Maybe it was time to step out of the shadows. To take a chance. To risk it all.

A scream ripped his thoughts apart and in an instant, everything changed. Again.

Five stitches, three hot chocolates and one Christmas tree later, they were in the great room, watching the lights on the big pine in the front window shine. They'd used the strings of lights Joy had hung on the walls in their room, and now the beautiful pine was dazzling. There were popcorn chains and candy canes they'd bought in town as decorations. And there was an exhausted but happy little girl, asleep on the couch, a smile still curving her lips.

Joy brushed Holly's hair back from her forehead and kissed the neat row of stitches. It had been a harrowing, scary ride down the mountain to the clinic in town. But Sam had been a rock. Steady, confident, he'd already had Holly in his arms heading for his truck by the time Joy had come downstairs at a dead run.

Hearing her baby scream, watching her fall and then seeing the bright splotch of blood on the snow had shaken Joy right down to the bone. But Holly was crying and reaching for her, so she swallowed her own fear to try to ease Holly's. The girl had hit her head on a rock under the snow when she fell. A freak accident, but seeing the neat row of stitches reminded Joy how fragile her child was. How easily hurt. Physically. Emotionally.

Sam stood by the tree. "You want me to carry her to bed?"

"Sure. Thanks."

He nodded and stalked across the room as if every step was vibrating with repressed energy. But when he scooped Holly into his arms, he was gentle. Careful. She followed after him and neither of them spoke again until Holly was tucked in with her favorite stuffed dog and they were safely out in the great room again.

Sam walked to the fireplace, stared down into the flames as

if looking for answers to questions he hadn't asked, and shoved both hands into his pockets. Joy walked over to join him, hooked her arm through his and wasn't really surprised when he moved away. Hurt, yes. But not surprised.

She'd known this was coming. Maybe Holly being hurt had sped up the process, but Joy had been expecting him to pull away. To push her aside. He had been honest from the beginning, telling her that they had no future. That he didn't want forever because, she knew, he didn't trust in promises.

He cared for her. He cared for Holly, but she knew he didn't want to and wouldn't want to hear how much she loved him, so she kept it to herself. Private pain she could live with. She didn't think she could bear him throwing her love back in her face and dismissing it.

"Sam…"

"Scared me," he admitted in a voice so low she almost missed the words beneath the hiss and snap of the fire.

"I know," Joy said softly. "Me, too. But Holly's fine, Sam. The doctor said she wouldn't even have a scar."

"Yeah, and I'm glad of that." He shook his head and looked at her, firelight and shadow dancing over his features, glittering in his eyes. "But I can't do this again, Joy."

"Do what?" Heart aching, she took a step toward him, then stopped when he took one back.

"You know damn well what," he ground out. Then he took a deep breath and blew it out. "The thing is, just before Holly got hurt, I was thinking that maybe I could. Maybe it was time to try again." He looked at her. "With you."

Hope rose inside her and then crashed again when he continued.

"Then that little girl screamed, and I knew I was kidding myself." Shaking his head slowly, he took another deep breath. "I lost my family once, Joy. I won't risk that kind of pain again. You and Holly have to go."

"If we go," she reminded him, "you *still* lose us."

He just stared at her. He didn't have an answer to that, and they both knew it.

"Yeah, I know. But you'll be safe out there and I won't have to wonder and worry every time you leave the damn house."

"So you'll never think of us," she mused aloud. "Never wonder what we're doing, if we're safe, if we're happy."

"I didn't say that," he pointed out. "But I can block that out."

"Yeah, you're good at blocking out."

"It's a gift." The smile that touched his mouth was wry, unhappy and gone in an instant.

"So just like that?" she asked, her voice low, throbbing with banked emotions that were nearly choking her. "We leave and what? You go back to being alone in this spectacular cage?" She lifted both hands to encompass the lovely room and said, "Because no matter how beautiful it is, it's still a *cage*, Sam."

"And it's my business." His voice was clipped, cold, as if he'd already detached from the situation. From *her*.

Well, she wasn't going to make it that easy on him.

"It's not just your business, Sam. It's mine. It's Holly's. She told me she asked you to be her daddy. Did that mean nothing to you?"

"It meant *everything*," he said, his voice a growl of pain and anger. "It's not easy to turn away from you. From her."

"Then don't do it."

"I have to."

Fury churned in the pit of her stomach and slid together with a layer of misery that made Joy feel sick to her soul. "How could I be in love with a man so stubborn he refuses to see what's right in front of him?"

He jolted. "Who said anything about love?"

"I did," she snapped. She wasn't going to walk away from him never saying how she felt. If he was going to throw her away like Mike had, like every foster parent she'd ever known had, then he would do it knowing the full truth. "I love you."

"Well," he advised, "*stop*."

She choked out a laugh that actually scraped at her throat. Amazing. As hurt as she was, she could still be amused by the idiot man who was willing to toss aside what most people never found. "Great. Good idea. I'll get right on that."

He grabbed her upper arms and drew her up until they were eye to eye. "Damn it, Joy, I told you up front that I'm not that guy. That there was no future for us."

"Yes, I guess I'm a lousy listener." She pulled away from him, cleared her throat and blinked back a sheen of tears because she *refused* to cry in front of him. "It must be your immense load of charm that dragged me in. That warm, welcoming smile."

He scowled at her.

"No, it was the way that you grudgingly bent to having us here. It was your gentleness with Holly, your sense of humor, your kiss, your touch, the way you look at me sometimes as if you don't know quite what to do with me." She smiled sadly. "I fell in love and there's no way out for me now. You're it, Sam."

He scrubbed one hand across his face as if he could wipe away her words, her feelings.

"You don't have to love me, Sam." That about killed her to say, but it was truth.

"I didn't want to hurt you, Joy."

"I believe you. But when you *care*, you hurt. That's life. But if you don't love me, try to love someone else." Oh God, the thought of that tore what was left of her heart into tiny, confetti-sized pieces. "But stop hiding out here in this palace of shadows and live your life."

"I like my life."

"No you don't," she countered, voice thick with those unshed tears. "Because you don't have one. What you have is sacrifice."

He pushed both hands through his hair then let them fall to his sides. "What the hell are you talking about?"

She took a breath, steadying herself, lowering her voice, *willing* him to hear her. "You've locked yourself away, Sam. All to punish yourself for surviving. What happened to your family was terrible, I can't even imagine the pain you lived through. But you're still alive, Sam. Staying closed down and shut off won't alter what happened. It won't bring them back."

His features went tight, cold, his eyes shuttered as they had been so often when she first met him.

"You think I don't know that?" He paced off a few steps, then whirled around and came right back. His eyes glittered with banked fury and pain. "Nothing will bring them back. Nothing can change why they died, either."

"What?" Confused, worried, she waited.

"You know why I had to drive you into town for Holly's sleepover?"

"Of course I do." She shook her head, frowning. "My car wouldn't start."

"Because I took the damn distributor cap off."

That made no sense at all. "What? Why?"

Now he scrubbed his hands over his face and gave a bitter sigh. "Because, I couldn't let you drive down the mountain in the snow."

"Sam..."

Firelight danced around the room but looked haunting as it shadowed his face, highlighting the grief carved into his features, like a mask in stone. As she watched him, she saw his eyes blur, focus on images in his mind rather than the woman who stood just opposite him.

"I was caught up in a painting," he said. "It was a commission. A big one and I wanted to keep at it while I was on a roll." He turned from her, set both hands on the fireplace mantel and stared down into the crackling flames. "There was a family reunion that weekend and Dani was furious that I didn't want to go. So I told her to take Eli and go ahead. That I'd meet her at the reunion as soon as I was finished." He swiveled his head to look at Joy. "She was on the interstate and a front tire blew. Dani lost control of the car and slammed into an oncoming semi. Both she and Eli died instantly."

Joy's heart ripped open, and the pain she felt for him nearly brought her to her knees. But she kept quiet, wanting him to finish and knowing he needed to get it all said.

"If I'd been driving it might have been different, but I'll never know, will I?" He pushed away from the mantel and glared at her, daring her to argue with him. "I chose my work over my family and I lost them. You once asked me why I don't paint anymore, and there's your reason. I chose my work over what should have been more important. So I don't paint. I don't go out. I don't—"

"Live," she finished for him. "You don't *live*, Sam. Do you really think that's what Dani would want for you? To spend the next fifty years locked away from everything and everyone? Is that how she wanted to live?"

"Of course not," he snapped.

"Then what's the point of the self-flagellation?" Joy demanded, walking toward him, ignoring the instinctive step back he took. "If you'd been in that car, you might have died, too."

"You don't know that."

"You don't, either. That's the point."

Outside, the wind moaned as it slid beneath the eaves. But tonight, it sounded louder, like a desperate keening, as if even the house was weeping for what was ending.

Trying again, Joy said, "My little girl loves you. I love you. Can you really let that go so easily?"

His gaze snapped to hers. "I told you that earlier today, I actually thought that maybe I could risk it. Maybe there was a chance. And then Holly was hurt and my heart stopped."

"Kids get hurt, Sam," she said, still trying, though she could see in his eyes that the fight was over. His decision was made whether she agreed or not. "We lose people we shouldn't. But life keeps going. *We* keep going. The world doesn't stop, Sam, and it shouldn't."

"Maybe not," he said softly. "But it's going to keep going without me."

CHAPTER TEN

JOY SPENT THE next few days taking care of business. She buried the pain beneath layers of carefully constructed indifference and focused on what she had to do. In between taking care of her clients, she made meals for Sam and froze them. Whatever else happened after she left this house, he wouldn't starve.

If she had her way, she wouldn't leave. She'd stay right here and keep hammering at his hard head until she got through. And maybe, one day, she'd succeed. But then again, maybe not. So she couldn't take the chance. It was one thing to risk her own heart, but she wouldn't risk Holly's. Her daughter was already crazy about Sam. The longer they stayed here in this house, the deeper those feelings would go. And before long, Sam would break her baby's heart. He might not mean to, but it was inevitable.

Because he refused to love them back. Sooner or later, Holly would feel that and it would crush her. Joy wouldn't let that happen.

She would miss this place, though, she told herself as she packed up Holly's things. Glancing out the bedroom window, she watched her little girl and Sam placing yet another fairy house in the woods. And she had to give the man points for kindness.

She and Sam hadn't really spoken since that last night when everything had been laid out between them. They'd sidestepped each other when they could, and when they couldn't they'd both pretended that everything was fine. No point in upsetting Holly, after all. And despite—or maybe because of how strained things were between her and Sam—he hadn't changed toward Holly. That alone made her love him more and made it harder to leave. But tomorrow morning, she and Holly would wake up back in their own house in Franklin.

"Thank God Buddy finished the work early," she muttered, folding up the last of Holly's shirts and laying them in the suitcase.

Walking into the kitchen of her dreams, Joy sighed a little, then took out a pad of paper and a pen. Her heart felt heavy, the knot of emotion still stuck at the base of her throat, and every breath seemed like an event. She hated leaving. Hated walking away from Sam. But she didn't have a choice any longer. Sitting on a stool at the granite counter, she made a list for Sam of the food she had stocked for him. There was enough food in the freezer now to see him through to when Kaye returned.

Would he miss her? she wondered. Would he sit in that dining room alone and remember being there with her and Holly? Would he sit in the great room at night and wish Joy was there beside him? Or would he wipe it all out of his mind? Would she become a story never talked about like his late wife? Was Joy now just another reason to block out life and build the barricades around his heart that much higher?

She'd hoped to pull Sam out of the shadows—now she might have had a hand in pushing him deeper into the darkness. Sighing a little, she got up, stirred the pot of beef stew, then checked the bread in the oven.

When she looked out the window again, she saw the fairy lights had blinked on and Holly was kneeling beside Sam in the snow. She couldn't hear what was being said, but her heart broke a little anyway when her daughter laid her little hand on Sam's shoulder. Leaving was going to be hard. Tearing Holly away was going to be a nightmare. But she had to do it. For everyone's sake.

Two hours later, Holly put on her stubborn face.

"But I don't wanna go," Holly shouted and pulled away from her mother to run down the hall to the great room. "Sam! Sam! Mommy says we're leaving and I don't want to go cuz we're building a fairy house and I have to help you put it in the woods so the fairies can come and—"

Joy walked into the main room behind her daughter and watched as Holly threw herself into Sam's lap. He looked at Joy over the child's head even as he gave the little girl a hug.

"Tell her we have to stay, Sam, cuz I'm your helper now and you need me."

"I do," he said, and his voice sounded rough, scratchy. "But your mom needs you, too, so if she says it's time to go, you're going to have to."

She tipped her head back, looking at him with rivers of tears in her eyes. "But I don't want to."

"I know. I don't want you to, either." He gave her what looked to Joy like a wistful smile, then tugged on one of her pigtails. "Why don't I finish up the fairy house and then bring it to you so you can give it to Lizzie."

She shook her head so hard, her pigtails whipped back and forth across her eyes. "It's not the same, Sam. Can't I stay?"

"Come on, Holly," Joy spoke up quickly because her own emotions were taking over. Tears were close, and watching her daughter's heart break was breaking her own. "We really have to go."

Holly threw her a furious look, brows locked down, eyes narrowed. "You're being mean."

"I'm your mom," Joy said tightly, keeping her own tears at bay. "That's my job. Now come on."

"I love you, Sam," Holly whispered loud enough for her voice to carry. Then she gave him a smacking kiss on the cheek and crawled off his lap. Chin on her chest, she walked toward Joy with slow, dragging steps, as if she was pulling each foot out of mud along the way.

Joy saw the stricken look on Sam's face and thought, *Good. Now you know what you've given up. What you're allowing yourself to lose.*

Head bowed, shoulders slumped, Holly couldn't have been more clear in her desolation. Well, Joy knew just how she felt. Taking the little girl's hand, she gave it a squeeze and said, "Let's go home, sweetie."

They headed out the front door, and Joy didn't look back. She couldn't. For the first time in days, the sun was out, and the only clouds in the sky were big and white and looked as soft and fluffy as Santa's beard. The pines were covered in snow, and the bare branches of the aspens and birches looked like they'd been decorated with lace as the snow lay on every tiny twig. It was magical. Beautiful.

And Joy took no pleasure in any of it.

Holly hopped into her car seat and buckled herself in while Joy did a quick check of everything stuffed into the car. Their tiny tree was in the backseat and their suitcases in the trunk. Holly sat there glowering at the world in general, and Joy sighed because she knew her darling daughter was going to make her life a living hell for the next few days at least.

"That's it then," Joy said, forcing a smile as she turned to look at Sam. He wore that black leather jacket, and his jeans were faded and stacked on the toes of his battered work boots. His hair was too long, his white long-sleeved shirt was open at the neck, and his brown eyes pinned her with an intensity that stole her breath.

"Drive safely."

"That's all you've got?" she asked, tipping her head to one side to study him.

"What is there left to say?" he countered. "Didn't we get it all said a few days ago?"

"Not nearly, but you still don't understand that, do you?" He stood on his drive with the well-lit splendor of his house behind him. In the front window, the Christmas tree they'd decorated together shone in a fiery blaze of color, and behind her, she knew, there were fairy lights shining at the edge of the woods.

She looked up at him, then moved in closer. He didn't move, just locked his gaze with hers as she approached. When she was close enough, she cupped his cheeks in her palms and said softly, "We would have been good for you, Sam. I would have been. You and I could have been happy together. We could have built something that most people only dream about." She went up on her toes, kissed his grim, unyielding mouth, then looked at him again. "I want you to remember something. When you lost your family there was nothing you could do about it. *This* time, it's your choice. You're losing and you're letting it happen."

His mouth tightened, his eyes flashed, but he didn't speak, and Joy knew it was over.

"I'm sorry for you," she said, "that you're allowing your own pain to swallow your life."

Before he could tell her to mind her own business, she turned and walked to the car. With Holly loudly complaining, she fired up the engine, put it in gear and drove away from Sam Henry and all the might-have-beens that would drive her crazy for the rest of her life.

For the next few days, Sam settled back into what his life was like pre-Joy and Holly. He worked on his secret project—that didn't really need to be a secret anymore, because he always finished what he started. He called his mother to check in be- cause he should—but when she asked about Joy and Holly, he evaded, not wanting to talk about them any more than he wanted to think about them.

He tried to put the two females out of his mind, but how could he when he sensed Joy in every damn corner of his house?

In Kaye's suite, Joy's scent still lingered in the air. But the rooms were empty now. No toys, no stuffed dog. Joy's silky red robe wasn't hanging on the back of the door, and that pitiful excuse for a Christmas tree was gone as if it had never been there at all.

Every night, he sat in the great room in front of the fire and looked at the tree in the window. That it was there amazed him. Thinking about the night he and Joy and Holly had decorated it depressed him. For so many years, he'd avoided all mention of Christmas because he hadn't wanted to remember.

Now, though, he *did* want to. He relived every moment of the time Joy and Holly had been a part of his life. But mostly, he recalled the afternoon they had *left* him. He remembered Holly waving goodbye out the rear window of her mother's car. He remembered the look in Joy's eyes when she kissed him and told him that he was making a mistake by letting her go. And he particularly remembered Joy's laugh, her smile, the taste of her mouth and the feel of her arms around him when he was inside her.

Her image remained uppermost in his mind as if she'd been carved there. He couldn't shake it and didn't really want to. Remembering was all he had. The house was too damn quiet. Hell, he spent every day and most of the night out in the workshop just to avoid the suffocating silence. But it was no better out there because a part of him kept waiting for Holly to rush in, do one of her amazing monologues and climb up on the stool beside him.

When he was working, he found himself looking at the house, half expecting to see Joy in one of the windows, smiling at him. And every time he didn't, another piece of him died. He'd thought that he could go back to his old life once they were gone. Slide back into the shadows, become again the man fate had made him. But that hadn't happened and now, he realized, it never could.

He wasn't the same man because of Joy. Because she had brought him back to life. Awakened him after too many years spent in a self-made prison.

"So what the hell are you going to do about it?" he muttered, hating the way his voice echoed in the vast room. He picked up his beer, took a long drink and glared at the glittering Christmas tree. The night they'd decorated it flooded his mind.

Holly laughing, a fresh row of stitches on her forehead to remind him just how fear for her had brought him to his knees. Joy standing back and telling him where lights were missing. The three of them eating more candy canes than they hung and finally, Holly falling asleep, not knowing that he was going to screw everything up.

He pushed up out of the chair, walked to the tree and looked beyond it, to the lights in the fairy houses outside. There were pieces of both of them all over this place, he thought. There was no escaping the memories this time, even if he wanted to.

Turning, he looked around the room and felt the solitude press in on him. The immense room felt claustrophobic. Joy should be here with him, drinking wine and eating "winter" cookies. Holly should be calling for a drink of water and trying to stay up a little later.

"Instead," he muttered, like the hermit he was, "you're alone with your memories."

Joy was right, he told himself. Fate had cheated him once, stealing away those he loved best. But he'd done it to himself this time. He'd taken his second chance and thrown it away because he was too afraid to grab on and never let go. He thought about all he'd lost—all he was about to lose—and had to ask himself if pain was really all he had. Was that what he'd become? A man devoted to keeping his misery alive and well no matter the cost?

He put his beer down, stalked out of the room and headed for the workshop. "Damned if it is."

Christmas morning dawned with a soft snow falling, turning the world outside the tiny house in Franklin into a postcard.

The small, bent-over tree stood on a table in the living room, and even the multiple strings of lights it boasted couldn't make it a quarter as majestic as the tree they'd left behind in Sam's great room. But this one, Joy assured herself, was *theirs*. Hers and Holly's. And that made it perfect. They didn't need the big tree. Or the lovely house. Or Sam. They had each other and that was enough.

It just didn't *feel* like enough anymore. Giving herself a mental kick for even thinking those words, Joy pushed thoughts of Sam out of her mind. No small task since the last four or five days had been a study in loneliness. Holly was sad, Joy was miserable, and even the approach of Christmas hadn't been enough to lift the pall that hung over them both.

Deb had tried to cheer her, telling her that everything happened for a reason, but really? When the reason was a stubborn, foolish man too blind to see what he was giving up, what comfort was there?

Ignoring the cold hard stone settled around her heart, Joy forced a smile and asked, "Do you want to go outside, sweetie? Try out your new sled?"

Holly sat amid a sea of torn wrapping paper, its festive colors and bold ribbons making it look as though the presents had exploded rather than been opened. Her blond hair was loose, and her pink princess nightgown was tucked up around her knees as she sat cross-legged in the middle of the rubble.

She turned big blue eyes on Joy and said, "No, Mommy, I don't want to right now."

"Really?" Joy was trying to make Christmas good for her daughter, but the little girl missed Sam as much as Joy did, so it was an uphill battle. But they had to get used to being without him, didn't they? He'd made his choice. He'd let them go, and she hadn't heard a word from him since.

Apparently Sam Henry had found a way to go on, and so would she and Holly. "Well, how about we watch your favorite princess movie and drink some hot chocolate?"

"Okay…" The lack of enthusiasm in that word told Joy that Holly was only agreeing to please her mother.

God, she was a terrible person. *She's* the one who had allowed Holly to get too close to Sam in the hopes of reaching him. She had seen her daughter falling in love and hadn't done enough to stop it. She'd been too caught up in the sweetness of Holly choosing her own father to prepare either of them for the time when it all came crashing down on them.

Still, she had to try to reach her baby girl. Ease the pain, help her to enjoy Christmas morning.

"Are you upset because Santa couldn't bring you the puppy you wanted? Santa left you the note," Joy said, mentally thanking Sam for at least coming up with that brilliant idea. "He'll bring you a puppy as soon as he's old enough."

"It's okay. I can play with Lizzie's puppy." Holly got up, walked to her mother and crawled into her lap. Leaning her head against Joy's chest, she sighed heavily. "I want to go see Sam."

Joy's heart gave one hard lurch as everything in her yearned for the same thing. "Oh, honey, I don't think that's a good idea."

"Sure it is." Holly turned in her lap, looked up into her eyes and said softly, "He misses me, Mommy. It's Christmas and he's all by himself and lonely and probably crabby some more cuz we're not there to make him smile and help him with the fairy houses. He *needs* us. And we belong with Sam. It's Christmas and we should be there."

Her baby girl looked so calm, so serious, so *sure* of everything. The last few days hadn't been easy. They'd slipped back into their old life, but it wasn't the same. Nothing was the same anymore. They were a family as they'd always been, but now it felt as if someone was missing.

She'd left Sam to protect Holly. But keeping her away from the man she considered her father wasn't helping her either. It was a fine line to walk, Joy knew. She smoothed Holly's hair back from her face and realized her baby girl was right.

Sam had let them leave, but it was Joy who had packed up and walked out. Neither of them had fought for what they wanted, so maybe it was time to make a stand. Time to let him know that he could try to toss them aside all he wanted—but they weren't going to go.

"You're right, baby, he *does* need us. And we need him." Giving Holly a quick, hard kiss, she grinned and said, "Let's get dressed."

Sam heard the car pull into the drive, looked out the window and felt his heart jump to life. How was *that* for timing? He'd just been getting into his coat to drive into Franklin and bring his girls home. He felt like Ebenezer Scrooge when he woke up on Christmas morning and realized he hadn't missed it. Hadn't lost his last chance at happiness.

He hit the front door at a dead run and made it to the car before Joy had turned off the engine. Snow was falling, he was freezing, but he didn't give a good damn. Suddenly everything in his world had righted itself. And this time, he was going to grab hold of what was most important and never let it go again.

"Sam! Sam! Hi, Sam!" Holly's voice, hitting that high note, sounded like the sweetest song to him.

"Hi, Holly!" he called back, and while the little girl got herself out of her seat belt, he threw open the driver's door and pulled Joy out. "Hi," he said, letting his gaze sweep over her features before focusing back on the eyes that had haunted him from the first moment they met.

"Hi, Sam. Merry Christmas." She cupped his cheek in her palm, and her touch melted away the last of the ice encasing his heart.

"I missed you, damn it," he muttered and bent to kiss her.

That first taste of her settled everything inside him, brought the world back into focus and let him know that he was alive. And grateful.

"We're back!" Holly raced around the car, threw herself at Sam's legs and held on.

Breaking the kiss, he grinned down at the little girl and then reached down to pick her up. Holding her tight, he looked into bright eyes and then spun her in circles until she squealed in delight. "You're back. Merry Christmas, Holly."

She hugged his neck tightly and kissed his cheek with all the ferocity of a five-year-old's love. "Merry Christmas!"

"Come on, you two. It's cold out here." He carried Holly and followed behind Joy as she walked into the house and then turned for the great room. "I've got a couple surprises for you two."

"For Christmas?" Holly gave him a squeeze, then as she saw what was waiting for her, breathed, "Oh my goodness!" That quick gasp was followed by another squeal, this one higher than the one before. She squirmed to get out of Sam's arms, then raced across the room to the oversize fairy castle dollhouse sitting in front of the tree.

Beside him, Sam heard Joy give a soft sigh. When he looked at her, there were tears in her eyes and a beautiful smile on her amazing mouth. His heart gave another hard lurch, and he welcomed it. For the last few days, he'd felt dead inside. Coming back to life was much better.

"You made that for her."

He looked to where the girl he already considered his daughter was exploring the castle he'd built for her. It was red, with turrets and towers, tiny flags flying from the points of those towers. Glass windows opened and closed, and wide double doors swung open. The back of the castle was open for small fingers to explore and redecorate and dream.

"Yeah," he said. "Holly needed a fairy house she could actually play with. I'm thinking this summer we might need to build a tree house, too."

"This summer?" Joy's words were soft, the question hanging in the air between them.

"I've got plans," he said. "And so much to tell you. Ask you."

Her eyes went soft and dreamy and as he watched, they filled with a sheen of tears he really hoped she wouldn't let fall.

"I can't believe you made that for Holly," Joy said, smiling at her daughter's excitement. "She loves it."

"I can't believe you're here," Sam confessed, turning her in his arms so he could hold her, touch her, look into her eyes. Sliding his hands up her arms, over her shoulders to her face, his palms cradled her as his thumbs stroked gently over her soft, smooth skin. "I was coming to you."

"You were?" Wonder, hope lit her eyes, and Sam knew he hadn't blown it entirely. He hadn't let this last best chance at love slip past him.

"You arrived just as I was headed to the garage. I was going to bring you back here to give you your presents. Here. In our home."

Her breath caught and she lifted one hand to her mouth. "*Our* home?"

"If you'll stay," he said. "Stay with me. Love me. Marry me."

"Oh, Sam…"

"Don't answer yet," he said, grinning now as he took her hand and pulled her over to the brightly lit Christmas tree. "Just wait. There's more." Then to the little girl, he said, "There's another present for you, Holly. I think Santa stopped off here last night."

"He *did*?" Holly's eyes went wide as saucers as her smile danced in her eyes. "What did he bring?"

"Open it and find out," he said and pointed to a big white box with a red ribbon.

"How come it has holes in the top?" Holly asked.

"You'll see."

Joy already guessed it. She squeezed Sam's hand as they

watched Holly carefully lift off the lid of the box and peer inside. "Oh my goodness!"

The little girl looked up at Sam. "He's for me?"

"She is. It's a girl."

Holly laughed in delight then reached into the box and lifted out a golden retriever puppy. Its fur was white and soft, and Holly buried her face against that softness, whispering and laughing as the puppy eagerly licked her face. "Elsa. I'm gonna name her Elsa," Holly proclaimed and laid out on the floor so her new best friend could jump all over her in wild abandon.

"I can't believe you did that," Joy said, shaking her head and smiling through her tears. "Where did you find a white puppy? I looked everywhere."

Sam shrugged and gave her a half smile. "My sister knew a breeder and, well… I chartered a jet and flew out to Boston to pick her up two days ago."

"Boston." Joy blinked at him. "You flew to Boston to pick up a Christmas puppy so my little girl wouldn't be disappointed."

"*Our* little girl," he corrected. "I love her, Joy. Like she's my own. And if you'll let me, I'll adopt her."

"Oh my God…" Joy bit down hard on her bottom lip and gave up the battle to stem her tears. They coursed down her cheeks in silvery rivers that only made her smile shine more brightly.

"Is that a yes?"

"Yes, of course it's a yes," Joy managed to say when she threw her arms around him and held on. "She already considers you her father. So do I."

Sam held Joy tight, buried his face in the curve of her neck and said, "I love you. Both of you. So much. I won't ever let you go, Joy. I want you to marry me. Give me Holly. And give us both more children. Help me make a family so strong nothing can ever tear it down."

"You filled my heart, Sam." She pulled back, looked up at him and said, "All of this. What you've done. It's the most amazing moment of my life. My personal crabby hermit has become my hero."

His mouth quirked at the corner. "Still not done," he said and drew her to the other side of the tree.

"You've already given me everything, Sam. What's left?" She was laughing and crying and the combined sounds were like music to him.

The big house felt full of love and promise, and Sam knew that it would never be empty again. There would be so much light and love in the house, shadows would be banished. He had his memories of lost love, and those would never fade, but he wouldn't be ruled by them anymore, either.

When Kaye finally came home from her annual vacation, she was going to find a changed man and a household that was filled with the kind of happiness Sam had thought he'd never find again.

"What is it, Sam?" Joy asked when he pulled her to a stop in front of a draped easel.

"A promise," he said and pulled the sheet from the painting he'd only just finished the night before, to show her what he dreamed. What he wanted. For both of them.

"Oh, Sam." Her heart was in her voice. He heard it and smiled.

Joy stared at the painting, unable to tear her eyes from it. He'd painted this room, with the giant, lit-up tree, with stacks of presents at its feet, and the hint of fairy lights from the tiny houses in the woods shining through the glass behind it.

On the floor, he'd painted Holly, the puppy climbing all over her as the little girl laughed. He'd painted him and Joy, arms around each other, watching the magic unfold together. And he'd painted Joy pregnant.

There was love and celebration in every stroke of paint. The light was warm and soft and seemed to make the painting glow with everything she was feeling. She took it all in and felt the wonder of it all settle in the center of her heart. He'd painted her a promise.

"I did it all yesterday," he said, snaking both arms around her middle as they stared at his creation. "I've never had a painting come so quickly. And I know it's because this is what's meant to be. You, me, Holly."

"I love it," Joy said softly, turning her face up just enough to meet his kiss. "But we don't know if I'm pregnant."

"If you're not now," he promised, both eyebrows lifting into high arches, "you will be soon. I want lots of kids with you, Joy. I want to live again—risks and all—and I can only do that if you love me."

She turned around in his arms, glanced at her daughter, still giggling with puppy delight, then smiled up at Sam. "I love you so much, Sam. I always will. I want to make that family with you. Have lots of kids. Watch Holly and the others we'll make together grow up with a father who loves them."

"We can do that. Hell," he said, "we can do anything together."

She took a long, deep breath and grinned up at him. "And if you ask me to marry you right this minute, this will be the best Christmas ever."

He dipped into his pocket, pulled out a sapphire and diamond ring and slid it onto her finger while she watched, stunned. Though she'd been hoping for a real proposal, she hadn't expected a ring. Especially one this beautiful.

"It wasn't just a puppy I got in Boston," he said. "Though I will admit my sister helped me pick out this ring."

"Your family knows?"

"Absolutely," he said, bending to kiss her, then kiss the ring on her finger as if sealing it onto her hand. "My mother's thrilled to have a granddaughter and can't wait to meet you both in person. And be prepared, they'll all be descending after the holidays to do just that."

"It'll be fun," she said. "Oh, Sam, I love *you*."

"That's the only present I'm ever going to need," Sam said and kissed her hard and long and deep.

She'd come here this morning believing she would have to fight with Sam to make him admit how much he loved her. The fact that he had been on his way to get her and Holly filled her heart. He wanted her. He loved them both. And he was willing to finally leave the past behind and build a future with her. It really was the best Christmas she'd ever known.

"Hey!" Holly tugged at both of them as the puppy jumped at her feet. "You're kissing! Like mommies and daddies do!"

Joy looked at her little girl as Sam lifted her up to eye level. "Would you like that, baby girl? Would you like Sam to be your daddy and for all of us to live here forever?"

"For really?"

"For really," Sam said. "I'd like to be your daddy, Holly. And this summer, you and I are going to build you a fairy tree house. How does that sound?"

She gave him a wide, happy grin. "You'll be good at it, Sam. I can tell and I love you lots."

"I love you back, Holly. Always will." He kissed her forehead.

"Can I call you Daddy now?"

"I'd really like that," he said and Joy saw the raw emotion glittering in his eyes.

Their little girl clapped and grinned hugely before throwing her arms around both their necks. "This is the bestest Christmas ever. I got just what I wanted. A puppy. A fairy house. And my own daddy."

Sam looked into Joy's eyes and she felt his love, his pleasure in the moment, and she knew that none of them would ever be lonely again.

"Merry Christmas, Sam."

"Merry Christmas, Joy."

And in the lights of the tree, he sealed their new life with a kiss that had Holly applauding and sent the new puppy barking.

Everything, Joy thought, was *perfect*.

* * * * *

Christmas With
The Single Dad Doc

Annie O'Neil

Annie O'Neil spent most of her childhood with her leg draped over the family rocking chair and a book in her hand. Novels, baking and writing too much teenage angst poetry ate up most of her youth. Now Annie splits her time between corralling her husband into helping her with their cows, baking, reading, barrel racing (not really!) and spending some very happy hours at her computer, writing.

Books by Annie O'Neil

The Island Clinic
The Princess and the Pediatrician

Double Miracle at St. Nicolino's Hospital
A Family Made in Rome

Dolphin Cove Vets
The Vet's Secret Son

Miracles in the Making
Risking Her Heart on the Single Dad

Christmas Under the Northern Lights
Hawaiian Medic to Rescue His Heart
New Year Kiss with His Cinderella
In Bali with the Single Dad

Visit the Author Profile page
at millsandboon.com.au for more titles.

Dear Reader,

It may come as no surprise to my regular readers that I am a Christmas story superfan. When I was asked to be part of the Carey Cove Midwives "staff," I was absolutely over the moon. A Christmas nut in a beautiful seaside village? Perfection. With, of course, some emotional hurdles to leap, but my goodness, isn't it satisfying going on that journey from emotionally vulnerable to exhilarated to more vulnerable than ever, then…out there…on the horizon…is the happily-ever-after? Writing this story was a genuine pleasure. I hope you enjoy it and that it instantly makes you want hot chocolate and a candy cane. Thank you so much for being here. That is the best holiday present ever.

Xoxo *Annie O'*

To Nettybean, who has been with me
from the beginning…may it long continue!

CHAPTER ONE

'DASHING THROUGH THE…' Kiara stood back from the snow-flake stencil she'd taped to the window, then gave the aerosol can a good spray. 'Snow!'

She carried on humming the Christmas song as she filled in the dozen or so other gaily shaped stencils, until her windows were transformed into magical snow crystal portals. Seeing actual drifts of snow outside her house would've made the effect even more enchanting, but the one thing Kiara wasn't in charge of in her new life here in Cornwall was the weather.

Unless…

She could dip into her Christmas Decorations Fund just a teensy bit more than she already had and buy some fake snow. Or— Ooh! A rush of excitement swept through her. A snow machine! After all, she quickly justified, any expenditure would be worth it, considering she was doing all of this mad over-the-top decorating for charity.

As a midwife, she knew just how important funding for specialised equipment was, and First Steps, her chosen charity, was renowned for helping families in need to furnish their homes with the specialised equipment they needed to give their newborn the very best chance to live a happy, healthy life. Ventilators, specialist cots, apnoea monitors… They all made the world of difference to an infant…just like being at home did.

As such, she pulled out her phone and on her increasingly long 'Christmas Decorations' list tapped in *snow machine*.

With a grin, she perched atop the armrest of her new sofa and admired her handiwork. Inside, it already looked like the day before Christmas. Stockings? Check! Chimney. Check! Tree, plate of biscuits, nativity scene, miniature glittery reindeer and unicorns? Check!

Sure, it was only the beginning of November. And, yes, she was aware of the handful of side-eyes she'd already received from some villagers, clearly wondering whether the new kid in town was a bit bonkers. She wasn't bonkers. Just new, and a bit lonely. And making the cottage feel all cosy and set for the festive season was her way of settling in. Especially as the view outside her window was no longer the familiar bustling London high street.

She twizzled round so she could look out of her new front window. Through the prisms of faux flakes she could see that outside the clear blue sky shone brightly over a crisp and increasingly autumnal Carey Cove. The leaves had turned and, courtesy of the warm afternoon sunshine, were glowing in multicoloured hues of red, orange and yellow as they floated down in colourful drifts. Not so much that the trees lay bare, but just enough to ensure there were always plenty of leaves for her to skip through if no one was around, as she went on her daily trip into the village to explore the smattering of shops along the solitary high street. Which was blissfully far away from London.

London.

The word hardened like a shard of ice in her chest. This would be the first year ever she would miss the Christmas lights being switched on. There would be no bustling into a pub after, to raise a glass of festive cheer with friends and family. No walking around the twinkling streets of London arm

in arm with her boyfriend as all the shops decked their halls
with boughs of—

Stop!

She didn't live there any more. Or have that life. She lived
here, in the picture-postcard village of Carey Cove. A glorious
seaside village that didn't have a patch on big, old, overcrowded
London, where it was far too easy to fall in love with dazzlingly
talented surgeons. Surgeons who, along with having piercing
blue eyes and flax-coloured hair, were *liars, liars, pants on fire*.

As if sensing the vein of discord threatening to break into her
happy but still fragile new existence, her phone rang with her
mum's tell-tale ringtone: a Bollywood song her mother regularly sang in an off-key, happy voice similar to Kiara's.

'Hey, Mum. Perfect timing as ever.'

'Hello, darling…' Her mum's voice instantly thickened with
concern. 'Everything all right? This isn't a bad time, is it?'

'No, not at all. I meant it's just nice to hear your voice.'

And it was. Even though she was twenty-eight, and had lived
on her own for years now, she was an only child, and she and her
parents were very close. Her mum had stuffed countless tissues
into Kiara's hands over the past ten months. Nor had she been
shy about voicing her concern when Kiara had announced that
moving to a different hospital in London wasn't the solution to
her post-breakup blues. But a new home was.

A new home in a new village in a new county. Far, far away
from London. Even her father, a poster boy for Britain's renowned stiff upper lip, had expressed concern that moving a
five-hour train ride away from her family in London might not
be the wisest of decisions.

'Are you all right?' her mother asked, not even pausing for
breath as she added, 'It's not too late to back out, you know.'

'What?' Even the idea of leaving made her blood run cold.
'No, Mum. Honestly. I love it here. Not to mention the fact I've
already signed my contract for Carey House.'

Her eyes flicked up the hill and along the treetops where,

courtesy of some bare branches, she could just make out the golden stone chimney tops of the transfigured cottage hospital that commanded an arresting view of the harbour village. This was a new thing for her. Working somewhere small enough to actually learn everyone's name.

After her life had imploded last year, Kiara had felt cornered into leaving the enormous inner-city hospital where she'd worked for five years. Shame and regret had been powerful motivators. Anger, too. She'd begun what had become a long string of short-term posts in maternity wards across London, hoping to find something—*somewhere*—that would make her feel as if she was starting her life afresh. A life reboot.

She'd finally found it. Here in Carey Cove. And that was why she couldn't wait to start her new permanent midwife post at Carey House.

'I'm not backing out before I've even begun.' Kiara charged her voice with the confidence she knew her mum would be hoping to hear. 'The last thing Carey House needs is to be shorthanded when all those Valentine's babies arrive.'

Her mother made a confused noise. 'I'm sorry, love. I'm not making the connection.'

Kiara grinned, perfectly able to envisage her mother's bewildered expression. 'C'mon, Mum. You know how to add. A night out on February the fourteenth with wine and flowers and romance leads to what to remember late in the month of November...?'

'A baby!' Her mum laughed, but before it descended into silence she carefully began again. 'I just want to make sure you're feeling strong enough, after things with—'

Kiara cut in before her mum could bring up The Ex Who Should Not Be Named. 'All good! I love it here. And, hey... remember that charity thing I told you I set up with First Steps?'

'Oh, yes...?' Her mother said, her tone indicating that she clearly didn't remember.

Rather than mention her front garden, which was already

bursting with Christmas decorations, Kiara proudly announced, 'I've got a window's worth of snowflakes.'

'Is it that cold down there?'

Kiara laughed and told her mother it wasn't. After they'd nattered a bit more, she hung up the phone, then tugged the ever-present scrunchie off her wrist and made her practised move of pulling her long hair into a swishy ebony ponytail.

She'd inherited her Indian-born, English-raised mother's jet-black hair and her British father's golden-brown eyes. Of course she missed her parents, especially near Christmas, but last year, having the carpet ripped out from underneath what she'd thought was her reality, had been quite the eye-opener. Making this change was the best thing she'd ever done.

She'd only been here in Carey Cove a fortnight, but it had been love at first scone. She looked down at her tummy and gave it a poke. Yup. Definitely a wee bit bigger than it had been. It was little wonder the Cornish were proud of their baked goods. She'd never enjoyed so many fluffy, jam-filled, clotted-cream-dolloped treats in her life. It was a good thing she was starting work tomorrow, otherwise she'd be looking a lot more like a roly-poly Mrs Claus than the too-thin version of herself who'd skulked out of London under the shadow of romantic humiliation.

She gave herself a short, sharp shake and made herself resume her off-key singing. Sure, she was single, eight weeks before her favourite time of year. And, no, it wasn't snowing…yet. But everything else in her life was firmly under her control.

As if to prove her point, she sprayed one more snowflake into place. A level of snowflake excess her ex would definitely have rolled his eyes about. So wasn't it lucky she didn't have a boyfriend to be judgemental over everything she did any more?

She put her things away and then, after tugging on her favourite bright red gilet, went out onto the small thatched-roofed porch at the front of the cottage. The estate agent had promised that in the spring it would be bedecked with graceful strands of wisteria blooms, but right now it was swathed in garlands of pine and fir and wrapped in whorls of red ribbon and fairy lights.

Unlike Carey House, which was built of large butter-coloured stones, her cottage had been painted white, with beautiful green window frames and, of course, the traditional thatched roof. It was almost impossible to believe that selling her small one-bedroomed flat in London, perched above a busy sandwich shop, had bought her this amazing picture-perfect cottage.

Memories of her ex's flat—the one she'd thought was his home—flashed through her mind's eye. Glass. Steel beams. A preponderance of grey. Barely a personal item in sight. It was so obvious to her now why she'd been buffeted with frequent refusals to let her soften the place up with some cushions and a bit of bric-a-brac.

Anyway...

That was then and *this* was the build-up to Christmas. Kiara-style.

She stepped out onto the pavement in front of the house, which stood at the end of a lane about two streets up from the harbour. One of the many things that had attracted her to both Carey Cove and Mistletoe Cottage was the fact that all the homes had a front garden. Perfect for her ever-increasing display of Christmas delights.

She scanned the decor outside her new home with an exacting gaze.

Cuckoo for Christmas...but classy?

She pulled a *Who are you kidding?* face at the nutcracker figure standing guard at her front door. Classy only because it was for charity. This was pure unabashed devotion to decorations.

So far, she had three fairy-lit deer grazing outside the small porch. She hadn't yet decided on which sleigh she wanted to harness them to...or if she wanted to get a Rudolph to attach to it. Her first instinct had been to put a sleigh on the lawn, but... One on the roof would totally be better. Maybe if she met someone at work who was taller than her—which wouldn't be hard—she could get them to help her.

Her current favourites of all the decorations were the three penguins she'd bought with her loyal customer discount at an online Christmas store. Should she get more? Or plump for the snowman who did a little jig when you pressed his button nose? Decisions, decisions!

Perhaps a little sing-song would help.

She patted the pockets of her gilet and tugged out the remote control. After a surreptitious look around—although heaven knew why she was being shy about it...she didn't exactly know anyone here—she pressed the power button.

Her insides went all tingly with childlike glee. Who didn't love a singing and dancing penguin? If there were any Scrooges around she was determined to win them over with her pure, un-adulterated love of Christmas. Which reminded her... She had some huge fake candy canes she wanted to attach to the little white fence that ran along the front of her garden, leading peo-ple to the miniature Santa's Workshop donation box she'd af-fixed to her front gate. And those snowflake baubles. And the first of three living Christmas trees she wanted to decorate—all before she started work tomorrow.

She kept the penguins switched on while she ran into the house to get the other decorations. They would keep her com-pany while she worked. Who knew? Tomorrow at work she might even start to make some friends who could actually talk back to her.

'Harry! Remember what I said about going too far ahead on your scooter.'

Lucas's daredevil three-year-old slowed down for about two seconds, and then...because little boys would be little boys... began to speed up again. Uphill.

Despite his concerns, Lucas laughed. He knew exactly what

he'd fed his son for breakfast, and it certainly hadn't been rocket fuel. 'Harry! What's the name of the game?'

His son stopped abruptly and, with one foot on his scooter, one foot on the ground, turned round. His blond hair fell in soft curls beneath his bright red helmet. The same helmet Harry had spent the morning begging his father to refashion into a Santa's hat, even though they'd only just had Halloween.

His son's grey eyes, a reflection of his own, glittered with fun. Then he unleashed an arrestingly warm smile that could only have come from his mother, gave his father a stately salute, and pronounced, 'Safety first, Daddy.'

He smiled back, despite the sting of emotion tugging at the back of his throat as he remembered Lily's long list of things he wasn't to do once she was gone. No smothering. No overcoddling. No imposing his awareness of how fragile life could be on this little bundle of energy whose only perspective on life was that it was endless.

And, of course, the kicker: no more wearing his wedding ring after the first year.

He'd cheated. A bit. And by 'a bit' he meant an extra year and a half.

He'd taken it off when he'd been greasing up Lucas's scooter and seen that the ring was loose because he still hadn't got around to taking that Cooking Healthy Meals for your Child class the ladies at the Women's Institute kept tempting him with. The moment it had left his finger he'd realised it wasn't what connected him to his wife. His heart was. And that would be with him wherever he went, so the ring had finally gone into the keepsake box. The one his wife had started when they'd first met at uni. First cinema tickets. First airline tickets. And now first and very likely only wedding ring.

Lucas jogged up, his arms weighted with his son's all-weather coat, his backpack, his lunch, and pulled his little boy in for a hug. 'That's right, son. Safety first.'

He gave the top of Harry's helmet a loving pat and then, after giving him one more reminder about speed and distance, they set off again towards the nursery—which was, conveniently, only a hop, skip and a scooter ride from work.

Lucas stemmed another cautionary call when Harry added leaf-catching to his repertoire.

For the billionth time, man! Life isn't full of assurances. Plasters exist for a reason. Knee patches. Helmets. And doctors.

He, of all people should know that. Not just as a doctor, but as a husband. How could he forget the cancer he and his wife had convinced themselves would go into remission—

'Harry! Not too far.'

'I'm not too far, Daddy! I can still see the whiskers on your chinny-chin-chin!'

'Hey! I shaved this morning!'

Hadn't he? He put a hand up to double-check that he hadn't missed anywhere. *Struth*... He hadn't shaved. So much for being on the top of his game again. At least stubble was considered trendy. Not that his looks were a priority. His son was. Their routine. Getting their lives on a forward trajectory. And, of course, his job. The one thing besides his son that brought a smile to his face.

Since they'd relocated here to Carey Cove from Penzance, where there were far too many memories, he'd finally cracked getting their lives up and running. Morning story and cuddle in bed with his son. A shower for him while Harry played. Nursery 'uniform', such as it was, ready to be stepped into one leg at a time, then arms up overhead for the logoed sweatshirt, collar out. Hair semi-tamed into submission. Check. Check. Check.

Why had things gone wrong this morning?

Socks.

That was it.

They had a massive pile of socks and yet somehow, against the odds, there hadn't been a pair amongst them.

Note to self: buy more socks.

He had to laugh. So much for having their lives back on track.

If something as simple as locating a pair of matching socks threw a spanner into their entire morning routine—

Be kind to yourself.

Another one of his wife's reminders. And, to be fair, he hadn't forgotten to shave in well over a year. Nor, as he'd done two and half years ago, had he completely given up, using what energy he had to try and soothe a crying baby whose mother would never hold him in her arms again.

'Daddy, look!' Harry pointed towards the end of the lane where...yes...there it was. Mistletoe Cottage.

And that was when the lightbulb went on. This house—a homage to Christmas—was yet another reason his so-called 'game' was off-track right now.

The cottage all but screamed a daily reminder of the countdown to Christmas, and it was a time of year he found impossible to enjoy. Not because it had been Lily's favourite, or because it had been when they'd lost her. No. She'd lost her life in the throes of the most beautiful spring either of them had ever witnessed. It was more that Christmas was about *family*. And the most important member of their family wasn't there any more. Never would be.

And even though he'd promised himself he would make this a Christmas to remember for Harry—who, to all intents and purposes, was finally old enough to truly understand and fall head over heels in love with Christmas—he simply couldn't light that same flame of enthusiasm burning inside Harry in himself.

Thank goodness there was someone else in the seaside village who was feeling it as much as Harry. Not that they'd seen the new owner of Mistletoe Cottage yet... The 'For Sale' sign had come down a few weeks back, but it had been two weeks ago when the decorations had begun appearing. First a little Santa's house. Then a few evergreen swags. Then wreaths and baubles and a preponderance of fairy lights. Every day there was something new. Including today when... Were those *dancing penguins*?

'Penguins!' Harry crowed.

Okay. Now there were penguins. What next? Waltzing polar bears?

If Lucas had thought Harry was hot-rodding before, he'd been wrong. One sighting of the bum-wiggling penguins and his son took off, one foot madly pressing the pavement behind him, as if his life depended on it.

Lucas quickened his pace, eyes trained on his son, until something in the corner of his eye caught his attention. A woman was coming out of the front door of Mistletoe Cottage holding a box of decorations in her arms. Petite. Dark-haired. He was too far away to make out anything else.

'Aah-ow!'

Lucas's blood instantly roared in his ears. One second with his eyes off Harry and, as he'd feared, boy and scooter had parted ways.

His speed-walk turned into a run. With the low hedge in the way, he'd lost sight of Harry. But he could see the woman's head snap back as she dropped her box of decorations on the porch and raced towards his son.

By the time he reached the cottage there were no yowls of pain. There were voices. The woman's and his son's. And then... there were *giggles*.

Harry was still on the ground, and although he'd definitely grazed his knee, he somehow seemed entirely unfazed by it. Normally there would be howling by now. But the woman crouching down, face hidden by a sheet of glossy black hair, was somehow engaged in a greeting ritual with his son.

'How do you do, Harry?' She shook his hand in a warm, but formal style. 'It's such a pleasure to meet someone who loves Christmas as much as I do.'

If she was expecting Lucas to join in the I Love Christmas Every Day of the Year Club she was obviously recruiting for, she had another think coming. It was only November. He had enough trouble mustering up excitement for the day of December the twenty-fifth.

Clearly unperturbed by his lack of response, she smiled at Harry and pointed at his grazed knee. 'Now... Important decision to make. Do you think you'd like a plaster with Santa on it? Or elves?'

'Elves!' Harry clapped his hands in delight.

The woman laughed and said she would run into the house and get some, as well as a cloth to clear away the small grass stains Lucas could see were colouring his son's little-boy knees.

Her voice had a mischievous twist to it, and underneath the bright, child-friendly exchange was a gentle kindness that softened his heart.

'I'm ever so sorry. Harry is just mad for—' Lucas began, but when she looked up and met his gaze anything else he'd planned on saying faded into nothing.

Though he knew beyond a shadow of a doubt that they'd never met, his body felt as if it had been jolted into a reality he'd always been waiting to step into. Every cell in his body was supercharged with a deep, visceral connection as their eyes caught and held. Hers were a warm brown...edging on a jewel-like amber. Her skin was beautiful, with an almost pearlescent hue. Glowing... Cheeks pink. Lips a deep red, as if they'd just received a rush of emotion.

Perhaps it was the unexpected excitement of a three-year-old boy careering into her front garden. Perhaps it was the fresh autumnal weather. Or maybe...just maybe...she was feeling the same thing he was. A strange but electric feeling, surging through him in a way he'd never experienced before.

She blinked once. Then twice. Then, as if the moment had been entirely a fiction of his own creating, realigned her focus so that it was only on Harry. Pulling him up, dusting off some invisible specks of dust, she walked him over to the steps of her small, elaborately decorated porch and sat him down, asking if he could count how many seconds she'd be away while she ran into the house to get a plaster, and starting him off with a steady, 'One...two...three...'

She was back as Harry began to stumble over his elevens and twelves, and without so much as a glance at Lucas she turned her back and knelt down in front of his little boy. She began to clean his knee in preparation for the plaster.

Feeling weirdly blind-sided, Lucas made a lame attempt at conversation. 'Quite a display you've got here. I'm guessing you like Christmas?'

'It's for charity,' she said. 'First Steps. Do you know it?'

'I like Christmas,' Harry said.

Though Lucas couldn't see her smile, he could hear it in her voice as she answered his son. 'It's a pretty special time of year, isn't it?'

'It's when Santa comes!' Harry said.

'And who doesn't like Santa?' Lucas tacked on, feeling stupidly left out, but also completely out of his element. He wasn't into Christmas. Not at all. He wanted to make it fabulous for his boy, but...

He forced a limp smile onto his lips. The woman gave him a quick glance. It was dismissive, in the way someone might try to figure out where a fly was buzzing and then decide the fly wasn't worth her attention. Or maybe she'd seen right through him. Knew he was more *bah-humbug* than *ho-ho-ho*.

Either way, he'd definitely imagined whatever it was he thought had passed between them. It might have been electricity, but it certainly wasn't the type that led to candlelit dinners and—

Whoa!

He clearly hadn't screwed his head on straight this morning. His life was about his son and himself and making sure they were healthy and happy. End of story.

'Daddy?'

Lucas's son's expression was all the confirmation he needed

that he'd definitely woken up on a side of the bed he'd never woken up on before. The cuckoo side.

'Right!' The woman stood up and briskly zipped her rather professional-looking first aid kit. 'That's you sorted, young man.'

'Say thank you to the nice…erm…' Lucas left a blank space, so that the woman could fill in her name, but no luck.

'Thank you!' Harry beamed up at her and received a warm smile and a miniature candy cane 'for later' in return.

'Have fun today,' she said, her eyes on Harry, and then, without so much as a glance at Lucas, she disappeared into her house, leaving nothing but air and mystery between them.

CHAPTER TWO

AFTER APPLYING A couple of coats of 'first day at the new job' mascara to her lashes, Kiara tugged the maroon scrunchie off her wrist and swept her hair up into a high ponytail. Her hands went through the motions intuitively, but as she got to the part when she grabbed two fistfuls of hair to cinch the ponytail tight her brain immediately flashed back to yesterday morning, when that poor little boy had crash-landed in her garden.

Though everything had happened super-quickly, she had felt as though she'd crammed an entire new relationship—highs and lows and finished—all in a matter of seconds. Somehow, when she'd come out of the house with the decorations, her scrunchie had caught on a one of the pine branches, yanking her head back, pulling her hair out of her ponytail, before she'd lurched forward to help the boy—only to look up and see that the gorgeous little boy belonged to the hottest dad in the whole world.

Deliciously chestnut-coloured hair that, despite a clean, short cut, held hints of moving round his ears and collar in the same soft curls his little boy had if he were to let it grow. Amazing grey eyes. The perfect amount of tall. She was guessing he was spot-on six foot. Anything else would require her to have a step-stool for kissing him. There had been dark shadows under those dark-lashed eyes of his. Shadows that hinted at something that might be troubling him.

But he was a dad—meaning he very likely had a wife or partner somewhere. Which, of course, made him totally off-limits for ogling, wondering how tall she'd have to be to kiss him, or imagining him wearing absolutely nothing but a Santa hat and a sprig of coyly placed mistletoe.

She'd learnt that lesson the hard way. So she'd shut down faster than Santa could put someone on the naughty list for kicking a puppy.

You'd think after what she'd been through, she would have been able to put two and two together a lot more quickly than she had. Little boy plus father equals married man.

The fact that the man was seriously hot and had a haunted little-boy-lost lost look that made her want to make him warming winter stews set off alarm bells she couldn't ignore.

She knew exactly how things would pan out if she succumbed to one solitary, forlorn *woe is me* smile. Because she'd travelled down that path before.

I'm so lonely. All I do is pour myself into work, saving children with my incredible surgical skills, and there's no one there for me at the end of the day. Just an empty flat...with an empty bed...

Pfft. She gave herself an eye-roll, then forced herself to realign her focus on the fact that she'd both physically and emotionally moved on from the hurt and shame and, yes, the heartbreak she'd endured, and that today was the first day of the rest of her new professional life. And no matter what, it was going to be a good one.

A walk up the hill in the crisp autumn air was all Kiara needed to get those endorphins flowing again. The leaves were colourful heralds of a happy, shiny, fresh start. And why shouldn't they be? She was heading to her new job in a new village in a new nook of England, and one solitary spotting of a gorgeous dad whose adorable son clearly loved Christmas as much as she did wasn't going to throw her off her stride. No way!

When she finally reached the top of the gravelled front drive, and could soak in the full glory of her new workplace, her heart did a little jig right there in her ribcage.

Carey House could not have been a more perfect place to start her life over. There was a small general practice there, but the bulk of the hospital's business was delivering happy, healthy babies.

Helping women bring babies into the world in a cottage hospital overlooking the sea, with a gorgeous, picture-postcard village below...

Perfection.

All but skipping up to the front door, she was virtually bursting at the seams with excitement to get started.

Cheerfully wondering when—or if—the powers-that-be at Carey House would decorate the place for Christmas, she pulled open the door and saw Hazel, the warm-hearted receptionist, chatting to someone tucked just out of her line of vision in the GP's waiting room.

At the sound of the door opening Hazel turned and smiled. 'You'll be needing Nya. Hang on a minute, love, I'll fetch her for you.' She gave Kiara a wiggly-fingered wave, then held a solitary finger up to indicate she'd be over in just a moment.

Kiara grinned. She'd met Hazel Collins when she'd come down for her interview, and she was every bit as warm and welcoming as Kiara remembered. The sixty-something woman could have been a stunt double for Mrs Claus any day of the week. She had a beautiful billow of white hair, done up in thick plaits and pinned atop her head, pink cheeks, and a smile that would warm the coldest of hearts.

Hazel claimed she had worked in the building since it had been built. This, of course, was patently untrue. What might be true was the fact that her ancestors had worked here. Formerly a large family home, Carey House had been put together, stone by beautiful stone, at least two hundred years ago…if not more. It had been converted into a cottage hospital in 1900, to help improve maternity services in the area.

At that time, pregnant women who lived here, or in the more remote islands off the Cornish coast, had often struggled to find quality medical care. These days they had St Isolde's Hospital over in Falmouth to take on any high-risk pregnancies or oversee unexpected complications, but with Head Midwife Nya Ademi in charge here at Carey Cove, suffice it to say, they delivered a lot of babies there. The vast picture wall of beautiful little faces was testament to that.

Kiara allowed herself to get lost in the myriad of tiny little button noses and tightly clenched eyes and teensy fingers clutching pastel-coloured swaddling until she heard Hazel approach.

'Gorgeous, aren't they?' said Kiara.

'They certainly are,' said a very male voice. One that spilled down her spine like warm caramel. One that certainly wasn't Hazel's.

Kiara whipped round and found herself nose to chest with Extremely Hot Dad.

A short, sharp intake of breath only made it worse. He smelled *delicious*. Like molten butter on a loaf of bread fresh out of the oven. Fresh air and—*mmm*—nutmeg.

Sweet mother of God. The man smelled like French toast in the Alps.

Her knees threatened to buckle. Her tongue turned leaden. Which was probably just as well, because the first words that popped into her head were highly inappropriate: *I'd like to climb you like a tree.*

Whatever that meant.

As it dawned on her that she was leaning in to inhale more of him she jerked back, her heart somersaulting and then lurching up into her throat. Because looking up into his face from this proximity was even better than smelling him.

He was clean-shaven today. She wasn't even sure she'd realised he'd been all rough chestnut stubble yesterday until now, when he wasn't. Would it feel good to run her fingertips along the softness of that stubble? Or would it be abrasive?

Come to think of it, how had this stranger managed to imprint himself so thoroughly on her subconscious that she was desperately trying to memorise even more of him now?

She made the mistake of looking up.

His eyes were a mesmeric grey. Like multilayered storm clouds. Each tiny sector was a different shade, demanding and receiving her full attention. Dark lashes gave them added punch. If he had been evil they would've been like little Venus flytraps, waiting to snap and snare her into his power. But something told her he wasn't evil. The tumult she saw in his eyes wasn't of his own making…it was life. And that was something she could definitely relate to.

Her gaze slipped away from his eyes, down along his nose, and landed soundly on his mouth. One of his front teeth was caught on his bottom lip—as if he, too, was struggling to figure out how to make his brain and body work together again.

Where her heart had once been, a glitter bomb had detonated. One filled with gold and starlight and warm bursts of response in her erogenous zones. Which instantly filled her with horror.

She had made a solemn promise to herself that there would be no glitter bombs detonating anywhere near her for at least a year—and *definitely* not for an insanely attractive man who was already taken.

A burning hot rage replaced the glitter bomb. This was *her* place. *Her* new sanctuary. *Her* new job. *Her* new colleagues, populating *her* new world, and despite all the precautions she'd taken to stitch her heart back together, after such an ignominious and insulting end to the love affair she had thought was real, she was keenly aware of how loose that stitching had been.

A physical ache clawed at her chest as she stepped away from him and demanded, 'What are *you* doing here?'

* * *

Lucas almost laughed. Not because Miss Mistletoe's face was full of delight or warmth or joy. More because he'd never met someone so free with their distaste of him. He couldn't exactly say he liked it, but...

Her nose crinkled in frustration as she waited for him to answer.

Crikey.

He rubbed at his jaw, perplexed to find himself in such a peculiar scenario.

He'd never seen anyone so openly repulsed at the sight of him before. And on two separate occasions. Perhaps he had a doppelgänger out there? Someone who'd caused this poor woman pain? He hoped not, for her sake, but he did kind of hope it was true for *his* sake. Because... Dammit, he didn't know why. But he wanted to get to know this woman. And the reasons were slightly too potent to explain. Particularly in this scenario.

If he were to tell her he'd had one of the most erotic dreams of his entire life last night—starring her—he imagined he would win himself a slap on the face. Deservedly so. He didn't even know her name, let alone just how soft the curves of her breasts were, or whether or not she would groan his name when he licked them and then drew her nipples into his mouth as his hands teased and...

'I'm sorry,' he began. 'I think you might be mistaking me for someone—'

'No. There's no mistake. You're you. I mean—'

She pulled her hair out of her ponytail and then swiftly re-did it, splitting her dark hair into two thick shanks and tugging it tightly into place, so that it swung from shoulder to shoulder after she'd freed it from her grasp.

His awareness of her hair, how it would feel if he ran his hands through it, was so visceral he could almost have sworn he'd done it before. Surely he must be imagining it?

His body was telling him otherwise. His fingers were twitching, as if they hungered to touch. He almost physically felt the silky strands sweep against his skin, even though she was nowhere near him. It was like a memory freshly resurfacing after having long been buried. He closed his eyes and an image passed behind his lids that should have made him blush.

She'd found her voice again, and in a crisp, clear tone he imagined would be fitting for a Victorian schoolmarm, chastising a naughty young boy who'd been pulling faces, asked, 'I meant who are you and why are you at Carey House?'

Her eyes flicked away from his before he could answer. He pounced on the free moment to scan her features—an unguarded instant to try and find something, *anything*, to divine where this open hostility had come from. But before he could find much they were back on him like golden-brown searchlights.

Even so, she had looked away long enough for him to see that her charged tone was actually fuelled by insecurity. And... worse...by fear. It made his heart clench tight for her. Never, ever would he want anyone to be frightened of him. Had it been Harry's crash? Had she— His breath caught in his throat. He hoped to God she hadn't lost a child. Losing his wife had been like being eviscerated, but losing his son... He couldn't even begin to imagine the horror.

'I'm sorry.' He held out his hand. 'I'm Lucas Wilde. The GP here at Carey House.' He pointed towards the room Hazel was just coming out of, her hands full with two plates of biscuits. 'That's the surgery in there.'

She stood there and blinked uncomprehendingly at him, as if his offering a hand to shake was the most peculiar thing she'd ever seen. What was he meant to have done? Gone in for a cheek-kiss?

'Ah! Kiara!' Hazel cut in. 'I see you've met our Dr Wilde.'

'Er...' Kiara managed.

'Oh, deary me, Dr Wilde,' Hazel chastised him warmly. 'Did you not introduce yourself to our newest midwife? This is Kiara

Baxter. Kiara—this is Dr Wilde. He's our main GP here at Carey Cove.'

She carried on talking about locums, visiting GPs and the specialist doctors who sometimes came in from St Isolde's, but it all became a low buzz to Lucas, who was still trying to separate his wickedly sensual dream about a version of this woman—Kiara—from the woman who was staring at him as if she were a bull preparing to charge.

'I've just put a fresh plate of biscuits in your surgery...' He heard Hazel's voice come back into focus. 'Kiara, you're welcome to grab one from there if you like or—' She stopped herself. 'Better yet, why don't you take this plate? You're going up to the lounge, are you not? Where the lockers are? That's where you store your handbag and personal items.'

Kiara's eyes darted between the two of them as if she was trying to figure out whether or not this was some sort of joke, but then, looking down at her hands, she moved forward to accept a plate of what Lucas knew to be Hazel's secret recipe ginger biscuits.

'You'll definitely love getting your teeth into one of those,' he said, giving the side of his nose a tap and unleashing a cheesy grin.

Now Hazel was looking at him as if he had sprouted antlers as well. If he could, he'd roll his eyes. Going back to sleep and starting this day over again would be an ideal option if only the idea of going to sleep and having another one of *those* dreams was something he had any sort of control over.

They all stopped short when a cry came from just outside the building. Plates of biscuits were quickly deposited on the reception desk, and the sound of running footsteps began echoing through the corridor as Kiara raced out through the front door with Lucas quick on her heels.

A woman was virtually doubled over on the driveway, with her arms wrapped round her large, very pregnant belly.

This wasn't an infrequent occurrence on the drive of Carey

House. Often Lucas found there was an ashen-faced father racing up holding a jumble of the expectant mother's handbag and overnight bag and anything else she'd demanded he bring. The staff here encouraged all expectant women to make the birth experience as personalised as they wanted. Down in his surgery he sometimes heard drifts of music coming from what he privately called 'the contractions playlists'.

Kiara had reached the woman and helped ease her back up to stand, but their conversation was too low and too far away for him to grasp.

Wait a minute.

Though he couldn't see her face, Lucas recognised the petite figure. Her stylishly cut blonde bob was masking her features, but he was sure of it now. The woman clearly in the throes of a contraction was Marnie Richards, one of the hospital's own midwives. Lucas ran across to join them.

'Hello, love. I'm a midwife here. My name's Kiara. I'm guessing you're in labour?'

'Good guess!'

Kiara laughed good-naturedly. She'd clearly been through a fair few of these tightrope walks before, Lucas thought. The kind where the expectant mother was thrilled to be having a baby but experiencing feelings she'd never had before, so was lacking her usual charm and warmth—characteristics Lucas knew Marnie had in spades, despite her reputation as the hospital's most fastidious midwife.

'I've texted Nya—she's my midwife. Hopefully she'll figure out that I haven't quite made it indoors yet.'

'I can run in and fetch her if you like,' Lucas volunteered. 'I'm sure Kiara here would be more than happy to— Oh! Oh, dear... Another contraction?'

As Marnie let out a growl of pain Lucas took one of her hands in his and made swift introductions. And as Kiara coached her through her breathing techniques, he gave Marnie an impressed smile.

'You've got quite a grip, Marnie. I'll be picking you to be on my tug-of-war team at next year's summer party.'

Marnie laughed and said, 'Just you wait until the contractions start—oh! Coming—oof! Faster!'

'I think we might've hit that moment.' Lucas threw Kiara a pained look he hoped she'd know was for comedic effect.

She gave him a shy smile, cheeks lightly pinkened, then looked away.

As he and Kiara gently escorted Marnie, step by careful step, towards the door, Marnie huffed out her answers to Kiara's questions in short, sharp, staccatos.

Lucas caught, 'Waters broken…' 'Contractions…' and something along the lines of 'Time for this baby to enter the world now'. But perhaps not put quite as politely.

'Marnie!'

Lucas looked up to see where the new voice had come from.

Nya Ademi, the head midwife, was rushing out through the door towards them. With an apologetic smile, she nudged Lucas out of the way. 'I'm pretty sure you've got patients waiting, Dr Wilde?'

Lucas knew it wasn't a chastisement. It was Nya doing what she did best—exemplifying the Six Cs the staff at Carey House embodied. Compassion, care, competence, communication, courage and commitment.

She gave Marnie's arm a squeeze and took over the hand-holding without so much as a wince. Nya's hands must be made of steel. 'Hello, love. We didn't expect you so soon. Why didn't you ring? We don't want you having the baby out here on the drive, now, do we?'

'Ow!' howled Marnie, stopping in her tracks, trying and failing to breathe through a fresh contraction. When it had passed she gave Nya a look already tinged with fatigue. 'To be honest with you, I don't care where I have it. If I was up a tree right now, I'd have it there!'

Kiara's eyes flicked to Lucas. He shot her a questioning look.

Her cheeks flushed with streaks of red. She swiftly returned her attention to Marnie.

What was that about?

A mad thought occurred to Lucas. Had she had a naughty dream about *him*? Now, that would be an interesting turn of events...

Surprise darts of heat arrowed below his belt line. The idea that she had spent some of her nocturnal hours dreaming of being tangled up in the sheets with him held appeal. Too much appeal.

He forced his concerned doctor face back into place and, spying a duffel bag a few metres back, jogged to get it.

'Up a tree? You don't want to copy that nursery rhyme, do you?' Kiara lightly teased Marnie. 'Someone's already rocked their baby on a treetop and it didn't end well. I think the Carey House birthing centre is a far more comfortable option.' Kiara counted through the breaths with her until Marnie's contraction had finished, then pointed towards the building, now only a handful of metres away. 'Let's get you inside, where we can get some monitors on you and the baby out.'

'Dr Wilde?' Hazel called from the front door. 'I'm ever so sorry, but your nine o'clock appointment is here and looking a bit anxious.'

'Be right there, Hazel. Just ensuring our number one pregnant midwife is all tickety-boo.'

'I'm perfectly all right, Lucas. Go in and see your— Sweet crumbs and empty biscuit tins!' wailed Marnie. 'No one said it would hurt like *this*!'

Kiara laughed again—a warm, inclusive laugh that said, *I hear you*. Lucas liked it. He was beginning to like a lot of things about this woman.

He opened the front door, placed Marnie's bag inside, then called to a colleague to find a wheelchair, half listening while Kiara gave Marnie some more cues on her breathing as another contraction struck when they were only a few footsteps away from the entrance.

While Marnie trained her focus on blowing slow, steadying breaths, Kiara playfully lectured her. 'As you're a midwife yourself, I'm pretty sure somewhere along the line you were warned about the pain. In fact...' she flashed Marnie a cheeky grin '... I would lay money on the fact you were.'

Kiara looked up again as Lucas ushered them in, and, for an instant he was caught in the flare of one of those genuine smiles of hers. It felt like being bathed in sunlight. Then, as if it had been an accident, and her brain had suddenly told her who she was smiling at, her attention was quickly redirected to Marnie. Which, he sternly reminded himself, was where it belonged.

A volley of questions ensued.

How long had Marnie been having contractions?

How many minutes in between the contractions?

Was there anyone they should ring?

'Just get me inside! I don't want to miss the window for getting an epidural.'

Kiara shot a look at Nya, who had run inside to steer the wheelchair to the door, and then to Lucas. The look spoke volumes. The window for that kind of painkiller had opened and shut a while ago.

Again, his eyes caught hers, and this time something entirely different passed between them. Trust. A shared understanding that what was happening was well within Kiara's toolbox. Not that he'd doubted it, of course—Carey House only hired the best. But in his experience everyone began their first day at work in a new hospital in a completely personalised way. Some people—like Kiara—were clearly the 'in at the deep end' type. Others liked to observe. Some insisted on leading, to prove right off the bat that they knew their stuff. He liked where Kiara sat on the spectrum. She was comfortable with her skills and neither needed to showboat nor defer to anyone.

'Dr Wilde?' Hazel called him again, this time tapping her watch.

He ducked his head so that Marnie could see him. 'Are you three going to survive without my alpha male cheerleading?'

Marnie huffed out a laugh. 'I don't know. If it comes without painkillers maybe not!'

CHAPTER THREE

KIARA LAUGHED AS Lucas accepted Marnie's insistence that she was fine, and that he really should go and tend to his own patients now.

As schoolgirlish as she knew it was, she had to look back as he disappeared into the GP surgery. And, to her surprise, she was rewarded with another one of those soft smiles of his as he glanced back too. The kind of smile that ribboned round her heart and freed a chorus of invisible birds, singing as if it were the first day of spring and not the beginning of November.

Sweet crumbs and empty biscuit tins, indeed!

It wasn't a saying she'd heard before—and maybe Marnie had made it up, to prevent herself from swearing too much, as many mothers in labour did—but it actually suited what she was feeling. The two encounters she'd had with Lucas—her new colleague, no less—had been like delicious crumbs, strewn on a path that only led to danger. For her anyway.

Yes, he was gorgeous. And, yes, it was a bonus that he worked in the health profession—she'd learned early on in her dating 'career' that not many people understood the strange demands of a midwife's role. It wasn't as if babies worked to a schedule when they decided to appear. But those alarm bells had rung for a reason when their paths had all but literally collided yesterday. Lucas Wilde was a father. And where there were fathers there were usually mothers. And mothers very rightly didn't like it when their husbands wove them a tale of deception in order to woo a twenty-something midwife who thought she might be starting a family of her own one day...

Nya's steady voice pulled her attention back to where it needed to be. On Marnie.

'That's right, love. Let's get you in here and pull off some of these layers before— Oh! Easy, there, darling... Kiara, do you think you could help Marnie get her things off while I run and let the desk know we're here and ready for action?'

'Absolutely,' Kiara said, guiding Marnie over to the bed. 'Why don't we get your coat off? Then you can have a seat and I'll help you with everything else.'

'None of it's gone according to plan!' Marnie panted. 'I have lists. I have charts. I do this for a *living*! I thought I was the one in control.'

We all think we're the one in control.

Kiara stemmed the quip. It wasn't what Marnie needed or wanted to hear. It also referred to a dark mark on her own past that she wanted to leave behind. Which was exactly why she needed to remember to give Lucas the cold shoulder whenever their paths crossed again. But smiling at him was so easy! She hadn't noticed yesterday that there was a twinkle in his eyes when he tried to be funny. How he could make dad jokes sexy was beyond her. Dad jokes should never be sexy. Especially to her.

She knelt down and got to work on Marnie's winter footwear. 'That's right...just sit back against that big, snowy mound of pillows while I get these boots off for you.'

'Sorry about all the laces,' Marnie apologised. 'Again—not part of the plan.'

Kiara smiled up at her before putting both the boots in a small cupboard ready for the expectant mother's personal items.

'It'd be great if babies listened when we told them the plan, wouldn't it?'

Marnie laughed appreciatively. She gave her belly an affectionate rub. 'I was out for a walk. I thought it'd be good for the baby and my swollen ankles if I had some gentle exercise. I had my first contraction when I was out on the beach, but I thought it was a Braxton Hicks so decided to ignore it. If I'd known it was the real thing I would've worn some slip-ons.'

Marnie gave a self-deprecating chuckle, then sighed.

'Heaven knows why I thought I'd be the one in charge of all this.' She pointed at her stomach, and for just a moment her smile shadowed as she said, 'I guess it's because I'm the one who organised this whole scenario. Her,' she corrected herself, her smile warming again. 'She's not a scenario. She's a her.'

'Oh?' Kiara said, keeping her tone light, but neutral.

She'd learnt hundreds of babies ago that it was always best to leave the baby's origin story to the mum to tell. Not every family came pre-packaged with a fairy tale romance, a diamond ring and a baby nine months after the honeymoon.

Another contraction hit before Marnie could explain, but once it had passed, and Kiara had got Marnie out of her clothes and into one of the soft hospital gowns, she glanced at the empty chair usually occupied by the birth partner and thought it was safe to ask, 'You didn't say before, but is there anyone you'd like me to ring?'

Marnie's cheeks coloured. 'No,' she answered curtly, and then, her forehead creasing apologetically, added, 'Sorry. Sorry... I'm pregnant on my own through IVF treatment— which most people already know. I haven't had to explain how I got to look like a beached whale without having a boyfriend in a while.'

'You just let me know what I can do to help, okay?'

Kiara meant it, too. Having a baby was a big step. Having it on your own was even bigger. It took courage to do what Marnie was doing and she definitely wasn't judging. Everyone's path was of their own making, and Marnie's voice was rock-solid. She wanted a baby and now she was having one. Exactly the same way Kiara wanted to celebrate this Christmas with complete and utter abandon.

Okay, fine… It was a little bit different. But the endgame was the same. She and Marnie were living their lives by their own rulebooks. And she respected that.

Kiara silently began hooking Marnie up to the relevant monitors, making it clear that it was up to Marnie how much she did or didn't say.

'Do you mind if I take a little look,' she asked eventually. 'See how far along you are?'

'Please,' Marnie said. 'I'd do it myself, but…' she pointed at her large belly '…this is in the way.'

Kiara glanced at the door, certain that Nya would be re-appearing any minute. 'I know you work here, but I think that if there was a day of all days when Nya would be happy for you to sit back and let someone else do the work, today would definitely be the day.'

The women shared a warm smile. And Kiara thought she'd look forward to working with Marnie when her maternity leave was finished.

'Nya's probably got stuck at the desk answering four million questions. If you want to take over for her, please feel free.'

'Are you sure? If she's your midwife—'

Marnie gave a combination of a laugh and a moan. 'When you work as a midwife *everyone's* your midwife.' Her smile softened. 'Nya has been the one to do all the exams, but it's shift-change time, so honestly… Oh!' Her hands flew to her belly. 'You can go ahead. Please.'

'Right you are, then. But if you want me to step aside for Nya, just say.'

Kiara gloved up, put some gel on her hand and pulled a stool over so she could do a quick examination.

Rather than flinch, as many patients did at the first touch,

Marnie suddenly beamed a big, huge, beautiful smile. 'I'm going to be the mother of a little baby girl!'

'You are!' Kiara beamed back. 'And...' she finished her examination '...by the looks of things, you'll be holding her in your arms and picking out the perfect name any minute now.'

'Sorry...sorry!' Nya appeared at the door, her smile mischievous as she briskly walked to the wall-mounted glove dispenser. 'A woman having twins cornered me on the way here, but I knew I'd left you in capable hands.' She gave Marnie a discerning look. 'You're choosing names already, are you?'

Marnie nodded and then, as a contraction hit again, somehow managed to get out, 'I know—I haven't—physically experienced—this—before—but I'm pretty sure—'

'You're crowning!' Nya and Kiara chorused in tandem.

At Marnie's request, Nya took on the hand-holding role. Then, after two, possibly three minutes of encouragement, some deep guttural cries and some concentrated pushing later, Kiara was holding Marnie's baby girl in her arms.

'She's a beauty!' Kiara held her up so Marnie could see, and as if on cue the little girl uttered a loud cry, announcing her arrival in the world.

They all laughed and, exhausted, Marnie fell back against her pillows.

Nya and Kiara cleaned and dried the baby, then placed her in Marnie's outstretched arms so that they could share that all-important skin-to-skin contact both mother and baby craved organically.

Kiara was relieved at how easy it had been to fall into a rhythm with Nya who, despite being her boss, was treating her as an equal, only taking the lead when it came to finding things—which, to be fair, was something Kiara did need guidance with.

'Nothing like starting your first day with a baby born in the first ten minutes,' she said, and grinned.

Nya shared a complicit smile with her. 'It's the best way to start a new post, isn't it? One perfect baby on a beautiful day.'

Nya prepared a Vitamin K injection and Marnie reluctantly handed her little girl over to Kiara for weighing and measuring. They dealt swiftly with the umbilical cord and the placenta, offering Marnie a local anaesthetic for the inevitable pain she felt, and finally moved the new mother and her freshly swaddled daughter to a bright, clean bed.

'I can see why new mums sometimes get teary at this part,' Marnie said, blinking back her own tears.

Kiara gave her a warm smile. 'There are a billion hormones running rampant in your body right now,' she told her. And she was also alone. There was no one special to share this life-changing moment with.

She pictured this moment for herself. Her brain summoned the images and she was shocked to see that Lucas was the one standing in the room next to her—not her ex, Peter. It wasn't so much a clear image of Lucas as a doting father, but more his presence she imagined. That calm, warm, humour-filled aura that had surrounded him from the moment they'd discovered Marnie on the driveway.

'I know…' Marnie sniffed, already holding out her arms for her baby again. 'I've known all that professionally for years, but now I feel like I truly *know* it. In here.' She tapped her heart. 'I don't know how she's done it, but this little girl has made me complete. I feel like I've just become the person I was always meant to be.'

Kiara smiled, but said nothing, knowing that her voice would squeak up into the higher registers if she did. She knew the feeling of knowing there was something missing in her life…not yet having it. She also knew that the sense of wholeness had to come from within. That more than likely whatever had led Marnie to go through IVF and have this baby alone had been a step in the process of recognising and owning the type of woman she wanted to be.

Kiara wanted to be a woman who could trust and love a man again. She wasn't going to tar all men with the same brush her ex had been lavished with, but...

Again, an image of Lucas flashed up in her mind's eye.

She tried to bat it away but it wouldn't go.

This was insane. She'd barely met the man. And yet just a few moments in his presence and she'd known instinctively that he was someone she could rely on. Professionally. Obviously. Just because looking at him set butterflies loose in her tummy, it didn't mean she couldn't take a step back and acknowledge that, at her place of work, he was a good man to know.

The thought snagged.

Having a doctor's respect meant a lot to her. Perhaps that was why she'd been so smitten by her surgeon boyfriend. A surgeon dating a midwife... It was so clichéd. But that first time Peter had asked her opinion about something and nodded along, as if she'd just offered him the most valuable insight ever, had thrilled her. The 'respect' had turned out to be just for show, of course. Peter had only ever valued Peter's opinion.

But with Lucas the respect had seemed genuine. The man had surely delivered a few babies over the course of his training, if not during his career as a GP, and he had seemed completely at ease leaving Marnie's care to Kiara. She hadn't got the impression from him—even for a nano-second—that he considered her less than capable of looking after her patient. She respected him for that.

And it spoke of the self-confidence he possessed that he hadn't felt the need to micro-manage her—a stranger whose skills were completely unknown to him. A stranger who had kind of been a little bit rude to him, now that she thought of it. She'd been warm and kind to his son, but she'd been crisp and dismissive of him...right up until they'd shared *that* look. The one that had turned her insides into a warm cupcake.

'Are you all right, Kiara?' asked Marnie.

Kiara shook her head, as if that would shake away the image

of Lucas now firmly embossed in her brain. 'I'm just really delighted that your baby was the first one I helped to deliver,' she said.

'You and Lucas saved me from having her outside!' Marnie laughed, then gave a sigh that was difficult to read. 'Have you had a chance to chat with him yet?'

Kiara shook her head, even though it wasn't strictly true. He had tried to chat, but she'd shut it down.

'He's such a good man,' Marnie continued. 'Not everyone would be as kind and thoughtful as he is, given his situation.'

Kiara's eyebrows drew together. 'What situation?'

Marnie's eyes darted to the open door, then back to Kiara. 'It's not really my place to say, but a good man like that deserves to meet someone really special.'

Like me?

Marnie was making poor work of stifling a yawn.

'Why don't you have a rest?' Kiara helped Marnie arrange her covers and pillows just so, unable to stop her smile twitching into something broad, as if she'd just received the best Christmas present ever.

Lucas Wilde wasn't married!

She tried to pull her smile into some sort of control. Boyfriend-shopping was not on her list of things to achieve here. Delivering babies and decorating her house to collect money for charity were. And looking after herself. That was it.

Even so...just a handful of minutes with Lucas today had shown her a side of him that she really liked. Beyond the sexy hair, the beautiful grey eyes and those lips that really did look inviting enough to kiss...

A good man like that deserves to meet someone really special.

An image of her wearing a sexy elf costume, one leg wrapped seductively round a giant candy cane, popped into her head. And Lucas was wearing nothing more than a Santa hat...

Kiara! Stop it. He's a single father, not a boy toy.

She wrapped things up with Marnie, who looked more than ready for a sleep, especially now that her daughter had nodded off, and headed down to the central desk to do her notes.

'Well, that's a new way to approach the desk!' Nya smiled as she approached. 'It's not often someone skips to come and do their notes.'

'Was I skipping?' Kiara hadn't even noticed. The Lucas Effect? 'It was a great delivery,' she said. 'Always gives me a boost.'

'You're certainly in the right job if delivering babies gives you added pep!' Nya gave her arm a squeeze, then showed her where to do her notes, telling her the two of them would soon sit down to discuss her future patients.

Kiara started filling out her forms, but she couldn't stop her mind from wandering just a bit. Had Lucas Wilde really made her *skip*?

Sure, he was great. But finding out he was single couldn't be the main reason she was so happy. She'd already had a three-year run at having a man as the centre of her universe. It had blown up in her face in spectacular style. And that was the thing she needed to remember. Along with the fact that perhaps she didn't need to be quite as cool a customer when it came to a certain Dr Wilde...

Lucas scanned his patient's test results, together with the symptoms she'd described, and gave her the information he knew she didn't want to hear. 'I'm afraid you have entered the phase of life known as perimenopause, Mrs Braxton.'

'Oh, please...' The forty-seven-year-old woman batted away his formal address, reaching for one of the tissues out of the box Lucas had extended to her. 'Call me Becky. Everyone else does, and it's the one thing that still makes me feel young. Well... that and my thirty-something boyfriend.' She threw him a watery smile, dabbed away a few tears, then blew her nose, sitting back in her chair with a sigh. 'It was a bit mad thinking I still might be...you know...'

Lucas did know, but he thought it best to let Becky say the words herself.

'Able to have a baby. At my age.'

He held out the tissue box again. 'It isn't an impossibility, but I will caution you—'

'That pregnancy at my age comes with added risk.' She threw her hands up and gave a tearful laugh. 'I know. Down's. High blood pressure. Gestational diabetes.'

'There are risks for both you and the baby, so if you are sexually active and still trying for a child it's worth remembering the possible risks that could arise from a geriatric pregnancy—'

'Oh, God! Let me stop you there.' She repeated the words *geriatric pregnancy* with a tone of pure horror. 'It just sounds so...so...*old*.'

'Eighty-eight is old,' Lucas said with a gentle smile. 'A hundred and three is old. And, for the record, I have seen patients of both ages earlier this morning—both of whom, I am happy to report, are fit and well despite their additional life experience.'

Lucas hoped his smile would say what propriety wouldn't allow him to. Becky Braxton was an attractive, intelligent woman, who was clearly in a happy, healthy sexual relationship with a younger partner who adored her, seeing as he'd texted three times already during her visit.

Children might not be on the cards for her, but that didn't mean she had to buy herself a wheelchair and consider her life over and done with.

He tapped the test results he'd just printed out. 'You are healthy and fit. Those are valuable assets.'

He was about to say she would have decades of other experiences ahead of her, but he knew first hand that life didn't always work out like that. So he gave her a couple of pamphlets and said he was more than happy to talk through some of the physical changes she could expect over the coming years, or offer a referral if she preferred to discuss it with a woman doctor.

'Heavens, no!' Becky pooh-poohed the idea. 'You're ever so kind, but I suppose… Oh, I do hate to be personal, but when I heard about your situation, and saw you were getting on with your life, I thought, *If young, handsome Dr Wilde can take one of life's more serious blows on the chin and pick himself and get on with it…so can I.*' She pressed her fingers to her mouth, then let them drop into her lap, her expression anxious. 'I hope that isn't too intrusive? It's just—you know—it's a small village, and people know things about people here. In a friendly way.'

'I know,' he said. 'It's a very welcoming place.'

More than enough stews and casseroles had been left on his front porch when he'd first moved in, to make it clear that life in Carey Cove was about being part of a community. Not hiding away and licking his wounds as he had back in Penzance, when he'd been not even thirty, the father of a six-month-old son and newly widowed.

He'd learnt the hard way that life after a bereavement was not about forgetting—because how could you forget someone you'd promised to love till death parted you? You couldn't. Nor could you stop loving them. Especially when you woke up to a three-year-old version of that person every single morning.

'How do you do it?' Becky asked. 'Get on with life when it's not going to be remotely like the one you thought you'd be living?'

'Good question,' he said, doing his best to lean into the question rather than avoid it. People came to their GP when they were feeling vulnerable. Frightened. He knew he couldn't give her a perfect answer, but he could explain what he'd done. 'For me and Harry—my little lad—it was finding a way to live with our new reality. It was less difficult for him, of course, but—'

'I'm sorry,' Becky cut in. 'That was extremely personal of me. I suspect I need to go home, have a bit of sulk and a think, and then just get on with it. That's what we British do, isn't it?'

'As long as you're not letting anything fester,' Lucas said, meaning it.

He'd known that if he'd stayed in the house he and Lily had thought was to be their 'for ever' home he'd have been tending wounds that would never heal. The move here had felt like a physical necessity.

'If you need a referral to talk to someone, or would like some phone numbers of charities, I'm happy to pass them on.'

A thought caught and snagged his attention. He didn't know what it was, but something told him Kiara's move to Carey Cove had been for exactly the same reason his had. To give herself a clean slate. A fresh start.

Losing his wife had been a gut-wrenching loss, but he'd at least been able to pour his love into their son, ensuring that Harry felt as safe, happy and secure as they had wanted all their children to feel—*their child*, he silently corrected. Because there wouldn't be more children, would there? Not without falling in love again, trusting his heart again. Taking the risk of stepping off the edge of a cliff and believing, once again, that this time he would actually get to spend the rest of his life loving and caring for someone who felt the same way about him.

He stemmed the thought.

Once in a lifetime had been a blessing.

Harry was a blessing.

Kiara was just—

Wait. What? Kiara wasn't mean to have entered that particular thought process. Particularly when he was thinking about falling in love again.

He realigned his focus to where it should be. On his patient. 'Have you considered adoption? Fostering?'

She shook her head. 'No, not really.' She grabbed another tissue, dabbed her eyes clear of mascara, and popped on her usual bright smile. 'Anyway, it's simply too embarrassing, sobbing my heart out in front of you. I'll figure something out.' She gave his hand a pat, as if their roles had suddenly been reversed and she was the one consoling him. 'Thank you, Dr Wilde. No disrespect, but I hope our paths don't cross again too soon. Unless—' her smile genuinely brightened this time '—it's down at the harbour? They're turning on the Christmas lights tomorrow night. Your little one might like that. It's always such a lovely evening. Mulled wine, mince pies, and of course all the lights.'

'That sounds wonderful.'

Lucas saw her out of the surgery and as it was now lunchtime thought he'd pop upstairs to the room Nya had told him Marnie was in. He'd rung earlier, to see how the labour had gone, and had been delighted to hear she'd delivered her healthy little girl in record time.

A few minutes later, he was just about to enter the room when Kiara came out, chart in hand. Her eyes brightened at the sight of him. It was a nice change from the cool reception he'd been given the first couple of times their paths had crossed. Perhaps he'd surprised her, or caught her out... Who knew? There were a million reasons why someone's initial encounters with another person might not be perfect.

'I take it she's sleeping?' Lucas said in a low voice.

Kiara's dark brown eyes flicked back towards the bed. She nodded, and gently pulled the door shut behind her. 'Like a baby,' she said. '*With* her baby,' she added with a soft laugh, her gaze dipping and then lifting to meet his.

Something hot and bright flared between them, causing them both to look away. There was something both of them were shy of, Lucas thought. Was it something neither of them had expected or wanted?

It was a question he couldn't answer.

'How are you getting on?' He gave a teasing glance at his watch. 'What's it been? Four hours? Delivered any more babies?'

Kiara shot him a shy grin. 'Not yet. Although there have been a couple more December babies added to my roster, so

I'll definitely be looking forward to swaddling them in seasonal blankets.'

Lucas threw her a questioning look.

Kiara led him over to the supplies cupboard and pointed to a couple of fresh stacks of swaddling blankets with a variety of patterns: Santas, elves, holly and ivy, even bright red reindeers in a Nordic design.

'I didn't even realise we had seasonal swaddling,' Lucas said.

Kiara flushed and admitted, 'That would be my fault.'

'How?'

'Back in the hospital where I used to work, we would sometimes get samples from companies wanting to sell these. When I knew I'd be moving here at Christmas time I contacted one of the suppliers to see if there were any samples available, and they sent this huge box full. They're last year's designs, so...'

'So Carey House is the lucky recipient?' Lucas said. 'I'm impressed. You're not just a fan of Christmas at home, you spread the joy.'

Again, her gaze dropped, then lifted to meet his. The compliment—however generic—had obviously touched her. Her response, lightly pinkened cheeks and a tooth snagging on her lower lip, made his heart skip a beat.

Something—or more likely someone—had hurt this woman. Made her feel less valued than she should be.

'Well...' Kiara finally broke the silence. 'I wanted to do something to show how appreciative I am of being taken on as part of the team here.'

'Christmas swaddling blankets was a nice choice,' Lucas said, and then, because he couldn't help himself, asked, 'You worked in London before, right?'

Kiara let out a low whistle. 'Word travels fast in these parts.'

Lucas gave her a knowing grin. 'Tell me about it. When I moved here—'

He stopped himself. He wasn't ready to bring up the cancer,

the months of praying that this time, this check-up, his wife would get the all-clear.

He began again. 'When I moved here, I received a very warm welcome. There are fewer folk to spread the news to, I guess. Fewer than up in London, anyway.'

The expression on Kiara's face suggested to him that she'd seen the dark shadows flit through his eyes when he referenced his move. Or perhaps she'd read him like a book the moment she'd met him. Seen the light blue shadows that had taken up residence under his eyes in those last heartbreaking days of Lily's life and refused to leave. Sensed the void in his life he didn't know how to fill or what or who to fill it with.

But instead of trying to prise more information out of him, Kiara volunteered, 'I worked at London Central.'

Lucas looked impressed. 'You'd certainly get your daily steps in at that place. I mean—' He stopped, smacking himself on the forehead with the heel of his hand. 'Not that you need to count steps. Midwives are some of the most active people I've ever met, and you're obviously very fit and slender and—' He was about to say *beautiful*, but something stopped him, so he faked a cough and asked, 'Did you enjoy your time there?'

Kiara quite happily pretended she hadn't noticed his weird gaffe. She was obviously private, too, but she did volunteer, 'It was amazing. I started there straight out of university, and it was trial by fire, really. But the care there is much more doctor-led. Not to diminish what you do—obviously it's super-important. But I guess before I did the job I had imagined that being a midwife would be more like it has been here from the moment I arrived.'

Lucas felt himself caught in her enthusiasm. The warm glow of her smile. 'You mean pregnant women appearing on the driveway about to give birth?'

Kiara shot him a cheeky grin. 'If she'd been riding a donkey and had a man in hessian robes alongside her it would've been even better.'

He gave her a disbelieving look.

'No!' She was laughing as she waved the nativity image away. 'I was obviously delighted we got to Marnie in time, and that we didn't have to worry about there being no room at the inn. It was more… Well, you, for example. You saw that the midwives had things under control and honoured the fact that it's our area of expertise.'

'But it *is* your area of expertise.' Lucas felt he was missing something here. 'That's the point of midwifery.'

'I know!' Kiara laughed and clapped her hands. 'Exactly. It's just…lots of times in the London hospital there were incidents when male obstetricians would elbow us aside although we were perfectly capable of handling the situation. Women helping women, you know?'

Lucas scanned her expression, looking for something that might signal that she disliked or mistrusted men in general, but found nothing. Maybe there'd been a bully in her department? Or perhaps it was simpler than that? Perhaps she was referencing the traditional customs of childbirth that went back much further than modern medicine did?

Kiara must've sensed that she needed to explain herself a bit more, so she continued, 'I like being a woman's wingman. And her partner's—if there is one,' she added hastily, with a quick glance towards Marnie's room. 'Being with her almost from the beginning as she rides the world's most exhilarating and terrifying rollercoaster of all. Bringing someone new into the world…'

Her passion spoke to him. It was akin to his love of being a GP. Helping people throughout the various stages of their lives.

'You look like someone who loves her job very much,' he said.

'I do. I love it. Absolutely. And I just know I'm going to love it here too.'

Her eyes shone bright. To the point where Lucas knew he'd be caught in their brilliance for longer than was appropriate.

So again he resorted to the fake cough manoeuvre and excused himself.

He was responding to Kiara in ways he'd never thought he'd experience with a woman again. Curious to know more. Wanting to be around her. Hyper-aware of himself when he was. And that wasn't even counting the starring role she'd had in the erotic dream he'd had last night.

It scared him. He and Harry had only just got themselves into a steady, workable routine. He wasn't sure he had it in his emotional toolbox to change things yet again. Not in this way.

He could feel her eyes on him as he left the ward…and for the first time in years he liked knowing that someone was looking.

He kept his pace slow and steady—and then, when he hit the stairs, surprised himself by hoisting his bum cheek up onto the banister and sliding all the way down.

When he got to the bottom, he was smiling.

And so was Nya, who'd seen the entire thing.

CHAPTER FOUR

JUST AS SHE was about to do her first lash, Kiara gave her mascara wand the side-eye and then, after one long hard stare, set it back down. She wasn't going to dress up for her second day at work, and she definitely wasn't dressing up for Dr Lucas Wilde. Even if he did make her skip along the corridor at work and think surprisingly saucy thoughts as she slipped into bed.

Even so, when she went out to her front garden—coat on, backpack loaded and ready to go to work—she found herself accidentally on purpose dawdling. Changing the angle of the dancing penguins by a smidge. Realigning a couple of waist-high candy canes that were listing ever so slightly in the crisp breeze coming in straight off the sea.

She had all the lights on already. With the mornings dark for so long, she thought it might be fun for the hardworking fishermen to look back to the coast and be able to spot her home, shining bright like a Christmas lighthouse, welcoming them back to the beautiful little harbour below when they brought in the morning's catch.

She turned and looked out to sea, just making out the skidding movement of white horses atop the waves. When she turned back around, the twinkling delights of her decorated cottage hit her afresh. It looked like a real-life gingerbread house.

One that was hosting visitors from all over the North Pole. She tapped the black nose of the polar bear she'd set up last night after work. He was standing guard over a pile of 'presents'— colourfully decorated weatherproof boxes, arranged in an artful tumble and coming out of a huge Santa sack.

She'd checked with the neighbours first, assuring them that she wouldn't have the house flashing and blinking like a Vegas casino, and had been thrilled to discover they were all collectively delighted with her efforts. They'd even pledged to donate to First Steps in the name of Mistletoe Cottage.

It wasn't the glory she was after…it was knowing that something she'd done would be bringing care and solace to families unable to afford medical equipment for their poorly newborns. Life was hard enough when you brought a child into the world. Having medical problems to take on board when your finances were tight was even worse.

She shouldered her backpack, locked the front door, and gave her home an appraising look. It looked spectacular. If you loved Christmas, that was.

Her gaze drifted down the lane to where she had first seen Lucas and Harry, but it was completely devoid of human life. Just a few leaves scudding across the pavement.

A strange feeling of emptiness threatened to nibble away at the glow of anticipation she'd woken up with. She'd practically bounded out of bed. And it wasn't just the joy of going to work at Carey House she'd been looking forward to. It was the giddy sense of excitement about who she was going to see at Carey House. Today, she'd vowed silently, she would be less wary of Lucas Wilde and more…

Hmm… She'd have to work on that part, because obviously pouncing on the man and kissing him was out of the question. No. That sort of 'staff Christmas party' behaviour was not going to be a part of her strategy. As if she were as calculated as that. She wasn't. Not in the slightest. What she really needed here in her new home was a friend. Independent of her attraction to him, Lucas Wilde seemed like excellent friend material. And also a very, *very* sexy dad.

A sound at the end of the lane caught her attention. As if thinking about his father had magicked him into appearing, a familiar looking blond boy, kitted out in a red woolly hat and a matching puffer jacket, came careering round the corner, one foot madly pushing away at the pavement that stood between him and her increasingly over-the-top Christmas display.

Her heart softened.

Harry.

With or without the sexy dad he was a darling little boy. Precocious. Full of beans. And clearly as in love with Christmas as she was.

'Morning, Harry! Remember to slow down for the corner— Oops! There you are. Nice one. You're getting better at stopping, aren't you?'

'Penguins!' he cried, as the timer she'd set clicked into action.

She gave him a complicit grin and readjusted his knitted hat as he leant his scooter against the fence. 'Want to take a closer look?'

Wide-eyed with a combination of disbelief and pleasure, he looked up at her, his big grey eyes a carbon copy of his father's. 'Yes, please.'

'Well, go on, then. They were asking for you this morning.'

'They were?' Harry's eyes grew even bigger.

'Absolutely.' She put on a funny voice she hoped sounded like a penguin. '"When's Harry coming over for a dance?"'

Harry needed no further encouragement.

'Good morning, Kiara.'

Lucas's butter-rich voice all but physically pulled her up to stand. When she met his gaze, she was delighted to see it was matched with a smile. Less dubious than it had been yesterday at Carey House. There was warmth in it. Comfort. And, if she wasn't mistaken, a hint of that same fizz of anticipation she knew was glittering in her own eyes. They held one another's gazes for a moment, the atmosphere between them teetering on the precipice of too nice for Kiara to be able to resist and… *uh-oh*…blushing.

'Morning.' She feigned a crucial readjustment to her bobble hat and pointed to the lane. 'Off to work?'

Of course he is, you idiot! He's not heading to the zoo.

Lucas nodded, his eyes skidding from one decorative tableau to the next. 'And to the childminder's. Harry insisted we left early enough to visit The Christmas Lady.'

His face became less easy to read. Though he was obviously trying to fulfil his son's wishes, something about her or Christmas wasn't letting his smile reach his eyes.

'Are you not a fan of Christmas?' she blurted, instantly regretting it when he winced.

'Is it that obvious?' He waved the words away. 'That's not exactly the case. It's more—' His phone beeped and he pulled it out. The wince turned into a frown. 'Sorry. We've got to get going.' He took in her hat, the bag on her shoulder and the winter coat as if seeing her for the first time. 'Want to join us?'

Yes. Absolutely, she did. But if this was precious father-son time she didn't want to intrude. 'If you're sure…?'

Lucas's smile was genuine now. 'I am. Sorry. It's just—' He did a quick scan of her house and called Harry over with a loving, 'Time to go now, son.' Then, 'I don't have the best relationship with Christmas, and as this is the first one this little monkey is going to properly remember I'm trying to plumb some of the Christmas spirit by proxy.'

Kiara took this as her cue. 'You want Christmas spirit by proxy? I can do that. In spades.' She gave him a little salute. 'Christmas spirit by proxy, at your service!'

Lucas gave a good-natured laugh and then, to her surprise, reached out and gave her candy-cane-striped scarf a little tug. 'If it's anything like your midwifery I'm sure you'll be an excellent guide.'

Her blush deepened. 'You hardly saw me do anything.'

'I saw enough to know that you're good at your job. And, perhaps more importantly, that you love it. Have you had any updates on your patient?'

She pulled out her phone and thumbed up the photo she'd asked one of the night nurses to send her. Marnie and her baby nuzzling one another's noses. It was a really sweet photo, and unexpectedly tugged at a longing she didn't dare give voice to. She was around babies every single day and had never before had this response to a mother-baby moment. Not even with her ex. What had changed?

'Hold it up a bit?' Lucas was asking, putting his hand under hers to bring it to his eyeline.

Again, that twist of longing swept through her, but this time it came with glittery sparks of delight whooshing through her bloodstream. Sparks that had absolutely nothing to do with the tall, dark and handsome doctor with a snowman backpack hanging from his arm, leaning into her personal space to look at the photo.

God, he smelled good.

This morning he was more like vanilla latte with hints of cornflakes and berries than the sexy woodcutter aroma he'd left in his wake yesterday. Not that she'd be smelling him every time their paths crossed. Much. But that was hardly her fault. He was like the scented version of a kaleidoscope.

When he pulled back, she instantly missed his proximity. She'd never known lust at first sight to be so potent.

'They look well. I'll have to check in on them today,' Lucas said, mercifully having missed the twist of her features as she took a final look at the photo and then closed it down.

She wasn't jealous of Marnie. She was happy for her. Though she hadn't yet heard her whole story, Marnie seemed a picture of contentment…just her and her baby.

Kiara had always pictured something different for herself. Something like what her parents shared. A happy, solid friendship that had led to a loving marriage. They'd had their ups and downs through the years—she was beginning to learn there weren't many couples who enjoyed entirely smooth sailing once they vowed to spend a lifetime together—but they had always dealt with their problems together. As a family. She admired them for that, and knew that her ideal relationship would contain those core principles of love and respect.

'So...' Lucas began after they'd walked in silence for a bit. 'Do you always decorate for Christmas like this?'

She barked a laugh. 'No. This is new. I don't think the rest of the tenants in my building in London would have taken to me turning their homes into a great big flashing Christmas orgasm. Oh, God!' She clapped her hands over her mouth. 'I'm sorry. I don't know what made me describe it that way. Especially in front of your son—' She squeezed her eyes tight in humiliation. 'I'm making this worse. Much, much worse. The more I talk, the worse it gets. Please save me from myself!'

Lucas, to her relief, was laughing rather than looking horrified. He lowered his voice and, as if they were sharing a secret, leant in and intoned, 'Maybe in future you could use the phrase "festive wonderland" when Harry's within earshot?'

Her cheeks burnt with embarrassment. 'I am so sorry. I'm not really getting off on the right foot as your number one Christmas spirit guide, am I?'

He shook his head, but didn't look annoyed or even put off by her series of verbal gaffes. 'This is the childminder's.'

She stood back as the carer came out of her lovely rambling home, tucking a well-loved cardigan around herself as she greeted them with the news that the children would be having a biscuit-making party after lunch today.

Harry cheered, then waved to Kiara. 'I'll make you a Santa biscuit!'

She grinned, and pressed her hands to her heart in thanks. She looked across at Lucas, whose expression had suddenly gone blank. Unreadable. He seemed to be actively avoiding eye contact with her.

Had she done something wrong?

He knelt down in front of Harry and gave him loving but stern reminders to wear his coat when he was playing outdoors and to listen to the childminder—especially when she said it was time for a nap. He gave him a kiss on the forehead and tugged one of the little blond curls peeking out from under his hat. And then, as if it had suddenly become physically painful for him to leave his little boy, he briskly rose, turned, and walked back out to the pavement, where he instantly set off at a clip.

Kiara wasn't sure what had just happened. Was that sort of a goodbye normal for them? Maybe it had been a bit stiff because she'd been watching. Or was it because Harry had offered to make a biscuit for her?

This and a thousand other questions clamoured for supremacy as she jogged up to him and, in as light a tone as possible, asked, 'Are you upset that you're not going to get to go to the biscuit-making party? I get it. I love making and decorating biscuits—all those hundreds and thousands...'

He stopped and threw her a look saturated with sadness. His grief was so pure, so undiluted, it tore her own heart open with compassion. Whatever was haunting this man was big. Well beyond anything she'd endured. And that wasn't slighting what she'd been through at all.

It had been life-changing. And not in a good way.

But it had led her here...

'I really want to give Harry a special Christmas this year,' Lucas said finally, his brow furrowing tight. Not really the expression someone should wear when announcing they wanted to spread cheer and joy for Christmas.

'Like I said, I'm completely happy to be your Christmas elf.'

Lucas shot her a sharp glance, slowing his pace as if he was genuinely absorbing her offer. To her surprise, he pointed towards the village below them. 'They're turning the Christmas lights on down at the harbour tonight. Harry's never experienced anything like that, and you're new here in Carey Cove... You wouldn't, by any chance, possibly—'

'Yes,' Kiara interjected, hoping she was putting him out of his misery. 'I would love to go.'

He looked horrified.

Oh, no. She hadn't put him *out* of his misery—she'd thrown him straight into a pit of despair. She was clearly meant to have said no.

She tried to backtrack. 'I mean... I'll go as a friend. Because I'm friendly. But not overly friendly. I don't even have to stand with you, if you don't want. Like a date would. Because it wouldn't be a date.'

Lucas was now looking both horrified and confused.

She soldiered on. 'Unless you mean would I go as Harry's friend? In which case I'm totally on board with— I'll stop there. This talking thing always gets me into trouble at moments like this.' She laughed nervously. 'A *date*!' She feigned disbelief that the word had even been on the table. 'We wouldn't want to start any undue gossip at Carey House, now, would we?' Again, she popped her hands over her mouth, then muttered, 'Please stop talking...please stop talking.'

He looked at her, seriously for a moment, as if actually considering her question, then nodded. 'Good. Grand. Harry will love that. Right!'

He clapped his hands together, as if to bring an end to all the awkwardness, and to the clear relief of both of them they arrived at Carey House, where a shift-change meant there was enough hustle and bustle for her to wave him a quick goodbye and pretend she hadn't just humiliated herself as much as she thought she had.

Lucas closed the door to his surgery and silently banged his head against the wall—one, two, three times—before leaving it there as a low moan escaped his throat.

She didn't think it was a date, did she?

Did he?

No. He wasn't a dater. Not now, anyway. Not even when their chemistry was—

Hang on. Did he *want* it to be a date?

No. Absolutely not. She was a colleague. He was a widower. He had a son to look after.

He thought of the way his body had responded when their hands had inadvertently brushed as they'd both reached to pull shut the small gate at the childminder's. It had been an electric connection. Through *gloves*. Well... In her case mittens. Bright red things, with tiny white reindeer and Christmas trees knitted into the pattern. Not that he'd been staring at her hand and wondering what it would be like to reach out and weave his fingers through hers.

Another low moan emptied out of his chest.

His wife had been right. He was horrendous with women. Terrible at asking them out. Making them feel at ease. In fact, if memory served, he was fairly certain it was Lily who had asked *him* out first back in time. Not that he'd meant to ask Kiara out. This was for Harry. For Christmas. For Harry and Christmas.

He rubbed his hands over his face and shook his head.

The fact he'd managed to woo and win his wife's hand in marriage was a miracle. One miracle in a lifetime was more than enough. Unless you counted Harry, and then that gave him two. Falling in love again was one miracle too many to wish for.

Right?

'Let yourself love again. Don't be afraid to let someone else into your and Harry's lives. And remember to give her flowers.'

His wife's words came to him unbidden. A reminder that he was in charge of his heart. He'd barely registered them at the time. She'd been so very ill, and devoting himself to anything other than their infant son and her care had seemed an impossibility. He'd felt so helpless. So lost. Umpteen years of medical training hadn't prepared him to endure witnessing the woman he'd begun a family with waste away to nothing. So how on earth could he absorb dating advice from that same woman? It had seemed impossible at the time.

So he'd done what he'd imagined any grieving husband might. Closed down the option of ever loving again. And yet here he was, almost three years after losing her, remembering her wish that he and Harry would find room in their hearts for someone else.

Was Kiara that someone?

Eight hours later, as he pulled on his coat and walked to the new mothers' ward, he was still asking himself the same question. Usually a full roster of patients enabled him to push uncomfortable thoughts out of his mind—but not today. Then again, he didn't usually have a date—*not* a date!—waiting for him at the end of the day.

He popped his head into Marnie's room, pleased to see the tell-tale glow of motherhood lighting up the room as Marnie took her daughter into her arms for a feed. Not wanting to interfere with this private moment, he left them to it and headed to the central desk, where he saw Kiara doing a handover with Nya and another midwife—Sophie French. All three of them were wearing multicoloured reindeer antlers. Kiara's were flashing. She leant in and said something in a low voice to the women and they all gave a knowing laugh.

In-jokes already? Only two days on the job and she seemed completely at ease. The fact that she was a good midwife was not in doubt. It was more... Her aura embodied something less tangible. There was a heightened sense of presence about her behaviour that spoke of a feeling of gratitude. He didn't know why, but he got the impression she needed a place like this. Not just Carey House, but Carey Cove.

When he'd moved here with Harry he had been feeling lost, overwhelmed, bereaved. Then he'd driven in along the coastline, seen the beautiful village laid out in lanes that worked their way up the hillside to where, on top, was the golden stone former manor house that was now the cottage hospital. He'd instantly felt as though he'd entered a place of solace. Warmth. Not necessarily a place to forget his past, but a place to heal and then, one day, move forward.

The second Kiara laid eyes on him her expression changed from smiling and bright to purposeful. For reasons he couldn't pinpoint, the shift in mood put him at ease. It was as if she'd read and processed this morning's gaffe over the date/not date invitation and repurposed their outing into what he had intended it to be: for his son.

She shared a quick look with the other women and he didn't miss the mischievous expression Nya sent his way when Kiara disappeared into the midwives' lounge to get her things. He was guessing her humour-filled smile was largely fuelled by his out-of-character slide down the banister yesterday.

'I'm guessing both you and Harry will be hungry,' Kiara said through the muffle of her thrice-wrapped scarf as they left Carey House and headed towards the childminder's. 'If you like, I can meet you down at the Harbour at six. That's when the lights are going on, apparently.'

Her smile was soft and warm. There was no expectation in it and for that he was grateful.

'He's usually had some sort of afternoon snack at the childminder's that tides him over. It's the days at nursery when he needs immediate feeding. I can assure you…a hungry Harry is not a beautiful sight to behold.' He pulled a monster face as evidence.

Kiara put on a shocked expression. 'What? A three-year-old not being beautifully behaved at all times? I refuse to believe it.'

They shared a companionable laugh and carried on walking, the question of when and where to meet still unresolved.

It struck him that she was leaving it up to him. Not in a helpless way. More in the kind of way that meant she wasn't going to push for something that wasn't there. Had her heart been broken, too? Surely not in the way his had. But he sensed a vulnerability in her…a spirited type. One that wasn't going to allow anyone to take command of her heart and treat it without due care.

'Maybe…' he began, just as she started to say something.

A ridiculous politeness pile-on ensued.

'You go…'

'No, you go…'

'Really…'

'Please…'

'You first. I insist.'

Eventually they got to the point where they both stopped talking—although, if he wasn't mistaken, Kiara had succumbed to a case of the giggles behind that extra-long scarf of hers.

Crikey. He was making a right hash of this. He steeled himself and asked the question that had been poised on the tip of his tongue. 'Would you like to join us for supper? Nothing fancy. Or homemade.' He grimaced apologetically. His cooking still had plenty of room for improvement. 'We could have fish and chips down by the harbour?'

Kiara shot him a look, clearly trying to ascertain if she needed to read anything into the invitation. He smiled and held out his hands, as if that was an indicator that he really meant it.

He must have made a convincing show because her smile brightened. 'I do love a hot packet of fish and chips all wrapped up in paper.'

Lucas's smile matched hers in enthusiasm. 'It's great, isn't it? Shame it's not newspaper any more. Sometimes the traditional way of doing things is the best.'

Her smile faltered, then regained purchase so quickly he wouldn't have noticed it if he hadn't been looking. 'Right. That's settled, then. Fish and chips down by the harbour followed by some festive lights.'

She let out a whistle. 'Look at you, getting into the Christmas spirit.'

'It helps having you guide me on the way,' he said, pointing at her antlers. 'Both literally and figuratively.' And he meant it, too.

They collected Harry, who had made and decorated not one, but several gingerbread biscuits. He was instantly bewitched with the blinking antlers. Without a moment's hesitation Kiara switched them from her head to his, sending an *Is this all right?* glance back at Lucas as she did so.

Of course it was. And it also made him want to kick himself. It was magical flourishes like this that his little boy was missing out on by having *him* as his only parent.

After stopping to admire Kiara's dazzling display of Christmas delights, they dropped the biscuits and Harry's backpack off at his house—which Lucas suddenly felt a bit ashamed of. Not because of the house itself. It was a beautiful stone cottage, in keeping with the rest of the village's solid but welcoming aesthetic. It was because it was entirely bereft of Christmas decor. When Harry asked why their house wasn't more like Kiara's, he muttered some excuse about things being lost in the post, but it was, of course, a fiction. The simple truth was that he didn't know how to celebrate Christmas any more.

Kiara didn't comment on it, but he could see that she'd clocked the absence of decorative Christmas cheer and his awkward way of explaining it away.

No wonder his little boy adored her. She embodied the spirit of the season. Warm, generous, kind.

Beautiful.

The thought pulled him up short. She didn't look a thing like Lily—which, if he were psychoanalysing himself, made his attraction to Kiara feel less like a betrayal and more a biological reality.

He buried his head in his hands, grateful that Kiara and Harry were walking ahead of him.

What a Casanova!

If, by some extraordinary turn of events, whatever was happening with Kiara evolved into something romantic, he would have to find a way to express his admiration for her with better word-choices. 'Biological reality' wasn't really a turn of phrase that made a woman swoon. Besides, his response to her was more than biological. It was... It was that same ethereal thing that drew any two strangers together. Kismet? The stars? The spirit of Christmas? He didn't know. All he knew was that it was too strong to ignore. For Harry's sake, obviously. Kiara was the key to making this Christmas a truly memorable one for his little boy.

To his relief, Kiara and Harry commandeered the evening and, mittened hand in mittened hand, led the way down to the harbour, where there was already a small crowd gathering, many with fish and chips.

'Guess we aren't as original as we thought,' Lucas said as they joined the queue.

Kiara's mood only seemed further delighted by his observation. 'It's wonderful being part of something bigger than yourself, isn't it?'

He looked around the harbour area and suddenly saw it through her eyes. She was a stranger here, and yet the atmosphere was anything but exclusive. As people milled in the cobblestoned square, he saw a sea of smiles lifted by a soundscape of laughter and excited chatter. It was a happy place, made cheerier with each new arrival.

One of the retired sailors who was often seen propping up the bar in the local pub was roasting chestnuts in a large metal drum on the harbour's edge. The publicans had set up a stall outside The Dolphin Inn—aka The Dolph—for mulled wine, and from the looks of the number of families in the queue something for the little ones as well. Cornish apple juice with a bit of cinnamon, he guessed from the waft of aroma coming his way.

'You know, you're right.' He smiled down at her as he drew his son in for a hug. 'It feels infectious. In a good way,' he hastily tacked on.

She laughed. 'I would hate the Christmas spirit to be infectious in a bad way.' She threw him a look that was equal measures delight and caution. 'I meant what I said this morning. I'm happy to help.' She lowered her voice so Harry wouldn't hear. 'If you want me to take Harry to anything that's not appealing to you...' She rattled off a list of events happening around the area, including a Christmas train ride, a nearby Christmas fair and a Christmas-decoration-making afternoon at the weekend.

Lucas laughed. 'You really do love Christmas, don't you?'

She smiled brightly, but her voice was serious and her dark eyes shadowed when she said, 'I love being able to celebrate it as wildly and with as much joy as I want.'

There was a story there. One she clearly felt happy to allude to, but not offer specifics on. He got it. He had his story, too. Moving here hadn't just been about getting out of the house where he'd nursed his wife through to her final moments. It had been about being able to go to the village shop and not have people stare at The Widower. Or having all his patients offer their condolences when he was the one who was meant to be caring for them. He knew, as well, that his son had to be allowed to be Harry Wilde, the energetic little blond boy with curls and a smile to soften even the steeliest of hearts. Not Harry Wilde, the poor little boy who'd lost his mum when he was only a baby. It was a fact. Yes. Just as it was a fact that Lucas was a widower. But he had known they couldn't continue having their loss be the defining factor of who they were and who they might one day become.

'These are amazing!' Kiara beamed when they'd finally got to the front of the queue and were each holding warm bundles of freshly fried fish and deliciously moreish chips doused in salt and vinegar. 'Harry...' Kiara dropped Lucas a complicit wink. 'If you hold on to my hand, I bet I can take you to the best spot to watch the Christmas lights being turned on.'

Harry looked from Kiara to his father, then back again. 'Can we?' he asked his father.

'By all means,' Lucas said, bewildered as to how Kiara managed, after little more than a fortnight in the village, to know already the best place to sit—especially with just about the entire population of Carey Cove being present.

She led them out to the small stone quay where a smattering of sailing and fishing boats were moored. After a quick word with a young man sitting on the back of a mid-sized fishing trawler that was alight with multicoloured lights spanning across its rigging, she stood back, pointed up to the Navigation Bridge, which was strewn with unlit fairy lights, and with a swirl of her free hand announced, 'Ta-da! Your viewing platform, gentlemen.'

Harry looked wide-eyed with disbelief. Lucas realised he probably did, too. 'How on earth—'

She explained as they climbed aboard. 'The captain's wife had a baby yesterday.'

'And you delivered it?' Lucas finished.

She smiled and nodded. 'Her regular midwife had been held up with a more problematic birth, and she kindly agreed to let me step in and help.'

'And somehow, in between teaching her breathing techniques and delivering the baby, you managed to find out that her husband had the best spot to see the Christmas lights.'

She smiled up at him, and yet again Lucas felt that warm glow of connection light up his chest—one that went beyond the parameters of friendship.

'I call it The Distraction Technique,' she quipped, then added, 'She said her husband had decorated the boat specially for her. However, the one scent she hadn't been able to stomach ever since falling pregnant was...' She looked down at what remained of her meal and then grinned at him.

'Fish?' Lucas finished for her, popping the last piece of his battered cod into his mouth with a smile. 'Well, lucky us.'

'Yes...'

Kiara's smile softened and then, as a light flush caught the apples of her cheeks, she looked back to the village just as a

swell of music filled the air. A hush spread across the crowd all
the way out to where Lucas, his son and Kiara were perched in
the trawler. Lucas hoisted Harry up on to the captain's bench
so that he could see the magic of the lights as they came on in
their full festive glory.

His fingers twitched with an instinct to take her mittened
hand in his. As if sensing the impulse, she glanced over at him
and then, clearly feeling the same reticence he was, looked back
to the lights, glittering away with nothing but promises of the
season yet to come.

CHAPTER FIVE

'HERE YOU ARE, Bethany.' Kiara lifted one tiny swaddled bundle and handed it to the new mum, then once she was settled asked, 'Are you ready for your second son?'

Bethany threw her an anxious smile, tears suddenly blooming in her eyes. 'I guess...' She gave a watery laugh. 'I think I might be missing Graham.'

Kiara smiled warmly and said, 'It's perfectly normal to feel overwhelmed. It's such a shame this is his busy season, but the way your phone keeps pinging to check on you is proof that he wishes he was here instead. And remember...' she tapped the side of her nose '...you can blame hormones for all sorts of things for a while yet.' She handed her a tissue.

Bethany laughed and wiped at her eyes, then held her free arm out to accept her son's twin brother. 'I suppose I'm going to have to get used holding both of them with Graham at work so much.'

'It has only been a day,' Kiara said gently. 'There's no need to be hard on yourself. Motherhood is one of the steepest learning curves there is.'

Kiara caught Bethany's quick glance at her bare ring finger and felt the absence of the natural follow-up question: *Do you have little ones yourself?*

The question had never stung before, when it had felt like such a future certainty. But for the last year it hadn't felt certain—and, although she never begrudged new mums their children, she was beginning to feel the sting of being a singleton.

Kiara stayed close until she was certain Bethany had good purchase on both of her children and then pulled two tiny little elf hats out of her pocket. 'Ready?'

In a sudden about-face, Bethany giggled. 'This is so silly. I mean, they're not even going to remember their first Christmas.'

'But you are! And so is your husband. They're memories for you to share with the boys as they get older.' A thought pricked and lodged in her mind. She had no idea what had happened in Lucas's past, but she was curious as to why Lucas was trying to make Christmas so special for his son but not for himself. Was the fact he hadn't had a spouse or a partner to share his son's earlier Christmases what made it so difficult?

She knew why *she* was marching all guns blazing into the Christmas season. Her ex hadn't just been a married liar. He had been a bit of a control freak—and a snob too. Apparently highly successful surgeons didn't drink cranberry-flavoured cocktails with glittery salt round the edges of the glass, or dance around Christmas trees in Covent Garden for the sheer joy of it.

'Is this okay?' Bethany asked, slipping her own elf hat over her head at a rakish angle.

'Perfect!' Kiara beamed, grateful for the reminder that her life was here in Carey Cove now.

She took a few shots, all at different angles, then, just as she was popping the phone on Bethany's bedside table, heard a soft knock on the doorframe.

Lucas.

Her insides went warm and sparkly.

'Those will be nice additions to the family album,' Lucas said.

Bethany beamed. 'You think?'

'Absolutely.' He indicated the twins, who Kiara was now

gently easing back into their shared bassinet. 'It's a nice starter pack of elves you have there.'

Against the odds, Bethany's smile grew even brighter. Kiara gathered up her tablet and a couple of other items and wished Bethany a good night, along with giving her a reminder that her husband would be calling in for a visit in an hour's time.

'Nice day?' asked Lucas.

'Very.' Kiara beamed. 'We have a dozen new November babies and it's only a few days into the month!' She laughed and gave him a wink that halfway through took on a flirtatious flare she'd never known she possessed. 'Valentine's Day has got a lot to answer for.'

Lucas smiled, then slowed his pace. 'Speaking of Valentine's...'

Kiara's eyes shot to his. Was he going to ask her out for next February? That was forward planning on a whole new level. However, they did say good things came to those who waited, so...

Lucas must have seen the confused look in her eyes, because he pulled a face of his own and rubbed his hand along his jaw—clean-shaven again today—and then dropped it. 'That was a terrible segue. I wasn't meaning to talk about Valentine's at all.'

Her heart surprised her by plummeting. Of course he wasn't. She was stupid to have even gone there in her mind. Stupid winking...turning everything ridiculously flirty. She made a silent vow never to wink again.

He paused, and then clawed one of his hands through his hair as he started and stopped talking a couple of more times.

Kiara gave him a sidelong look. 'I'm not so scary that you can't just ask me something outright, am I?'

'No, I—'

Kiara bit down on her lip as her heart skipped a beat. He was going to ask her out on another date/not a date!

'I was wondering if—'

'Yes!' she blurted. 'I mean...if it's more Christmas stuff with

Harry, I'm in. Like I said the other day… I'm your Ghost of Christmas Present.'

The instant she said the words she regretted them. There was very clearly a Ghost of Christmas Past in Lucas's life…just as there was in hers…only his seemed more ingrained in him.

'I mean… Sorry… I…' She pulled a face, then said, 'Should we start this whole conversation again? My mum calls them do-over moments.'

Lucas's lips twitched into a grateful smile. 'Your mother sounds like a very wise woman.'

To Kiara's delight, his eyes grew bright as he lifted his eyebrows and cupped his chin with his hand, a finger tapping away on his cheek, as if he was in thoughtful consideration of how one commenced a 'do-over', then abruptly turned and walked away.

'Hey!' she called after him. 'Where are you going?'

Quick as a flash, he whirled around and with a warm, confident smile said, 'Oh, hi, Kiara. I'm glad I caught you here. Harry and I were thinking of heading over to the Christmas market and fair a bit further down the coast tonight. We were wondering if you'd care to join us.'

Happiness bubbled from Kiara's toes all the way up to the sparkly Santa hat she was wearing. She felt as if Lucas had dropped a bath bomb in her insides. 'Excellent do-over,' she said, impressed.

'You think?' He doffed an invisible cap. 'I aim to please.'

Their eyes caught and held. For a precious moment Kiara felt linked to him in a way she hadn't imagined ever feeling with a man again. Not after last year. The energy between them had built into something almost tangible. A magnetic force connecting them in a way that surely had to make their trip to a Christmas market and fair more date-like than not.

And then Nya appeared.

'Hello, you two.' She looked much more amused than bemused as she asked, 'May I ask if you plan to hold your little staring contest here in the corridor for the foreseeable future? Or is it just a temporary thing?'

Kiara, who heard the teasing tone in her voice, turned to her and pointedly blinked her eyes. 'That's us done.'

'We're heading off to the Christmas fair just outside Mousehole,' Lucas said. 'For Harry.'

'Yes,' Kiara pounced on the much less date-sounding description. 'Harry does love his Christmas bling.'

Nya gave an approving nod, then shooed them out of the corridor towards the stairs, her voice taking on the tone of a concerned mother. 'Two nights out in the same week? That little boy's going to be over the moon. You'd best get a move on. Here's your coat, Kiara. Lucas, make sure you wear a hat. Set a good example for your son. On you go, now, and make sure you get Harry home early. It's a school night!'

When Nya had finally headed back to her desk, Kiara and Lucas shared a giggle. 'Well, that's us told, then,' said Kiara.

They laughed again, and expressed their mutual admiration for Nya. Kiara felt no compunction about enthusing about her being a good boss. The best she'd had, actually. Warm, but exacting. Generous and humane. It made working here really feel like being part of team rather than the cog in a huge machine that she'd sometimes felt like back in London.

Exchanging information about their days at work, they briskly made their way down the hill, collected Harry and, at Kiara's suggestion, enjoyed some cheese on toast at her house, with the added bonus of Harry being allowed to help Kiara select which box of decorations to put out next. Then they set off down the road towards Mousehole.

Before they'd even rounded the corner to the next cove they could see the lights. Harry, who seemed to be filled with jumping beans tonight, was clapping his hands in anticipation.

When they got out of the car they walked to the central green, where the Christmas market was being held, they all held their breath as one.

In the very centre of the square were three enormous ice sculptures—a snowman, a reindeer and, tallest of all, a huge, jolly Santa Claus with an enormous bag of presents slung over his shoulder. Kiara had no idea how they'd done it, but frozen into the 'bag' were actual toys. A nutcracker, a teddy bear, a doll, and a dozen or so other old-fashioned toys that made the visual display all the more remarkable. The sculptures were illuminated, so that they sparkled like diamonds.

Harry's eyes were so wide, Kiara could actually see the sculptures reflected in them. She knelt down so that she was at eye level with Harry. 'Which one's your favourite?

'The reindeer,' he said after a moment's hesitation. And then, 'The snowman.' He threw her a panicked look. 'Can't I love all of them just the same?'

'Of course you can!' Kiara laughed pulling him in for a cosy hug. 'You've got a huge heart, haven't you, Harry? Such a big, huge heart.'

She let herself fall into the moment. Enjoy the little boy arms around her neck. His energy. His scent. A little boy elixir made up of crisp cheese, earth and soap. She looked up and realised Lucas was watching the pair of them with an intensity the moment didn't necessarily warrant. But…who knew? Maybe it did.

A memory of her reaction to seeing Lucas that very first time he'd loomed above her sprang to mind. It had been visceral, her response to him. Core-deep. As if somehow she'd been waiting to meet him for her entire life.

She felt a shift then. Something in her gave way. Something that hadn't managed to move since her relationship had come to such an explosive end. It felt as if light was pouring into the little cracks and crevices inside her. Fissures she'd thought she'd blocked, so that she wouldn't ever allow herself to feel so hurt again. But this feeling was different. There was a vulnerability to it, yes. But there was also hope and possibility infused with the warmth that she knew came from meeting Lucas.

He held out a hand and helped her to stand up, and although

they didn't continue to hold hands as they walked around the fair, with Harry running from stall to stall, intent on sampling all the Christmas treats, she still felt the strength of his hand as it had wrapped round hers for those few seconds. And something deep inside her told her she would miss that touch for evermore.

'You all set, mate?'

Harry wobbled uncertainly in Lucas's hands for a moment, and then, when one of the teenaged girls hired as a coach for the special pre-schoolers' skate session held out both of hers for Harry to join the rest of the little ones on the ice, Harry took them without so much as a backward glance.

Despite the hit of loss, Lucas had to smile. His son's first moment on skates...

'It's amazing how they take to it, isn't it?' Kiara appeared beside him, holding two steaming mugs. 'Hot chocolate to keep you warm?'

He took the mug gratefully. 'They've really done this whole event up to the nines, haven't they?'

It was truly magical. But rather than agree, Kiara let out a contented sigh and took a big sip of her hot chocolate, which left an impressive dollop of whipped cream on her nose.

'Here. You've got some...' He dug into his pocket and pulled out a clean handkerchief. Their eyes locked as he held it just above her nose, poised for action, and asked mischievously, 'Unless you were keeping it for later?'

'Hmm...' she began, as if considering the option. 'I do like a bit of whipped cream before bed, but...' Her tongue swept across her bottom lip just before her upper teeth caught it tight. Her cheeks pinkened, as if she'd admitted something slightly too intimate for the occasion.

He took a step back and offered her the handkerchief instead of wiping the cream off himself, as he had planned to, suddenly aware of how many of their interchanges bore the hue of flirtation about them. Interchanges neither of them had pushed beyond a glance or a flush of acknowledgement.

He felt an abrupt and urgent need to explain where he was in life. How meeting her had opened up a rush of feelings and… yes…he'd admit it…an attraction he hadn't thought he'd ever experience again.

Before he could stop himself, he said, 'Harry's mother would've loved to see a moment like this.'

He nodded out to the ice rink, where Harry was now holding hands with a little girl, her hair in near identical blonde curls to his peeking out from underneath a knitted cap with snowflakes woven into the design. The two of them looked like a Christmas card.

He tried to say more, but the words caught in his throat. Because if his wife had lived, he wouldn't be here with Kiara— he'd be here watching Harry, and one of them would most likely have a baby strapped to their chest. Perhaps a little girl. Or another boy. It wouldn't matter. They'd said they wanted children, not boys or girls. Because it hadn't mattered if they'd be picking up mud-splattered jeans or tutus. What had mattered was family. Having babies, then toddlers, then school kids, then teens, to nurture and love until one day they had children of their own. He'd seen it all so clearly back then, but now the future…it was a blank slate. One that, courtesy of a Christmas-mad midwife who'd just happened to move to the same tiny village in the same nook of Cornwall as he had, was now bathed in possibility.

He looked into Kiara's eyes and saw nothing but compassion there. And a thousand questions he realised he was going to have to answer.

'She passed away,' he said simply. 'Cancer,' he added by means of explanation. It had been one that had crept up on them a matter of weeks after they'd found out Lily was pregnant. The malignant cells had attacked and reformed into tumours with such ferocity it had completely blindsided them. 'Gestational trophoblastic disease.'

Kiara gasped. It was clear from the expression on her face—and the fact she was a midwife, so probably had encountered similar cases—that there was no need to explain about this particular, quite rare form of cancer.

He gave a few details. The discovery of the cancer. His wife's refusal to have chemotherapy, terrified that the treatment had the potential to compromise their son's welfare. Their disagreement. Their ultimate compromise... She would get treatment as soon as Harry was born. And then, to their horror, the realisation it was far too late.

Lucas knew that his normal voice had been replaced by the strange, automated version of it that had come to him in the days and weeks following the funeral, but he wasn't sure what would happen if he allowed even an ounce of the emotion he was feeling to sneak to the surface.

A little voice rose loud and clear in his subconscious. *You'll bend or break, Lucas. And I know which way I think you'll go.*

His wife had believed he had the power to bend and bounce back. He'd tearfully told her she had more faith in him than he had in himself. That there would be no regrouping from a loss like the one he and Harry were about to endure. The day she'd died he'd felt as if his entire body had been filled with darkness. It would have consumed him if he hadn't had his son. This tiny creature, only a few months old, wholly dependent upon him.

Throughout his explanation Kiara stood solidly, her eyes glued to him as he spoke, her attention unwavering, her hot chocolate untouched. He knew she was there for him. One hundred percent. And, as if her strength of character was physically supporting him, for the first time since he'd lost his wife he spoke freely about what he'd gone through.

He hadn't bounced back. He'd felt as if he'd been cleft in two...one half of him with his wife and the life they were meant to have led, and the other half desperately trying to gain purchase on the life Harry deserved to be living. One in the here and now.

'Truth be told,' he said to Kiara, 'I just never imagined doing anything but breaking into a thousand pieces if a scenario like this one ever arose.'

'What do you mean?' Her brow furrowed in confusion.

'I—' he began, and then backtracked. 'Being out with a woman,' he said. Then, when her response was one difficult-to-read blink, he added, 'You know... Not on a date, but in a situation where people who didn't know we weren't on a date might think we were together.'

'Oh...' Kiara's voice drew the sound out as if the thought had never occurred to her. She let her gaze drift out to the rink, where Harry was, once again, picking himself up off the ice.

Her reaction threw him. It *was* mutual, wasn't it? The attraction they shared? And, to be honest, to him this felt like a date.

A swift, icy-cold spear of panic lanced through him. Had he read this situation entirely incorrectly? Had she genuinely meant that she wanted to give Harry the best Christmas ever and that was where it ended? Perhaps he was the one desperate for a connection and had been dotting 'i's and crossing 't's where there hadn't been any.

Or maybe...

He looked at her. Really looked at her. And saw what he hadn't before. A desire to listen and be there for him but a wariness not to overstep. A nervousness about crossing that line.

To be fair, it was a big ask. To pour his heart out about losing the love of his life to someone with whom he shared a physical and increasingly emotional attraction and expect her to say, *Oh, that's sad...do you want to kiss me?*

Not that Kiara would ever do anything as crass as that, and not that he was even close to ready to be stripping off and jumping in the hay with her except in his dreams, but he'd dreamt a very erotic dream about her. And each time they'd met he'd felt a magnetic energy shift between them on more than one occasion. Including tonight, when he'd pulled her up to stand and been so tempted to keep her mittened hand in his.

And now he was throwing a bucket of ice on what should, by all counts, be a romantic evening.

Was he self-sabotaging?

Or testing himself?

He hadn't cracked into a million tiny shards of glass. Or lost himself in a sea of misery and grief. He hadn't run. Or broken down. Or lashed out at the world around him for the cruelty that was cancer.

Quite the opposite. He was standing in front of a woman he shared an undeniable attraction with. His feet were solidly on the ground. He was, to his astonishment, offering Kiara what he hoped was a smile. It was the least and the most he could offer her at this moment. And he hoped to heaven she could see that.

When she returned his cautious smile, his heart bloomed and began pounding out large, approving thumps against his ribcage.

Maybe he was doing it right. Maybe, after a loss like his, you just took it step by step. One sip of hot chocolate after the next. One walk home under a starry sky with her mittened hand tucked in his.

One first kiss?

He almost stumbled back a step at the thought, then forced himself to regroup. Life was precious. He of all people should know that. It wouldn't just be stupid to crumble at this, the first and probably most important hurdle of his friendship with Kiara. It would be a form of self-sabotage that would serve no purpose.

If he was being truly honest with himself, he knew Lily would've liked her. They weren't peas in a pod. Not by a long shot. But Kiara championed everything he valued and was everything he had sought in a woman when he'd been a young singleton back in med school. Honest. Kind. Infused with strong family values.

Kiara brought a smile to his lips more often than not. His son thought she was on another level. She was incredible at her job. She'd brought more Christmas cheer to her home than he'd seen anywhere in a lifetime of celebrating Christmas.

'And that,' he said, with a weird half-bow he hoped would break the awkwardness of his confession, 'is our origin story. What brought us here to Carey Cove, anyway.'

Kiara pressed her free hand to her mouth, her red-mittened fingers pushing the colour out of her lips. Her cheeks, so recently flushed with pleasure, were now pale. 'I'm so sorry, Lucas. I didn't know.'

He shook his head. 'You're possibly the only one in a ten-mile radius who doesn't.'

'Did you want it to be a secret?'

Her question was a genuine one.

'No,' he answered truthfully. 'It was more that we put ourselves on a path that led forward, you know?'

Kiara shook her head. Unsurprisingly, she was clearly unable to understand his feeble attempt to explain what he'd wanted from the move. He realised this was actually the first time he'd tried to put it into words. He took a sip of his hot chocolate and gave her a smile before refocusing his gaze on his son—the reason behind the move.

'Everyone knew Lily where we were. I guess, rather than having Harry live in the shadow of someone he was never going to meet, I wanted him to live in the light. I thought moving would help us both focus on what we did have. Not on what we didn't.'

He tried to keep his tone light, but it was impossible to keep the rough edges of emotion at bay.

'You two sound as if you were very much in love.'

Tears glistened in Kiara's eyes, and it surprised him to realise his instinct was to dab them away for her. To care for her. And not just as a friend. He wanted something more. He simply didn't know how to make that shift.

He nodded. 'Yes. We were.'

He took the handkerchief which Kiara had balled up in her hand and folded it into a neat triangle with the bit of whipped cream tucked on the inside. He handed it back to her and pointed to her eyes.

'I suppose the main thing I have is that I've known true happiness. So should it ever cross my path again...'

He left the sentence hanging, but when the atmosphere between them threatened to shift into something that felt more intimate than any other silence they'd shared, Kiara asked, 'Did Harry...? I mean, how has he dealt with things?'

Lucas shook his head and gave his jaw a rub. 'He was only a few months old when Lily died, so he doesn't have any memories of her apart from what I've told him.'

His eyes scanned the rink until he found Harry who, in a moment of bravery, had broken away from the chain of youngsters only to end up falling on his bum.

Lucas gave a little laugh. 'That's roughly what it's been like for the pair of us. Falling down. Getting up. Falling down again. Finding a new way to get up. Well...' He shot her a self-effacing smile. 'That's mostly been me. Harry grabs on to all of the happy things in life and runs with them. I'm still learning from him, to be honest.'

'I can't even imagine...'

He could tell from the depth of emotion in her voice that she was feeling his pain as if it was her own. 'Thank you,' he said, meaning it. 'I dare say there are a few things I could learn from you, too.'

Their eyes caught and held. He felt as if he could see straight into her heart then. And what he saw was pure and kind.

'Has moving here helped?' Kiara asked, and her question was weighted with something else. Something personal.

'Yes,' he answered simply, hoping his straightforward answer would help with her unasked question.

Will it help me, too?

'The people at Carey Cove are so kind,' he continued, returning his gaze to his son. 'And, of course, so are the folk up at the cottage hospital. I only worked in one GP surgery before—before we lost Lily—and I feel like I've really landed on my feet here.'

'I'm so glad. I can't even imagine… Especially with Harry being so young.' She made a quick correction. 'I can't imagine going through what you have at any phase of life. Losing someone you clearly loved so very much. I'm guessing that might be why you find celebrations hard? Christmas, anyway…' She gave an awkward laugh. 'Seeing as it's the only time of celebration I've known you.'

He was gripped with an unexpectedly intense desire not only to see Christmas through her eyes, but all celebrations. New Year's Eve, Easter, Valentine's Day…

That last one caught him up short. Was he really feeling this? Attraction and interest in a woman to whom he was explaining about his deceased wife?

'Don't be afraid to let someone else into yours and Harry's lives. And remember to give her flowers.'

Lucas stared at his son for a few concentrated moments, allowing himself to absorb just how easily his son had taken to Kiara in their handful of outings. He leant in close, letting their shoulders brush against one another's, and said, 'Thank you for showing me how special it can be.'

'Pleasure,' she whispered back.

It's all mine, he thought.

Acting on an impulse, he put his arm around her shoulders and pulled her close to him for a hug as they both watched Harry fall once again and then, with an ear-to-ear grin, get back up again and wave to the pair of them as if he'd been doing it all his life.

CHAPTER SIX

'ARE YOU SURE this is all right?' Kiara winced, not wanting to overstep. She held out the flyers so Hazel could take a proper look. Not that they were hard to read even from a distance. She'd made them bright and cheery—Christmas colours, of course—and the font was extra-large.

Mince Pies at Mistletoe Cottage!

She realised it was short notice, but last night, when she hadn't been able to sleep and had been decorating inside her home, she'd decided a mini gala in the form of mulled wine, mince pies and, of course, a huge swag of mistletoe would give the fund she'd been accruing for First Steps an added boost.

'Of course, love.' Hazel dug around in the reception desk drawer for a moment, obviously looking for a couple of drawing pins so that Kiara could put her flyers up on the noticeboard. 'Who doesn't love a mini gala?' Then she gave Kiara a slightly confused look. 'Although, come to think of it, I don't think I know what a mini gala is, so I'll have to go just to satisfy my curiosity. Ah! Here we are.'

Kiara beamed as Hazel handed across a small clear plastic box of pins. They were tiny little Christmas trees! 'Aw...

Thank you. And you do know it's for charity? This definitely isn't for personal gain.'

'I do, love, and let me assure you the enjoyment the villagers are getting from your incredible decorations is—well, it's like nothing Carey Cove has ever experienced before. You're a wonder.'

Kiara flushed and, to her embarrassment, felt the opening prickle of a rush of emotion tease the back of her nose. She swallowed it back, but felt it lodge somewhere between her heart and her throat.

Taking the pins, Kiara quickly turned away and, with a fastidiousness the task didn't really warrant, began to display her flyers.

She was just feeling sensitive this morning. Perhaps a bit *too* sensitive after her night out with Lucas and Harry.

It had been lovely, of course, but finding out about Lucas's wife and seeing first-hand how much he'd loved her had stuck a pin in the elation she usually felt whenever their eyes met. She was positive she hadn't been imagining it—that electric connection she felt each time they looked into one another's eyes—but there was no chance she would be able to find herself any room in a heart that was clearly filled to the brim with love for another woman.

And no chance she would even try.

Elbowing out Harry's mother to make room for herself?

Not a chance.

She'd unwittingly already played that game, and had definitely not come out the winner. She'd spent the past year re-inflating her crushed hopes, dreams, ego...you name it. All of them had been smashed beyond all recognition. The woman she'd rebuilt herself into was someone she liked. But no matter how brave a face she put on she was still fragile. And she certainly didn't want to experience heartache like that ever again. So from here on out she'd wear the firmest of emotional armour when she was around Lucas. She'd keep her heart safe…like Rapunzel in her turret.

As if to prove it to herself, she took a hold of her ponytail and twirled it into a very self-contained bun. *There.* No princes would be climbing up her hair. Not tonight. Not ever.

'Mince pies at Mistletoe Cottage, eh? Sounds like a dream evening. Are father and son duos invited?'

Lucas's warm voice wound its way round her spine like molten caramel. She steadied the wobble in her knees and smiled brightly, hoping her face didn't betray how she was really feeling. 'Yes. Everyone's welcome.'

Lucas's smile stayed put, but he frowned at her comment, the creases in his forehead actively registering the statement she was really making: *You're not a special guest.*

'Ooh! Mince pies at Mistletoe Cottage?' Sophie, her fellow midwife, joined them at the noticeboard. 'Is this for everyone?'

'Absolutely! The more the merrier,' chirped Kiara, and then, remembering how cool she'd just been with Lucas added, 'All for charity.'

Cringe!

'Hey, Lucas…' Sophie's bright blue eyes suddenly widened. 'Are you going to see Santa tonight? You and Harry?'

Lucas looked at Kiara first, as if to double-check that he hadn't forgotten any plans they'd made, then shook his head. 'I hadn't heard Santa Claus was coming to town. I'd better watch out!'

'Ha-ha. Very funny.'

Sophie rolled her eyes and Kiara choked on a genuine laugh. The joke was silly, but funny. To her, anyway. She'd always imagined having a boyfriend who told goofy jokes. Dad jokes, really. And that the boyfriend would become her husband and a father one day.

Despite her best efforts to keep the image at bay, a mental list of the ways in which Lucas was absolutely perfect for her unfurled in her mind like a list of Christmas wishes.

'What about you, Kiara? A bunch of us are going to be there. Want to come?'

'Oh, I…' She looked at Lucas. His expression was quizzical, as if he was looking to her for a read on the situation. She didn't blame him for being confused. Yesterday Kiara would have pounced on the invitation and insisted Harry and Lucas join her. How on earth was he to understand why today Kiara was hesitating?

But, as if reading her mind, Lucas said, 'Harry has had quite a few nights out this week. Perhaps a night off—'

'But it's Santa!'

The words were out before Kiara could stop them. It appeared giving Harry the world's best Christmas experience trumped her own discomfort.

Lucas's smile brightened, the light returning to those grey eyes of his. 'You sure? He might get cranky.'

She pursed her lips. 'Cranky-schmanky. If I can handle women giving birth on a near daily basis, I can handle an overtired little boy. Besides…' she looked to Sophie '…if it's for the little ones, it isn't going to be late, is it?'

Sophie said no, and filled them in on the time and place. A village green about five miles further down the coast. 'So, see you there?' she asked.

'Yes, definitely,' Kiara answered, with a confidence she was trying to get the rest of her body to feel.

Sophie said she was off early, so would meet them there, then went off to the birthing wing where a patient was waiting. Which left Kiara and Lucas standing there on their own.

'You sure you're okay with this?' Lucas asked. 'I don't want to strong-arm you into anything.'

'Yes, of course.' She couldn't let Harry down just because his sexy dad was off-limits. It wasn't fair. And if she'd learnt anything over the past year, it was that happiness came in the smallest of moments. 'I can't wait to see his little face light up when Santa arrives. I wonder how he'll do it. There isn't any snow forecast, so...will he arrive by boat?'

Lucas shrugged, his smile now more relaxed. 'Who knows? We'll all have to wait and see. I'll pick you up after your shift?'

Her resident butterflies lifted and did a few gentle laps of her tummy. 'Sure. Sounds good.' Then, as if to prove to herself he was only a friend, she added, 'See you then, mate.'

If Lucas thought her turn of phrase was peculiar—which it was—he didn't let her see it. Instead, he gave her a little salute and disappeared into the GP surgery.

At which point, she finally let her knees wobble.

It was going to be a long day...and an even longer night.

'Ooh!' Harry was all eyes, and his mouth was a big round O as they took in the scene.

It seemed every village form Carey Cove to Land's End and back again was doing its utmost to celebrate the arrival of Christmas. Even Lucas, who was now happy to admit he'd been Christmas resistant, was feeling a buzz of excitement as more and more children's excited chatter filled the air.

'Daddy. I can't see.'

'Would he like to ride on my shoulders?' Kiara asked, a hint of shyness tinging her voice.

Lucas bent down to pick up his son, hoping to hide his reaction to the walls that seemed to have appeared between them since he'd told Kiara about Lily. He hated it that she felt awkward around him, and wondered if this was what it would be like if he were to proactively go out and start dating.

He checked the thought, and with it felt a new understanding take purchase in his chest. He didn't want to proactively start dating. Downloading apps. Letting the kindly women at the bakery who'd been all but begging him to let them set him up with their daughters organise a few 'chance meetings'.

But he did want to see Kiara. And not as a colleague. Or even as a friend. More as...a possibility.

But he found it impossible to say as much.

'How about we take turns?' he suggested. 'I'll do round one.'

He dipped his head to see if he'd hit the right note and was rewarded with one of those soft smiles of hers. The kind where her teeth skimmed along her bottom lip as if she wasn't going to allow herself a full grin. Feeling as though he was at least heading in the right direction, he popped Harry onto his shoulders so his son could properly ogle the huge throne where Santa would be sitting when he arrived.

Kiara shot him another one of those shy smiles, then shifted her gaze towards the huge tree at the edge of the green, its thick evergreen boughs expertly swirled with festive lights and topped with a sparkling star.

'Have you two got your tree up yet?' she asked.

Lucas's smile turned guilty. 'Not strictly speaking.'

'Are there plans to put one up?'

Again, out of Harry's earshot, he had to confess, 'It's not exactly on my "To Do" list.'

A purposeful look wiped away any shyness she'd been carrying in her features. 'I am afraid I'm going to have to stage an intervention. Three-year-old boys who love Christmas as much as your son does should have a Christmas tree.'

'Oh, no. You've already done so much for—' He stopped himself. 'That would be great. We'd really like that.'

She beamed and gave Harry's foot a tap. 'You all right up there? Not too cold?'

Harry bounced his feet up and down, clapping his hands and singing, 'Happy! Happy!'

Kiara laughed as well, her smile softening into something so pure Lucas felt as though its warmth was physically touching his heart.

He had to admit, Christmas fan or not, he was moved by the way Kiara behaved with his son. Her heart was completely open with him. When Harry laughed about something she joined in completely organically. When he was hurt—as he had been that first day, after their literal run-in—her immediate instinct was to wipe away his tears and bring a smile to his face. To care for him.

The ache in his heart doubled.

He'd never imagined another woman caring for his son as a parent, but here was proof it could be done. With both ease and grace. And perhaps, one day, with love…?

Kiara must've felt his gaze, because she turned to him and said, almost apologetically, 'I'm so grateful that you and Harry are letting me tag along on your Christmas adventures.'

'What?' Her comment was seriously out of left field. 'Not at all! It's us who should be thanking you.'

She scrunched her nose up, clearly unconvinced.

He was about to ask her where all this was coming from, but he thought he knew the answer.

It had come from him.

Even thinking it brought a thousand emotions to the surface. His body felt as if it was being torn in two directions.

This was it. The turning point he'd heard other widowers describe.

The moment when he could choose to devote himself to a familiar but heartbreaking past—or look, at long last, towards a new future.

'You're the one who's making this season special for Harry,' he said. 'For both of us,' he added, a second too late.

She blinked, and her gaze shifted from him to Harry, then back to the hum of human life around them. Families, mostly. He watched an invisible cloak of loneliness wrap around her as she took it all in. Mothers dabbing bits of food off their children's faces or clothes. Fathers doing the same as he was, hoisting their children up onto their shoulders or giving them a piggyback. Older children helping little ones with their mittens or hats.

He knew in that moment that whatever it was that had happened to her in London had stolen this from her. Being part of a family. And, worse, she'd been made to feel ashamed for wanting it. His heart ached for her. He might not have his wife, but he had his son, and the power of that was incalculable.

Could he offer her a cobbled-together version of a family? The thought all but knocked him sideways.

He *really* liked her, and it wasn't just as a new friend and colleague. But he was still brand-new to navigating the world as a single dad. His flirting skills were properly rusty—and there was also the fact that he had no idea what he could promise.

Listen to your heart, you idiot! Life's full of risks.

An epiphany struck. Loving Lily had been one of those risks.

Aren't you happy you loved her when you had the chance? If you hadn't, you wouldn't have Harry.

The voice in his head had a point. But on the flipside... His number one responsibility was Harry. What if he got attached to Kiara? Too attached? And what if things didn't work out? Kiara was obviously trying for a fresh start in life and who knew? Maybe Carey Cove was all well and good for her right now...but would it be always?

Not everything's an 'always'. That doesn't mean it's wise to run away from life. Run to it. You've only got this one chance to be you.

Rather than ignore the voice in his head, Lucas reached out and did what he should have done the other night. What he should be doing right now. He took her hand in his, then gave it a light squeeze. 'I appreciate everything you're doing for me. It's not easy bringing Christmas cheer to a bah-humbugger like me.'

She looked at him, startled, but then, as his words registered, her lips began to twitch with hints of a smile. 'Anyone would be happy to do it,' she countered.

'Rubbish. Harry deserves the best and we got the best.' He saw her smile flicker with pride. 'We wouldn't be having nearly as much fun if you weren't our festive Christmas guide. Would we buddy?'

He looked up at his son, who had been distracted by a loud hum overhead. One that was growing louder by the second.

When he looked back at Kiara, she too was looking up at the sky, but he could feel her fingers lightly pressing into his palm. A calmness came over him. A peace he hadn't expected to feel when he touched another woman in this way.

Suddenly it was as plain as day: Kiara felt the same way about him as he felt about her. There was a shared attraction. But they had both been hurt. Possibly in very different ways. So they'd have to tread carefully. Respectfully.

He returned the gentle squeeze, half tempted to put his arm round her and pull her in close, when all of the sudden a huge searchlight appeared from the ground, illuminating the tell-tale red and white of one of the local Search and Rescue helicopters. The door swung open as the helicopter expertly hovered overhead.

To the crowd's delight, Santa Claus appeared, one foot already stepping onto the guard rail as he hooked himself onto a winch, and then slung an enormous red bag over his shoulder.

'Oh, my *days*! I can't look!'

Lucas and Kiara dropped their linked hands as their colleague Sophie's voice cut into the warm bubble of calm surrounding them. He wasn't sure who had let go of the other first, but it was clear neither of them wanted the rumour mill to include the two of them.

'Everything all right, Sophie?' Kiara put an arm around the other woman's shoulders, the concern in her voice taking the lead.

'No. Seriously…no.' Sophie shaded her eyes and looked down at the ground as the crowd cheered. 'How can they all watch?'

Lucas looked up to see what could be causing her such distress. Santa was being winched down…no surprise there…

'Ooh, I can't look!' Sophie repeated, looking down at the ground and stamping her feet, as if willing herself into another time and place.

'Are you afraid of heights?' Kiara asked, dipping her head so her colleague could see her face.

'Big-time. That Santa's either insane or more intent on spreading good cheer than any other Santa I've ever seen in my life. I mean—' She threw a panicked look at Harry, who had just looked down at her. 'Not that I've met any different Santas. That's Santa. Obviously.' She winced. 'Are you sure you're all right up there, Harry?'

Harry clapped his hands, then pointed up to the sky. 'I want to be up *there*!'

Sophie gave a low moan.

Lucas gave her back a gentle rub. 'You're looking a bit pale, Sophie. Can we get you something?'

'I can take you somewhere to sit down and get you some water if you like,' Kiara offered, throwing Lucas an *Is that all right?* look.

Of course it was. Anything Sophie needed. Poor woman. He had the opposite situation going on. A three-year-old boy bouncing on his shoulders with sheer delight, begging to climb up and meet Santa.

Kiara put a hand on his arm and in a low voice said, 'I'm going to take Sophie away from the crowd for a bit. If we don't catch up at the end of the event, I'll figure out a way to get back to the village on my own.'

'Don't be silly. We wouldn't leave you here.'

Her eyes snapped to his as if he'd said something much more personal. More intimate. And he wondered again what on earth had happened to her back in London to make her so grateful for simple kindnesses.

But maybe they weren't simple. Perhaps those were the moments that should be cherished the most. Fingers brushing. Eyes locking. Heartbeats pounding out the beats as a reminder that you were alive. After all, those few precious moments when their fingers had been interlocked were still buzzing through his bloodstream like a brand-new life force.

Later, after Santa had handed out small gifts to all the children and heard their wishes, then been winched back up to the helicopter to the cheers of the crowd, Kiara found her way to them. She said she'd walked Sophie to her car in the end and, after ensuring she felt well enough to drive, had left her to go home.

Harry fell asleep almost the instant he was buckled into his car seat, the brand-new teddy bear from Santa clutched in his arms.

They drove home in relative silence, and when they stopped at her house—a beacon of Christmas cheer that now instantly brought a smile to his lips because he knew who was behind it—Lucas decided to tell Kiara just how much having her in their lives meant to him.

Just as he began to stumble through some words, Kiara unbuckled her seatbelt and quietly eased herself out of the car with her finger to her lips. She pointed to Harry with a whispered, 'See you in the morning.'

He waited until she got to her front door, and when she waved goodbye and disappeared behind it an emptiness filled him he hadn't expected to feel.

When he got home, and was tucking Harry into bed after their usual night-time story, Harry curled up to him and asked, 'Can Kiara stay here sometimes? I think she'd be good at telling stories, too.'

The question knocked the air out of him. It was an innocent enough question for a child. His little boy could hardly know about Lucas's very adult dream and nor would he. Harry was simply stating a fact: He liked it when they were all together.

He wasn't trying to replace Lily. To be fair to his son, he didn't even remember her enough to miss her. He'd only ever known life with the two of them, and yet he seemed instinctively to know there was something missing in their lives. One more piece to the puzzle they had yet to complete.

Instead of answering—because he simply didn't know how—

Lucas kissed his son's head, wished him sweet dreams and told him to sleep well so they'd be on time to pick Kiara up in the morning.

'But that's hours away!' Harry whined through a yawn. And then, as exhaustion took over, he fell asleep, his new teddy tucked beneath his hand.

A restless sensation took hold of Lucas. He wandered through the house picking things up and putting them down somewhere else, then returning them to their original position. He turned on all the lights. He turned them off. Pulled the curtains shut. Opened the curtains. Rather than seeing the things he had done, he saw all the things he hadn't. There were beds, and sofas, and even a throw cushion or two. But it didn't feel like his child-hood home had done, with designated places for all the furniture to be rearranged to make room for the Christmas tree. The presents. The space where he and his siblings would play with their toys for days after, until his mother, fed up with tripping over train tracks or dolls' houses, finally made them take their shiny new possessions up to their rooms.

It didn't feel like a home at all.

And, although he'd managed to pick up the pieces after Lily's death—raise his son, find a new job, find a new house—he still seemed to be missing one elemental part of himself.

The next morning was a disaster. He and Harry had both slept poorly—to the point when Harry had left his own bed and crawled in with Lucas…something he hadn't done for months. Once sleep had finally come, they'd both slept through the alarm.

Getting themselves together had been chaos. And now Harry was overtired and cranky. Irritable to the point where Lucas wondered if he was coming down with something. At least he was with the childminder today and not at nursery. The calm atmosphere there would do him good.

When they reached Kiara's house, Harry dropped his scooter and ran to the door, demanding that Lucas pick him up so he could reach the bell. After several unanswered ding-dongs they were forced to accept that she wasn't at home, and Harry had a proper meltdown.

There were tears. Wailing. Tiny fists pummelling the artificial snow blanket laid out beneath the dancing penguins. If he hadn't been so tired himself, Lucas might've tried to console his son more than he did. Instead, he knelt down in the 'snow' beside him, rubbing his back and saying on a loop, 'I know, son. I know...'

He wished she was here, too.

After he'd finally managed to soothe Harry, he dropped him off at the childminder, who assured him she'd dole out some extra TLC, and possibly an extra nap today. She also suggested a quiet night at home to counterbalance the excitement of the season. She said it kindly enough, but Lucas knew what she was really saying: *Are you sure you're prioritising your son?*

By the time he'd greeted Hazel at the hospital, taken off his jacket and made himself a cup of tea he thought he had regrouped enough to be as present for his patients as he needed to be. The childminder was right. He'd leapt too far, too soon, with this whole Christmas thing with Kiara. His son was only three. He didn't need all the bells and whistles. Especially when there was confusion. He'd dial it back...maybe get Harry a snow globe or something to tide him over until the big day. And then, one day when Harry was older, they'd set about figuring out how to do Christmas their way. Whatever that was.

But when he opened the door to his surgery, his resolve to face the season on his own disintegrated instantly.

There, on the table, was a tiny living Christmas tree, all decorated, with a small handwritten note that said simply:

A starter tree for the two Wilde men in my life. K x

CHAPTER SEVEN

KIARA SHOWED HER patient the blood pressure gauge. 'WE can do it again if you like, but I think it might stress you out more.' She released the cuff and untagged the Velcro from around the woman's arm. 'It is worth bearing in mind that one fifty-nine over one ten is edging on severely high.'

Audrey Keene gave her arm a rub where the cuff had been and blew out a breath that clearly didn't calm her in the slightest. The poor woman was all nerves.

'Would you like to call your husband?' asked Kiara.

'Can't.' She said briskly. 'He's away until Crimbo.'

'And he's out of touch until then?'

'Oil rigs. His is way out. He can send texts sometimes, but I don't want to tell him this in a text.' She pretended to type on her phone. *'Hey, babe. Your wife and child might be dead by the time you get back. Merry Christmas!'*

'Hey...' Kiara soothed. 'No. We've got this.'

She took the phone out of her patient's hand, put it on the desk, and then took both of Audrey's hands in hers. She looked her straight in the eye. This was her first child, and she was only young. Twenty-three. Having a husband who worked out on the oil rigs most of the year didn't help either.

'There are risks with any pregnancy but being aware of

what's happening with you and the baby is half the battle. You're at the best midwifery centre in the area. And there's a hospital nearby if—'

'Hospital!'

Audrey paled further, and Kiara could actually see her pulse pounding in her throat. Oh, crumbs... Were they were heading for a panic attack?

'We're here now. Look at me, Audrey. Focus on my eyes. Breathe in and out. Nice and slow. That's it. Now, is there anyone else we can ring for you?'

Audrey pressed her lips together, then pushed them out, her face contorting as if she were about to cry. 'I'd really feel happier if my GP was aware of this.'

'Not a problem.' Kiara's heart went out to Audrey. She picked up a pen. 'Just give me the number and I'll give them a ring as soon as we're done.

'I mean...' Audrey squeaked. 'Right now. I think we should tell them right now.'

Kiara and Audrey stared at the blood pressure machine. It was telling both of them the same thing. Audrey's blood pressure was way too high and she was potentially staring down the barrel of pre-eclampsia—something definitely worth avoiding. Professionally, Kiara knew she was spot-on with her diagnosis. And years of experience had taught her that trying to talk a frightened pregnant woman out of something when she was feeling alone and vulnerable was a bad idea.

'Not a problem,' she said again. 'Shall we get a urine sample and take a blood test first?' she suggested. 'That way we can give her a fuller picture of what's going on and—'

Audrey cut her off. 'My GP's a he—not a she.'

'Sorry.' Kiara pressed a hand to her chest. 'My bad. I shouldn't have assumed.'

Her thoughts instantly pinged to Lucas. She wondered, if he had become her GP, would she have wanted to stay with him because he was a good GP, or run for the hills. Because how on earth could she tell him if she had…um…warts, for example? She didn't, but…

Her frown tipped into a smile as it occurred to her that Lucas was a man she could probably say anything to, no matter how embarrassing. He had a way about him. A calmness that assured her she wasn't being judged. Or dismissed. Or being kept in a tiny corner of his life so that he had plenty of room left to lead his real life.

In inviting her to help him steer through Christmas with Harry, he had invited her into the heart of his life, and she knew it had taken a lot of trust for him to do as much. Being with them brought her so much joy… Although maybe leaving the Christmas tree on his desk had been a step too far. There was hanging out together and there was inserting yourself into someone's life far more than they wanted.

Which was how Peter's wife had found out she existed. Kiara had made him a playlist and sent it to his phone. His wife had found it when she'd been going through his messages… The thought mortified her. If she'd been suspicious enough to be going through his phone messages, there was no chance Kiara had been his first affair. It was just too humiliating to think about.

She pushed the thoughts way back into the recesses of her mind and reminded herself that she'd only done the Christmas tree thing as her way of drawing a line in the sand. Or should that be putting a piece of tinsel on the snow?

Either way, whatever she thought had been buzzing between them hadn't been real.

She refocused on the situation at hand. Audrey and her high blood pressure. Pre-eclampsia was no joke, and they needed to get to the bottom of this.

Kiara softened her tone even further and, putting away the blood pressure equipment, said, 'Right, my dear. Are you happy to do bloods today? See if we can get a better picture of what's going on?'

'Um...' Audrey fretted her fingers into a weave, then shook them out as if they had ants on them and began tapping her index fingers against her chin as she spoke. 'Please don't think I'm only second-guessing you. I'm second-guessing everyone. You can't even begin to imagine what I'm putting my husband through. He was just home, and I'm pretty sure I'm the one who drove him back out to the rig. The poor man didn't know whether to buy me pickles or peanut butter or ice cream. No wonder he left!' Tears bloomed in her eyes and her voice lurched up an octave into a wail. 'I'm *impossible* to live with! How is he going to want to live with me when I have the baby?'

'Hey...' Kiara soothed, handing her a tissue as the tears began to fall. 'You're a mass of hormones. Don't give too much weight to the micro-moments. It's the big picture you need to keep in mind.'

It was advice she could do with listening to herself. Whenever she was near Lucas, she, too, was 'a mass of hormones'. A *mess*, more like. Especially as she had to keep reminding herself, *He's not available. His heart is already full and there's no room at the inn for you!*

As a result, teasing reality apart from fantasy after they'd spent the evening together had become her number one pastime. And the number one thing she'd tried not to think about at work. Even so...

She curled one of her hands into the other, feeling her body instinctively pulling up the memory of Lucas taking her hand in his and giving it the lightest of squeezes. It could have meant nothing. It could have been an accident. It could have just been a friendly thank-you. Or it could have meant he was feeling that same electric connection she was every time they were together.

She looked from her hands to Audrey's and realised her patient's hands were trembling. 'Audrey, I'm here for you. I am your midwife and we've got this. We're going to do the tests and sort everything out—all right?'

'No!' Audrey snapped. 'No. It's *not* all right. *Nothing's* going to be all right.' A look came over her face that was almost frightening. 'I can't do this on my own. I never even have the right food in the house. How on earth am I going to grow this baby properly, let alone *have* the baby. What if I die? I might die!'

Audrey was definitely having a panic attack. Kiara wondered if she'd had more than one—hence the high blood pressure.

She got down on her knees in front of Audrey and covered her hands with her own. 'Audrey? Can you look at me please?'

Audrey began to shake her head back and forth, muttering something she couldn't quite make out. Her breathing was coming in short, sharp huffs now.

'Audrey? Audrey... I need you to look at me. We're going to slow down your breathing, otherwise you might get dizzy.'

Audrey kept murmuring the same thing. The words had a familiarity Kiara couldn't quite work out, until all of the sudden she heard it loud and clear: *'Dr Wilde.'*

'Is Dr Wilde your GP? Dr Lucas Wilde?' She had to keep repeating his name, all the while reminding herself that she shouldn't let it taste so sweet on her tongue.

Eventually she got a nod of affirmation out of her patient.

'Would you like to see him?' Kiara asked.

'Yes!' Audrey was all but pleading.

Kiara's body flooded with an energy that didn't know what to do with itself. She had a patient who needed help. From Lucas. The one man in the world Kiara loved to be with but also didn't. Because whenever she was with him her emotions took on a life of their own. One minute they were demanding she give him a Christmas tree. The next they were regretting it because of the ample opportunity to misread the gesture.

Was it friendly? Or over-friendly? An invitation to throw caution to the wind and see what all the crazy frissons buzzing between them were about? Or the total opposite? Which, of course, made a whole other set of feelings burst to the fore. Because whenever she looked into Lucas's eyes she felt something so much more powerful than anything she'd ever felt when she was with Peter. It terrified her—because how would she ever survive another broken heart?

She wouldn't. Not to mention the fact that there wasn't a storage unit large enough for all her Christmas things, let alone the decorations she had yet to buy. And, of course, she'd have to find a new place to live and a new job—which she didn't want because she completely loved it here. And Harry! She couldn't even get started on how she felt about Lucas's son, because just when she thought she'd tapped into the bottom of her emotional well, it became insanely apparent that there were fathoms of emotions yet to go.

'Kiara?' Audrey's expression was a mix of concern and confusion as she continued to fight for breath. 'Do you not like Dr Wilde?'

'No! I mean yes. Of course. Why would you ask that?'

'Your face has gone all funny.'

Kiara's cheeks burned with embarrassment, and she made a heroic effort to refashion her expression into something vaguely approaching professionalism—because her focus shouldn't ever have veered from Audrey.

See? This is why you don't get all gooey over colleagues who aren't available. You take your eyes off the ball and go into a tailspin whenever their names are mentioned.

She gave her spine a sharp wriggle and took hold of Audrey's hand again, all the while lobbing her swirling mass of mixed emotions into the ether. And hopefully beyond.

'Let's call him right now. He's only downstairs.'

She took the phone and coached Audrey through some more steadying breaths as she rang down to Reception.

'Hi, Hazel? Is there any chance you could put me through to Dr Wilde?'

Hazel said she'd just seen him heading to the break room— most likely for a cup of tea. 'Would you like me to fetch him for you, love?'

'Yes, please. And can you tell him it's quite urgent? It's about one of his patients.'

Right. Excellent. That was more like it. Patients first. Totally uncontrollable emotions squished. Job done.

Lucas flew up the stairs, skipping every other one. He had seen enough of Kiara at work to know she would only call for help if she really needed it. But if it was extremely urgent, there were people closer to hand than him.

Hazel hadn't mentioned who the patient was, and he could only guess that the omission meant Kiara was honouring patient confidentiality. Whoever it was, she must be one of his.

The door to her room opened just as he was about to knock.

Kiara's expression was focused and in control. Before she stepped aside, she quickly explained. 'I've got Audrey Keene with me. A discussion about her high blood pressure has escalated. I've been trying to steady her breathing, but she kept requesting you, so I thought I had better defer to the patient's wishes.'

He walked into the room with a nod of thanks as Kiara closed the door behind him.

Seeing her like this, charged with energy and drive, reminded him anew of just how fundamental a response he had to her. It wasn't just Christmas trees and dancing penguins that had drawn them together. It was more visceral than that. They were a match. In good times and, if her expression was anything to go by, in bad.

Before Kiara could say anything else, Audrey began wheezing. Lucas took two long-legged strides and was soon squatting down so that he was at eye level with her. 'Audrey? It's me. Dr Wilde.' To Kiara he said, 'Can you find me a small paper bag?'

She nodded and went straight to the supplies cupboard, returning seconds later with a plain white bag. After she'd handed him the bag, she scribbled something on a bit of paper and held it up out of Audrey's eye line.

Panic attack?

He nodded. Audrey had been prone to them even before she fell pregnant. He was surprised Kiara hadn't noticed the mention of them in her notes. He had definitely made a record of them. Then again, Kiara was new here. Perhaps Audrey had staggered in this way, already mid-flow. Or, more likely, they'd been going through her notes together as Kiara got up to speed and, unfortunately for Audrey, a case of the nerves had leapt to the fore.

'Audrey?' Lucas put a hand on her shoulder, 'It's Dr Wilde,' he repeated. 'Kiara and I are both here to help you. Did you come in this way? Feeling anxious?'

Audrey reached out a hand and gripped his, as if trying to physically channel some of his easy, steady breathing into her own lungs.

In a low, steady voice, Kiara said, 'Audrey came in to see Marnie, not realising she was on maternity leave. She and I came in here to go through her notes and I thought her blood pressure was a bit high.'

'What were the numbers?'

She told him, and in that same, low, steady voice went on, 'Her husband's away working and it doesn't sound like there's anyone else to ring. Do you think it might be something else? Should we run an ECG?'

He shook his head. 'Not just yet. But you're right. We should definitely do some tests before she leaves.' He added some sunshine to his voice and said to Audrey, 'Sometimes we take a little walk when things get too intense—don't we, Audrey?'

She was staring at him, wide-eyed with fear, one hand on her belly, one holding the paper bag to her mouth.

'That's right... Slow and steady... One...two...three...four... And hold for one...two... Excellent.' He sat back on his heels, listening as Audrey's breaths started to come in short staccato bursts again. 'Audrey? Kiara and I are concerned about you and the baby. We're going to breathe with you, okay? All three of us breathing together... One, two, three...'

After a few moments, Kiara shot him a look. It wasn't helping. Their eyes locked, and in the few seconds their gazes held they exchanged a raft of information. These short, sharp exhalations of hers were pushing all the CO_2 out of her body. The absence of CO_2 would make her blood more alkaloid, which would then kick off a domino effect on the metabolism of calcium, which she would feel in her hands, then her feet, and then, unless she could regain control, her heart.

'Shall we see if we can get you up and walking?'

Lucas took one of Audrey's hands in his and wrapped an arm around her shoulders as she pushed herself up and out of the chair with the other hand. He signalled with his eyes that Kiara should take Audrey's other hand, which she did, wrapping an arm around the back of her waist as she did so. Which was just as well, because the moment she rose out of the chair Audrey gave a precarious wobble.

They steadied her as if they were one, exchanging glances and unspoken thoughts as organically as if they'd worked together for years.

'Thank you for the Christmas tree,' he whispered as Audrey regrouped for a moment.

Kiara's eyes lit up in surprise and then softened with pleasure. She gave him a smiley nod but said nothing, pressing her lips tight together as if she was holding his thanks inside herself like a present.

Audrey began to pull at her collar, as if she were trying to get fresh air on herself. Beads of sweat began to present on her forehead.

'Audrey?' Lucas turned his full attention back on to their patient, an idea growing from seeing the gesture. 'Let's get outside in the sunshine, shall we?'

Audrey managed a nod, which was good. It was progress. It meant she was breathing slowly enough to be able to listen.

Lucas began to guide them towards the stairs, anxious that taking the lift might trigger more panic. Their progress was slow. From the looks some of their colleagues were throwing them, Lucas was beginning to wonder if he'd made the right call, but the first thing Audrey did when they finally were outside in the beautifully manicured gardens, lit golden by the winter light, was take a huge, relieved breath. As if it was being indoors that had been the source of her anxiety and nothing more.

Relief flooded through Kiara's features. She wore an expression which no doubt matched his own. It was always a tenuous call—leaving behind the myriad of machines they could hook her up to and the medicines they could give her to calm her down. But he knew Audrey well enough to go with his gut, and it had paid dividends.

He and Kiara pointed out various things in the garden: bright yellow winter jasmine, the colourful cyclamen beds, a low hedge made of orange and red dogwood boughs, glowing with the same colours. There were holly trees weighted with berries. And, of course, a huge evergreen, circled from bottom to top with fairy lights.

'Are you looking forward to Christmas, Audrey?'

Kiara's own excitement shone through, instantly bringing a smile to Lucas's face.

'I love the simplicity of this tree…' she pointed to the towering evergreen '…but I think Dr Wilde can confirm that my love of Christmas is…erm…'

'Not exactly subtle?' Lucas supplied, when Kiara failed to find a description of her glittering love of the festive season.

'Oh. My. Gawd.' Audrey stopped in her tracks, as if the entire panic attack had never happened at all, then threw up her hands and clapped them together as if she'd just discovered Kiara was a rock star. 'Do you live in that adorable cottage that looks as if it's straight out of the North Pole?' she asked.

'Guilty.'

'Why guilty?' Audrey looked at Lucas, as if trying to garner support. 'That place is pure magic! Right? I mean, I'm to-tally right. Magic,' she reiterated, with a stern look at Lucas as if daring him to contest her.

How could he? Kiara's love of Christmas was what had first put them in one another's path, and he had to admit this Christmas season so far had been his best in years—if not ever.

Lucas and Kiara shared a smile as Audrey began a long, de-tailed explanation of how much she adored Mistletoe Cottage, and how she'd been making sure to walk past it every day since the first set of decorations had gone up. It reminded her of her love of Christmas as a young girl, and she'd been hoping that whoever lived there would decorate it that way for ever, so she could walk her baby past, and then her toddler, and then hope-fully, because of Mistletoe Cottage, her baby would love Christmas as much as she did.

Suddenly aware that she'd been gabbling on, she clapped her fingers to her mouth, pressing a giggle into submission. 'I'm sorry. I didn't— Hey!' She widened her hands and grinned at the pair of them. 'The panic attack is gone! Your Christmas cottage cured me!'

Laughing, the three of them headed back into the warmth of the hospital. Lucas noted that a swag of mistletoe had ap-peared in the doorway to the staff lounge as they made their way to Kiara's room.

'I'm happy to stay while Kiara takes your bloods and other stats,' Lucas began, but Audrey stopped him.

'I'm good. Kiara and I need to discuss the merits of seasonal glitter balls.'

'And you'll make sure to ring one of us if you ever feel pan-icky again?' he asked.

'Better than that!' Audrey beamed. 'I'm going to take my-self on a walk to Mistletoe Cottage next time. How could I not relax, looking at all of that joy?'

Kiara grinned at him as she pumped up the blood pressure

gauge, and to their collective delight he saw that it was significantly lower than it had been the first-time round.

Lucas headed to the door, but before leaving he ducked his head back in and asked Kiara, 'Hot chocolate later?'

She scrunched her nose. 'I can't.' She threw a look at Audrey, then explained, 'I'm having an open house tomorrow night.'

'Oh, yes. Of course. Harry ensured I put that on the calendar.' He was about to offer to help, but as Audrey was there decided now wasn't the time.

He gave her a wave goodbye just as Kiara was explaining to Audrey about the charity she was collecting money for, and then he heard Audrey's squeals of delight as Kiara started telling her about her festive cushion collection.

He hadn't realised how broadly he was smiling until he passed the main desk, where once again Nya was giving him that mischievous smile of hers. Rather than look bewildered, as he had before, this time he gave her a jaunty salute and danced what he hoped looked like a small but carefree Christmas jig.

CHAPTER EIGHT

MINCE PIES?

There were scores of the star-topped, sugar-dusted beauties, fresh out of the oven, covering every platter and plate Kiara owned.

Mulled wine?

Gallons of it. The warm, enticing scent of cinnamon, cloves and allspice was almost literally wrapping her house in an extra layer of magic.

She had even warmed up some apple juice as well, and lightly spiced it with cinnamon. And she'd made gingerbread men and put out bowls of nibbles just in case anyone happened to stay into the early evening.

She'd also put up countless more baubles, but…

She went outside to look at her cottage with fresh eyes. It was all there. The dancing penguins. The snowman and his pals. Stars. Candy canes. Huge gingerbread men. Even Santa was up there on her roof now, courtesy of the man who'd come to adjust her television aerial the other day. And a few elves.

The decorative trees in her front garden had twirls of lights on them, as did all of the super-sized candy canes and the wicker reindeer. There were moving light displays too, that made it look as if the house was being softly blanketed by huge, decorative snowflakes. And there were fairy light angels who, when a button was pressed, sang Christmas carols. There were super-sized 'presents' and glittery bell baubles.

Every single Christmas decoration she could think of.

She had set up several fake gingerbread houses, which were actually coin collectors, at the front gate, by her front door and on the kitchen counter, all with pamphlets explaining about First Steps and why it was such a great charity. She'd already managed to collect an impressive amount of money in her little Santa's workshop donation box, and was hoping today would put her at her target goal.

But still there was something missing. And she didn't have a clue what it was.

Night fell early this time of year...in the afternoon, actually. And she had taken the day off especially to make sure her open house was truly open to the public by the time schools let out. She knew Harry and Lucas wouldn't be coming until later, but from the moment people started arriving—first in trickles, then in a steady flow—she simply couldn't stop scanning the crowd, looking for that tidily cropped head of brown hair attached to a man she knew she really shouldn't be falling for but, against her better judgement, had already fallen for.

'Kiara!'

Before she could register who had said her name, Kiara was being wrapped in the arms of a definitely pregnant woman. She realised it was Audrey, her patient from yesterday. She looked an entirely changed woman. Her dark hair was twisted up underneath an adorable knitted cap in green and white stripes with a line of reindeer knitted along the base and a huge gold bauble on top. Her cheeks glowed with health and her eyes were sparkling bright. But it was her smile that was the best thing to see.

Still holding on to one another's arms, they pulled back and grinned at one another. 'You look amazing,' they both said at the same time, then laughed.

More seriously, Kiara asked, 'Are you feeling all right?'

'Much better.' Audrey's voice was ripe with gratitude, and once again she pulled Kiara in for a hug. 'I can't thank you enough for everything you and Dr Wilde did for me.'

'Uh-oh! What have I done now?'

Lucas's buttery voice swept with warm caramelly magic down Kiara's spine, swirling and dreamily pooling in her tummy, where... Yes, there they were...the Christmas butterflies had taken flight.

Their eyes connected and that increasingly familiar buzz swept through her, as if a thousand fireflies were heralding the arrival of her soulmate.

Which, of course, was completely ridiculous.

He'd loved his wife. Who he couldn't be with any more. So he would not love another woman. No matter how right it felt when they were together.

Lucas's lips parted, his expression soft, as if he, too, was going through a similar internal checklist.

I like her, but I don't love her. I can't love her.

Before he could say anything, Lucas was being wrapped in one of Audrey's heartfelt bear hugs.

'Kiara!' Harry appeared from around the other side of the picket fence and dropped his scooter, running and jumping up into her arms as if he'd done it a thousand times. He was wearing a knitted beanie that looked like a gingerbread man, his blond curls peeking out from beneath the hat and a bright red yarn bobble topping it all off. He looked adorable. And so, so lovable. She hugged him close, cherishing his little boy scent. She didn't care what the nursery rhymes said. This little boy smelt of sugar and spice and everything nice.

'Daddy!'

Kiara looked up to see that Lucas was standing in front of them, holding out his arms for his little boy.

'Here. I'll take him.' He was smiling, and his expression was kind, but there was something about the gesture that cut her to the quick. It was as if he was reminding her that Harry wasn't hers to love. Not in the way a mother would. Just like her ex's wife had.

'You think you can have what we have? A family? You'll never have a family. You'll never know this kind of love.'

Lucas's brow crinkled and he stepped in closer. 'He's a bit heavy for you, isn't he?' He angled his head to try and meet her gaze. 'Kiara...?'

The movement, his proximity and the scent of him—juniper and pine—jarred her into action. 'Yes. Of course. You're right. I tell everyone I need to build up my upper body strength. Ha-ha! You'd think carrying babies around all day would do the trick, but nope!' She handed Harry over and gave her bicep a little squeeze. 'Nothing there but flimsy noodles! Protein...' She tapped the side of her nose in an attempt at a wise gesture. 'I have it on good authority that I should eat more protein.'

Oh, God. If the earth could open up and swallow her whole right now, she'd be nothing but grateful.

Lucas shifted Harry onto his hip and gave one of his little boy's hands a kiss before giving her a slightly perplexed smile. 'You don't need to change a thing, Kiara.' Lucas seemed genuinely confused by her peculiar monologue. 'You're perfect as you are.'

What? He thought she was perfect? No one in the history of her entire life had ever called her anything close to perfect. Did that mean—

Lucas made his voice bright and childish as he gave Harry's hand a jiggle. 'Isn't she Harry? We wouldn't want our new friend any other way.'

'Happy...happy!' sing-songed Harry.

Of course. Perfect as a friend. Well, that was her solidly placed in the Friend Zone.

A sinkhole clearly wasn't going to help her out here. Panic began to grip her chest in the same way she'd seen it take hold of Audrey yesterday. But this was not the time or place to have any sort of meltdown.

Having her emotions split into a kaleidoscope of conflicting emotions by a man who had unwittingly swept into her heart and made her feel whole again was a brand-new level of heartache she wished she didn't know existed.

'Um… Mince pies.' She pointed randomly over her shoulder and then said, 'Apple juice,' before quickly excusing herself, refusing to register the bewildered expression playing across Lucas's face as she turned away and quickly absorbed herself into the crowd.

An hour later, as the crowd began to clear, Lucas appeared in front of her with a broom and dustpan and a very sleepy Harry at his side. 'I thought maybe we could help you clean up.' Harry unleashed a huge, unprotected yawn. Lucas gave him a fond look. 'And by "we" I mean me. Any chance I could put this guy in the spare room for a nap?'

'Oh, gosh…' She pulled a face. 'You don't have to stay and help. That's ever so kind—'

Lucas held up a hand. 'It's the least we can do after all the joy you've brought us.'

Harry leant against his father's leg and wrapped his arms around it, looking as if he might fall asleep on the spot. The complication of emotions she'd felt earlier suddenly lost their relevance. How could they be relevant when Harry so clearly needed to be sleeping? Besides… Even though adrenaline was still running through her from an evening spent mostly trying to avoid Lucas, she had to admit an extra set of hands to help with the clearing up would be genuinely useful.

They cleaned the place as if they had been doing it together for years. Intuitively knowing when the other person needed a hand or when it would be all right to head off to another room and tidy up there.

'Gosh!' Kiara looked around her living room with a smile. 'It looks as good as new.'

She smiled at Lucas, who was standing by her wood basket. He was so handsome. So kind. It tore at her heart that she had found someone so perfect to love and yet her love was so destined to be unrequited. A loneliness crept into her bones. She didn't want to give it space, but despite her best efforts to push it away she shivered.

'Shall I pop a couple of logs on the fire?' Lucas asked.

'That'd be nice. Kiara smiled in gratitude and then, suddenly wanting more than anything not to have this moment end, blurted, 'You wouldn't want to stay for a quiet glass of wine and a final mince pie, would you? Something to fortify you before carrying that son of yours home.'

What the *hell*? Had she gone *mad*?

The good fairy on her shoulder—the responsible one—was looking at her as if she'd just grown an extra head. Women who'd had their hearts crushed by one married man did not invite emotionally unavailable sexy dads to stay and drink wine on their sofa with them.

That naughty fairy—the one who was greedy and wanted to spend just a few quiet moments with Lucas before she officially called the evening to a close—didn't think there'd be much harm in just one more glass of mulled wine by the fire, with only the twinkling lights of the tree lighting up the room...

The good fairy prepared herself to stage an intervention.

'That sounds like a great idea.'

Lucas was already putting logs on the fire, and from this angle she had a really good view of his very pinchable bum.

He turned back and smiled at her. 'Thoughtful of you to give Harry some extra sleeping time.'

Ha! Yes. Totally *not* what she'd been thinking. But she made a vague noise, indicating that that had definitely been her intention.

She was going to make a joke about trying to lift a sleeping Harry and failing, but thought better of it. Rehashing her more humiliating moments in front of the man she wished she could love was an exercise in self-defeatism she didn't need to subject herself to.

She bustled around a bit, until finally presenting Lucas with a plate laden with mince pies, some cheese and crackers, as well as the promised glass of wine.

He noticed she was now empty-handed. 'You're not having anything?' he asked.

Unlike the first time her ex, Peter, had taken her to the pub, and she'd agreed not only to a second but a third glass of wine, this evening the imaginary good fairy had proactively taken her by the shoulders and shaken her when she'd pulled a second glass from the cupboard just now. Tipsy and besotted were not a good combination. Not for her. Not at any time of year. But especially not at Christmas. And super-especially not with Lucas Wilde sitting on her sofa looking like the Christmas card of her dreams.

She shook her head. 'I have enough Christmas cheer running though me already.' She pointed back at the kitchen, where the kettle was coming to a boil. 'I'm on the herbal tea now. Christmas spice.'

She waggled her hands and Lucas laughed.

'Leave it to you to find Christmas tea. What is it? Gingerbread-flavoured?'

'Close!' Her voice matched his playful tone, and despite her effort to keep herself in the Friend Zone she heard herself walking a fine line between fun and flirtation. 'Spiced apple.'

'Sounds good.' He rubbed his tummy.

And, as ridiculous as it was, she loved the homeliness of the gesture. It was so Papa Bear.

To stop herself from throwing herself at him, ripping his shirt off and begging him to tell her if his emotional landscape was as tumultuous and horny as hers, she went back to the kitchen and stuffed her head in the freezer for a count of ten deep breaths.

But even that didn't work. As she prepared her tea, and a small plate of snacks, she let an image of the two of them as a couple slip into her mind. Right here in Mistletoe Cottage. It was still decorated for Christmas, but maybe not quite to the level she'd done it this year. They'd have just had a dinner party, maybe. Or, like tonight, a neighbourhood open house, ripe with laughter and community spirit. They'd be keeping their voices low as Harry slept, aware of his building excitement for Christmas. Come Christmas Eve they'd be hanging three stockings by the chimney with care. Laying out surprise Christmas presents. Curling up on the sofa together...

She balled her hands into fists and mentally tried to knock some sense back into her head. Being with Lucas wasn't her reality, and it definitely wouldn't be her future.

'You're the one who invited him to stay, but it isn't your fault he said yes and then looked all sexy and desirable,' said the naughty fairy.

'You're the one who will sit at the opposite end of the sofa and eat mince pies with him and talk about the joys of getting urine samples...then stand as far away as possible as you wave him off when he and his son go back to their own home. Their real home,' said the sensible fairy.

'That plan is stupid,' said the naughty fairy, pouting.

'Everything all right?'

Lucas was at the doorway, concern creasing his features as he took in the mad vision of Kiara clutching her head. And very possibly talking to herself.

'Good! Fine! I—' she began, and then, hoping her parents wouldn't mind, she covered the moment with a half-truth. 'Just missing my family, that's all.'

Lucas pressed one of his hands to his chest in a gesture of undiluted empathy. 'I hear you... It can really hit you out of the blue this time of year, can't it?'

She nodded, grateful that he understood. And doubly grateful that they now had a sort of neutral topic to discuss. One that wasn't about the two of them, anyway.

Lucas crossed over to her and picked up her plate, the gentle waft of his man scent obliterating anything the sensible fairy had suggested from what was left of her brain.

'C'mon. Grab your tea and let's get you settled on the sofa for a well-deserved break.'

When he turned his back to lead the way into the living room, Kiara feigned a swoon. How could someone so perfect be so far out of reach?

Because he's not meant to be yours. So suck it up and eat a mince pie.

Kiara settled on the sofa, popping a Santa face cushion on her lap to stand in as a table. When she looked up to find him looking at her, a rush of shyness swept through her. They'd never sat like this before and just…talked. There was always some sort of festive buzz happening around them. Or work things. It didn't surprise her, though, to realise that it felt as natural as if they'd been doing it for years.

'Does your family do a big Christmas?' she asked, after a few moments of contented munching.

Lucas shook his head. 'Not so much these days.'

Kiara nodded, more interested in what he wasn't saying than what he was. 'Is that recent?'

He gave a forlorn huff of a laugh. 'If you mean is it since Lily died? No. It was before that. I guess the Wilde family were never really wild about Christmas.' He quirked an eyebrow at her. 'See what I did there?' He waved off his silly pun, then explained more seriously, 'My parents retired to France a few years ago, and my sisters go there for Christmas. Lily's parents took to going on cruises once the children had flown the coop, and I was usually working right up until "the big day", so I never made too much of an effort to get down to France. And once the little guy was born… I guess it was just another excuse to stay put. Sort things out as best we could.'

Kiara frowned. 'Do you all get on? Your families?' She shook her head. 'Sorry… That's quite a personal question.'

'Oh, yes we do.' His response was genuine. 'Seriously, I didn't mean to give you any "crazy family" vibes. I suppose we're more significant birthday types than Christmas types, that's all.' He leant forward to give her knee a tap and his smile warmed. 'I think this is the first year I can genuinely say I have been properly infused with the Christmas spirit.'

Despite her silent warning to herself that this was just a friendly chat, she blushed, flattered to the core by the compliment. And then the rush of feelings she'd been trying to keep at bay swept in and filled her body with a warm glow she never wanted to shake.

And why should she?

Here she was, on the sofa with a man she admired and was stupidly attracted to. His son was sleeping peacefully in the spare room. A fire was crackling away. There was wine and herbal tea and snacks, and the energy of a genuinely gorgeous evening all around them, but…

Sensible fairy piped up. *'Your heart will be broken in the end, Kiara. Pull the plug now.'*

'Are you happy here?' Lucas asked.

He'd thought she must be, but there was something that was suddenly missing in that soft smile of hers. *Her eyes*, it occurred to him. *The light hasn't reached her eyes.*

She thought for a moment before she answered, and when she did her voice was steady, but it bore an undercurrent of emotion that lifted and rose into her cheeks. 'I love my house.' She grinned and put her hands out, as if she were a model in a showroom. 'I also love my job and my colleagues,' she said in a more heartfelt manner, and then, as if realising he was one of her colleagues, she looked away and sighed.

'What?'

He tipped his head to one side and looked at her. Really looked at her. She was such a beautiful woman. Sitting here in the glow of the firelight, with the lights from outside the window providing a soft fairy lit warmth around her. It was a reflection on her overall aura. She was a kind woman whose personality instantly drew people to her. She'd lived here less than a month and already she had the entire village eating out of her hand. In contrast, he'd come into town under the radar. On purpose.

Everyone loved Mistletoe Cottage and its dazzling decor. And the fact that she was doing it all for charity. They loved *her*. But he could see now, in this moment of vulnerability, that she wasn't as brave as she seemed. Nor as happy. And that cut him to the quick. This was a woman whose heart was so generous, so empathetic. She deserved all the happiness she desired, and yet something was keeping her from attaining it.

A need gripped him to do anything he could to help. 'There's something missing, though, isn't there?' he asked. 'Is it your family? The distance from London?'

She shook her head, her smile tinged with melancholy. 'No. I love my parents, but I moved out of their house years ago, so we're used to living our independent lives. Although we talk all the time. No, it's more...' She picked at the tufty white beard sown onto her Santa cushion and then gave an embarrassed smile. 'It's more they thought I'd be married by now. Having children. Setting up house. The whole nine yards, as they say.'

'And you? Is that what you thought?'

She met his gaze. 'I thought so as well.'

There was something about the way she said it that suggested she'd been on track for exactly that, but it had been stolen from her. 'Was there someone specific you thought you'd be married to?' he asked.

She turned crimson.

He was feeling the heat of the question as well. It wasn't his business, and he wasn't even certain he wanted to know the answer. The idea of Kiara, dressed as a bride, walking down the aisle towards someone who—well, someone else, tugged at a part of him that hadn't seen oxygen in years.

She took a sip of her tea and then, as if having made a decision, set it down and looked him square in the eye. 'I did have a boyfriend. We were together for three years.'

'Sounds serious...' Lucas took a sip of wine and then put it to one side. He didn't want to get tipsy listening to this story. He wanted to be as present for her as she had been for him when he'd told her about Lily.

She nodded in acknowledgement of his comment, then continued in a way that suggested she hadn't talked about this in a while—if ever. As if she needed to get it out quickly…as if letting the words loiter in her body for a moment longer than necessary would cause her physical pain.

'He worked at the same hospital as me. He was—is—a surgeon.'

Her brow crinkled, as if remembering caused her pain. Lucas wanted to reach out to her, comfort her, but he knew this was a story she needed to tell from the safe nook of her sofa, with her cushion taking the blows as her fingers clenched and unclenched against it.

'We flirted at work, and that led to drinks afterwards, which led to…other things. And soon enough we were an item. Our schedules were always busy, so it was a bit haphazard as far as a traditional courtship goes. I'm sure you can imagine…'

Her eyes flicked to him, as if hoping for an acknowledgement but not a judgement, so he nodded. He understood. Surgeons worked mad hours, as did midwives. Babies didn't keep to a nine-to-five schedule.

'Anyway…' she continued. 'We did some of the normal boyfriend-girlfriend stuff. Dinner dates. He met my friends. He met my parents. They thought he was brilliant. My mother kept saying things like, "Our daughter…marrying a surgeon!"' She pulled a face, as if to say they'd been as deluded as she had.

Lucas felt ire raise in him. Whoever the hell this guy was, he certainly hadn't deserved Kiara. And no way did she deserve to hold this amount of pain and, if he wasn't mistaken, shame.

'We had weekends away and so on. But we never spent Christmas together. Last Christmas I asked him—*again*—if maybe this year we'd be spending Christmas together, and again he put off making a final decision. Later that night my phone rang.' Saying the words seemed physically painful for her. 'It was his wife.'

She paused for effect, but he could see tears bloom in her eyes. He ached to go to her. Move in close and wipe them away and curse this creep of a man who'd led her on. It was cruel, what he'd done to her.

Kiara's face was pure anguish as a solitary tear trickled down her cheek. 'I had no idea. If I'd had even the slightest of clues that he was married...'

She couldn't finish the sentence, succumbing to long-held-off sobs.

Lucas no longer checked his instincts. He moved across the sofa and held her close to him. He didn't offer trite words of consolation that wouldn't mean anything. Instead he just let her cry, expel the grief that she'd so clearly held inside.

Eventually, when the tears had gone, she pulled back and said, 'The worst part is, my parents don't even know.'

'What? Why not?'

'I was too ashamed.' She buried her head in her hands, then peeked out between her fingers. 'I was too humiliated to tell them that the man I'd been so cock-a-hoop for was a liar. Not to mention his poor family. I mean—he has *children*!' Her eyes flicked to the corridor which led to the room where Harry was sleeping.

Lucas's heart slammed against his ribcage. He felt humbled and moved that she should be thinking of others before herself when she had been so very wronged.

'He was a con man,' Lucas said indignantly. 'He took advantage of you. He was only thinking of himself. No one else. You can't possibly blame yourself for his selfish, heartless inconsideration.'

Kiara dropped her hands from her face, tears still glittering in her eyes. 'I just feel so stupid, you know...? Those first few months after we broke up I went over and over everything, trying to figure out if there had been signs. Things I should have noticed. Like him not ever wanting to share Christmas with me.' She huffed out a laugh that—incredibly—wasn't embittered.

His heart went out to her. 'A man like that—' he began, and then stopped himself. Slandering someone he didn't know wasn't the point. Ensuring Kiara knew that this wasn't her fault and that she should not carry one ounce of the burden of guilt was. 'You are not to blame. He presented himself as a man who was available.'

Kiara cringed. 'But seriously… After three Christmases, when he knew how much I loved Christmas, why wasn't I able to figure it out?'

Lucas thought of the last two years, when he hadn't been able to see the joy in the festive season no matter how much he had tried to talk himself into a bit of Christmas cheer. In little more than the blink of an eye Kiara had effortlessly all but transformed it for both him and Harry. She'd made this season that he found so troubling a time of generosity and joy. It was fun! She was a woman who should be made to feel amazing for the happiness she brought to people. And, of course, at work she brought calm. She was a rare breed of woman, and it killed him that someone had made her feel otherwise.

'You're a good person, Kiara. You didn't deserve to be treated like that.'

She blinked up at him, her lashes stained pitch-black with spilt tears. 'Thank you for not judging me.'

'Of course not,' he whispered. 'It wasn't even an option. Listen…' He took her hands in his and rubbed his thumbs along the back of them. 'You're one of the most extraordinary women I have ever met. If it were two hundred years ago I would definitely be threatening a duel with this scoundrel!'

His bravura won a smile and a hiccoughing laugh from her, which melted his heart even more. He liked being the man who'd brought that smile to her lips. His eyes dropped to her mouth and remained on it. She looked down, then back up at him. The atmosphere between them shifted in that instant. Energy surged from the pair of them and met in the ever-decreasing space between them.

He became acutely aware of her presence in his arms. The fabric of her Christmas jumper...the curve of her arm beneath it. The shift of her shoulder blades. The cadence of her pulse. He felt her as she presented to him: as a woman.

He'd often wondered about this moment. The one where he'd take a step away from his past and towards a different future. One he had never entirely been able to imagine. But maybe that was what life would be like with Kiara. One welcome surprise after the other.

Though his pulse had quickened, and his body had begun to feel heat travelling in darts of approbation to areas that hadn't been lit up for a long time, the moment also felt perfectly natural. It was as if she had belonged here in his arms all along, but that they'd each needed to follow the paths life had put them on to eventually guide them to one another.

Sweeping aside a few strands of hair that had stuck to her tear-streaked face, Lucas closed the space between them, feeling their shared energy come to fruition in an explosion of heat as their lips connected in a long-awaited kiss.

CHAPTER NINE

KIARA DIDN'T KNOW if she was in heaven, on earth, or in some magical place in between. Wherever it was, she didn't want to leave.

This was the stuff of fantasy.

A glittering Christmas tree. A heartfelt, meaningful talk with a man she was not only attracted to, but whom she respected. A man who not only refused to pass judgement, but who openly wanted to champion her. To kiss her!

The moment his lips touched hers she felt as if the final piece of the year-long puzzle she'd been piecing together had been completed. Cornwall plus Carey Cove plus Lucas was everything she'd ever wanted.

'You all right?' Lucas whispered against her lips.

'Mmm…' was all she managed.

Kissing Lucas was like finding herself anew. There was no comparing him to any other. Nor being drawn back to a time and place where she'd been in another man's arms. A man who had made her feel the very worst kind of humiliation. She'd thought she would panic if a man ever tried to kiss her again, but Lucas's kind words had served as a balm to the thoughts that had kept her up more nights than she cared to acknowledge.

The pain of discovery and subsequent fall-out had taken a

physical toll on her. She hadn't realised how fragile she'd felt, starting this new existence. How much courage it had taken to sell up, find a new job, move across the country and start again...and not in a mild, self-recriminating way. In a way that announced who she was and how she wanted to live her life. And, against the odds, it had led her to Lucas. A man who had borne his own heartache and, if his tender touch was anything to go by, who was also looking for a foothold on a new future.

A shiver of delight whispered down her neck when Lucas traced his finger-pads along her cheeks as if he had mandated himself with a mission: to explore her, inch by careful inch.

'You're so beautiful,' he murmured as he ducked his head to the soft crook between her ear and her chin, dropping velvety kisses along her neck.

Her body absorbed his attention like sunlight. His finger-tips traced her jawline, the backs of his palms brushed the fine hairs of her cheek and his soft stubble grazed her delicate skin as his lips touched, explored, tasted...

But each time she tried to take the reins, return the exquisitely detailed attentions he was giving her, he'd murmur, 'No. Me first. I want to know everything about you.'

It was a level of care she hadn't realised she'd hungered for. As if being cherished was an essential nutrient she'd not known she'd been missing all along. Vitamin Lucas.

No. Not even that was right.

He didn't complete her. He made her life better. And that was the key difference. Another person didn't make you whole... they admired you for everything you were and didn't hold you to ransom for the things you weren't.

The nanosecond of dark thought she'd permitted to enter her system must have translated into hesitation to him. He pulled back, his expression wreathed in concern. 'Are you sure this is all right?'

It was more than all right. It was soul-quenchingly delicious.

'Yes,' she said, cupping his cheeks in her hands and looking him straight in the eye. 'More than.'

'Good.' He pulled her to him and drew a long, luxurious kiss from her. The kind that made time irrelevant.

'And you're okay?' she asked, when a natural pause introduced itself.

It was important to her to check. This was as much a first for Lucas as it was for her. Just as importantly, Lucas didn't just have himself to think about. He also had to consider his son, sound asleep in her guest room.

'I'm okay,' Lucas assured her, running his fingers through her hair and down her back.

The sensation was both new and familiar all at once. As if he'd been doing it for years and might for years yet to come.

'Better than okay.' His smile was warm. Genuine. 'Best Christmas party I've ever been to.'

This time his smile was wicked. The lights reflected in those grey eyes of his glimmered with something more heated than she'd seen there before.

If someone had told her she was made of starlight and fairy dust right now she would have believed them.

Her response to Lucas went beyond the elemental aspects of their very obvious chemistry. He *appreciated* her. And, more importantly, he wanted to make sure she knew it. Not to make her feel lucky that she'd been graced with his presence, as her ex had. She refused to allow herself to feel that shame again, even as she recalled how desperate she'd been for his attention. How grateful she'd felt when he'd deigned to shine his light on her. She saw it clear as day now. Her ex had been an arrogant, self-serving, egocentric jerk. His pleasure hadn't been to make her happy. His pleasure had been to hold power over her and his wife. Doling out his attentions as if they were fine gifts.

She felt a shift in her body chemistry as Lucas pulled her closer into his arms. *This* was genuine affection. This was what being cared for felt like. This was what she had wanted all along.

She untangled her limbs from his and, when he protested, put her index finger on his lips and said, 'My turn.'

She was smaller than him, so arranging herself on his lap so that her legs wrapped around him was not a problem. When she wriggled her hips and bottom into place her lips twitched with delight as Lucas gave a low moan of satisfaction. She reached for the top button of his shirt, desperate to feel her skin on his. He caught her hand in his, giving the back of it a kiss as his eyes darted to the corridor.

'Is there somewhere more private?' he asked.

The implication of his question exploded in her like lava. He wanted more.

She rose from the sofa and held her hand out to him. 'Follow me.'

Lucas felt more alive than he had in years. As if he could pinpoint each cell in his body and tell it where to direct its focus. His energy levels were soaring, as if they were absorbing the hyper-real sensations coursing through his bloodstream.

It was, he realised, the power of two.

Two hearts. Two minds. Two people attracted to one another on multiple levels.

Sight. Sound. Touch. All his sensory capabilities were focused on one thing: Kiara.

Holding her in his arms without a stitch of fabric between them was on another level. As if he'd never touched warm, soft skin before.

Being with her was nothing like what he'd thought making love to someone who wasn't Lily would feel. Truth be told, he'd not let himself consciously consider being intimate with another woman. But, courtesy of his deeply erotic dream, being with Kiara felt more natural than he could have imagined. As if the dream had somehow prepared him for this different realm of pleasure with a woman.

There was no point in comparing, he'd realised, as slowly

and purposefully they had taken one another's clothes off. They were both adults. People with pasts. With experience. And yet… this felt brand-new. As if the slate hadn't been washed clean, exactly—their histories would always be a part of them—but more as if one chapter had ended and another had begun.

He groaned in equal measures of loss and pleasure as Kiara pulled away from him, then made it clear it wouldn't be for long. She twirled her finger, indicating he should lie on his back, then slowly walked to the end of the bed where she stood, her brown eyes scanning the length of him as if he were a Christmas present she'd never imagined receiving.

She climbed onto the mattress on all fours, hovering over his legs and then, tantalisingly, his midsection. He was leaving her in no doubt that he desired her. She bent at the elbows, her breasts brushing the length of his chest as she swept her body along his, eventually lowering her lips to his for a hot, succulent kiss that magnetically arched their bodies against one another.

If the beginning of this chapter was anything to go by, he never wanted it to end.

Kiara pulled back a little…just enough so that the feather-soft warmth between her legs slid along the length of his erection. She was ready for him. If she wanted him.

Her eyes met his, as if asking him the same question, and there was only one answer. Yes. A thousand times yes. He wanted her as much as she seemed to want him.

She pushed herself up, her hands reaching for his. Their fingers wove together as the tip of his shaft met the heat of her feminine essence. The contact shot flames through him. It wasn't the length of time between now and the last time he'd made love…it was the intensity of the sensation, incinerating everything he'd used to be and rebuilding him into this new version of himself. He felt desired in a way he'd never known before. Cared-for. Appreciated fully for the man he was today.

It was an extraordinary feeling. Knowing he was made of so many elements different from the person he'd once been awed him. And that he was sharing it with this woman—this beautiful, kind, incredible woman—was as humbling as it was empowering. He came with baggage. A lot of it. But today he felt as if he could handle it all. The past, the present and, more importantly, the future.

Time took on an otherworldly type of energy. The air around them was charged with more than oxygen. There was hunger... and need. And yet there wasn't any urgency about it. No voraciousness. There was a softness to their movements. A smouldering, slow burn shared between two people who wanted one another but felt no crush of pressure to do everything all at once. As if hurrying things would take away from the intensity of each touch and caress they shared.

After a delectation of time, they seamlessly moved and shifted into place, teasing and pleasuring each other to the point that he had a physical need to feel himself inside her. He confessed to not having any protection. She whispered that she was on the pill.

They exchanged a look. One charged with purpose and intent. Heated by desire. But their decision to go forward was a deliberate one, and that made the emotional impact of it even larger. He wanted her in a way he'd never wanted a woman before, and with her nod of consent he let the rest of the world fade away into nothing so that it was just the two of them.

He placed his hands on her hips and, after checking once again that she was happy to be with him like this, guided her down the length of himself.

His body was bombarded with sensations. Heat. Liquid pleasure. Movement undulating like the sea. It was a rhythm he realised he was participating in as Kiara rocked her hips in sync with his, their fingers woven together, their eyes locked on each other's, until at last he sat up and pulled her close to him, her taut nipples grazing his bare chest as he said, 'Wrap your legs around me.'

He didn't need to repeat himself. With a reserve of strength he hadn't realised he possessed, he picked her up and reversed their positions, so that he was on top. With her legs still around his waist he began to slowly recapture the rhythm, as if it had become a part of him. A part of them both.

Neither of them spoke again. It didn't seem necessary. All the time he'd spent with Kiara seemed to have built to this—a pure, unadulterated connection. He felt the intensity grow in him, and with it a shift in Kiara's energy, as if she felt it, too.

They clung to one another as their bodies took over. Movement overpowered thought as they merged into one beautiful, shared sensation of pleasure which built moment by moment until it did, finally, become urgent. The swell of accumulated potency finally reached its pinnacle and waves of pleasure washed through them both. The strength of their shared orgasm seemed inevitable and yet also to take them by surprise.

After a few moments Lucas lay down beside her and held her close, her heartbeat translating through to his until, after some long, lingering kisses, the pair of them fell asleep.

Before Kiara even opened her eyes she knew something was different about her bedroom. It wasn't that Lucas was there—because there was no way the evening they'd just shared wasn't going to be imprinted on her mind for ever. It was that he wasn't.

An icy slick of fear shot through her, holding her heart's ability to beat properly in its arctic hold. She forced herself to be still. To listen. Perhaps it wasn't that at all. Perhaps...

Again a glacial wave of panic swept through her as flashbacks to all the mornings she'd woken up alone came back to her. Mornings alone that she now knew hadn't been due to her ex's calls to the surgery ward, but to his family home.

No. Stop it. Lucas isn't like that. He let his son stay here, for heaven's sake.

She forced herself to take a slow breath, calming her hammering heart enough to let her listen to any sounds that might be coming from beyond her closed door.

Perhaps he'd thought a nice cup of tea in bed would be a lovely way to cap off a magic night. Or coffee? A mince pie? She sniffed the air for hints of any or all three. Listened for the tell-tale rumble of the kettle. The clink of spoons on the big chunky mugs she'd bought. The ones with Christmas trees and Santa faces and—her and Harry's favourite—the one with Rudolph the Red-Nosed Reindeer.

There was one sound. But it wasn't from the kitchen. It was the sound of a little boy, still drowsy and confused.

Shockwaves of fear reverberated through her. What was happening?

She pulled on some thick flannel pyjamas and a dressing gown and ran out into the corridor and downstairs where, in her small entryway, she saw Lucas zipping Harry into his winter coat.

He looked up but said nothing. He didn't need to. His expression said it all.

He regretted his night with her.

She stumbled back a step, the humiliation hitting her like an avalanche of pain. She'd thought she'd moved on from her past. Learnt her lessons. Buried her shame and remorse at having been so unwittingly played. But she hadn't. She hadn't come even close. It had all been right there, just below the surface, waiting for her.

Something must've played across her features and spoken to Lucas, because out of the silence and through the roar of blood pounding through her head she could hear him muttering something about nursery, change of clothes, a bath...

They were all legitimate reasons to take his son home. Definitely. But before he'd even woken up? The poor little boy was leaning against his father, half asleep, as Lucas fitted on him first one boot and then another. The sweetest little pair of boots that until now Kiara hadn't realised she'd loved seeing lined up next to her bigger boots and, next to them, Lucas's even larger ones. It had made her little cottage look more like a home than a dream. A hope.

And that was when it really hit her. This beautiful cottage that she loved so much, that she'd lavished with Christmas decor and scented candles and cushions and more fairy lights than the rest of the homes in Cornwall put together... She could have given all the money directly to charity rather than spending it on blinging up her house on the premise of raising awareness. She'd been showboating after all. Advertising her hunger to be a part of something. Anything, really. And the mortification that she'd been so public about her loneliness threatened to crush her.

'I'll see you later at Carey House?'

She saw the comment form on his lips...was not even certain she'd heard it. He certainly didn't mean in a romantic context. They wouldn't be dipping into the supplies cupboard and having a quick snog. Not the way this was going.

'Sure,' she managed. 'Of course.'

'And are you all right if we...you know...keep last night between us?'

He had the grace to wince at his request, but there was no chance he could know just how much it hurt her.

She couldn't begrudge him his behaviour. Not on a logical front. He was a widower with a young son to think of. Harry's welfare was paramount, and dragging him round the village on one-night stands was definitely not how Lucas operated. Even through her pain she knew this to be true. He might not want her any more, but he wasn't a cruel man. And she couldn't hold him to ransom for being the same level of Machiavellian as her ex.

But it didn't make it hurt any less. Or ease the pain she felt. With an apologetic flick of his eyes, he lifted his son into his arms and opened the door... The cold air was a mirror of the cold blood running through her veins.

The moment the door closed behind them she let the truth settle into her bones.

She was going to be someone's dirty little secret again.

* * *

How she'd managed to get into work that morning was a complete mystery.

'Everything all right?'

She stopped in the entryway, turned and saw Hazel's expression laced with concern.

'Fine!' She forced herself to give a bright smile, then tapped her head. 'Just…you know…recovering from yesterday.'

'Too much mulled wine?' Hazel asked with a knowing grin.

Kiara smiled back. She'd seen Hazel make a couple of return trips to the punch bowl as well. But she'd also seen her drinking water, and excusing herself to get home for 'something sensible to eat' afterwards.

The fact she was here with a smile on her face indicated that Hazel knew when enough was enough. Something Kiara wished she knew about falling in love. Because that was what had been happening to her these past few heady days. She'd been falling in love with Lucas—and with Harry—even though there was a part of her that had known all along that she shouldn't.

They weren't hers to love. They were on their own journey. One that didn't include her. Not in public, anyway. Not for Lucas. And there was no way she wanted to be someone's dirty little secret again.

'I've got some paracetamol if you need any…' Hazel began to dig in the reception desk drawer.

'No, no…' Kiara took a couple of steps up the stairs towards the midwives' lounge but then, remembering her manners, turned to offer a smile of thanks. The kind of pain she was enduring wouldn't respond to any kind of medication.

At just that moment Lucas came through the front door.

She froze in panic.

'Good morning, Dr Wilde!' Hazel greeted him cheerily. 'And how are we this morning? Full of festive cheer?'

Kiara almost physically felt the flash of panic that crossed Lucas's face.

Oblivious, Hazel danced knowing looks between the pair of them.

As if he was literally drawing a line under the days they'd spent together, Lucas said, 'Oh, you know... That's more Harry's department. Christmas isn't really my thing.'

And there it was in a nutshell. The addition of the insult to the injury. He might as well have had the message printed on a banner and flown it across the sky for the impact it had. She'd been a fool to fall for him. He'd only done all this for his son's sake. Played along. The kiss and then the lovemaking had all been a mistake. *She'd* been a mistake.

And as the true impact of what she'd done hit her she turned and took the stairs two at a time, unwilling to let him see just how much the loss of him had devastated her.

CHAPTER TEN

'MAKE SURE YOU take them every day—all right, Mr Thomas?'

Lucas's patient screwed up his face as if he'd just spoken to him in Martian.

'He will. My poor man can't hear without his hearing aids, and he didn't want to wear them—what with the infection and all.' Mrs Thomas gave her husband's leg a pat and then shouted, 'You'll be taking your medicine every day!' She tapped the prescription Lucas had just handed them. 'Right up until Christmas Eve.' She turned to Lucas; her face suddenly stricken. 'Will that mean no Christmas cheer for him?'

Lucas made a remorseful expression. 'I'm afraid not. Not with antibiotics.'

'Oh, well!' Mrs Thomas turned to her husband again, turning her speaking volume up to eleven. 'It's a good thing we went out to Mistletoe Cottage for the mince pies and mulled wine—isn't it, love?'

Lucas rubbed his chin…hastily shaven and with a couple of nicks. Something he hadn't done in a long time. He didn't remember seeing the couple there. Which shouldn't come as a surprise to him. He'd only had eyes for Kiara.

The thought stung as an image of her face when she'd seen

him this morning, a wretched mix of fear and sorrow, flashed across his mind's eye.

Mr Thomas grinned. 'It certainly is.' He patted his tummy. 'Those were the finest mince pies I've had in yonks. And imagine…eating them for charity!' A look of panic zapped across his face. 'I mean, they were the finest apart from *yours*, love. Obviously.' He leant across and gave his wife's sweet, dried apple face a kiss.

Mrs Thomas's features softened. She put her palm on her husband's cheek and then gave it a gentle pat before turning to Lucas with a happy smile. 'Forty-seven years of marriage and I've finally got him trained.'

Something in Lucas's heart twisted, unleashing the raft of feelings he'd been trying to keep at bay all day. The reaction went well beyond the parameters of witnessing a lovely moment. It was a combination of loss and hope. Loss that he'd never share that sort of exchange with Lily, and hope that—

He cut the thought off. He'd been an absolute idiot this morning. He'd seen Kiara plain as day in Reception, and when he'd had a chance to extend some sort of olive branch to her he'd stuck his foot in it.

Christmas isn't really my thing.

What had he been thinking?

No prizes for answering that. He hadn't. From the moment he'd woken up he'd stopped thinking, and his body had gone into the mode it had been in during Lily's final months: simply reacting.

Holding Kiara in his arms, smelling the soft perfume of her shampoo as her hair tickled his chin and his chest, feeling safe and warm and part of something bigger than himself—all that had awakened something in him he'd thought he'd left in the past. Happiness.

He'd felt happiness. Pure, wonderful, undiluted happiness. It hadn't been frantic, or wild, or just beyond his reach. It had been right there in his arms and it had smelt of cloves and cinnamon sugar and mint. And its name had been Kiara.

As soon as the sensation had registered, the guilt had poured in.

He'd never imagined himself feeling that way again. At peace with someone. As if he were part of a team. A future. And yet there he'd been, less than three years after his wife had died in his arms, holding another woman and never wanting the moment to come to an end.

The realisation had savaged him.

It was nothing to do with Kiara. Well... It was everything to do with Kiara. Or, more accurately, with his reaction to her. His feelings for her. The fact he'd wanted nothing more than to make love to her last night and had done so without a thought for how he might feel in the morning.

She was entirely faultless in this. It was one hundred percent him, and the fact that he'd never imagined caring for someone in that way ever again. He'd not known what to do with the new raft of feelings. Happiness. Contentment. Actual joy.

Feelings that had slammed up against his past so hard and fast he'd barely been able to breathe.

He'd had everything he'd ever wanted with Lily, and then she'd been taken away from him. In such a cruel way.

Harry hadn't been old enough to know the loss, but now he was. He adored Kiara. Loved everything about her. When he was with her, he glowed with happiness. He couldn't risk his son experiencing the level of loss Lucas had when he'd lost Lily. Not that Kiara was sick—but you simply didn't know, did you? Anything could happen. Sickness. Car crashes. Freak weather events...

His mind had run wild with the thousands of reasons a man could end up standing at a graveside with nothing but a pathetic flower in his hand. A paltry show of feeling for a love that had been his life force. He didn't know how to love someone without loving them completely. With his whole being. Body. Heart. Soul.

Burying Lily had been like burying a part of himself. Even considering the possibility of experiencing that level of loss again was driving large wedges of ice straight into his heart. Fear. Panic. Confusion. Pain. Each one darker than the next to the point where he'd been completely and utterly panicked, convincing himself that his future had already been laid out for him.

He'd been so certain that his future was with Lily and life had showed him otherwise. He didn't know anything. He was destined to be alone. The perfection he'd shared with Kiara was not his to take. Not with what she'd already been through with her ex. What he'd been through with his wife. He was in no place to make promises for the future when he knew first-hand that the future was not in his control.

So he'd left. Convinced himself that he was doing it for Harry. That if, perchance, his son had found him with Kiara it would have confused things. And now here he was, face to face with a couple who, by the look of things, had enjoyed forty-seven years of marriage and were still smiling.

'What's your secret?' Lucas asked.

'For a good mince pie?' Mrs Thomas asked.

'What's that?' Mr Thomas leant in closer to his wife.

'He wants to know what my secret for a good mince pie is, Harold!'

They shared a look, then began to cackle. Low at first. Then building to a high fever-pitch of giggles.

'She buys them, lad! She buys 'em down the shops and pretends they're home-made.'

They laughed until they wiped tears away, and once again Lucas was struck by how wonderful their companionship seemed. Multifaceted, and at its very core a deep well of love.

'I meant the secret of your marriage,' Lucas persisted. He'd take any advice he could get. Living his life half in the past and half in the present wasn't working. He had to find a way to go forward—only he didn't know how. 'What's the secret to staying so happily married?'

'Agree with everything she says,' Mr Thomas said, still laughing, and then putting on a placating voice. 'Yes, dear. That's right, dear. Anything you say, dear...'

Mrs Thomas swatted at him. 'If only it was that easy.' She leant forward and said conspiratorially, 'You'll not even come close to guessing the tricks I'll have to play to get him through these antibiotics. He's stubborn as a mule, he is. I had to promise him a steak pie tonight just to get him to come and see you.'

'That's just because I wanted steak pie!' Mr Thomas gave his wife a little tickle, then sobered as he turned back to Lucas. 'The real reason I came is because I want to make sure I'm around as long as she is. Drives me bonkers with all her energy—but, by God, it doesn't half keep me going. Wouldn't have lived a day of my life without this woman. Worth her weight in gold, she is.' He leant forward and in a stage-whisper said, 'The real secret is making it clear to everyone around you that you won the lottery the day she agreed to marry you.'

The look Mrs Thomas gave her husband was so tender and full of love it nearly broke Lucas in two. He'd thought he was on track to have what they shared years back, when he'd asked Lily to marry him, but life had moved the goal posts for all of them. Lily, Harry and himself. And now, because of his poor behaviour this morning, for Kiara.

He had destroyed the very beginnings of something without even giving it a chance.

He had no idea how to shift the course of his own path to cross with Kiara's. Perhaps that had been the problem. Their fleeting connection had been a lesson to him to exercise more caution. Show more care. And never, ever again to hurt a woman who'd been so open, sharing with him her deepest humiliation only to feel it again by his own hand.

He owed her an apology. But words weren't going to be enough. The old saying was right. Actions did speak louder than words. And he had to make sure he was matching whatever apology he made to his intentions.

Until he knew what those were he was right back where he'd begun. Caught between his past and the present, not knowing which way to turn.

When Kiara opened the door for her next patient, Catrina, she was shocked to see Lucas, chatting away with her.

Not so much because it was weird for a GP to be speaking to a patient, but because it was weird for him to be outside a door he knew she'd be opening when he'd made it crystal-clear yesterday that he wanted nothing more to do with her.

She ran her thumb along the jagged remains of her festively decorated fingernails...all nibbled down yesterday.

He hadn't been *that* awful.

Despite her nerve-endings still burning like a bee sting, she had to concede that he hadn't cold-shouldered her or anything. He obviously just didn't want what had happened between them to happen again. Or, if he did, he wanted it to be between them. A secret. And if there was one thing she'd promised herself when she left London it was that she'd never again let someone treat her the way her ex had. As a secret.

'Hey, Kiara.' His grey eyes met hers. 'All right?'

'Fine, thanks,' she chirped, although the subtext was clear: *No thanks to you*. 'Catrina! So lovely to see you. Gosh... The twenty-eight-week appointment! If I didn't have it right here in black and white, I wouldn't have believed it from the size of you.'

'I know!' Catrina ran a hand over her neat bump then grinned, 'But look at me from the side!' She turned and jutted out her belly—which, to be fair, did look bigger from that angle.

Lucas hadn't moved a centimetre during this exchange and Kiara could feel him watching her. Was he inspecting her to see how she really was? Well, tough.

'Excellent.' She flicked her eyes to his and then to her patient's. 'Shall we get you out of the corridor and talk privately?'

It would be obvious that she didn't want him there, but she couldn't help it. Her response to Lucas was visceral. She wanted to touch him. Smell him. Taste him again. But wanting all those things rose like bile in her throat as she remembered his expression when he'd first laid eyes on her the morning after they'd had sex.

It might have been subconscious, but she'd seen the way he'd pulled Harry just that little bit closer to him, hunched his shoulders that extra centimetre lower... Small but unmistakeable visual cues that had told her he thought he'd made a mistake. That moment had shot her straight back to the day she'd cheerfully answered her phone and listened with dawning understanding as an unfamiliar female voice had informed her that her 'boyfriend' had a wife and children.

She'd never felt more humiliated and ashamed.

And that doubled the pain. Because she knew in her heart that Lucas wasn't anything like her ex.

Peter had been a self-serving, duplicitous married man with a God complex.

Lucas was a widower with the kindest, most gentle spirit. A protective father who'd taken his very first steps into having a relationship. Not to mention the best kisser she'd ever met.

She squashed the physical response that came with those memories and forced herself to be practical.

Deep down, she knew he wasn't the sort of man to go around kissing people willy-nilly. Or to blank them the next day. They'd had a connection. He'd acted on it. Then he'd realised he'd made a mistake.

Perhaps the simplest explanation as to how they'd ended up in bed the other night was that they'd both had too heavy a dose of Christmas magic. But that somehow made it hurt that much more. Being someone's mistake.

Catrina, who was standing and waiting to go into the room, but couldn't because Kiara still hadn't moved, gave her an inquisitive look. 'Everything all right?'

Kiara popped on a chirpy smile she knew didn't reach her eyes. With a level of defiance she knew would travel all the way to the tall, dark and handsome GP whose eyes were glued to her, she said, 'Fine. Never been better. Sorry... I should be asking you if you're all right. Okay, then...away we go.'

Kiara stood to one side to let Catrina enter the room and, despite trying not to, looked at Lucas as she pulled the door shut.

There was something in those grey eyes of his she couldn't read. Remorse? An apology? She didn't know. Whatever it was, she didn't want it anywhere near her. She couldn't go down that road again. No matter how much of her heart she'd already lost to him. She'd simply have to soldier on until she grew yet more scar tissue.

And with a simple click of the door she promised herself that that would be that.

But of course it wasn't.

A few hours later she was on the phone to both of her parents, in a video call so they could witness her ugly crying in High Definition. She told them everything. About Lucas and Harry and how she'd fallen for them both. About how much she'd enjoyed doing all the festive events with them. About how things had gone further with Lucas but that it had obviously been a step too far for him. Whether it was because he was a widower or because she just hadn't been a good fit, she didn't know, but it had brought up all sorts of feelings and memories, and she'd thought she should tell them everything.

They sat silently, compassionately, and listened as she told them about Peter. About how he'd courted her. Wined and dined her straight into her own bed. Occasionally a hotel bed. But never his. Until, three years later, she'd found out why.

Her parents were shocked, but not disappointed in her as she'd expected. They comforted her, and called him a scoundrel and a rake and a couple of other words she hadn't realised her parents knew, and eventually her tears began to dry.

'Would you like to come home for Christmas, love?' her mum asked.

She had to admit she was tempted. To have hot water bottles magically appear in her childhood bed each night. To have that wonderful mish-mash of Indian cuisine from her mother's childhood and English from her father's on the Christmas dinner table after hours of laughter and fun in the family kitchen. Board games. Sentimental films.

But the idea of leaving her cottage—her new home—made her feel worse. As if 'The Incident' with Lucas, as she was now calling it, was driving her out of the new life she'd carved out for herself here in Carey Cove. Leaving, she realised, would be the worst thing she could do.

'I think I'll stay here,' she said.

'We can always come down to you, you know.'

Her spirits brightened at that. And without her having to say a word, her parents began to plan. Her father pulled a notebook on to the kitchen table as her mother rattled off a long list of things they mustn't forget to bring.

Before she knew it, Kiara was laughing. 'They have shops here in Cornwall, you know, Mum.'

Her mother feigned shock, then laughed as well. 'You know, love, we're more than happy to come. We want to come. But if you happen to chat to your young man and…you know…decide you'd like to celebrate Christmas in a different way, we're happy to go with whatever decision you make.'

Kiara scrunched her nose, feeling the sting of tears surfacing again. 'Thanks, Mum. But I think it'll be just us Baxters opening presents around the Christmas tree this year.'

They chatted a bit more, then said their goodbyes. Wanting to recapture a bit of the Christmas magic she'd lost over the past twenty-four hours, she went and got her duvet and made a little nest for herself on the sofa. She put on a Christmas film—the kind where brand-new work colleagues turned out to be princes from far-off kingdoms—and snuggled in for the evening.

A bit of fiction never hurt a girl. Especially at this time of year.

'I can't get any of the candy canes to stick!' Harry dropped the red and white striped sweets onto the table and folded his arms across his chest in a disgruntled huff.

'Come on, Harry. You said you wanted to decorate a gingerbread house.'

Lucas picked up a candy cane, squirted some of the white icing onto it, as the woman leading the workshop had instructed, and then, lacking the will even to try, ate it in one go.

'Can I have one?' Harry said, his lower lip beginning to tremble.

'Sure.' Lucas took another candy cane out of its protective wrapping and handed it to him.

'No! With icing on it, like you had!'

Lucas didn't fight it. He did as his son instructed and together they sat, side by side, amidst tables full of happy families merrily constructing gingerbread houses out of every sweetie known to mankind.

Lucas watched as Harry chomped and then swallowed his minty treat without so much as a glimmer of a smile. It wasn't top parenting. It wasn't even top adulting. Lucas knew he sounded as dispirited as his son.

Harry looked up at him, his big grey eyes a reflection of his own, his blond curls an echo of his mother's. 'I thought Kiara was going to be here.'

Lucas had too. And to be honest he was doing a terrible job of keeping up his part of the bargain: playing along. 'C'mon, son. She can't be with us for all our outings.'

'Why not?'

There were myriad reasons she couldn't accompany them absolutely everywhere, but the number one reason she wasn't here right now was because of the way Lucas had behaved. He'd panicked, and it had come across as cruel. He'd dug a hole for himself he didn't know how to get out of—because the truth was he didn't have the answers. He'd never been a widower before. Never fallen for anyone other than Lily...

He closed his eyes and instantly saw Kiara's expression when she'd found him bundling up a half-asleep Harry and listened to him muttering nonsense about getting him home for uniform and the right socks. It had been ridiculous and she'd known it. Of course Harry had needed those things, but usually a good parent would wait until their child had had a full night's sleep before taking them out of their girlfriend's—

The thought caught him up. He'd been thinking a lot of things about Kiara over the past couple of days. Thousands of them. How kind she was. How generous. Thoughtful, beautiful, strong... The list went on. But he'd never once thought of her as his *girlfriend*.

Was that what she'd become to him? It wasn't as if he was a Jack the Lad, jumping into bed with every woman who took his fancy. He'd not actually been with or wanted to be with anyone until Kiara had lit up his life—*their* lives—both literally and figuratively.

'It's not as much fun without Kiara,' Harry said mournfully.

'You're right,' Lucas conceded. 'It's not.'

And he'd pulled the plug on the possibility of Kiara being with them ever again. The way he'd treated her, he deserved the icy glances she'd been sending his way. But he simply didn't know how to come back from that. Not after what she'd been through.

He forced himself to try and look enthused about the unadorned gingerbread house sitting in front of them. 'But she couldn't make it today, so what do you say we make the best of it, eh? How about these chocolate buttons? Should we try putting some on the roof?'

Harry looked at the buttons and then up at his father, tears welling in his eyes. 'Why didn't we go past Mistletoe Cottage today?'

Another good question with a host of bad answers.

'I—' Lucas began, and then, not knowing how to explain to his son how he was feeling torn between his past and a future that felt as if it would betray the past, he began eating the chocolate buttons that were meant to be tiling the gingerbread house neither of them had any interest in.

'Daddy?' Harry tugged his father's arm. 'I want to see Mistletoe Cottage.'

Lucas's heart felt punctured by the request, because he knew the subtext. Harry wanted to see Kiara. And so did he. The days weren't as nice without her. Not as bright. They were certainly bereft of any Christmas spirit. But if they went past the cottage there was every chance they would run into Kiara, and he simply didn't know how to put into words what he felt.

He dropped a kiss on top of his son's head and pulled him in for a hug. Sitting here being more miserable wasn't helping anyone. 'What do you say we go out to the harbour and see if we can get a glimpse of her house from there?'

It wasn't the perfect solution, but if they walked out on to the quay Lucas was pretty sure Kiara's spectacularly decorated house would be shining away, a beacon for all who could see it.

They bundled up, and after making their excuses to the woman hosting the gingerbread-house-making went down to the harbour.

'Daddy?' Harry gave Lucas's hand a tug.

'Yes, son?'

'Why did you tell the lady I wasn't feeling well?'

'Ah, well...' Crikey. Now he was going to have to explain about white lies. Tonight was going down as an epic fail in the parenting department.

'Is it because we don't feel like smiling when Kiara's not here?'

The question pierced straight through his heart. He stopped

where they were and dropped down so that he was face to face with his son. 'Hey… Hey, bud. Do you feel that sad without her?'

Harry nodded. 'And you do, too, Daddy.'

Lucas frowned, humbled by his son's observation and how accurate it was. He didn't feel good without Kiara. In fact, he felt downright miserable.

A thought suddenly broke through the fug of gloom he'd been wandering around in for the past couple of days. Was he paying a penance for loss that he had never actually owed? Lily had been clear with him. He wasn't to hold back from life. Not for her. Or for Harry. More to the point, he was to live life to the fullest *for* Harry. Living life mired in the past was something she had never wanted for her son. Or for Lucas.

Harry took his index fingers and put each one on the edges of Lucas's lips, first pushing them up, then down, as he said, 'When we're with her we smile, and when we're not all we want to do is be with her.'

Lucas sat back on his heels and looked at his wise three-year-old. That was pretty much it in a nutshell.

'Do you—' he began, and then stopped as a swell of emotion hitched in his throat.

He was about to ask his son a big question, and putting it into words felt as powerful as pulling his own heart out of his chest and asking for advice on how to go forward. How to live their lives.

'Would it be all right if—' Again the question caught in his throat.

How did you ask your child if it was all right to date someone who might possibly never want to see him again? Particularly when that little boy had never really known his mother's love. Two women loved Harry. Only one of them was here, up in that thatched-roofed, ornament-laden, fairy-lit testament to joy.

This was the decision Lily had wanted him to make. Accepting the joy. Loving another woman wasn't about forgetting his past. It was being grateful for it and then, with care, being willing to open his heart to yet more love. More joy. More happiness.

He no longer battled the emotion bursting in his chest. 'You know your mummy loved you very much, don't you?' he said.

Harry nodded, then pointed at his heart. 'That's why she lives here.'

'Yes. Yes, that's right. And if I were to ask Kiara to spend a bit more time with us—'

Harry beamed and clapped his hands, 'You mean a *lot* more time with us?'

Lucas wiped away a couple tears of his own and said, 'Hopefully. If Daddy hasn't mucked it up.'

Harry's little eyebrows drew together and he asked, 'Did you tell Kiara we weren't feeling well, too?'

Lucas had to laugh. 'Something like that. And now we have to find a way to let her know we're feeling better and that we'd love to see her again.'

A fresh burst of energy sent an empowering charge through his entire body. He rose and took his son's hand in his.

'C'mon, Harry. Daddy's got an idea. Shall we go and see if we can make it work?'

His son's cheers were all the encouragement he needed.

CHAPTER ELEVEN

KIARA'S NEWEST PATIENT and friend, Liane, was glowing with excitement. And it wasn't just her baby she was excited about. Kiara was about to unveil yet more decorations for her house, as it was now only forty more sleeps until Christmas.

Not that she was counting.

She was absolutely counting.

'Honestly,' Liane said to Kiara. 'This is the absolute best Christmas I've ever had. The whole of Carey Cove thinks so, if I'm honest. Will you be doing this every year?'

Kiara made an indeterminate gesture that she hoped said *Sure!* And also *There are no guarantees in life!* What she really wanted to say was *Absolutely, yes, but my heart's not in it nearly as much as it was back when Lucas and Harry were—*

She cut the thought short. Lucas and Harry weren't anything any more, apart from Lucas-and-Harry-shaped holes in her heart. As much as she wanted it to be otherwise, it simply wasn't to be.

She'd never been more grateful for a weekend in her life! It wasn't so much that she wanted to avoid Lucas… Well… She *did* want to avoid Lucas, because no matter how hard she tried she still couldn't shake the feeling that there was something unfinished between them. Just as there was that mysterious *some-*

thing missing from her home's over-the-top decorations which, like the final piece of a puzzle, would make it perfectly perfect.

'C'mon!' Liane rubbed her hands together, clearly beginning to feel the cold of the crisp, bright winter's day. 'I'm going to turn into an icicle if you don't choose soon.'

'I can't choose!'

Kiara's face stretched into a helpless expression. If this had been three days ago she knew who would be choosing. Harry. She swallowed back the lump of emotion and brightened her tone.

'You choose. Which one?' Kiara held up a star and then an angel.

'The angel, for sure.' Liane's grin widened. 'She looks just like you.'

'Ha!' Kiara smirked, holding up the blonde, blue-eyed archetypal angel and then giving her dark ponytail a flick. 'Maybe if I did this…' She lifted the angel above her head and struck a beatific pose, then, as she looked at her new friend, realised she was properly freezing. 'Wait there!'

She ran into the house and grabbed a cosy blanket off the back of the sofa, desperately trying not to remember the last time she'd been on it, her limbs tangled with a certain tall, dark and handsome GP.

She ran back, flicked the blanket out to its full length and wrapped it round Liane's shoulders. 'There you are. Got to keep you and your little one cosy.'

Liane laughed, said thank you, and then, as she pulled the blanket close, her expression turned earnest. 'Seriously, Kiara. I mean it. I know you're my midwife, and all, and that we haven't known each other that long, but I hope you know I count you as a friend. I mean—you're amazing. You achieve big things in small amounts of time.'

Like falling in love with the one man she shouldn't? Yup. She'd certainly done that straight away. Tick! Done and dusted.

'Hardly,' she said, instead of pouring her heart out to her

new friend and telling her about everything the way she'd done with her parents. With Lucas. The pain she had tried to keep at bay was threatening to burst through her mental blocks. This moment was proof that she didn't have to rely on Lucas for friendship.

Liane held her hands out wide. 'Look at what you've done in the last two weeks! I haven't managed to do anywhere near the same in ten years of living here! I hope you stay. I hope you stay for ever and we grow up to be old ladies in wheelchairs, admiring Carey Cove's famous Christmas lights at Mistletoe Cottage.'

Kiara pressed her hands to her heart, truly touched and then she said, more mischievously, 'When we're that old we'll have to hire some strapping young men to put up all the decorations!'

'Ooh...' Liane's eyes lit up. 'Why wait until we're old? We could hire some now.' She suddenly pulled a face. 'Do you think my husband would mind?' And then she burst out in hysterical laughter, pretending to be in a panic that he might have heard. 'Aw... Bless... He's the best-looking man in the village for me—and that's what counts, isn't it?'

Kiara nodded, absorbing the sight of her friend's face turning soft with affection as she no doubt conjured an image of her husband wearing a tool belt or possibly nothing, while her own thoughts instantly pinged to the man she would happily have as her Mr January through to December if she could. But she couldn't.

'I guess we'll have to leave it until we're older, then, before getting some young men to put up the rooftop decorations.'

They both looked up to the roof, no doubt imagining entirely different men up there, doing alpha male things in various stages of undress.

'And I guess I'd better get back and make tonight's tea.' With a small, contented sigh, Liane began to fold up the blanket Kiara had handed her, and then she asked, more seriously, 'Do you have any more decorations you want putting in awkward places?

I'm happy to ask Gavin if you need me to. He's not brilliant at DIY, but he is happy to give things a go.'

Kiara did want more decorations, but she just couldn't put her finger on what was missing. She looked up at Santa on the roof of the cottage. He was by the chimney, posed to look as if he was about to climb down with a big bag of presents. The orange and red glow of the sunset was disappearing in the sky, and the lights she had strung like rows of icing along the house were beginning to offer their warm glow to the fast-approaching darkness. She heard jingle bells and smiled. Christmas really had gone to her head!

'Did you hear that?' Liane asked, cocking her head to the side. 'Are those...*jingle* bells?'

Kiara started. So it hadn't just been her. She tilted her head to one side, as if that might be the best way to hear something better, and, yes... It was faint, but there was the unmistakably cheery sound of jingle bells rising up from the main road at the port. The way the road was angled made it possible to see whoever was coming once the vehicle came round the first bend.

'It must be someone with bells attached to their car,' Kiara said, feeling a shot of festive adrenaline spiking through her.

'No...' Liane's voice was awe-filled. 'It so much better than that.'

Kiara couldn't even speak and agree. Liane was right. It was a million times better than that.

It was Lucas. And Harry. On top of a flatbed truck that was somehow transporting the most beautiful sleigh with a full complement of reindeer hitched to the front.

How he'd found a sleigh—glittering and twinkling in the approaching darkness—let alone reindeer tame enough to be hitched to a sleigh with full swags of jingle bells was beyond her. She felt as if she was in the middle of a Christmas miracle.

She clearly wasn't alone. She could see front doors being flung open and children and adults alike running out into their gardens to cheer and sing snippets of Christmas songs as the enormous truck—bedecked in fairy lights, no less—slowly worked its way up the hill until, with a great sense of purpose, it came to a halt right in front of Mistletoe Cottage.

Lucas and Harry were in the driver's seat of the sleigh. Harry was bouncing all over the place, waving and pretending to steer the reindeer, and generally enjoying being the centre of attention, but it was Lucas Kiara was watching... Because his eyes—his entire energy—was solely on her.

She felt his gaze as if it were a sparkling Christmas elixir... magic from a fairy godmother's wand. Only he was no godmother, and the look in those grey eyes of his would enchant her for ever. He cared for her. She could see it now. And, more importantly, she could feel it. For Lucas, a hugely private man who'd endured so much emotional turmoil over the past few years, to make such an enormous, public, *festive* show of affection meant only one thing: he was falling in love every bit as much as she was.

What they'd shared was now the opposite of a secret. It was out there for the whole of Carey Cove to see.

The only question was...could she trust it?

Before an ounce of doubt that the gesture was genuine could creep in, Harry was out of the sleigh and clambering down onto the flatbed, where an obliging neighbour swung him off as he cried, 'Kiara! Kiara!'

Her heart filled to bursting as he ran and leapt up into her arms as if they'd been parted for an eternity. She buried her head in his little-boy scent as he wrapped his arms round her neck. He smelt of Christmas trees and cloves and winter mint. He smelt of love.

Eventually, he pulled back and asked, 'Do you like it?'

'I love it,' she answered honestly, as the pair of them turned and looked up at the sleigh where Lucas, still aboard, was looking down at the pair of them.

As their eyes met, her heart near enough exploded. His expression was a charged mix of hope and concern. Affection and intent. She could tell he wanted to talk, and she did, too... But it appeared having a sleigh arrive in front of her house warranted action, not a quiet conversation by the fire with a cup of hot chocolate which was what she really wanted.

Lucas was charged for action...and yet standing up here on the flatbed, watching his son run into his girlfriend's arms—for that was what Kiara was to him if she'd forgive him—made him feel more complete than he'd felt in years.

Everything about this moment was unbelievably outside the box for him. Making a gesture so epic, not only to show Kiara he knew he'd made a mistake, but that he cared for her, was definitely not in the emotional toolbox he'd left home with when he'd set off for medical school all those years ago. Life had changed him. He now knew how precious it was. How foolish it was to let fear and pride make decisions for him when really, all along, he should have been listening to his heart.

He wanted to go to her, pull her into his arms and whisper apologies, tell her how much she'd changed his perspective on both life and love, but it seemed when you drove a sleigh and reindeer up to the home of the woman you hoped loved you as much as you loved her, you weren't the star attraction. The sleigh and the reindeer were.

The whole of Carey Cove appeared to have gathered outside Mistletoe Cottage and somehow, magically—Kiara would definitely have said magically—everything began to move into place as if the entire thing had been planned.

Kiara's little red car was relocated to a neighbour's drive. The snowmen were rearranged. The dancing penguins were put into action, wiggling their little animatronic bums as if they, too, had been waiting for the sleigh and reindeer to appear.

Davy Trewelyn, the publican, a tall, portly, white-bearded man, turned up with a 'Ho-ho-ho!' in a perfect Santa suit. And his wife, the rosy-cheeked and ever-smiling Darleen, showed up in a Mrs Claus outfit complete with a huge tray of ginger-bread men.

The village's children were beside themselves, but between the schoolteachers, the firemen, the local bobby and, of course, the parents, who had all gathered to see Santa's sleigh and reindeer, a jolly kind of order was formed out of the chaos.

The sleigh and reindeer were unloaded and set up in Kiara's drive, flanked by a row of living Christmas trees, lined up in red pots and each decorated with a whorl of fairy lights and topped alternately with stars and angels. But there was only one true angel in his eyes: Kiara Baxter. The woman who had touched his life in a way he hadn't thought possible.

He kept trying to get to her, but across a fence of jumbo candy canes they shared a look of mutual understanding: their talk would have to wait.

Eventually, when the reindeer had had their fill of carrots and Mr and Mrs Claus needed to go back to their 'day jobs' at the pub, and the children's tummies began to grumble for their suppers, the crowd began to thin.

One of the mums from the local playgroup asked Lucas in a knowing tone if Harry would like to come to supper at theirs. 'It's spaghetti tonight, and bowls of vanilla ice cream for afters. Nothing fancy, but—'

'Spaghetti's great,' Lucas said, not even looking at her.

His eyes had been glued to Kiara all night and, as if they'd been sharing the same enriched pool of energy, hers had been locked on his. Except for this exact moment now, when his son was barrelling into her for another hug.

The look on their faces as they wrapped their arms around each other made him feel as if his thirst was being quenched with a life-affirming soul juice. As they waved goodbye to each other, and promised to see one another soon, it was as if a multicoloured aura surrounded them. One made up of hues of pure joy, contentment and peace. That Christmas song about peace on earth came to him, and in a moment's stillness he caught himself mouthing the words, about how the place love and harmony had to come from was within.

That was when he knew. Straight down to his marrow he knew he was in love with Kiara. And if she would have him, she was his future.

He reduced the space between them in a few long-legged strides and pulled her into his arms. She didn't push him away or demand an explanation. She just held him, and their bodies exchanged energy, heartbeats. When at long last, arms still wrapped round each other's waist, they pulled back to look at one another, Lucas knew she felt the same way, too.

Not even caring about the wolf whistles the few remaining Carey Covers were sending their way, he kissed her. By the time they parted there was no one else around. It was as if they'd been left in a snow globe entirely of Kiara's creation. And he loved being a part of it.

'Are the reindeer going to be all right?'

Lucas grinned, turning her so that his arms were still around her, but his chin was resting on her silky hair, her ponytail tickling his neck. They watched as the reindeer dug into the bags of hay they'd been left.

'The owner is coming to collect them soon. They'll be back with their manger tonight.'

Kiara twisted herself so that she could shoot him one of her trademark cheeky grins. 'Their manger, eh? I thought you were immune to Christmas magic.'

'Not with you in my life.'

She pulled back then, and asked the question he'd seen in her eyes all night. 'Am I in your life? Is that what you want?'

He nodded, and then gestured towards her cottage. 'Shall we go in? I can grovel inside so you don't freeze to death.'

She laughed and blew out a little cloud of mist, as if to affirm that inside would definitely be a better choice. Then she hesitated a moment. 'Grovelling won't be necessary, but...' her top tooth captured her lower lip for a moment as she sought and found the best word-choice '...honesty will. One hundred per-cent honesty, okay?'

He crossed his heart and held up his hand in a Boy Scout's salute. 'I promise nothing less.' He flattened his hand against his heart. 'I owe you nothing less.'

'You don't owe me anything, Lucas. That's the point.'

She didn't sound angry or vindictive. She sounded deter-mined. Resolute. As if she was showing him where she'd set her moral compass and it was up to him if he was on the same trajectory as her.

He let her comment hit its mark and then settle as they went into the house. She excused herself to make some warm drinks, assigning him the task of lighting a fire. As he went about mak-ing a pile of kindling and putting the logs in just the right place, he realised she was absolutely right. A relationship wasn't about obligation. It was about choice. And he chose loving Kiara over not loving her.

When they were settled on the sofa, a fire crackling away in the fireplace and warm mugs of hot chocolate complete with marshmallows in their hands, he took a sip, then set down his mug and turned to her.

'First and foremost, I would like to offer you an apology for my behaviour the other day.'

Kiara nodded, neither refusing nor accepting his apology. She was waiting for the explanation.

'You're the first woman I've felt like this about since...'

'Since Lily,' she filled in for him. 'She's not a secret, Lucas. She's part of who you are. Part of who Harry is.'

It was a generous gesture. Openly acknowledging the woman he'd loved and then lost to a terrible disease. The woman who had given him Harry. A boy without whose energy and verve he might not have survived her loss as emotionally intact as he was.

'I thought I'd finished grieving for her.' He raked a hand through his hair and gave the back of his neck a rub. 'Meeting you taught me I still had another step to take.'

She nodded, openly and actively listening.

He gave a little laugh. 'I actually needed to take her advice. She wanted this...' He moved his hand between the two of them. 'For me to fall in love again.'

Kiara's breath hitched in her throat. 'Is that what's happening?'

Lucas gave a proper laugh now. 'It's what's *happened*! I'm in love with you, Kiara Baxter.'

'But...?' She said it without malice, but she was still waiting for her explanation and she was right. He owed her the truth.

'At first I thought it was betraying Lily to love another woman the way I love you. But then...' His breath grew shaky as he rubbed his hand against the nape of his neck once more. 'The truth was I was scared. Loving someone—loving *you* the way I do... I can't do it half-heartedly and that frightened me. I didn't want to lose sight of myself the way I did before. But I realised fear and vulnerability are all part of loving someone. Love isn't about limits. It's about opening up. Expanding your heart, not blocking it off.'

He stroked the backs of his fingers along her cheek.

'It's about being brave with someone. Trusting someone enough to believe that whatever you do, no matter how frightening, it'll be so much better facing those things together. I want to be brave with you.' He pressed his hands to his heart. 'You've made me realise my heart has a much greater capacity for love and resilience than I thought. Harry adores you. I adore you. I mean...' He held his hands out wide. 'If you can get *me* to enjoy *Christmas* you're obviously a miracle-worker.'

Kiara was smiling now, and laughing, and crying, and moving across the sofa to climb onto his lap and receive the kisses he was so hungry to give her.

After a few moments she pulled back, and without words began to trace her fingers along his face. His forehead, his cheekbones, his nose and chin. As if she were memorising him.

As if she was finally believing that she didn't need permission to love him—she just needed to love him. And that was when it hit him. She had been every bit as frightened as he was.

'It takes courage, doesn't it?' he asked. 'To love after being so badly hurt.'

She nodded, and he saw a swell of emotion rushing through her eyes. 'It does.' She scrunched her nose and gave it a wriggle. 'I guess after you left I felt as if my future was destined to always be somebody's secret, and I didn't want that.'

'I hate it that I made you feel that way.'

Again, she scrunched her nose. 'The way you left did hurt me, but really I think I'm the one who made myself feel that way. I could've called you on it then and there. I knew in my heart you weren't a "love 'em and leave 'em" kind of guy, and that there had to be something else going on, but I let my past experience colour how I responded.'

'Hey...' He ran his fingers through a lock of her hair, then brushed her cheek with his fingers. 'I made a bad call. I was scared and I acted like an idiot, and that behaviour triggered the fears and hurt embedded in you. It was a not-so-perfect storm.'

'One that's blown over?'

'One that's definitely blown over,' he confirmed solidly.

'Should we seal that with a kiss?'

A smile teased at the corners of her lips, and then blossomed into a full-blown grin as he tugged her in close to him again.

'I think we should seal it with a thousand kisses. Maybe more?'

She giggled and asked, 'Just how long do you think it's going to take Harry to eat some spaghetti and a scoop of ice cream?'

'Long enough for me to do this...' Lucas said, scooping her up and laying her out on the sofa where, smiling and laughing, they tangled their limbs together and enjoyed a good old-fashioned kissing session...as if they were teenagers.

And that was how he felt. Young again. Unweighted by a past that he didn't know how to move on from. Stronger for having Kiara in his life. For accepting and giving her love. Their strength united in loving his son.

This, he realised as the twinkle of the star atop her tree caught his eye, was the true meaning of Christmas. And he was excited to be celebrating it with a full heart for the rest of his life.

EPILOGUE

'WHO WANTS TO put the star on the Christmas tree?'

'Which one?' Harry and Kiara asked in tandem, instantly dissolving into fits of giggles.

Lucas pretended to look confused, and then rotated in a slow circle to see where not one, nor two, but seven full-sized Christmas trees circled the front garden, with five more to come. They'd decided their famous decorations—famous for Cornwall, anyway—should come with a new twist this year.

The first tree was covered in ornamental partridges made of every material imaginable. Felt, papier mâché, glass, plastic, wood… They were all decorations that visitors had brought to be part of the Mistletoe Cottage Merry Christmas Fest. Some of the decorations had been handmade by people of all different ages. One artisan glass blower had even made the tree-topper for that one. A robust, but beautifully ornamental partridge that glowed in the wintry sunlight.

Today, of course, was swans, and the tree glowed with all of the offerings from both near and far.

While the stream of visitors was steady, it still felt very much as if this was the same small local project that Kiara had begun in the name of charity. The fact that she'd been able to give First Steps healthy donations every year for the last few years on behalf of the wider community was just the icing on the gingerbread man.

But, more than that, now that Harry and Lucas had moved in Kiara's house no longer felt like her little cottage—it felt like a home. A family home for her, and Lucas, and Harry—whom she'd now officially adopted—and their latest addition, a precocial curtain-climbing kitten called Holly.

'Oof!' Kiara's hands flew to her tummy, extended to accommodate a thirty-seven-week pregnancy.

Lucas was by her side in an instant, putting Harry in charge of holding the star. 'Everything all right, love? Is it time?'

Kiara shook her head, although she was uncertain if this was the real thing or not. 'You'd think with my experience I'd know!'

Lucas laughed and said, 'Remember Marnie? She said pretty much the same thing when her baby was due.'

Kiara nodded, breathing through a pain that was mixed with the pleasure of knowing their baby would be with them at Christmastime. She already had a list of Christmas-themed names she hoped Lucas would like. And Harry, of course.

He was hopping up and down, singing, 'Baby! Baby! I'm going to get a baby for Christmas!'

Lucas gave his son's head a playful rub and said, 'Yes, you are, son—but should we maybe get Kiara to the sofa, so she can have a rest before we figure out if we need to take her up to Carey House?'

Kiara grinned. 'I think the fact that we have a midwife "just popping in to see the decorations" on the hour every hour will probably stand us in good stead.'

'That's a good point. Do you want to ring Nya?'

They shared a smile. Nya was the one who'd had the very first inklings of their romance, and as such, when they'd found out Kiara was pregnant earlier this year, they'd thought it only fitting to ask if she'd be their midwife.

'I'll ring her when the next one— Oof!' Kiara flinched again.

Harry's eyes went wide. 'Daddy, quick! Get the sleigh to

come! The one with the reindeer! Then we can *fly* Kiara to the hospital!'

Lucas gave him a hug, told him it was a great idea, and then pretended to think a minute before suggesting, 'Why don't you grab Kiara's bag and we'll go the normal way?'

'Walking?' Harry looked confused. 'Can she do that?'

'It's what every good midwife recommends,' Lucas said. 'I have that on good authority.' He tapped the side of his nose, then gave Kiara's cheek a kiss. 'Unless you want to kill me for saying as much and put you in the car like any normal panicked father?'

Kiara grinned, every bit as thrilled and panicked and having no more idea what to do than her 'men'.

'Walking's fine. It's a beautiful day.'

And it was. She gave her husband a kiss and then, because he looked as if he was feeling left out, dropped a kiss on Harry's forehead.

She loved being his parent, and a wife to his father. And she couldn't wait to have this baby so that they could all enjoy the Christmas season as one big happy family.

* * * * *

A Secret Christmas Wish
Cathy McDavid

Since 2006, *New York Times* bestselling author **Cathy McDavid** has been happily penning contemporary Westerns for Harlequin. Every day, she gets to write about handsome cowboys riding the range or busting a bronc. It's a tough job, but she's willing to make the sacrifice. Cathy shares her Arizona home with her own real-life sweetheart and a trio of odd pets. Her grown twins have left to embark on lives of their own, and she couldn't be prouder of their accomplishments.

Books by Cathy McDavid

Wishing Well Springs

The Cowboy's Holiday Bride
How to Marry a Cowboy

The Sweetheart Ranch

A Cowboy's Christmas Proposal
The Cowboy's Perfect Match
The Cowboy's Christmas Baby
Her Cowboy Sweetheart

Visit the Author Profile page
at millsandboon.com.au for more titles.

Dear Reader,

Sometimes, a story takes a completely different direction than what I had planned. *A Secret Christmas Wish* originally had a hero I described as a horse trainer who was hired on part-time at Your Perfect Plus One. He'd been saddled (pun intended) with some expensive medical bills and needed extra income. At his first job, a wedding, he'd meet my heroine, Maia, a competitive trail rider and single mother who also worked part-time for the same company. The book was going to be light with a touch of humor.

While there are still moments of humor—nothing like an adorable toddler's antics to make you smile—a different Brent took shape on the pages when I started this book. For a long while now, I've been wanting to write an outwardly strong character with a hidden disability. Brent is that character. His private battle with depression has brought him to a low point in his life, largely because he's in denial. A possible future with Maia gives him a reason to get better, but alas, that's easier said than done.

I hope you enjoy reading Brent and Maia's journey, not only of love and growth but also of healing and understanding, as much as I enjoyed writing it.

Warmest wishes,

Cathy McDavid

PS: I love connecting with readers. You can find me at:

CathyMcDavid.com

Facebook.com/CathyMcDavidBooks

Twitter: @CathyMcDavid

Instagram.com/CathyMcDavidWriter

This book is dedicated to everyone who's struggling with depression or has struggled in the past. You aren't defined by your illness, you should never be judged by it and, most importantly, you aren't alone.

CHAPTER ONE

STARING AT AN attractive cowboy across the way while on a date with someone else probably wasn't considered good manners. Maia MacKenzie imagined her mother rolling her eyes and announcing she'd raised her youngest daughter better than that.

But, Maia rationalized, this wasn't a real date. Yes, technically she'd arrived with the man sitting to her left. And, like all the guests at Wishing Well Springs wedding barn, she waited for the familiar strains of "Here Comes the Bride." But at the end of the reception, they'd part ways and never hear from one another again.

Her date—Kenny Haselhoff, she reminded herself—seemed nice, if a bit nervous. She sent him her best you've-got-this smile. He fidgeted in response, his knee bobbing up and down.

According to the bio she'd been provided, Kenny worked as a project manager for a large flooring company, liked to golf and jog, was a newly divorced father of two and had season tickets to the Arizona Cardinals games. In the story outline he'd created, they'd been seeing each other for the past two months and weren't yet serious.

In truth, Maia had just met Kenny for the first time thirty minutes ago. In the rear parking lot of Payson Feed and Hay, of all places. He'd chosen the discreet location, insisting they not be glimpsed by anyone attending his cousin's nuptials. As Maia had learned this past year working for Your Perfect Plus One, people were funny when it came to weddings. They had no problems going solo to any other activity. Nightclubs. Parties. Sporting events. Movies. But somehow, arriving alone at a wedding screamed *loser* with a capital *L*.

Which explained why her older sister's wedding-and-event-date company had doubled in size since opening and why Maia was busy most weekends. Weddings were big business in this tourist town. More than ever since Wishing Well Springs had opened its doors. Getting hitched or hosting a family reunion in a glamorously rustic barn with an adorable Western-themed miniature town next door appealed to a lot of people. Particularly over the holidays.

Personally, Maia wouldn't want to get married on Thanksgiving eve, but to each their own. The turkey with all the fixings dinner reception at Joshua Tree Inn next door did promise to be delicious. She had that to look forward to at least.

Her gaze traveled again to the attractive cowboy in the pew across the aisle. He looked vaguely familiar, though not in an I-know-you way. More like an I've-seen-you-somewhere way. Hmm. Maybe his name would come to her before the end of the wedding.

"Who are you looking at?" Kenny whispered.

Caught off guard, Maia swallowed a groan. Busted. She was here as his date and a representative of Your Perfect Plus One. He was entitled to her undivided attention for the duration of the wedding and reception.

She pinned a pleasant expression on her face and turned toward him, vowing to do better. It was unlike her to slip. She prided herself on her four-point-eight-star client-satisfaction rating.

"The decorations," she murmured. "They're lovely."

She wasn't lying. Not about that. The wedding barn had been transformed to reflect the fall season and Thanksgiving. Shades of gold, orange, yellow, deep browns and reds abounded. At the end of each pew hung a cluster of tiger lilies tied with a satin ribbon. On the table behind the altar, a festive array of pumpkins, gourds and dried rainbow corncobs spilled from a wicker cornucopia flanked by vases holding enormous bouquets of fall flowers. Multicolored dried oak leaves were scattered on the carpet leading to the altar, left there by the flower girl.

The effect was magical. Maybe Maia would consider a Thanksgiving wedding after all.

"When I introduce you to my cousin," Kenny said, "don't forget to say we met at a golf tournament where you drove me around in the VIP van."

His nerves were showing again.

"I won't."

Maia wasn't sure about the necessity of adding a VIP van to the story. But whatever. Her job was to go along with the role the client chose for her. Many of which were far removed from her often-boring real life as a hardworking single mom to a young toddler. On some of her more memorable wedding dates, she'd been a cemetery-plot salesperson, a phlebotomist, a fish-hatchery technician and a travel blogger. That last one had been something she wouldn't mind trying in real life. The traveling part.

Your Perfect Plus One was *not* a matchmaking service and certainly *not* a hire-for-the-evening service. Maia's assignments lasted only for the wedding and reception or event, during which she'd sit beside her date, show interest in him and engage in friendly, casual conversation with the other guests. She'd leave at the end with people convinced he'd found a nice gal. What he told his friends and family later about their fictitious breakup wasn't her concern.

Music started, and everyone shifted as one to watch the bride and her father proceed down the aisle. A small lump formed in Maia's throat. It happened every time, regardless if she knew the couple or not. Something about witnessing the happiest day of two people's lives brought out her sentimental side.

The moment was also a small reminder of her own thwarted wedding. She no longer pined for her former fiancé. Hardly! She more often wanted to boot him from here to the next county for all but ignoring their son. But she'd once almost been this stunning bride, and the memory strummed those tender heartstrings.

After the ceremony, the newlyweds practically floated down the aisle. They were followed by the wedding party and close family members. One by one, the pews emptied. When their turn came, Kenny took Maia's arm.

"This okay?" he whispered.

"Of course." She smiled. "I'm looking forward to meeting your family."

Minimal, appropriate and respectful touching was allowed. Also dancing. Again, respectfully. Only once had Maia's date gotten a little handsy with her. She'd politely and firmly reminded him of the client contract terms, and he'd backed off. He'd even given her and the company a glowing review. Good thing. A bad review could reflect negatively on her sister's fledgling business.

Outside, Maia listened with half an ear while Kenny chatted about both the fun and trouble he and his cousin had gotten into as teenagers. She couldn't shake the sensation that someone was staring at her. As she and Kenny entered the receiving line, she glanced behind them—and immediately locked eyes with the attractive cowboy. He grinned.

Wow! He'd donned a tan Stetson that showed off his navy Western-cut suit and emphasized his ruggedly handsome features.

She spun back around, her insides fluttering and her cheeks growing warm.

"You ready?" Kenny said as they took another step forward.

What? Right. The receiving line. "Yes."

Focus, she reminded herself. She had a job to do and company policies to uphold. No flirting or romantic fraternizing with any of the guests topped the list. That would be the end of her lucrative part-time job, and she needed the extra money. Winning the Diamond Cup without a new competition saddle would be difficult, and they didn't come cheap.

Besides, the cowboy was with somebody. Maia had caught sight of a turquoise dress and blond hair. His wife or girlfriend, no doubt.

Steeling herself, she silently counted to ten and smiled at Kenny. "Sounds like you two had a great childhood."

He looked at her strangely. "I was talking about my dog."

Was he?

"Murphy. My goldendoodle."

Maia nodded. "Your cousin gave him to you as a puppy."

"His mom did. My aunt. For my kids."

She ground her teeth together. What was the matter with her? She normally didn't botch dates.

"I'm sorry," she said. "I won't mess up again. I promise."

And she didn't. When the receiving line advanced, and they greeted the bride and groom, she offered a warm handshake, made the appropriate comment about where she and Kenny had supposedly met—which earned him a fist pump from his cousin, the groom—and, lastly, expressed her very best wishes for the newlyweds.

"Thanks," Kenny said in a low voice once they'd moved away.

"Did I pass?" she joked.

"With flying colors."

They gathered in front of the wedding barn with the other guests milling beneath the yellow, orange and green crepe-paper bells strung in the branches overhead. Maia slipped into the velvet wrap she'd been carrying. Payson could turn cold in late November. Rain wasn't uncommon. Today, the elements had cooperated and gifted the newlyweds with unseasonably mild weather to go with a shimmering blue sky.

She and Kenny made small talk while they waited. To be honest, Kenny did most of the talking with Maia chiming in now and then and always sticking to the script. A few times, the cowboy drifted into her line of vision. She diligently avoided eye contact.

Okay, maybe not that diligently. The petite blonde clung to the cowboy's arm, her grip borderline possessive. Funny, mused Maia, they didn't look like they belonged together. Not that a person could tell from appearances. But they gave off an undeniable vibe of being mismatched.

"You simply must check out the miniature Western town around the corner," a middle-aged woman in Maia's circle commented.

"It's adorable," she replied. "I love the jail and the general store."

The woman's glance flitted between Maia and Kenny. "I thought Kenny said you were running late and didn't have a chance to see it."

Beside her, Kenny tensed.

"I...um..." Oops. Maia thought fast. "I attended a friend's wedding here this past summer."

She'd actually attended six weddings here during the last year, not to mention several dozen more at different locations, some as far away as Phoenix. All in the role of a client's date. Her sister was extremely careful and usually sent Maia on weddings for nonlocals, minimizing the risk she'd be recognized and have some explaining to do.

"Yes," the woman in her circle agreed. "Wishing Well Springs is very popular."

Whew! Kenny must have experienced the same relief, for he relaxed.

Not long after that, the bride and groom announced that everyone should head on over to the inn across the way for the reception. They and the rest of the wedding party would be along once they'd finished with the photographer.

Maia and Kenny rode the short distance in his car. He didn't say much until they were in the parking lot searching for an empty space.

"That went okay," he conceded.

"I'm sorry I got distracted."

"Yeah."

Was he accepting her apology or just acknowledging her admission? She let the subject drop. No sense rehashing her blunder. Better she spend the remaining two hours being the best wedding date possible. Surely in that short amount of time, and in a space the size of the dining room at the inn, she could avoid the cowboy.

She and Kenny met up with some of the other guests during their stroll inside. On a credenza to the right of the dining room entrance, they located their meal tickets and table assignment. He led the way, weaving in and out of the growing throng of people and pausing periodically to say hello to someone.

Midway across the room, he pointed. "There we are. Table eighteen." After covering the few remaining feet, he pulled out a chair for Maia.

"Thank you," she said and lowered herself onto the plush cushion.

Removing her wrap, she looked up—right into the compelling hazel eyes of the attractive cowboy sitting directly across from her.

Brent Hayes had arrived in Payson a little before eleven that morning, driving straight through from Tucson where he'd been staying with an old rodeo friend. He'd left at the crack of dawn, pretty sure his friend had been happy to have his couch back after three weeks and not unhappy to see Brent's truck backing out of his driveway.

He had that effect on people, the last couple of years, anyway. He'd worn out his welcome at more places than he could count, including his mom's and cousin's.

In the two hours since he'd hit town, he'd met with the owner of Your Perfect Plus One and completed the required paperwork. He'd taken a preemployment drug test three days earlier while still in Tucson, the same day as his online interview and background check. The drug testing company had forwarded his results to Your Perfect Plus One, and Brent had received the official offer via phone call yesterday.

Are you sure you can handle this? the owner had inquired after giving him a brief orientation and set of instructions.

Yes, ma'am. He'd flashed his winningest grin. *I'm a fast learner. I won't let you down.*

I hope not.

By the way, is there somewhere I can change?

She'd escorted him to a dressing room where he traded his jeans and faded work shirt for his one good suit. After that, she'd sent him off with a worried smile, admitting she was in a bind and didn't have much choice.

Brent had driven straight to the prearranged meeting location where Bobbie-Ann waited. The two of them had then headed to Wishing Well Springs, arriving in plenty of time despite her concerns they'd be late.

She was a talker, which was fine with Brent. He hadn't expected to know any of the wedding guests except Bobbie-Ann, and had no problem with her taking the lead in their conversations.

Another benefit to sitting quietly was Brent could people watch. It remained a favorite pastime from his days on the rodeo circuit.

The woman with the mink-brown waves and even darker eyes had caught his attention from the second she'd walked into the wedding barn. No denying her prettiness, but it was her animated expressions that had kept him seeking her out. She spoke volumes without saying a word, and he was listening. The guy with her didn't stand a chance. She clearly wasn't into him.

Brent and the woman sitting across from each other at the

reception had been a stroke of good fortune, and his long-dormant interest was piqued. Not that he'd ditch Bobbie-Ann. No way. Or be less than the attentive and affable companion his job required of him. But his obligation to her extended only until the end of the reception.

"Hi. I'm Bobbie-Ann and this is Brett," Bobbie-Ann said, greeting the two new arrivals and using the fake name Brent's new boss had selected for him. "Isn't that cute? Bobbie-Ann and Brett. We sound like a singing duo. Are you on the bride's side or the groom's? She and I roomed together in college."

"Groom's," the guy answered. "He's my cousin." He indicated himself and then his companion. "Name's Kenny and this is Marla."

"Nice to meet you," Brent said, speaking to the guy but looking at Marla. Funny. She didn't look like a Marla.

Introductions continued with their four tablemates, and conversation flowed. The women discussed the wedding ceremony, the bride's dress, the elaborate multitiered cake in the corner and the newlyweds' honeymoon plans. The men stuck to sports and Kenny's new Lexus sedan.

Brent replied when asked a direct question. Otherwise, he listened and fulfilled Bobbie-Ann's need of the moment—fetching her a drink from the bar, locating her a fresh linen napkin when she dropped hers and making sure the server got their correct meal tickets. In between, he studied Marla.

"We've been dating a couple months," Kenny answered in response to another guest's question. "We met at a golf tournament. Marla was the VIP driver who took me around."

"That's cool," the young man said.

"Yeah. It is." Kenny's gaze went to Marla.

She smiled in return. A platonic smile, though Brent doubted anyone else noticed.

"You must meet a lot of interesting people driving for events," Brent said.

"Um, no." Marla shook her head, sending her long brown

waves into motion. "I… It was a one-time job. A friend convinced me." She laid her hand on Kenny's arm. "Which turned out well for us."

"What's your regular nine-to-five?" Brent asked and then gave himself a swift invisible kick when Bobbie-Ann stiffened.

He really needed to keep his mouth shut. Except he hadn't enjoyed himself this much in months. No, longer than that. Certainly not since before the National Finals Rodeo two years ago, when he realized his bull- and bronc-riding career had tanked with zero possibility of him rebounding.

Marla blinked, hesitating. Her glance cut quickly to Kenny. When he and everyone else remained silent, she finally answered.

"No one wants to hear about me."

"Yes, we do," the women nearest her insisted.

Bobbie-Ann remained uncharacteristically quiet.

Marla let out a long, indecisive breath. "I'm a competitive trail rider."

"No fooling!" Brent didn't know a lot about the sport, other than it required a tremendous amount of athleticism, strength and hard work on the part of both horse and rider. "That's impressive."

"Not really," she said, attempting to dismiss her accomplishments.

But Brent observed a slight squaring of her shoulders he could only describe as satisfaction or pride.

"Have you won any events?" the woman asked.

"A few. Not in a while, though. I took a break from competing. Life got in the way. I just recently returned."

"Good for you." The woman smiled approvingly. "I admire anyone who can return after a setback."

Brent did, too. He knew firsthand how hard that was, having tried himself and failed. He liked to think he was at long last moving out of the dark place and that life would improve in Payson. At least he was getting out of the house, seeing new sights, meeting new people, trying new things. A definite improvement.

As was landing gainful, permanent employment. Working sporadically for these last two years had drained his bank account. The full-time wrangler job at Mountainside Stables was right up his alley. A wedding date for hire? Not so much. Still, he couldn't complain. The part-time gig paid well.

"I'm trying to get Marla to take up golf," Kenny said, and then went on to describe a nine iron he'd purchased the previous week.

Marla appeared relieved to no longer be the center of attention.

Kenny's lengthy description of his new golf club was thankfully cut short when the servers materialized with their food.

Brent savored every bite of his delicious turkey dinner, which would be the closest he'd come to celebrating Thanksgiving. If he wasn't working tomorrow at Mountainside Stables, he'd spend the day staring at the walls. Much the same as he'd done last Thanksgiving. And Christmas. And every other major holiday.

The remainder of the reception progressed as expected. After their meal, toasts were made and the cake cut. A DJ took to the small stage, and guests joined the bride and groom on the dance floor.

Brent turned to Bobbie-Ann. "Would you like to dance?"

"Yes!" She jumped to her feet.

They hit the floor a total of six times—Bobbie-Ann more often than that, pairing up with friends and participating in the boisterous line dances. Brent took advantage of the breaks to resume people watching or engage in casual chatter with other guests at the table. Sadly, Marla didn't return, Kenny apparently keeping her busy elsewhere.

Just as well. She had a boyfriend. And, besides, Brent wasn't in any kind of emotional place to consider a relationship, committed or casual. Hopefully, that would change along with his new jobs and new address.

It was time he got his act together. Past time. Problem was, he had almost no motivation. What had once been easy for him now required tremendous effort. Brent didn't like labeling his problem. Men didn't suffer from depression. Especially big, tough, physically strong men like him. Men who rode bulls and broncs for a living. In his mind, he should be able to just shake it off. Except he couldn't.

He woke up most mornings with little desire to crawl out of bed. When he eventually did, he dragged through his day as if wearing a hundred-pound chain around his neck and cement shoes. The idea that he might need professional help often occurred to him. His ego refused to let him seek it.

Instead, he put on happy face and pretended everything was fine. Maybe one day, he'd start to believe it and feel better for real.

Sometime later, the DJ announced the last dance. Bobbie-Ann found her way back to the table, her complexion glowing from mild perspiration, her eyes bright and a grin stretching from ear to ear. The wedding had been winding down for the past forty-five minutes, but not Bobbie-Ann.

"One final spin?" Brent asked.

"Love to."

The DJ played a slow number.

"Guess it's time to go," Bobbie-Ann said on the way to the table.

"Guess it is."

She glanced toward the door and then back at Brent, her eyes hopeful. "I don't suppose we could go somewhere else?"

The owner of Your Perfect Plus One had prepared Brent for just this possibility, and he let Bobbie-Ann down gently. "I wish I could. I have an appointment at five."

"Another wedding date?"

He said nothing, neither denying nor confirming. There was a limit to how much personal information he'd reveal.

"Got it." She nodded resignedly.

Brent kept a lookout for Marla while crossing the room toward the exit. She wasn't anywhere to be seen. Neither was Kenny. They must have left. Brent snuffed out the slight stab of disappointment.

He and Bobbie-Ann drove to the shopping center where they'd met up and where Brent had left his truck.

"It was nice to meet you," he said reaching for the door handle. "Happy Thanksgiving."

She surprised him by leaning over and throwing her arms around his neck. "Thanks. You were a great date. Really wonderful."

"You take care, Bobbie-Ann."

"You, too."

Once in his truck, he called Your Perfect Plus One and reported in to the owner, who was pleased to hear the date went well. Next, he plugged his destination into the GPS app on his phone.

While he followed the voice's directions, he mentally prepared for his second job interview today. Mountainside Stables was located on the grounds of Bear Creek Ranch, a four-star resort north of Payson. And while situated on the resort grounds, the Stables was independently owned and operated. Brent had talked with the owner of the trail-ride outfit twice already on the phone, and the man had assured him today's interview was a formality. Brent had the job if he wanted it, which he did.

But first, he needed to escape the exhaustion pulling him down and down. The long day of driving, combined with the wedding and his constant battle to present a cheerful front, had worn him out. One more hour, he told himself, then he could surrender to the depths until tomorrow.

Twelve miles north of Payson, he spotted the monument sign

for Bear Creek Ranch. As he executed the turn, the GPS voice informed him that he'd arrived.

Though not yet five, the sun had already dipped beneath the nearby mountains. The sky hung in that drab place between dusk and nightfall. Brent related. He felt that way most of the time. Though, there'd been a bright spot today: sitting across from Marla during the reception.

He exercised care on the long, winding dirt road. Sharp bends could easily hide people on foot, riders on horses and nocturnal critters in search of food. He crossed a narrow bridge traversing Bear Creek, the origin of the ranch's name, according to their website. Every building at the hundred-year-old vacation lodge was constructed of logs, from the main office to the dining hall to the quaint guest cabins.

Arrows pointed the way to the stables, and he followed them. A red barn appeared at the bottom of the hill, off to the side and nestled against a stand of tall pine trees. Horses of varying sizes, colors and breeds ate contentedly in the large enclosure beside the barn, their noses buried in three communal feed troughs. Brent parked next to the hitching post and got out. A man he judged to be in his early sixties emerged from inside the stables.

"Evening," he called. "You must be Brent."

"Ansel?"

"In the flesh. Welcome to Bear Creek Ranch."

The two shook hands. Ansel's roughened palm and weathered cheeks belonged to a man who'd spent his life outdoors rather than tied to a desk. His amiable grin put Brent instantly at ease.

"A pleasure to meet you, sir."

"Channing speaks highly of you. It's on account of his recommendation I'm offering you the job."

"He and his family are good people. I've known them a lot of years. Competed against Channing on the rodeo circuit. He won more than I did."

Ansel chuckled and went on to explain the requirements of the job as guide for the mounted trail rides. In addition to weekly wages, Brent would be given a bed in the employee bunkhouse and three squares a day. He'd be up with the sun and work until it went down, five days on followed by two days off. If there were no customers to take out on the trails, he was expected to clean tack, make repairs, train the livestock, run errands and whatever else Ansel required of him. Brent's free time was his to spend how he saw fit.

"I like to stay busy," Brent said. Staying busy kept his mind occupied and kept him from sinking into the dark place.

"Trust me, that can be arranged." Ansel chuckled again.

Before he could continue, a figure emerged from the stables, the two-story building casting her in shadows. She'd changed from her pale gold dress into jeans, and it took Brent a few seconds to recognize her. When he did, his pulse spiked.

Marla!

She recognized him, too, her brown eyes widening with surprise.

"Brett?"

"Hi."

"You two know each other?" Ansel asked.

"We met this afternoon," Brent said. "At a wedding. And the name's actually Brent."

"Oh. I apologize." She looked chagrinned. "I must have misheard."

He didn't explain the use of a fake name for his wedding-date side gig.

A movement drew his attention, and he realized Marla wasn't alone. A child, a boy of one or maybe two, stepped out from behind her. After giving Brent a cautious once-over, he tipped his head way back and lifted his arms to Marla.

"Mama. Up. Up."

Mama? Well, thought Brent, that was unexpected.

"What are you doing here?" she asked him, her tone curious rather than alarmed as she stroked her son's head.

"He's our new wrangler," Ansel said and turned to Brent.

"Maia's my daughter. And this here young whippersnapper is TJ, my grandson."

"Mama. Up."

"Maia?" Brent asked. "This is embarrassing. I thought *your* name was Marla."

She laughed. "It's Maia. But sometimes Marla. It's a long story." She bent and lifted the boy into her arms, settling him on her hip.

He grinned, his previous exhaustion vanishing. This new job of his suddenly held much more appeal.

CHAPTER TWO

THE COWBOY WHO had distracted Maia at the wedding and the new wrangler her dad had hired were one and the same. What were the odds? She'd thought her eyes were deceiving her when she first stepped out of the stables and saw Brent. He'd discarded the tailored suit jacket he'd worn earlier in favor of a fleece-lined denim one and swapped out his tan felt Stetson for a weathered straw one. But there'd been no mistaking that engaging smile and those intense hazel eyes.

She noted he appeared more relaxed in these surroundings than at the wedding. Like he wanted to be here. Like he belonged.

"This is probably going to sound strange…" Maia hesitated and then blurted, "Have we met before? Other than at the wedding?"

"Don't think so." His voice took on a husky quality. "I'd remember you."

"I, ah, meet a lot of people because of work. I…guess you remind me of someone."

Brent's smile widened. "I get around. I suppose it's possible we've crossed paths."

She jostled TJ to quiet his fussing and her own mild disconcertion. Brent had attended the wedding with a date. Maia couldn't forget that very important detail. He and Bobbie-Ann were serious for all she knew, and she'd never infringe on an established relationship despite a mutual attraction.

Besides, between caring for TJ, working at Mountainside Stables—her parents' horse-rental outfit that catered to Bear Creek Ranch's year-round guests—and her demanding training schedule, she had zero free time for a man. More important, she wasn't about to get derailed again. Making a good life for TJ and winning a competitive trail-riding championship were her priorities. Not dating.

Real dating. Your Perfect Plus One didn't count.

"We have only one ride scheduled tomorrow because of Thanksgiving," her dad said to Brent. "You leave at eight sharp, which means you'll be saddling up at seven thirty. Which also means you need to be here by six for feeding and chores."

"Yes, sir."

"Maia, you go with him tomorrow. Show him the ropes."

She'd expected as much; she and her dad had discussed it before Brent arrived. But that was also before she'd learned Brent was her dad's new hire. Showing *him* the ropes added a whole new element to the ride.

"Mama, Mama." TJ leaned in, and, putting his face in front of hers, patted her cheeks with his pudgy hands. "Firsty."

"Hold on, sweetie."

Glad for the distraction, she reached into the fanny pack at her waist and extracted a baby bottle of apple juice she'd brought for exactly this occasion. Uncapping the bottle with a flip of her thumb, she handed it to TJ and then repocketed the cap. TJ watched Brent as he drank, his cherubic features reflecting a mixture of wariness and interest.

"How long is the ride?" Brent asked.

"This one is ninety minutes," Maia's dad explained. "We offer everything from an hour to a full day that includes a box lunch. My wife, Lois, Maia's mom, manages the reservations and the money. All our horses are dead broke, though a few can get testy now and then. You'll learn their different personalities and to match the horse to the rider based on their experience."

He spent the next several minutes detailing Mountainside's daily operations.

"Think you're up to the task? The days are long and the work hard."

Brent nodded. "I'm used to long days and hard work."

Maia's arms had grown tired, and she shifted TJ to her other hip. "You ever trail ride before?"

"Once or twice. When I was younger."

"You'll learn," her dad said. "I figure anyone who can score 91 in bronc riding can surely handle one of our fat, lazy horses."

Bronc riding! Of course. That was where Maia had seen Brent before. He used to compete at the Rim Country rodeo arena in Payson. If she remembered correctly, he was chasing a world title. Though, now that she thought about it, she hadn't seen him at the arena for quite a while.

"Aren't you friends with Channing Pearce?" she said, naming the rodeo arena manager.

"Guilty as charged."

"Channing's the one who recommended Brent for the job," her dad said.

"I see."

Only Maia didn't see why a professional bronc and bull rider would hire on with a horse-rental outfit. She loved Mountainside Stables and hoped to take over from her parents one day. But a wrangler/trail guide did seem like a step down for Brent. The qualifications weren't many. Her dad often employed high school students during the summer tourist season.

She supposed Brent had his reasons, and she didn't ask. Later, she'd pump her dad for information.

"Remind me, aren't you from Oklahoma?"

"Kansas. I grew up in Wichita." Brent's expression brimmed with aw-shucks charm. "Most of my family's still there."

It was on the tip of her tongue to ask how he knew Bobbie-

Ann if he wasn't from the area. She refrained. He had one friend in Payson: Channing Pearce. Obviously, he had another—this one a lady. Perhaps several lady friends. Handsome professional rodeo cowboys rarely lacked for companionship.

"I'd take you out myself tomorrow," Maia's dad said, "exceptin' I have plans."

"He volunteers at Payson Rescue Mission." Maia was proud of her dad and bragged about him every chance she got. "They put on a really nice holiday dinner for the residents. Dad's specialty is baked sweet potatoes."

"I like to pay it forward when I can. This community's been good to me and mine over the years."

Brent's smile lost some of its exuberance. "I'm sure the residents appreciate it. The holidays can be hard when you're alone and away from home."

He spoke as if from experience.

Her dad apparently had the same thought, for he said, "You should join us for dinner, Brent. That is, if you aren't busy."

"I'm not, but—"

"We'll sit down to eat around three, after I get back from the shelter. Arrive early. Lois puts out a bowl of homemade apple cider that's lip-smacking delicious."

"Thank you, sir." Brent shook his head. "I couldn't impose."

"No imposition. The more the merrier. My other daughter and her family will be there. A few of the neighbors. You'll fit right in."

"I'll just grab a bite at the dining hall or in town."

"Nonsense. I insist. Maia will give you directions to the house."

She'd expected Brent to say he was busy with Bobbie-Ann. Since that wasn't the case, she added a little arm twisting of her own. Why not?

"We invite all the new hires. It's kind of a tradition."

With a soft sigh, Brent relented. "Okay. For a little while."

Maia's dad clapped him on the shoulder. "Glad that's settled.

Now, Maia, honey, take him to the bunkhouse while I finish up here for the night."

She held back a protest. Was her dad matchmaking? It wouldn't be the first time since her almost marriage. Ansel MacKenzie was progressive enough to believe a woman should have the same opportunities as a man and traditional enough to think he wanted his daughters married to, in his words, *a good man of sound character.*

"Fine. Will do, Pops." Time for her to hit the road, anyway. Her mom, who babysat TJ while Maia worked or trained, had already fed him dinner. But he was an early-to-bed and early-to-rise baby and would tire soon. Then he'd become whiney and cranky, sort of like his mother when she got tired.

Her dad sauntered over, kissed her on the cheek and ruffled TJ's pale brown hair. "Night, little man. You behave for your mama."

TJ crinkled the fingers of the hand not holding the bottle. His version of a goodbye wave.

"I'm parked on the other side of the stables," Maia said to Brent and tilted her head in that direction. "I'll meet you out front, and you can follow me."

"Okay."

At her SUV, she loaded TJ in the car seat, her mind still on Brent. She didn't quite know what to make of him. He gave off an air of mystery that intrigued her. The only personal information he'd revealed was that his family hailed from Wichita. And he'd required considerable persuading before agreeing to attend Thanksgiving dinner—which struck her as strange, as he hadn't been the least bit antisocial at the wedding. Then there was the noticeable change in his mood at the mention of the holiday.

She motioned to him as she pulled onto the bumpy dirt road. In the back seat, TJ babbled and pointed out the darkened window. She had no idea what caught his interest, possibly his own reflection. At fifteen months old, his intelligible vocabulary was limited.

As she drove, a notification appeared on her vehicle display informing Maia of a text message and asking if she wanted to read or ignore it. The number of the sender belonged to her sister, Darla.

Maia hit the Read button and the vehicle's mechanical voice recited, *Call me. Smiley-face emoji.*

She hit Reply and said, "Later. Still at work."

The voice responded with, *Your message has been sent.*

Maia would phone her sister on the drive home or tomorrow morning. For now, she wanted to concentrate on Brent. Not on *him*, she silently correctly herself. On getting him situated in the bunkhouse. As her dad had asked.

She mulled over what little she'd learned of him. He hadn't been competing professionally for a while. He was agreeable to working at a job beneath his qualifications. He didn't talk a lot about himself. The air of mystery surrounding him deepened, and she was admittedly curious.

Approaching a sign saying Employees Only Past This Point, Maia turned right. A hundred yards beyond that, she stopped in front of a small cluster of private buildings—the largest two being bunkhouses, the smallest a storage shed. Brent pulled into a small clearing behind the bunkhouses where employees parked. She then opened the rear door, unbuckled TJ from the car seat and lifted him out.

After setting him on the ground, she took his hand in hers. Brent rounded the corner of the bunkhouse, a duffel slung over his shoulder, the pair of dress boots he'd worn to the wedding tucked under his arm and an undeniable spring to his step. Seemed whatever came over him at the stables had vanished during the short drive.

Must have been a momentary flash of homesickness, Maia decided. Well, she'd do her best to make him feel at home here. Strictly as a coworker, of course.

She had to remind herself of that twice more as he neared, his gaze not once wavering from hers.

* * *

During the drive to the bunkhouse, Brent had managed to vanquish the gloom that abruptly descended on him at the stables. It was often like that. He was struck down with no warning, the sensation like a sofa falling on him from a third-story window. Unlike tonight, he usually needed a day or two to crawl out from underneath the wreckage.

A desperate desire to not embarrass himself in front of Maia had given him the boost he needed.

"Hi." He put on a smile, the one he hid behind.

At his approach, her young son reached out his arm and gave Brent the same curling finger wave as he'd given his grandfather earlier.

"Hey, partner." Brent winked.

The kid uttered some gibberish in return that Brent translated to mean hello.

"This is the men's quarters," Maia said. "Next door is the women's."

The two buildings appeared identical, save the wrought-iron cowboy figurine mounted above the door on the men's building and a matching cowgirl figurine above the door on the women's.

Maia knocked and waited for a response. Getting none, she dug in her pocket for a ring of keys and unlocked the door.

Sticking her head inside, she called, "Anyone home?" When there was still no response, she entered.

TJ remained rooted in place.

"Come on, sweetie." She took his hand in hers.

He snatched it away and, pointing to Brent's boots, uttered more gibberish.

"Like those?" On impulse, Brent offered the kid a boot. "Maybe you can carry this for me. Be careful. It's heavy."

TJ clutched the boot awkwardly to his chest, his face alight with joy as if he'd won a prize.

"Wow." Maia stared at her son. "He's usually shy with strangers. You must have a knack with children."

"Not a knack. A little experience."

"Kids of your own?" Maia asked.

"What? No. I have some friends with kids."

"Nieces and nephews?"

"Not yet, and probably not for a while."

His younger brother and sister were still teenagers. A product of their dad's second marriage, they lived with him and their mother on the other side of Wichita. Brent seldom saw them.

His parents had divorced twenty-three years ago after a bitter falling out that had to do with his dad's chronic need to control. Sides had been drawn, and Brent, being only six at the time and having no choice, went with his mom. He and his dad saw each other once or twice a year, but the rift created by the divorce was too great to breach. His dad's constant attempts to tell Brent how to run his life rubbed him wrong. As a result, neither of them made more than a token effort.

If he ever had a family of his own, he was determined to be a better husband and give his children the kind of loving upbringing he'd missed out on.

"I think he likes my boot more than me," Brent said, referring to TJ.

Proving he was right, TJ shouldered his way past Maia into the house, dragging the boot behind him.

"TJ, don't," Maia chased after him. "You'll scuff it."

"He's fine," Brent assured her and followed them inside. "Let him have his fun."

Maia stopped and turned to face him, a question in her voice. "You sure?"

"That boot's been through far worse treatment than one little kid can inflict."

"O...kay." She winced as TJ inserted his entire leg into the boot. "I hope you don't regret it."

Brent doubted he would. Watching TJ's comical attempt to walk across the floor only made what had been his best day in a long time even better.

He looked around the bunkhouse. "Nice setup."

"Obviously, this is the communal kitchen and dining area." Maia gestured to a kitchenette complete with three-burner stove, microwave, refrigerator and four-person table and chairs. "There's the living room." A sofa and recliner faced a wall-mounted TV. "Internet's available, though the signal's not always the best out here. That door leads to the bathroom, and then there are the beds."

Six narrow beds sat perpendicular to the walls, each with its own nightstand, lamp and three-drawer dresser. Brent tried to remember the last time he'd slept on an actual mattress.

"Nothing fancy," Maia observed.

"Are you joking? This is great."

She tilted her head. "Looks like that bed over there's available."

The neatly tucked covers and a lack of any personal items cluttering the nightstand and dresser top supported her assumption.

Brent walked over and tossed his duffel bag onto the bed, set his cowboy hat atop the bag and his remaining boot on the floor. "Where is everyone?"

"Rowdy, he's our other wrangler, went to Show Low. He's spending the holiday with his girlfriend and her family. You'll meet him tomorrow when he gets back. Your other bunk mates all work in the dining hall. They won't return until late—they're prepping for the Thanksgiving dinner tomorrow. Sorry, but you'll have to make your own introductions."

"Are they expecting me?"

"Dad told them."

"I'm surprised Mountainside employees are allowed to stay in the bunkhouse," Brent said, "seeing as it's separate from Bear Creek Ranch. The owners don't mind?"

"Dad had that included in our contract with the owners. Some of our wranglers are nomads, for lack of a better word. No permanent roof over their heads."

Like Brent. "Does your family live here, too?"

"Wouldn't that be nice, but no. They have a house in town. Dad keeps his personal horses at the stables."

"I noticed a lot of vehicles on my drive through the ranch. I'm kind of surprised there are so many guests here. Don't most people visit family and friends over Thanksgiving?"

"Bear Creek Ranch is booked to capacity *every* holiday, including Christmas. People like to get away for all sorts of reasons."

Brent thought if he had the money, he'd spend the holidays somewhere fun rather than alone at home. Not that he called any particular place home and hadn't since he'd hit the rodeo circuit at nineteen.

"Like Dad said," Maia continued, "you get three meals a day. Just go the kitchen entrance behind the dining hall. Breakfast starts at five thirty. One of the staff will make you a plate. No limit on coffee, iced tea or soda, so don't be shy. There's also a coffee maker here." She indicated the counter. "If you have personal food you don't want to share, either put your name on it or store it in your dresser. Bunkhouse rules are posted on the wall by the bathroom. You'll find the guys friendly and respectful as long as you're the same."

"I spent the last ten years on the road, eight of those competing professionally. For most of that, I had to share a room with other guys. I think I can get along with everyone."

Her gaze cut to TJ, who was now pushing Brent's boot across the floor and making engine sounds as if the boot were a toy car.

"I suppose we should get going," she mused. "Let you settle in."

He didn't want to be by himself. Not yet. He wasn't ready for the gloom to creep slowly in and smother him. If he sat at the kitchen table, would they stay?

Pulling out a chair, he dropped into it. "Have you known Channing a long time?"

His ploy succeeded. She joined him, albeit hesitantly. "Most of my life. My family attends a lot of events at the arena. What about you? Known Channing long?"

"I started rodeoing shortly after he did. Like you, I've been to Rim Country more times than I can count."

She waited, perhaps for Brent to elaborate. When he didn't, she said, "I bought my competition horse from his girlfriend, Kenna."

"I've met her. A talented trick rider."

"She originally used Snapple for performing, but he didn't work out."

"Is he better at trail riding?"

"Not bad. Actually, in all fairness, Snapple's fantastic most of the time. Strong. Young. Athletic. Fast. Sure-footed. Amazing lung capacity. A real beauty. Everything I want in a competition horse. Problem is he has one bad habit. The same bad habit Kenna had with him and why she sold him. I hate giving up and selling him, not without first trying every technique I can think of. And if I did sell him, I'd have to start over again with a different horse. That would set me way back and undo all the progress I've made."

"What's the bad habit?" Brent removed his jacket and draped it over the chair beside him.

"Horses are judged on more than speed of recovery and endurance in trail riding. Good manners are a big part. Snapple sometimes reacts when a person or another horse gets too close to his lower left flank. He was bitten there as a yearling, and it left a nasty scar. He used to bolt and run away on Kenna. I've trained that out of him, but he shuffles sideways or dances on his front feet. Once in a while he bucks. Just a small hop. If that happens during a competitive ride, I'll lose points or risk disqualification."

"Maybe I can help."

Maia studied him. "You have a special technique to correct bad habits like Snapple's?"

Brent shrugged, keenly aware of her scrutiny. Rather than

feel uncomfortable, he returned it. "I've ridden a lot of reactive horses."

"Rodeo, right. Bucking broncs. But last I checked, cowboys encourage the broncs to buck. Not to behave."

"You aren't wrong. But I was part of a crew that broke and trained wild mustangs rounded up by the Bureau of Land Management. The mustangs deemed adoptable were then sold or auctioned off."

She sat straighter in her chair. "When was that?"

"Last year." Before she could ask for more details, he said, "The job was seasonal." He didn't admit to quitting. She might think he'd quit Mountainside Stables, too. Which he probably would at some point when the funk he refused to label as depression prevented him from performing his job. "I learned a few tricks."

"Okay. Worth a shot. Might help and probably can't hurt. Let's talk more tomorrow before the ride."

She slanted him a look. Something of a flirty look, if he wasn't mistaken. At the very least, an I-find-you-interesting look. His pulse spiked before he could caution himself to keep cool and not respond.

Except, like at the wedding today, he smiled back. It felt good, normal, to be talking with a pretty girl. Brent could forget for a few moments and just be his old self.

He took the flirting one step further by saying, "I could use something to fill my days off. Can't think of anything better than spending time with you."

"What about Bobbie-Ann?" she asked, a hint of reservation in her voice.

"Bobbie-Ann?"

"Doesn't *she* fill your days off?"

He chuckled. "She's not my girlfriend, if that's what you're asking."

"She's not?"

"Nope." He leaned forward. "I'm single."

Maia's smile returned, and she also leaned forward. "Me, too. Single, that is."

This piece of news cheered him more than it should, considering she could do a whole lot better than a flat-broke, has-been cowboy with little to show for himself.

Then he remembered. She hadn't attended the wedding alone. "Will Kenny object?"

"We're… It's nothing. Very, very casual. In fact, I doubt I'll see him after today."

"No?"

"Definitely no," she reiterated. "We were never going to last. I just agreed to be his wedding date."

Huh! Another crazy coincidence. Brent wasn't just cheered, his mood soared. Fate, it seemed, was smiling down on him for once.

He forgot all about being cautious and about being a lousy catch. "It's the same with me and Bobbie-Ann. Was the same, I should say."

"Really?"

"To be honest with you, I only just met her today."

Maia drew back, her expression incredulous. "You did? You just met her and she asked you to a wedding?"

Brent debated how much to reveal. He felt funny admitting his new side gig as a wedding-and-event date for hire. On the other hand, he wanted Maia to know beyond any doubt there was nothing between him and Bobbie-Ann. "Don't know how you'll take this, but here goes. She hired me. Besides Mountainside Stables, I also work for Your Perfect Plus One. They're a—"

"I know what they are." Maia blinked at him in disbelief, her smile dimming.

Did she think badly of him or the service the company provided? "Look, it's completely aboveboard."

"My sister owns the company. I work for her, too. Kenny hired me to be *his* date."

Now it was Brent's turn to draw back. The difference was his smile grew. "No fooling!"

"Working for her is how I pay for my competitive trail-riding costs."

"Small world. I plan on using the money to pay for extra costs, too." Okay, to pay down his maxed-out credit cards and the money he'd borrowed from his cousin. But those were technically extra costs, right?

"Darla doesn't usually send two employees to the same wedding or event," Maia said, a frown creasing her brow. "She must have been in a bind."

"She mentioned that when she hired me."

Darla's bad luck had been Brent's good luck. He shouldn't be happy. He had no business encouraging Maia or believing he was ready for a relationship. Except he was happy. This felt like exactly what he needed to lift himself out of the dark place he'd been living in for too long.

She suddenly stood, the frown expanding to include her mouth. "It's late. Come on, TJ."

It was getting late, though Brent didn't have much to unpack.

Maia went over to TJ. When he refused to abandon Brent's boot, she lifted him into her arms. He immediately burst into outraged tears.

"Shh, sweetie." She propped him on her hip and started for the door.

Brent went with her. "Look, I realize we only met today, and, well, I don't want to jump to any conclusions…?"

Maia blew out a long breath. With each passing second, Brent's stomach sank further. Had he completely misread her signals?

"We work together," she said at last.

"Yeah."

"Your Perfect Plus One has a strict no fraternizing policy."

"I swear, Bobbie-Ann and I aren't seeing each other."

"Not you and Bobbie-Ann. *You and I* can't see each other.

The company's no-fraternizing policy also extends to coworkers, for obvious reasons."

"It does?" If he'd read a clause in the employment contract about coworkers not fraternizing, or Darla had told him, he didn't remember.

"Yes."

He struggled to form a response. A low humming had begun filling his ears and interfered with his ability to think straight.

"I am glad that Dad and my sister both hired you," Maia said, sounding twenty feet away rather than two. "And I'm looking forward to any advice you have for my horse." She opened the door with the hand not holding TJ and stepped outside onto the stoop. "See you in the morning."

"See you."

Had Brent spoken? He wasn't sure.

His last sight of Maia before he closed the door was of her hurrying to her vehicle. A few minutes later he heard the sound of her engine starting. Eventually, that faded, and Brent was left alone.

He had more items in his truck to unload. A briefcase containing his personal papers, tablet and phone charger. A footlocker for shoes, boots and his buckle collection. A wheeled suitcase holding more clothes and a plastic crate with miscellaneous items. He didn't go after them.

Instead, he shuffled across the floor to his bed, removed the duffel bag and dumped it on the floor. After stripping off his shirt and removing his belt, he threw them on top of the bag. He then kicked off his boots and peeled off his socks before crawling beneath the covers.

There, Brent closed his eyes and listened as the humming grew louder and the familiar heavy weight pressed down on him.

Tomorrow. He'd wake up and face the day. Do what needed to be done. For now, though, he'd just lie here.

He was still awake when his bunk mates arrived a few hours

later, but he didn't get up. That required too much effort. Instead, he peeked his head out and muttered hello. Claiming he had an early morning, he rolled over and pretended to go to sleep. What they thought about him, he didn't care.

CHAPTER THREE

WHEN BRENT'S ALARM went off at 4:50 a.m., he was already awake and had been for most of the night. He quickly silenced his phone and scanned the darkened bunkhouse, noticing one of his bunk mates up and roaming the kitchen area. From their prone positions and soft snoring, the rest appeared to still be asleep.

Throwing back the covers, Brent sat up and swung his feet onto the floor. The thick cotton batting filling his head began to pulsate as blood moved through his veins. He shoved his fingers into his hair and massaged his temples. He would have liked to blame insufficient sleep for the lack of mental clarity, but he knew better. The reminder that he had nothing to offer someone like Maia—who deserved more than a guy the likes of him—was responsible for his fogginess.

With each high, he hit a little harder on the inevitable low and took a little longer to recover. His motivation dwindled, the road to recovery stretching further and further ahead. If not for friends like Channing—who'd given Brent a swift kick, along with a helping hand—it was anybody's guess where Brent would be today. Crashing on someone else's couch? Living in his truck? Staying at the shelter where Ansel volunteered?

He'd been given a chance to turn his life around and, by God, he wouldn't waste it.

Drawing on his slim supply of energy, he pushed to his feet, the effort akin to emerging from a pool of quicksand. Rummaging through his duffel bag, he extracted clean clothes for the day and his toiletries kit. With a mumbled, "Good morning," to his bunk mate, he ducked into the bathroom.

Twenty minutes later, he reentered the world, a shower and shave having marginally revived him. The smell of freshly brewed coffee also helped.

"Mugs are in the cabinet to your right," his bunk mate said in a low voice. Short, with jet-black hair, he sat at the table and scrolled through his phone.

"Thanks." Brent selected the largest mug and filled it to the brim.

"Name's Javier." The other man put his phone down. "Not sure I caught yours last night."

"Brent. Brent Hayes." He sat in the chair where his jacket still hung, his glance cutting to the other four men lying in their beds.

"Don't worry about them." Javier looked over his shoulder. "They can sleep through an earthquake."

"Sorry I wasn't more companionable when you came in. I had a long day. Drove up from Tucson and then—" he stopped short of admitting he worked for Your Perfect Plus One "—went to a wedding."

"It's cool. You hungry?"

"I could eat."

Brent's last meal had been at the reception around four. Too early to be called dinner.

"Dining hall opens about now."

"I can drive," Brent offered. "Just give me a few minutes."

"You got it, amigo."

While Brent finished his coffee, he attempted to tidy his bed and then checked his phone for texts and emails, answering only those he deemed urgent.

One of those happened to be a notice of past-due payment on his most overburdened credit card. With a few swipes of his finger, he processed the minimum payment. It was enough for now to keep the wolves away from his door. With room and board provided, Brent's monthly expenses would drop. And the money from his second job would soon make a dent in his debt.

He scanned an email from Darla, Maia's sister and his boss at Your Perfect Plus One. She'd forwarded the positive client satisfaction survey from Bobbie-Ann and asked Brent if he was available the Saturday after Thanksgiving for a wedding in the neighboring town of Green Valley. He answered yes.

Too bad Maia wouldn't be there. Then again, her absence was for the best.

He tried to focus on the positives. He had a new job—two new jobs—and would be helping Maia with her horse. His days had a purpose after going months and months without any. He put Thanksgiving dinner at the MacKenzies' out of his mind rather than risk his mood plummeting again.

"Are there a washer and dryer around here?" he asked Javier as they exited the bunk house.

"In the storage shed. That building on the end. Gotta provide your own laundry detergent."

"I read that in the rules."

Javier laughed as he buckled his seat belt. "Don't let them intimidate you. We're not sticklers here. We all live and work together. Might as well get along."

"When does your shift start?"

"Nine. I'm the lunch prep cook, though I assist with other meals when needed."

Brent checked the dash clock which read 5:32. "I need to be at the stables by six."

"I'll catch a ride back or walk."

"You sure? I can drop you off."

"Trust me, I'm sure."

Shortly after Brent pulled in next to the dining hall, he saw why Javier was in no rush to hurry breakfast. A tiny redhead in jeans and a bulky jacket jogged over as they approached the kitchen's rear entrance. She kissed Javier's cheek before linking arms with him.

"Hi. You must be the new wrangler. Javier told me Ansel hired someone. I'm Syndee." She then recited the unusual spelling of her name. "I work in housekeeping."

"I'm Brent. Nice to meet you."

Clearly, Bear Creek Ranch didn't have the same restrictions regarding coworkers fraternizing as Your Perfect Plus One. Not that it made any difference, Brent reminded himself.

Inside the kitchen, he was met by the enticing aromas of baking biscuits, frying bacon, grilling hash browns and tangy fresh-cut fruits. His stomach growled as they gave the prep cook their requests from the employee menu. Brent chose a side of pancakes to go with his scrambled eggs.

He, Javier and Syndee sat at one of the three scarred and rickety wooden picnic tables behind the dining hall reserved for staff. They were soon joined by several more employees, too many for Brent to remember all the names thrown at him. Everyone ate with speed, their meals growing cold because of the chilly morning temperature.

"Brent's taking his first group of riders out this morning," Javier said, repeating what Brent had told him on the drive. "Maia's going with him."

"Oooh. Maia." Syndee peered at Brent over her cup of juice and waggled her brows.

She couldn't be much more than twenty—the same age as Javier. Brent wondered if she resided in the women's bunkhouse then decided no. She and Javier would have come to breakfast together.

"Ignore her." Javier bit into a piece of toast. "She's always trying to fix up couples."

Syndee kissed his cheek again. "I just want everyone to be happy like us."

"Maia seems happy," Brent said in what he hoped was a neutral tone.

"She is." Syndee propped her elbows on the picnic table, fully embracing the conversation. "Now. She wasn't happy after sending her fiancé packing three weeks before the wedding."

Brent half expected Javier or someone else to caution Syndee about gossiping. No one did, and she continued.

"The sleazeball cheated on her. Not just with one woman but two. Two!" She held up her first and second fingers for emphasis. "Poor Maia had no idea. His sister found out and told Maia. Caused a real problem with his family, too. The sister did the right thing, though, if you ask me. Maia deserved to know. Soon as she found out…" Syndee exhaled a long breath. "It wasn't pretty."

"That's a shame."

Brent had his faults. Betraying the trust of someone he supposedly loved wasn't one of them, and he had no respect for those who did. His parents' failed marriage was the result of deep-rooted and irreconcilable differences, and he often felt his dad had bailed too soon. But there'd been no infidelity on either his mom's or dad's part.

"Yeah, Maia took it real hard," Syndee said. "She was super down in the dumps."

The observation earned her several murmurs of agreement from others at the table.

"And then, a week later, she learned she was having a baby. Can you imagine? Things went from bad to worse after that. Her sleazeball ex wanted nothing to do with TJ. I mean nothing. What kind of guy refuses to take responsibility for his child?" Syndee made a sound of disgust. "Maia's way better off without him. TJ, too."

"We don't know everything that happened between them," Javier cautioned.

"We know she had to take him to court to get child support. We also know he cheated on her with two, *two*, women," Syndee emphasized again. "And she's raising that sweet little boy on her own. No wonder she was a wreck for so long. She only started being her old self when she got back into trail riding."

Brent felt uncomfortable listening to his new coworkers discuss Maia despite his avid curiosity. She had a right to her privacy and might not appreciate people discussing her personal life or him listening.

He'd been the subject of many conversations when he'd left rodeo after finally admitting defeat. The pitying looks and well-meaning platitudes and attempts to bolster his flagging spirits had worsened his funk rather than improved it.

Grabbing his paper plate and plasticware, he stood. "Nice meeting y'all."

"See you at lunch?" Javier asked.

"Probably not. I have somewhere to be."

Syndee elbowed Javier in the ribs. "I'm sure he's got plans. Don't pressure him."

Brent didn't admit Ansel and Maia had invited him to Thanksgiving dinner. The way the employees talked, they would surely have a field day with that information.

"Catch you later," Syndee called, her goodbye echoed by the rest.

Brent returned his plate and silverware to the kitchen, offered a wave and then made a beeline to his truck. The chronic pressure eased as he started the engine. He wasn't sure if the change was because he'd left rather than stick around listening to more gossip about Maia or because he was about to see her again. Probably a little of both.

Would she be there waiting for him? If not, he'd poke around on his own. At the sight of Maia's truck, Brent smiled to himself. Climbing out, he activated the door lock, pocketed his keys and phone and jogged toward the stables.

She was in the horse pen, tossing hay from a wheelbarrow into the feed troughs. Brent entered through the gate.

"Sorry if I'm late."

"Morning. And you're not."

Her congenial smile contained not a single trace of the flirting from last night. Okay, they were going to be friends. Strictly friends. That was all right with him.

As he helped her with the hay, their glances connecting often, a thought occurred to him. If Maia shared his interest, and if his new purpose got him out from under the black cloud constantly hovering above, maybe he could quit Your Perfect Plus One. Then, they'd be free to see where things went.

His cheer lasted all of three seconds before he remembered his exorbitant debt and the payment he'd made this morning on his phone—just enough to save his credit rating from sinking below sea level.

Nope, he needed both jobs if he didn't want to put his entire financial future at risk and alienate his buddy who'd fronted him a loan. That meant he and Maia maintained the status quo. Now and for the foreseeable future.

"Let me introduce you to Snapple," Maia said when she and Brent had completed the morning chores.

"Lead the way."

He accompanied her to the feed trough where the big Appaloosa polished off the remaining morsels of his breakfast. She was eager to hear what Brent had to say. He had a lot of firsthand experience. Though others had offered their opinion of Snapple and his bad habit, they hadn't rehabilitated wild mustangs for the BLM, which elevated Brent a notch or two in her opinion.

All at once, Snapple swung his head around and tried to nip his nearest neighbor, an overweight bay mare who'd dared to cross an invisible line.

"He's not mean," Maia said, rushing to Snapple's defense. "He just likes to guard his food."

"Is that the same behavior he exhibits when someone or another horse gets too close to his scar?"

"No. Then he's nervous and fearful rather than aggressive."

"Okay." Brent rubbed a knuckle along his chin and continued to study Snapple.

Maia studied Brent in return. She still couldn't put her finger on what made him tick. Initially, he'd seemed happy to see her this morning. Now, however, he'd withdrawn. No, that wasn't the right word. He'd put up an invisible shield, not dissimilar to what had happened last night after they'd discovered they both worked for Your Perfect Plus One.

There it was; she'd answered her own question. She'd made a hasty retreat, letting him know there'd be no acting on their mutual attraction. As a result, he was respecting her boundaries. She should be appreciative. And she was.

The twinge of disappointment she felt was something she'd have to get over. She needed her side job at her sister's company and wasn't about to lose it for some cowboy who'd happened to wander into her life and might wander right back out.

"You free Saturday afternoon?" she asked. "We have two rides scheduled, both short. The last one finishes at four. We can work with Snapple after that."

"I have a wedding but not until the evening."

"Me, too. Not a wedding, a corporate holiday party."

"That won't give us much time. An hour, tops."

"I realize I'm being pushy," Maia admitted. "Problem is, I have only five months to train Snapple, and myself, for the Diamond Cup. That might sound like ample time, but most serious competitors train up to a year for a big event like this one."

"An hour's long enough for me to assess him."

"Thanks." She released a sigh of relief. "I should finish showing you around before our customers arrive. I need to leave as soon as we're done to pick up TJ."

"He's a cute kid."

"And a handful. A typical toddler intent on conquering the

world. Mom works out of a home office and babysits for me while I'm here or training. Which is no small task. I couldn't manage everything without her."

"He seemed pretty mellow last night."

"He was tired. He starts running out of steam by dinner. Thank goodness. I'd never get the laundry or dishes done otherwise."

"My buddy and his wife just had a baby girl. He tells me she keeps them awake all night."

Maia stopped herself from gawking. Here was the first bit of personal information Brent had revealed about himself. "Lucky for me, TJ is a good sleeper." She waited for Brent to elaborate about the friend with the new baby. When he didn't, she gave up. "Ready for the grand tour?"

She showed Brent the stables, pointing out the tack room, the equipment shed, the enclosure where they stored the grain, the first-aid supplies—both human and equine—and Mountainside's two ATVs parked beneath an aluminum awning. They ended the tour at the small office, a room barely larger than a broom closet. Maia brought out a three-ring binder containing maps of the various trails and gave it to Brent.

"People have the first right of way," she explained. "Horses are next, and vehicles last. But don't automatically assume drivers will yield to you and the riders. Always take extra precautions."

"Got it."

"You can borrow this for a few days if you want." She handed him the binder. "Study up. Though we always send out at least two wranglers on every ride, in case there's an emergency. You'll either go with me or Rowdy. Sometimes Dad. If the rides end early enough, I'll train even if only for an hour or two. I also train on my days off, of course."

"You go out alone?"

"Usually. Most people can't or don't want to keep pace with

me, either because their horse isn't capable of it or they're not. Why?" She grinned. "You thinking of coming along?"

"I'd like to see how Snapple reacts on the trail when another rider closes in on him. Is there a horse in your pen out there with enough gas and grit to match Snapple even for a mile?"

"Hmmm." She considered a moment. "Possibly Lone Star. He's half Thoroughbred. If not him, we could ask Channing to borrow one of the arena horses."

"I'd hate to trouble him."

"Oh, he won't mind. My dad and his dad are good friends and on the city council together."

The sound of an approaching vehicle alerted them their customers had arrived for the trail ride. Brent stood nearby and watched while Maia conducted a brief conversation with each individual—a mother, father, two kids, ten and twelve, a friend of the kids' and Grandma and Grandpa. She chatted about their level of experience while jotting down notes on the questionnaires they'd completed.

Then, while the family waited and petted the horses, she and Brent went into the pen, nine halters split between them.

"Let's use Shorty over there for the grandmother." Maia pointed to a stubby black gelding. "He's lazy as they come and a good match for someone who's nervous and hasn't been on a horse in years. We'll put one of the boys on Astro over there and the other on Golden Boy."

Brent collected the bay and palomino. Once they'd saddled all seven horses for the riders, they selected their own mounts. Brent chose Lone Star, and Maia approved. The two should get acquainted before going on a practice ride with her.

"You're not using Snapple?" he asked.

As usual, the Appaloosa had been following Maia around the pen like a devoted puppy dog. She hugged his neck, her heart filling with love. She had to find a way to correct his bad habit. Parting with him wasn't an option.

"He's strictly for competition," she said. "I can't risk injuring him on a nontraining ride. Neither do I want to confuse him by holding him back with these slowpokes and then pushing him for speed the next time."

Before long, they were mounted up and heading down the road away from the stables with Maia in the lead. She conversed with the group over her shoulder, reminding them of the rules—no galloping, no jerking on the reins, no kicking the horse, remain with the group, no venturing off the trail, no roughhousing. Upon learning the group was from Phoenix, she also shared interesting tidbits about the area and the history of Bear Creek Ranch.

She periodically checked on Brent way at the back of the single-file line. He looked good in the saddle. Tall and confident. She had to force herself to look away.

Hopefully, he was paying attention to her chatter as he'd be giving this same talk when it was his turn to lead a ride. Though, that would be a while. Until then, he'd learn from Maia and Rowdy.

The family appeared to enjoy themselves, laughing when they had to duck their heads to avoid being struck by a tree limb and gushing over the spectacular mountain views when they crested a hill. Pictures and videos were taken with phones, the boys teased the girl, and Grandma shrieked when Shorty stumbled while walking along the creek bank. Maia relaxed as her horse, a well-seasoned veteran of these trail rides, plodded along with almost no direction from her.

It was a far cry from when she rode Snapple. Then, she spent every second on high alert. This morning, she enjoyed the contrast between the chilly air and the sunlight filtering through the fragrant pines to warm her face.

Someday in the not too distant future, TJ would be old enough to accompany her on these shorter rides. She took him out occasionally around the stables on their most reliable horse, sitting him securely in the saddle with her. He loved it and cried when she lifted him down.

Turning east onto Nine Stones Trail, Maia led the group on the return trip to Bear Creek Ranch. At the stables, the riders dismounted. The adults complained their joints ached. The kids complained the ride wasn't long enough and asked to go again tomorrow. Dad complained about the cost but ended up saying he'd see.

When they'd gone, Maia and Brent unsaddled the horses, returned them to the pen and put away the tack.

"Well, what do you think?" she asked.

"About the ride? I enjoyed myself." A hint of the flirty smile that had gotten her attention at the wedding yesterday appeared. "What do *you* think? Have I got what it takes to be a wrangler?"

"You made the cut." Feeling the effects of his smile clear to her toes, she almost returned it before stopping herself at the last instant. Seriously, she needed to control her reaction to him if they were going to continue working together.

"Is that yours?" he asked, eyeing her competition saddle, with its distinctive design, on the rack.

"For now." She returned the saddle Grandma had been using to its designated spot. "I'm having a custom one made. It should be done after the first of the year."

"Nice."

"It is nice," Maia agreed. "And expensive."

She'd put half down when she'd placed the order for the saddle and set aside a portion of every paycheck from Your Perfect Plus One to cover the balance. If not for her part-time job, she'd be competing in her old saddle.

Granted, races weren't won or lost solely because of a saddle or any piece of equipment. But a custom saddle could make the difference between the competitor's legs giving out two-thirds into the race and making it comfortable to the end. Ninety miles in one day over rough terrain was no small feat. Every advantage counted.

When they were finished and the stables in order—her dad

would return after Thanksgiving dinner for the nightly feeding—Maia and Brent walked to their vehicles.

She unlocked her SUV. "See you at dinner."

"See you."

His response lacked enthusiasm, leaving her to wonder if he'd
back out at the last minute. She followed him up the road as far
as the turnoff for the bunkhouse. She kept going, leaving Bear
Creek Ranch and heading south toward Payson. She'd collect
TJ at her parents' house and take him home where they'd both
get ready for dinner. Her mom needed a break. Hosting twenty-
four people was hard enough without TJ underfoot. Besides,
she missed her little boy when away from him.

Voice activating her phone, she placed a call to her sister.

Darla answered with a huff. "Finally!"

"Sorry I didn't call back last night," Maia said. "TJ kept me
busy. And I'd have called earlier, but I know how you like to
sleep in on your days off. And then I was giving Brent a tour
of the stables. Speaking of which, did you know he was Dad's
new wrangler when you hired him?"

"That's why I called you last night." Static caused by the
Bluetooth garbled her sister's voice. "To give you a heads-up.
I didn't have a chance before the wedding."

"We figured it out after we met at the stables."

"Probably just as well you didn't know at the wedding. No
awkwardness."

If she had known Brent worked for her sister, she might not
have been initially attracted to him. On second thought, knowing or not knowing wouldn't have made a difference.

"Him working for Dad is a plus," Darla continued. "I figure
he's more likely to stay, if only so Dad doesn't give him grief.
I've had real trouble keeping guys on the payroll. Why they
seldom stay and gals remain is a mystery to me. And according to my client, he did great yesterday."

"I think so, too. From what I saw, she appeared happy."

"It's his cowboy charm and good looks, which I'm sure you noticed."

Maia didn't reply. Her older sister had been teasing her from the moment she'd learned to talk. If she discovered Maia liked Brent... Well, suffice it to say Maia would be hearing about it forever.

"Why the long silence?" Darla asked. "Is there a problem?"

"Nope. I was just thinking. You and Dad both hiring him was too much of a coincidence."

"Your friend Channing recommended Brent to me *and* Dad."

That made sense. "Why does he need a second job?"

"Why does anyone need a second job? But you'll have to ask for the specifics. I don't divulge an employee's personal information."

Maia wouldn't ask. Brent's need for extra money was his business.

"He's coming to Thanksgiving dinner."

Darla hesitated. "He is?"

"Dad invited him." *So did I.*

"O...kay."

"I get that you prefer to keep your personal and professional lives separate."

"It's easier that way. My clients need to trust me and feel confident I respect their privacy. Me socializing with employees could affect that trust."

"You socialize with me," Maia countered.

"You're my sister. That's different."

"Brent's new in town and had nowhere to go."

"And Dad has a soft spot for people down on their luck."

Maia heard the softening in her sister's voice. "Brent said he wouldn't stay long." The exit came into view, and Maia flipped on her right blinker.

A high-pitched screech sounded in the background, and Darla groaned. "Gotta run. The girls are at it again."

"Love ya," Maia said.

"Love ya, too."

She disconnected, turning in the direction of her parents' home and her own house a mile farther down the road.

Her sister worried dinner might be awkward, which Maia understood. She, on the other hand, looked forward to it. Holidays at the MacKenzies' were a big, happy and frequently raucous occasion.

Okay, yes, Brent would be there. Of course, he had nothing to do with the excitement building inside her. That was entirely due to her anticipation of seeing family and old friends and TJ having fun with his cousins.

Except it was Brent's face continually coming to mind as she drove the remaining distance.

CHAPTER FOUR

BRENT ARRIVED EARLY to the MacKenzies' home for Thanksgiving. Not for the hot apple cider, as Ansel had suggested, but to make points with his new boss. Brent had driven three miles out of his way to find a grocery store open and had purchased a bouquet of flowers for Maia's mom. His wallet complained about the loss of another twenty-dollar bill, but he didn't feel right about arriving empty-handed.

He found a place to park on the jam-packed country road—how many people were invited today?—and strode up the walkway leading to the MacKenzies' front door. He spent a full minute breathing deeply and letting the moment sink in before ringing the doorbell. For the first time in two years, he wasn't spending a holiday by himself. That had to be a step in the right direction.

One downside—he'd be sitting across from Maia again and reminding himself of all the reasons she was off-limits. On the upside, it was good practice. He'd never turn his life around if he didn't learn to navigate difficult and uncomfortable situations.

Besides, was seeing Maia outside work really that terrible? He liked her and enjoyed her company. She had a way of putting him at ease, and he sensed no judgment when she looked at him. Then again, she didn't know his full story.

As if hearing his thoughts, she, and not one of her parents, answered the door.

"Happy Thanksgiving." She beamed at him.

"Um, thanks," he muttered, her dazzling smile momentarily short-circuiting his brain.

She nodded at the flowers. "Those are beautiful."

"They're...for your mom."

"She'll love them." Maia turned and motioned to him over her shoulder. "Come on in. I'll introduce you."

In the large great room, with its vaulted ceiling, roaring fireplace and holiday music playing in the background, at least twenty people sat or stood in small clusters. Four children of varying ages tumbled about in the center of the floor. Brent recognized the youngest one, Maia's son TJ. Most adults held a glass or bottle of some beverage. Brent's mouth watered at the enticing aromas wafting from the kitchen.

"Hey, everyone," Maia called out. "I want you to meet Brent Hayes, our new wrangler."

The introduction was met with a chorus of hellos and nice-to-meet-yous.

Brent raised his hand in greeting. "Howdy. Happy Thanksgiving."

"You know Dad, of course. And Darla. Her husband, Garret, is around here someplace."

Maia's sister stepped out from around Ansel. "Good to see you again, Brent."

Was it good? He couldn't tell if the owner of Your Perfect Plus One was okay with him being at her family's celebration or not.

"Same here. And thanks again for inviting me, Ansel," Brent said before Maia whisked him off to the kitchen where her mom was readying dinner with the help of three other people.

"Mom, this is Brent."

"A pleasure, ma'am."

Lois MacKenzie wiped her hands on her apron and then reached out to Brent. Before he could shake her hand, she pulled him into a warm embrace.

"I'm a hugger. You'll have to get used to it."

Brent tried to recall the last time someone had hugged him with such exuberance. Lois was the first one to let go.

"Ansel told me your ride went well this morning." Her lively eyes resembled Maia's. Actually, there was a lot about Lois that resembled Maia, including her mannerisms.

"The customers didn't complain, I hope."

"Not to me."

He gave her the flowers. "These are for you."

"Oh, my," she gushed and accepted the bouquet. "Aren't they gorgeous." She then handed the bouquet to Maia. "Can you put these in water for me, sweetheart?" To Brent, she said, "I look forward to chatting later. For now, I have a turkey to carve and gravy to make."

"Don't let me stop you."

Brent excused himself and, on his own, returned to the great room, ignoring his ill ease at being in a roomful of mostly strangers.

"Help yourself to some cider," Ansel said and pointed to a side table holding trays of appetizers, a Crock-pot of cider and stacks of ceramic mugs. "You won't be disappointed."

Brent did as Ansel suggested, ladling a portion of the steaming beverage into a mug. He'd skipped lunch, not wanting to spoil his appetite for today, and considered filling a plate with stuffed mushrooms and deviled eggs. Before he could, he felt a heavy weight knock into him and almost spilled his cider.

Brent looked down to see TJ on his knees and clutching Brent's boot with his chubby arms.

"Hey, buddy. What's going on?" Brent set down his cider on the table.

TJ tugged harder on the boot, the same one he'd pushed around the bunkhouse floor the previous evening. "Want."

Brent understood that word well enough. "Maybe later. Not sure your grandma fancies me walking around her house in my socks."

TJ plunked down onto his behind, wrapped his legs around Brent and pulled with all his might, his small face turning nearly the same shade of red as his sweatshirt. "Want!"

Brent chuckled. "We're going to have to reach a compromise."

"TJ!" Maia hurried over. "I'm so sorry." She bent and retrieved her son. "He's been a little stinker since we got here. It's all the people and commotion and his older cousins roughhousing."

Cousins? Some of the kids playing must belong to Darla.

TJ squirmed and grunted in an attempt to break free of Maia's grasp. When she held fast, he started to cry. She put him down but kept hold of his hand.

"What am I going to do with you?" she complained with mock sternness, her expression filled with tenderness.

She wore a red sweatshirt identical to her son's. It was then Brent saw MacKenzie Family Thanksgiving printed on the front over a cartoon turkey. He glanced at Ansel and Darla. They wore the same sweatshirt, as did Lois and two of TJ's cousins.

Corny. Also kind of nice. Brent's family hadn't done those kinds of things, and until today he'd have cringed at the idea. Funny how one's perspective could change.

"Here." Brent slipped out of his denim jacket and extended it to TJ, who grabbed the jacket with the same joyous abandon he had Brent's boot.

Struggling with the cumbersome jacket, TJ managed to insert an arm into the sleeve. Before Maia could stop him, he scooted off, dragging half the jacket on the floor behind him.

"Come back." She went after him.

Brent waylaid her with a hand on her wrist. "It's all right."

"What if he—"

"He won't."

"He could."

"Then he does."

She shook her head and grumbled, "You're as bad as he is."

Only then did he notice his hand remained on Maia's wrist. Reluctantly, he let go. He'd been here less than ten minutes and already experienced human contact twice after an incredibly long dry spell.

Lois's hug had been nice, but touching Maia was far nicer. He wouldn't lie.

Darla appeared beside them. "Come on, you two. Dinner's ready. Didn't you hear Mom calling?" She gave them a curious look.

Brent motioned for the ladies to precede him and grabbed his cider off the table. He needed to be less obvious around Maia. Her sister, their mutual employer, had become suspicious and not without reason.

The dining room table wasn't large enough to accommodate all the guests. A second folding table had been set up adjacent to it, and everyone crowded together, elbow to elbow, their spirits high.

Like the few family functions Brent had attended while growing up, the youngsters sat at a table in the kitchen. They were supervised by Darla's mother-in-law, who had insisted, so that the remaining adults could enjoy their meal. She'd flown in from out of town and claimed to relish every moment spent with her darling granddaughters.

Brent found himself sandwiched between a friend of the MacKenzies and Ansel's nephew. Maia sat four seats away from him, too far to engage in conversation. It seemed to Brent that Darla rarely took her eyes off him from her catty-corner vantage point.

Conversation flowed as platters, bowls and trays were passed from one person to the next. Brent needed little encouragement and took one of everything. He contributed little, preferring to listen. Especially when the conversation turned to the subject of Maia.

"I'm so proud of her," Lois declared to the group. "She works her tail off. Hardly a day goes by she isn't training."

"How many titles did you win before you quit?" someone asked.

"She didn't quit." Lois huffed. "She simply took a little break."

"It's okay, Mom." Maia smiled. "Most everyone here knows my story. I had a hard time bouncing back when my engagement ended and again after TJ was born. It happens. Life kicks us down, and we can't always get right back up."

"You needed some time to heal. That's all."

"Which I did, thanks to you, Dad and Darla."

Lois sent Maia a fond maternal look.

Brent tried to recall an exchange between him and either of his parents that came even remotely close to this one. There weren't any.

Memories hovered at the edges of his mind. He wasn't the only one his dad had high, sometimes unreasonable, expectations for. He'd demanded a lot from his mom, too. She'd once told Brent his dad was hard to love and had gotten that from his mom, Brent's grandmother. She hadn't been a warm person and believed sparing the rod spoiled the child.

Hearing Maia's voice returned Brent to the present.

"And to answer your question." She addressed the person across from her. "I've placed in a dozen other competitions. But none as prestigious or challenging as the Diamond Cup."

"Doesn't that start in Globe?" a man two seats over asked.

"North of Globe, yes. And ends in Monument Park here in Payson."

"That's what? Sixty miles?"

"Closer to seventy."

"And you complete the entire distance in one day?"

Maia laughed. "One long day."

"Over mountains, I might add, and across some mighty rugged terrain," Lois said.

The man helped himself to more mashed potatoes. "That must require a lot of conditioning."

"For me and the horse," Maia said. "Luckily, there are plenty of trails around Bear Creek Ranch and up by Christopher Creek. Dad usually drops me off at one of the trailheads and I ride back to the ranch. Sometimes he picks me up at another location." She sent Ansel an appreciative wink.

"I fret with her out in those mountains by herself." The look he returned held pride and admiration rather than worry.

"I'd take you along if you and Tugboat could keep up with me."

"If he went with you, I'd fret more about that poor old horse than I would Ansel," Lois said.

A round of laughter accompanied her remark, and the dinner continued. Brent was still considering what Maia had said about having a hard time bouncing back. Why couldn't he do the same? He reminded himself that she had her family, who were obviously close-knit and loving. Brent couldn't say the same, and the fault didn't lie entirely with his parents. He'd seldom visited after leaving home and made no effort to mend their differences. How could he expect their help and support? Unless he moved back to Wichita...

He rejected the notion the instant it occurred to him. Besides his work commitments here, he hated returning to his hometown a loser when he'd once been a rising young rodeo star.

"Brent?"

Realizing the woman sitting next to him had been speaking, he roused himself from his mental wanderings. "I'm sorry. What did you say?"

"Ansel tells us you're a bull and bronc rider."

"Former."

"How long did you compete?"

"Professionally, about eight years."

"Why'd you stop?"

"The time came to move on," he said instead of admitting he just hadn't been talented enough.

"Ever win any titles?"

"Some. State and divisional championships." *Less and less as the years went on.*

"That's exciting."

"I had a good run." But not quite good enough to retire a champion.

What if he'd stuck with it a little longer? Would that have made the difference? He'd never know.

"And now you're working for Ansel." The woman said with polite enthusiasm.

"Yes, ma'am."

Brent knew she meant well and was just making conversation. The fact he felt like a failure and didn't want to have this conversation wasn't her fault.

Maia abruptly stood. "I'll clear the table. Come on, Darla, you can help. It'll give us a chance to see what trouble our precious offspring have gotten into."

She smiled sweetly at Brent as she carried a load of plates to the kitchen.

He wasn't sure if she'd sensed his discomfort and interrupted to spare him or was merely assisting with cleanup. Either way, he was grateful to her and relieved when Ansel drew him and several others into a conversation about the latest food drives for Payson Rescue Mission.

"What are you doing?" Darla whispered in Maia's ear.

"Um…breaking up a squabble?"

With dinner over, the kids had resumed playing—this time at the table in the kitchen. TJ had gotten into a tug-of-war with the neighbor's grandson over a plastic turkey centerpiece. Maia had been doing her best to intervene before the battle escalated to full-on warfare when her sister interrupted.

"Not them." Darla straightened, her hands propped on her hips. "With Brent."

Maia managed to extricate the plastic turkey from TJ and the little boy, who immediately lost interest. Scrambling off his chair, he disappeared into the next room, presumably to join his family. TJ began wailing, and Maia groaned. Honestly, he'd been a handful today.

"I don't know what you're talking about," she insisted.

"You were practically giddy when you introduced Brent to everyone," Darla whispered. "Then, you were cozying up together over appetizers."

"I was not giddy, and we weren't *cozying up.*" She'd been happy to see Brent. Nothing more. She'd also been happy to see her aunt Cecily and uncle Bennie. "We were just talking, and TJ started pestering Brent about his boots."

"His boots?"

"It's a long story." Maia resettled TJ at the table, giving him a stack of plastic holiday cups to keep him busy.

"I haven't seen you act like that since you and Luke were first dating."

Luke. Why did her sister have to mention her former fiancé? Maia couldn't imagine herself once giddy over him, but she supposed it was true. He'd been a charmer. He'd probably also charmed the two women he'd been seeing on the side while they were engaged.

"Brent's a nice guy," Maia said. "He doesn't know many people here, and I was putting him at ease."

"Did you forget this is me you're talking to?"

At a high-pitched squeal, Darla turned her attention to her youngest daughter who was tugging on her older sister's braid. Once peace was restored, she and Maia moved to the counter where they began transferring leftovers into food-storage containers. Maia was glad the lively chatter between their mom and the other two helpers drowned out her conversation with Darla. Just like Maia's dad, her mom was eager for Maia to dip her toe into the dating pool. If she thought for one second Maia fancied Brent, she'd needle Maia nonstop.

"Okay, fine," Maia said. "I confess. Brent's an interesting guy."

"And gorgeous."

"If you prefer the rugged outdoor type." Which Maia did.

"Look, I hate to be the romance police and ruin your fun, but he's your coworker. You shouldn't be seeing him socially. You can't see him. You signed a contract."

"I'm not seeing him. He offered to help me with Snapple's skittishness is all." At her sister's pointed stare, Maia added, "He used to work for the BLM, rehabilitating wild mustangs."

"I'm aware of that. It was on his employment application."

"I promise you," she said, sealing a cover on the remaining green beans and stacking the container atop the one containing sweet potatoes. "There's nothing between us."

"Other than you find him interesting. Which, last I checked, was potentially the start of a romance."

"I'm too busy for a boyfriend. And I'm not sure I'm ready for one, to be honest. But even if I am, I have to be careful. I'm not the only one who would get hurt this time. There's TJ to consider."

"Aw, sis. No one wants you to be happy and find a great guy more than me." Darla and Maia carried the many containers to the refrigerator and found places for them. "I'm just not sure Brent's right for you."

"Not that I care, but why?"

"He's..." Darla hesitated as if afraid of revealing too much. "At loose ends."

"You say *loose ends* like he's harboring a deep, dark secret."

"I have my suspicions."

"Of what?" Maia asked. "Did he commit a crime?"

"No, no. I wouldn't have hired him unless he passed a background check. Plus, Channing vouched for him."

"What then?"

"His… Oh, I shouldn't say." Darla turned away.

Maia groaned. "You can't drop a hint and then clam up."

"There are some gaps in his employment history. And that's all you're going to get out of me."

"Gaps?"

"Not enough to concern me or Dad as far as hiring Brent."

"But they concern you as far as potential boyfriend material."

"Can't help myself. I'm your big sister." Darla dropped the remaining rolls into a plastic bag and sealed the top.

"Like I said, I have no intention of dating Brent."

But if she did date him, that would be her business, not Darla's. As long as Maia wasn't employed by Your Perfect Plus One.

Her parents might also have an opinion on the subject, though they be less vocal than Darla. Like Darla, they'd become overly protective of Maia after she discovered Luke's infidelity and wanted to look out for her.

But one lapse in judgment didn't mean she'd make a second one. She'd learned her lesson, and her family knew that.

"I love you and worry about you is all," Darla said.

"I love you, too." Maia bumped shoulders with her sister.

With the kitchen cleaned, she took TJ with her to the living room. She wasn't searching for Brent. Nope, not at all.

She found him near the front door, glancing around and wearing an I'm-ready-to-leave expression. She hurried over with TJ in tow.

"There you are." She cleared her throat, attempting to mask her rising panic. "You're not leaving already?"

"Apparently not. I can't locate my jacket."

Whew! She'd caught him in the nick of time.

She lowered herself to TJ's level. "Sweetie, what did you do with the jacket?" Her son was at an age where he understood much of what was said to him even if he couldn't verbalize in return. Or, refused to.

"The jacket, sweetie. Where is it? Mommy's friend needs to leave."

TJ remained stubbornly mute.

"Hey, buddy." Brent winked at TJ. "Want to go outside with me?"

TJ whirled and stared up at him, his face bright with anticipation. He then hurled himself at the door and yanked on the knob with both fists. "Ya, ya, ya!"

"Okay. But you have to wear a jacket. It's cold outside."

TJ scurried off to the living room where he ducked behind a recliner in the corner. A moment later, he reappeared, dragging Brent's jacket by the sleeve.

Maia winced. "I'll pay to have it laundered."

Brent chuckled. "You worry too much."

When TJ reached them, Brent picked up the jacket and slung it over the boy's shoulders. The hem dragged on the floor.

"Let's go, buddy." He put a hand on TJ's shoulder.

Maia's heart melted a little. Luke wanted nothing to do with TJ, and here was a near stranger treating her son with kindness, patience and affection. What was wrong with Luke?

Worse, how could she have been so blind? She'd believed he loved her and that he wanted a family as much as she did. They'd often discussed the future during their engagement, sharing their goals and dreams—goals and dreams Maia had believed were mutual. And all that time, he'd been seeing two different women on the side. Her stomach still twisted at the memory.

He'd asked her forgiveness, claiming he was sowing his wild oats before settling down to a life of monogamy, and swore it wouldn't happen again. Maia thought she'd never heard such a load of hogwash. She almost hadn't told him about the positive pregnancy test. After several weeks of soul-searching, she had, resigned to allowing Luke a role in TJ's life, though not in hers. To her shock, he'd accused her of trying to trap him into marriage.

Trap him! As if she'd want him after what he did to her. She'd told the jerk exactly what he could do with his accusation in no uncertain terms.

A few weeks later, once she'd cooled off and had a long talk with her sister, she again contacted Luke. She'd kept him in the loop during her pregnancy and left the door open after TJ was born. If Luke chose not to see their son or have anything to do with him, that was his decision and his alone. The monthly child-support payments were appreciated, but no substitute for an involved and caring father.

She hoped Luke was losing significant amounts of sleep over abandoning their son. And if not, thank goodness TJ didn't have to deal with someone so incredibly selfish and heartless. Though, it pained her to think her darling baby boy would grow up knowing his father didn't want him.

Outside, Maia and Brent watched as TJ half walked, half crawled down the steps to the front yard.

"Your jacket's leaving without you," she said.

"Give him a few minutes to blow off some steam."

"He is overly excited today." Maia considered Brent's observation an astute one for a single man with no children. His lack of concern for his jacket showed an appealing good-naturedness. "Did you have a nice time? You seemed kind of quiet at dinner."

"I had a real nice time. I thanked your dad before leaving, but please give your mom my regards. She's an excellent cook."

"I will."

They were quiet for another minute while TJ leaped from one spot to the next on the front lawn. Maia was about to make some banal remark about the holidays and small children when Brent spoke.

"I don't talk much about my rodeo career."

"O...kay."

"People always ask me why I quit."

Ah. The conversation at dinner when he'd become visibly uncomfortable.

"I suppose they do. People are curious."

"Given the choice, I'd rather not say."

"All right." She wasn't sure how else to respond.

"But I want you to know."

"You say that as if you're warning me."

"I guess I am." Brent drew in a breath. "I quit because I wasn't good enough. And rather than continue to publicly embarrass myself, I walked away."

"Not good enough or did you burn out? I've seen that happen in competitive trail riding."

"I wish I had. Sounds better than admitting I lacked the talent."

"I doubt you lacked the talent. You qualified for nationals. Multiple times."

"And then, one year, I didn't. Or the next year. Or the one after that. My rankings fell. Even a nongenius like me could see the writing on the wall."

She heard the disappointment in his tone, saw it in his eyes and felt it in her own heart. "You're being too hard on yourself, Brent."

"I'm being a realist."

"What you are is going through a rough patch. And there's no reason you can't come back from it. Lots of athletes do."

He paused, and she waited for him to continue. From what she'd learned about him, he was slow to open up.

Finally, he said, "Apparently, I'm not the best at handling setbacks and, because of that, I…have some problems."

Was that what Darla had been alluding to?

"Can I ask, what kind of problems?"

"I had a plan, and when that plan failed to materialize, I fell into a funk. Truthfully, I'm still in it."

Maia considered before responding, thinking of her own circumstances. "Losses come in all forms. Relationships ending, which I can speak to from personal experience. Death of a loved one. Grown children leaving home, so my mom tells me. Being laid off work. A health crisis. The list goes on. And losses, regardless of their nature, require a certain amount of grieving in order for a person to recover."

"Five stages," he said with false mirth. "I've read about it."

She had, too, and instantly regretted playing armchair psychiatrist. "Sorry. Sometimes I talk too much."

"Hey, I'm the one who brought it up."

"No excuse for lecturing."

"You weren't. And I'm curious, how'd you bounce back when things got hard?"

"I had help. My family, for one."

"Yeah. That's not an option for me."

Maia might have inquired about his family, but his stony expression stopped her. "I found a purpose. First and foremost, being the best mom possible to my son."

"Also not an option. The purpose, that is. I haven't found one."

"I joined a support group after TJ was born for women dealing with the pressures of single motherhood. I got a lot out of it. I realize you're not a single mom, but there are several support groups at the Payson Rescue Mission. Flyers are in the lobby."

"I'm not ready for a support group."

"Okay."

He avoided talking about himself, and she doubted he'd do well in a group setting. In fact, she was surprised he'd admitted everything he had to her. He must do better one-on-one.

"Have you spoken with your doctor? I did with mine, and she prescribed—"

"I don't need medication." His features abruptly darkened. "I'm not that bad off."

"No, no. Of course not. I wasn't implying you were. My doctor was the one who suggested the new mothers group. It was there I learned I wasn't alone. I guarantee, you aren't alone, either."

He nodded but said nothing.

"We all get into temporary funks. It's normal and part of life. We just have to find the right remedy."

"I'm hoping working for your dad and sister does the trick."

Well, that explained why he'd taken a wrangler job far beneath his qualifications. "Work is good for the mind and body. Even if I could afford to be a stay-at-home mom, I'm not sure I would. I need new experiences and to engage with people. It's another reason I like working for Darla, but don't tell her I said that."

Brent didn't smile as she'd hoped.

"It's getting late," he said. "I should go."

"You need your jacket." Maia caught up with TJ. As expected, he pitched a fit at losing his prize and quieted only when she swung him high in the air.

"Thanks again for the invitation," Brent said, accepting his jacket.

"Remember, you're partnering with Rowdy tomorrow. I probably won't see you. I'm training most of the day."

"Good luck."

She watched him amble down the driveway, her lower lip caught between her teeth. She couldn't help thinking she'd made a mistake offering advice instead of simply listening. Depression, even in its mildest forms, often carried a negative stigma. There were people who looked down on those suffering from mental illness, and, as a result, those suffering refused to get the help they needed for fear of being judged. It was a terrible cycle.

Heading back inside, Maia ruffled TJ's hair. "Mommy owes our new friend an apology."

Except, how did she give one without making Brent feel worse than he already did?

CHAPTER FIVE

BRENT CHECKED THE LEVEL in the horses' water trough while Rowdy pushed the wheelbarrow to the Dumpster behind the stables where he'd dispose of the manure. The last ride for the day had ended almost an hour ago, after which Brent and Rowdy had cleaned the pen. Not the most pleasant daily chore but a necessary one with this many head. Any cowboy worth his lick had cleaned his share of pens over the years, including Brent.

He'd started as a kid under his dad's supervision. Everett Hayes had been a three-time world champion. Yet another reason Brent's failure to make a name for himself in rodeo had sent him sailing over the edge into an abyss. He'd been compared to his dad his entire career, and not favorably in the end.

Rowdy returned just as Brent was shutting off the water spigot. The young cowboy drove into the pen on the ATV hauling a small utility trailer loaded with hay. The horses mobbed the trailer as if they hadn't eaten in a week, squealing and nipping at each other and reaching in to grab mouthfuls.

Brent sauntered over to the metal feeder and waited for Rowdy. He'd met his coworker and bunk mate two days ago on Thanksgiving evening when Rowdy returned late from spending the holiday with his girlfriend. Brent had immediately liked the affable twenty-two-year-old whose slow drawl and bowlegged swagger belied an impressive intelligence. Rowdy planned to resign from Mountainside Stables next May when he obtained his degree and, if all went as planned, hired on with the forest service. Appearances could be deceiving.

What, Brent wondered, did people think when they looked at him? Did he give the impression of having his life together or were the deep cracks he tried to hide obvious to all?

Maia could see them; Brent had no doubt. That was one of the reasons he'd approached her outside her parents' house on Thanksgiving. He thought she might be more understanding than most. But the second she'd suggested he seek medical help, he'd shut down and distanced himself.

He *wasn't* crazy or a weakling, and he certainly *didn't* have a mental illness. He just struggled with periodic dark moments. And who wouldn't in his shoes?

The quiet voice inside his head tried speaking up. Brent silenced it, refusing to listen.

Rowdy hopped off the ATV, leaving the engine idling, and helped Brent transfer thick flakes of hay into the nearest feeder. The horses vied for position, with the smaller and less aggressive ones forced to wait on the second feed trough.

"You think we should put some salve on Shorty's leg?" Brent asked.

The small black had scraped his knee on a jagged branch during the afternoon ride. And while not serious, Brent thought the scrape would benefit from a dab of antibiotic ointment.

"Probably," Rowdy said. "There's some in the tack room."

"I'll get it when we're done here."

The two of them had gone out together on the three short trail rides yesterday and two longer ones today, each ride traveling a different route. This morning Brent had returned the binder Maia lent him, having memorized most of the material. He'd continued to bring up the rear on the rides like with Maia, and was content to do so because it required less work and gave him the opportunity to watch and learn.

Also, to study the horses. From his vantage point, he'd observed them responding to the riders and noted any particular behavior that would aid in matching riders to mounts on future rides.

Another benefit of caring for Mountainside's livestock, he'd gotten to know Maia's big Appaloosa. Snapple insisted on being in charge, which was typical for a horse of his size and strength and with his competitive nature. He was naturally curious and liked people, Ansel in particular. He wanted to be part of whatever anyone was doing, be that trimming manes or examining a loose shoe. He adored Maia above all others and had practically jumped into her arms when she'd fetched him from the pen yesterday.

That had been one of the few times Brent and Maia had crossed paths since their talk on her parents' porch. He'd begun to wonder if she'd canceled their scheduled training session with Snapple without telling him. Then, she'd arrived bright and early this morning while he and Rowdy were saddling horses for a group of waiting customers. With a "Meet you at three" from her, his question had been answered.

Snapple had been safely tucked in the horse pen when Brent and Rowdy returned a short while ago from their second trail ride. Maia was home. Rowdy had mentioned in passing that Ansel had driven her and Snapple to one of the trailheads south of Bear Creek Ranch toward Payson, making the majority of her practice ride uphill.

"You free for dinner?" Rowdy asked as he and Brent moved to the second feeder, the remaining horses plodding along after them. "Feel like heading to town for a burger and a beer? I'm buying."

"Sorry, man. Another time? Maia and I are getting together at three."

"That's right. You're helping her with Snapple."

"We'll see. I'm going to show her some of the techniques we used on wild mustangs when I worked for the BLM."

"No joke! You worked for the Bureau of Land Management? I need to hear about that."

"It's a long story. I'll tell you about it when you buy me that beer."

"I can wait until you and Maia are done."

Brent gave a casual shrug. "I have plans tonight."

"Ah…" Rowdy flashed a sly smile. "Do tell."

"She's just a friend."

A friend who happened to be a complete stranger. She and Brent would meet for the first time at a coffee shop near the wedding venue. Brent had already received her bio and an outline of the role he would play tonight—they'd been recently introduced by a mutual friend. That would explain both their limited familiarity with each other and the reason she'd give for their relationship "fizzling out."

Unlike Thanksgiving eve, this wedding was a small affair. Following the ceremony at a local church, they'd attend a catered dinner in the home of the groom's grandparents. Brent doubted he'd run into anyone he knew. Definitely not Maia.

"Another time, then," Rowdy said.

"Count on it." Brent pointed toward the stables. "I'd better get that salve for Shorty."

Ten minutes later, they were done with their chores and coming out of the stables when Rowdy suddenly stopped in his tracks.

"Looks likes your date's here."

Alarmed, Brent followed the younger man's gaze. Had his wedding date showed up here rather than the coffee shop?

But instead of—what was her name? Brent would have to reread the email—Maia jogged toward them, pushing TJ in one of those exercise strollers. Brent's alarm vanished, and a different kind of anticipation rushed in to fill the space. Maia slowed as she neared. From the looks of her flushed face and disheveled ponytail, she'd had a long run.

"Lucky you," Rowdy said to Brent, his drawl infused with innuendo. "Getting to work with her."

"Strictly business."

"Whatever you say."

Maia reached them, cutting off Brent's response.

"Hi, guys." She stopped near the hitching post, blew out a long breath and propped her hands on her slim hips. TJ squealed and waved his arms in the air from his seat.

"Hey, Maia." Rowdy flashed a big ole smile. "Had yourself a run."

"Yeah. Seven miles."

"Wow." Brent didn't think he could run more than two miles without collapsing. All right, three. And a half. "That's some serious distance."

Even more impressive considering she'd already ridden Snapple for several hours through the mountains.

"Competitive trail riding takes a toll on the rider, too," she said. "Not just the horse. I need to build my stamina, or I'll lose steam halfway through the day."

Brent had worked and trained hard at rodeo and spent entire days in the saddle more than once while working for the BLM. Not, however, while charging up and down rugged mountain trails. He liked to think he was stronger than a slip of a gal like Maia, but realized he wasn't.

"You ready to start?" she asked him.

It was Rowdy who answered. "I'm just taking off. Catch you later, Brent." He ambled past Maia and TJ. "Take 'er easy, Maia. You, too, little man." He held out his hand, palm up, for TJ to high-five.

"I'll get Snapple," Brent offered and went into the stables for a halter.

When he returned two minutes later, Maia was unbuckling a now-wailing TJ from the stroller. "He's going to keep crying unless I let him out."

"Should we wait? Snapple's mighty big and TJ's mighty little."

"Don't worry." She hoisted him into her arms. "I'll be diligent. And if he escapes, back into the stroller he goes."

Brent continued to the pen, not entirely comfortable with a small child on the loose during training. Snapple came willingly once Brent put on the halter. Outside the pen, he tied the horse to the hitching post.

"Don't come too close," he cautioned Maia and then proceeded to thoroughly examine Snapple, running his hand along the horse's flank.

As Maia had reported, Snapple shuffled nervously when Brent got near the gnarly looking scar.

"Must have been some bite."

"Yeah," Maia agreed, disengaging her ponytail from TJ's grip. "I'd be sensitive, too."

"Tell me about what happens during a typical judging interval."

"They're usually every hour. A horse is scored on their rate of recovery. A vet listens to their heart and lungs, taking specific readings. The faster a horse recovers, the higher the score and the sooner a rider can resume the competition. During the examination, the horse is expected to exhibit good manners and a calm disposition."

"If not, you're disqualified," Brent finished.

"Like I said, Snapple used to bolt. I've been working with him since I bought him, and now he just gets antsy and sidesteps. But if the vet can't obtain his readings, he can't determine Snapple's rate of recovery. There is no getting around it."

Brent flicked his hand near Snapple's ear, and the horse instantly jerked his head back. "Well, he can see fine. His reaction to the scar has nothing to do with vision loss."

"I figured as much. He's just never gotten over that bite. Equine PTSD."

"Look at it from his perspective," Brent said. "In the wild, horses are prey. Snapple has a hundred thousand years of survival instincts encoded into his DNA. Being domesticated makes no difference. Horses with impaired senses, like vision loss, become overly fearful and run at the slightest hint of trouble."

"Self-preservation."

"Exactly. Since loss of vision isn't the case with Snapple, we have to assume the memory of being attacked from behind is imbedded so deep, he shies first and evaluates the threat later." Brent demonstrated by coming at Snapple from the front. "Notice he has zero reaction when he sees me coming."

"I can't ask a judge to come at Snapple from a different direction." Maia made a face. "There's no special treatment. Not for bad manners."

Brent went around to Snapple's other side. When he repeated his inspection and ran his hand along the horse's flank, a disinterested Snapple merely lowered his head to the ground and sniffed the dirt. Brent returned to Snapple's afflicted side and stepped back to study him.

"We saw this same behavior a lot in the wild mustangs. Self-preservation. It'll be hard to retrain Snapple, though not impossible. What we need to do is desensitize him. Teach him that what happened once won't happen again."

"How did you desensitize the wild mustangs?"

"Different ways, depending on the horse and the problem. I'm partial to the fishing-pole-and-sock method."

"The what?"

TJ yapped loudly as if asking the same question as his mom.

"Tie a plain old white sock to the end of a fishing pole. I'll show you next time." Brent moved closer to Snapple. "You do have a fishing pole and sock?"

"Dad does."

Brent continued studying Snapple. "You've tried positive reinforcement? Rewarding him for good behavior?"

"I have. That's how we progressed from running off to just sidestepping. Took some doing. A lot of trust building."

Brent started whistling. When he had Snapple's full attention, he moved his hand close to the scar. He got a whole inch closer than the last time before the horse began snorting and prancing in place.

"Okay. Easy does it, boy."

"That was a little progress."

Brent patted Snapple's neck. "We might try some other distraction techniques. But first, the fishing pole and sock. He has to learn not to be afraid, and that's a process. Often a long one."

"Thank you."

The soft quality of her voice compelled him to meet her gaze for the first time since he'd begun working with Snapple. Light radiated from her smile, like sunshine in a bottle, and he wanted one for himself.

"I haven't done anything yet," he said, breaking eye contact. "Let's wait."

"I have a good feeling."

He wanted very much to live up to her expectations. He'd do anything if she'd just keep smiling at him like that.

"I'll put Snapple away," he murmured. "You have your hands full." He indicated TJ, who was doing his level best to twist free.

She gave TJ's ear a playful tug. "Then I can finally put this little wiggle worm down."

Inside the pen, Brent slipped the halter off Snapple and then once again tried distracting the horse with whistling. He was able to get his hand an inch closer before Snapple snorted and retreated several feet.

"Whoa, boy. Easy does it." He held out his palm.

After a moment's hesitation, Snapple approached and nuzzled Brent's fingers.

"There you go. Was that so hard?"

Snapple shook his head, spun and trotted off, his way of having the last word. Brent understood. There'd been a time he'd always wanted the last word, too.

"I'm impressed. You have a real knack with horses," Maia said when Brent returned. She'd put TJ down, and the boy played contentedly at her feet, stacking pebbles into a pile. "You could have your own YouTube channel or start a podcast."

"Funny."

"I'm serious."

His mood, previously good, took an abrupt dip. How did he respond to her? That besides having no postrodeo career plans, he had little motivation to do more than take vacationing Bear Creek Ranch guests on trail rides?

"Sorry. I need to get going," he said, desperate to safeguard what remained of his good mood for tonight. "I have a wedding to attend."

With a nod, he left, rounding the stables to where he'd parked his truck.

Another bullet dodged. Another question evaded. Another potential judgment averted.

Maia leaned back and centered her weight as Snapple carefully picked his way down the steep, rugged trail. She squeezed with her knees and grabbed the saddle horn to anchor herself when he hopped over a fallen branch. His metal shoes clanged on the sharp rocks, their slick surface causing him to briefly lose his footing. Maia gasped but didn't panic. Snapple knew his stuff, and she trusted him completely.

He continued his descent, moving faster than was safe. Faster than anyone would normally travel on such challenging terrain. One misstep, and they'd both tumble hard, sustaining serious injuries when they hit the ground. Or worse. Eleven hundred pounds of horse could easily crush a hundred-and-twenty-pound human. Maia and Snapple were taking their lives in their hands—and hooves.

Her heart thundered inside her chest, from excitement and

danger. She loved competitive trail riding. Snapple did, too. He attacked each new challenge like an invincible warrior. She didn't have to ask more from him; he willingly gave it.

She hoped Brent was doing all right. She heard him behind her on Lone Star. At least, she had heard him. She'd been too preoccupied during this very arduous descent to pay attention to anything other than her and Snapple.

If Brent and Lone Star fell, they might roll forward and crash into Maia and Snapple, causing a serious calamity. Lone Star, while a competent trail horse, was unused to rides at this demanding level. If he fared well, it would be entirely due to Brent's ability. So far, so good.

She straightened little by little as they reached the bottom of the mountain. Snapple leaped over the small creek, a tributary of nearby Bear Creek, and landed solidly on the opposite side. Only when they came to a stop did Maia look behind her.

Brent and Lone Star were about fifty yards up the mountain and doing all right from what she could tell. If they'd managed to keep pace with her and Snapple, she'd have been shocked.

"I slowed him down," Brent said after he and Lone Star had crossed the creek. Unlike Snapple, the lanky buckskin trudged through the water. "He was getting tired."

"What about you?"

"I could go another round." Brent grinned. "Not another fifteen miles. I'm not sure how you do it."

"Lots of practice." She patted Snapple's neck. Neither of them was breathing hard.

To be fair, neither was Brent. The same couldn't be said for poor Lone Star. His sides heaved from the unaccustomed exertion, and his head hung low.

"Can we take a short break?" Brent asked. "This guy did all the hard work and deserves one."

"You mind if we start walking back toward the ranch? I have a wedding this afternoon. We can go slow."

Brent nudged Lone Star forward. "Speaking strictly for my horse, we'd appreciate it."

She laughed at that, and he joined in.

They'd worked together almost every day this past week and had developed an easygoing friendship. Their mutual attraction had been set aside, though not forgotten. Maia still found Brent attractive, but she'd learned to temper her responses. Him, too, apparently.

The result? Things were much better now. Best of all, Darla hadn't mentioned Brent again.

Maia had also noticed he seemed to be in a better mood. There had been fewer sudden mood shifts and no withdrawing behind invisible walls. According to her dad, Brent was always on time, worked hard, complained little, learned fast and was good with the customers. Though quiet and private, he got along well with his bunk mates. Rowdy had reported that Brent created no problems and broke no rules. A model employee by all accounts.

"Did you learn anything about Snapple on our ride?" Maia asked. This was the first day they'd been able to go on a ride together so that Brent could gauge Snapple's responses.

"Well, you saw how he reacted at the start of the ride when I rode up behind you."

"I did."

Snapple had nearly unseated Maia when Lone Star nosed his tail. He'd kicked out and then bucked furiously. Maia was better prepared the second time.

"He didn't notice us at all when we were going down that last stretch of mountain," Brent said.

"He was too busy concentrating on what was ahead rather than behind. Heck, I didn't notice you until you called out to me."

"We have to figure out a way to combine distraction techniques with reprogramming his fear responses."

They discussed various training approaches for the next

fifteen minutes, with Brent telling her about a particularly stubborn mustang he'd rehabilitated for the Bureau of Land Management. Maia liked that he didn't once mention using force or punishment. She herself had never and would never inflict pain on a living creature, even if she lost her temper.

At the stables, they unsaddled and brushed the horses. While Maia returned Lone Star to the pen, Brent set up the fishing pole and sock that Maia had borrowed from her dad. He'd taken a group of riders out for a ride or he'd have been here, having expressed an interest in watching Brent. Maybe next time. Snapple would likely require several training sessions.

She returned to find Brent had already attached the lunge line to Snapple's halter and was walking Snapple in a slow circle at the end of the six-foot line. He held the fishing pole in his hand with the sock tied to the end, all the while talking to Snapple and encouraging him to relax.

"I'll just sit here," Maia said and plunked down on the bench beside the hitching rail.

Brent didn't appear to hear her. His focus remained riveted on Snapple. The horse's ears twitched, indicating he was alert and listening to Brent.

"That's right. Nothing to worry about." With his free hand, he lifted the fishing pole and slowly stretched the tip with the dangling sock toward Snapple. "It's just a sock, boy. Can't hurt you."

Snapple snorted and shook his head but kept walking.

Brent touched the sock to Snapple's hind end. The horse danced sideways for two steps before settling.

"Good job. See? Nothing there to hurt you."

Brent moved the sock along Snapple's spine toward his mane and then reversed direction, returning the sock to his rump. Snapple snorted again and abruptly stopped. Brent jiggled the lunge line and clucked to him. Snapple obediently resumed walking, turning his head and eyeing the sock with mild contempt.

This went on for five full minutes, until Snapple paid the

sock no heed. Then, Brent changed the game and lowered the sock to Snapple's side, close to his scar. Instantly, the horse huffed and shied away.

"Settle down," Brent coaxed. "Just a sock, remember?"

He tried a dozen more times. Snapple's response would lessen by small degrees and then, suddenly, he'd blow up again, snorting and kicking out his back feet.

"I think we've had enough for one day," Brent announced after three circles with no reaction. He set down the fishing pole. "We should end on a positive."

"Yeah, I agree," Maia said. "He's making progress already. Each time he gets upset, he calms down quicker than the last."

"Hard to say for sure. The proof will be our next training session. Does he remember what we learned today or revert to his old ways?"

She pushed off the bench and stood. "I need to hit the road. I'd like to stop at the folks' and spend some time with TJ before the wedding. I hate leaving him so much with my mom."

Though her son appeared happy and healthy and well-adjusted, Maia didn't want him growing up with a part-time mother on top of an absent father. Plus, it wasn't fair to her own mother, putting so much of TJ's caretaking responsibility on her.

The extra money from Your Perfect Plus One was hard to resist, however. Especially during the holidays. TJ was older this Christmas. He'd get a thrill out of opening presents and attending the different holiday events with Maia and the family.

Presents cost money. As did her saddle. She'd pay off the balance in a few months, in time to break in the saddle before the Diamond Cup.

She was also determined that Santa leave plenty of gifts under the trees. She'd need a heathy checkbook balance for that to happen.

While she placed Snapple in the pen, Brent took the fishing pole and sock into the stables to store for the next time. When he didn't come right out, she followed him inside to see what had become of him.

"You lost in here?" she called.

He stood near the office door, staring down at his phone. "Sorry, I got a text from Darla. She had an employee cancel at the last minute and wants to know if I'm free to take his place." He began one-finger typing a response.

"You saying yes?"

"I am. If I don't pay down my credit card balances soon, they'll send someone after me."

Credit card balances? Maia digested that bit of information. Did Brent's joke hide a truth? Was he working a second job to pay off his bills?

"I hear you," she said. "That custom saddle of mine is costing me a small fortune." When he didn't respond, she asked, "Where's your wedding?"

He paused typing to reread the original text. "Um... Valley Fellowship Church. The reception's at some country club."

Maia thought she must have misheard. "Valley Fellowship Church? That's where my wedding is. Are you sure? Darla wouldn't schedule us at the same wedding. Not again." Not unless she had no choice.

"Yep." Brent shrugged. "That's what it says. Should I tell her no? Will it cause a problem?"

Before Maia could respond, her phone pinged. She pulled it from her jacket pocket.

"What do you bet this is her?" She quickly read the text. "She's telling me you'll be at the wedding and reminding me to pretend we don't know each other."

It was followed by a trio of stern-face emojis and then a heart. Maia sighed.

Brent's phone pinged.

"Let me guess. Darla sending you the same text."

He grinned. "You can't blame her for covering her bases. She has a business to run. And we were a little chatty at Thanksgiving."

"Humph. I think I'm insulted."

Brent tapped a reply.

"What are you saying?"

"I told her she has nothing to worry about."

"I suppose I should do the same."

Maia did. When she finished, she stuffed her phone back in her jacket pocket. "Looks like I'll see you later tonight."

"I'll see you, but not talk to you, *stranger*."

Maia pretended to zipper her lips closed.

All kidding aside, she was serious about avoiding Brent and not disappointing her sister. Especially now that she knew he needed a second paycheck as much as she did.

CHAPTER SIX

EVERY ONE OF Brent's good intentions flew out the window the second he walked into Valley Fellowship Church. He immediately glanced around the foyer area for Maia. Had she arrived yet? Was she in the sanctuary or still outside?

"Thanks for filling in on such short notice," his date whispered.

"My pleasure—" he paused to think, relieved when his memory finally kicked in "—Lizzie."

She smiled.

"Hope I'll do. I know I wasn't your first choice."

"You're a guy, and you're here with me. That should be enough to stop my parents from nagging me about getting a social life."

Brent and Lizzie had met twenty minutes ago in the parking lot of the Mexican restaurant near her apartment building. He hadn't expected her to be so young—a grad student at Eastern Arizona College. Not that Brent was exactly old at twenty-nine, but he felt like he'd lived an entire lifetime longer than the elf-like woman beside him.

"They're convinced I'm too focused on school," she said.

"Getting an education is important."

Brent almost added he wished he'd gone to college, then remembered their cover story. They'd met at a robotics demonstration on campus. Lizzie was an engineering nerd who preferred designing prototypes to hitting the clubs or hanging out with friends. She cared nothing for fashion and had admitted needing to buy her outfit for the wedding—silver leggings and an oversize black sweater. Since a former professional rodeo cowboy was the last person on Earth she'd meet, much less date, Brent had left his cowboy hat and boots at home. But if her parents put him on the spot and expected him to talk knowledgeably about robotics, he'd be in trouble.

He and Lizzie sat in one of the pews on the groom's side. She'd explained her connection during the drive here. Brent had already forgotten. He'd been preoccupied thinking of Maia and looking forward to seeing her here tonight. In hindsight, he should have turned down Darla's request. Except she'd offered a nice bonus as incentive, and he could really use the extra money.

Lizzie wasn't inclined to chat much, which suited Brent fine. She introduced him to her parents when they appeared and sat down in the pew beside her. He made polite, nice-to-meet-you conversation. In the middle of her dad recounting a recent business trip to Seattle, Maia entered with her date. Everything Lizzie's father said after that became white noise to Brent.

Maia looked as perfectly matched to her date as he was ill matched to his. Tall and fit and oozing success, the man wore a tailored suit and sported a hundred-dollar haircut. He escorted Maia to a pew on the bride's side with an easy confidence Brent envied. Why he needed to retain Your Perfect Plus One, Brent couldn't guess. Guys like him didn't have trouble getting a date. Women asked them out.

When Maia smiled pleasantly at the guy, Brent's gut tightened. She was playing a role, he assured himself. Even so, she and the guy made an attractive couple, and Brent was jealous. He wanted to be the one sitting next to Maia and chatting amiably to the people sitting in front of them.

Except that guy was a far better choice for her than Brent

and, from all appearances, had a lot more to offer. What did Brent bring to the table? Periodic dives into an emotional murk. Substantial debt. A job that put a roof over his head and food in his mouth but had no advancement potential. And he had no long-term career plans. Everything he owned could be carried in his truck.

His mood started to plummet. He tried to listen to Lizzie's dad. Wait, her mom was the one talking. About…her…social group. They…read books. No, made scrapbooks. Brent offered a generic comment when one appeared to be called for.

There'd been a time he dreamed of being the kind of guy with Maia—wearing tailored suits and striding into rooms with confidence. Having world champion tagged onto his name, the title opening all manner of doors.

What if he could still be that guy? Granted, he was down on his luck right now. But there was no reason he couldn't pick himself up and start over. People did it all the time.

There, he supposed, was the rub. Picking oneself up required a direction. A goal. Brent had only ever wanted to be a competitive bull and bronc rider. He'd seen himself making appearances postretirement and lending his name to gear or clothing or perhaps appearing in commercials. The fellow who'd won the world title two years ago had recently landed a bit part in a movie.

Brent continued to watch Maia, unable to tear his glance away. Maybe she was the motivation he lacked. A reason to spring out of bed every day with enthusiasm rather than trepidation. Pay off his bills. Get his life on track. Reinvent himself.

"Oh, look!" Lizzie's mom elbowed her. "There's Dillon. Whatever happened between you two? Remind me."

"Mom." Lizzie made a sour face. "I'm here with Brad."

Brad? Oh, yeah. Brent's fake name for this date.

"I always liked him," her mom continued, a wistfulness in her voice as she stared at the gangly young man awkwardly scooting past a seated couple.

Lizzie inched closer to Brent as if to make a statement. "I apologize for my mom."

"It's okay." In any other circumstances, Brent would have laughed. Dillon looked to be Lizzie's other half. The à la mode to her apple pie. The yin to her yang. "Let me guess. He's also majoring in engineering."

Lizzie rolled her eyes. "Biophysics."

Brent had no idea what that was and didn't ask.

Shortly after that, the wedding started. Thirty minutes later, they were filing out of the church. Apparently because of her distaste for socializing, Lizzie avoided engaging guests in conversation. She insisted she and Brent skip the receiving line, citing they wouldn't be missed. Weaving through the throng of people, they headed toward the church entrance to wait for her parents. Suddenly, Dillon materialized before them—possibly, on purpose.

"Hey." His goofy face broke into a wide grin.

Lizzie sniffed. "Hello."

"Figured I might run into you."

"Well now you have, and we have to go." She grabbed Brent's arm and spirited him away.

"You still like him," Brent observed with mild humor when they reached the entrance and Lizzie stopped to breathe.

"I do not."

"Why'd you break up?"

"I don't know." Her shoulders slumped. "School. We both had heavy class loads."

"And now? You still have a heavy class load?"

"Yes." She looked down. "At least, I do."

"Sometimes couples drift apart."

"Yes. We drifted apart."

Her parents found them, and the four went outside. After separating in the parking lot, they met up at the country club for the reception. Lizzie had grown even quieter during the ride. Brent assumed she was dwelling on their run-in with Dillon and didn't press her for conversation.

Though only the first weekend in December, the country club was already decked out in holiday lights and decorations. A ten-foot Christmas tree occupied the main lobby, demanding attention. Imitation frost had been sprayed on the large glass windows. Christmas cacti with their cheery red blossoms had been placed on surfaces throughout.

The reception was held in a large banquet room where the holiday decor continued. In a corner of the room, a sprig of mistletoe dangled from a festive arch entwined with vines of green-and-red garland. Guests were already taking advantage of the photo op, snapping pictures with one-time-use cameras that instantly printed out a picture.

Lizzie and her parents found their seats. Brent fetched drinks from the bar, glad for something to do. On his return trip, he nearly collided with Maia and her date. The similarity to Lizzie and Dillon's meeting didn't go unnoticed by him.

"Oh, sorry," Maia said. "My fault. I wasn't looking where I was going."

He should excuse himself and continue on. He'd promised Darla he'd keep his distance from Maia.

Only he remained rooted in place. "The fault was mine."

She smiled. He did, too.

Her date didn't smile and, touching Maia's shoulder, pointed to a table on the other side of the room. "We're over there."

"Have a good evening," Brent said to their retreating backs.

Idiot, he thought as he made his way back to where Lizzie and her parents waited. Him, not the guy.

"Did you know them?" Lizzie asked when he set down the drinks.

"What? No. Never saw them before today."

"Oh. You looked like you recognized them."

"I was apologizing for nearly running them over."

The reception progressed much like the one last weekend.

Toasts were made before and after the buffet dinner. Tears of joy were spilled and humorous anecdotes shared, much to the bride's or groom's embarrassment. Guests mingled. Conversation and laughter filled the room with a noisy, happy din. Cake followed dinner, and dancing followed the cake. Once the bride had taken the floor with her dad, followed by her new husband, a group of eight guests donned Santa caps and broke into a choreographed routine that had everyone laughing.

"Would you like to dance?" Brent asked Lizzie when couples began drifting from their tables to the floor.

"Me?" She shook her head vigorously. "I don't dance."

"All right."

"Oh, Lizzie." Her mom let out a long, exasperated sigh. "You've got to let loose and have some fun."

"I am having fun."

Brent supposed she was, if staring at Dillon busting a move with not one but two women constituted having fun.

She suddenly sprang to her feet. "I've changed my mind. Come on."

Halfway through the lively number, Dillon approached, wearing the same goofy grin from the church and the Santa hat from the choreographed routine.

"Hey, dude," he said, addressing Brent. "Mind if I cut in?"

"That's up to the lady."

Lizzie huffed. "Seriously, Dillon?"

That was the extent of her objection. She said nothing else when he slipped his hand into hers and whisked her to another part of the dance floor. Chuckling to himself, Brent strolled back to his chair, feeling not the least bit insulted.

"She abandoned you?" Lizzie's mom asked.

"I think maybe the two of them have some unfinished business."

"You're taking this pretty well."

"Lizzie and I haven't been seeing each other very long."

"I figured as much. No offense, but there's a glaring lack of chemistry."

"No offense taken."

While she and Lizzie's dad chatted with the other guests at their table, Brent observed the dancers. He spotted Maia's date, surprised to see Maia wasn't with him. Scanning the room, he found her sitting alone at a table. Funny, once again their situations were similar. Both abandoned by their dates. Was hers dancing with an old girlfriend? He thought of texting Maia, then wisely reconsidered. Breaking their employment rules might jeopardize her job, not just his. He couldn't do that.

"Good grief. Is Lizzie *still* with Dillon?" her mom complained, peering at them huddled in a corner. "You should ask someone else to dance, Brad."

Brent grinned at her. "What about you?"

"Oh, for heaven's sake. There are plenty of much younger women sitting by themselves. What about her?"

She gestured to a woman who promptly sprang out of her seat and darted off as if she'd heard them.

"You don't have to worry about me. Honestly."

"Nonsense. You must be bored to tears. There. What about her in the green dress? She's been sitting alone for the last fifteen minutes and staring at the dancers."

Maia. Of all the wedding guests, Lizzie's mom would have to suggest her. Brent scanned the dance floor, locating Maia's date. He was with a different woman now, prompting Brent to wonder why he'd brought Maia only to leave her stranded at the table.

"I'm fine." Brent wanted to dance with Maia. But he didn't dare. "Really, I am."

Lizzie's mom got out of her chair and marched over to where her daughter stood with Dillon, their heads bent together. Her dad offered a resigned shrug. Brent shifted his attention away from the family drama and settled into watching the antics at the arch with the mistletoe. Everyone wanted pictures of themselves getting or giving a kiss. Most involved shenanigans.

In hindsight, he should have paid closer attention.

"Brad."

He turned when Lizzie's mom tapped him on the shoulder, his gaze locking with Maia's startled one.

Brent faltered momentarily, trying to make sense of the situation. Lizzie's mom stood in front of him, though he had eyes only for Maia.

"I found you a dance partner," the older woman said, flashing a smile outlined by heavy red lipstick.

"I'm...here with your daughter."

"Could've fooled me. She and Dillon mentioned leaving together." Lizzie's mom gripped Maia's arm, preventing escape. "Until they do, or don't, you should enjoy yourself with this lovely lady."

"I don't think that would be right, ma'am."

"My daughter abandoned you. What's the harm?"

If she only knew.

Maia appeared as uncomfortable as Brent felt. "This nice lady said she had someone she wanted me to meet. I had no idea it was you."

Brent pushed back in his chair and stood. Remaining seated seemed impolite. Big mistake. Lizzie's mom took that as him agreeing to her crazy scheme. She nudged Maia toward Brent.

"You two have fun."

Neither Brent nor Maia moved.

"Come on," the other woman implored. "One little dance."

"Her daughter's old boyfriend is here," Brent explained to Maia. "She wants them to get back together." And keeping him out of sight might assist with her cause.

"I see." Maia's features gentled. She was clearly a sucker for a happy ending.

"Enough chitchat." Lizzie's mom put a hand on Brent's and Maia's shoulders and pushed them toward the dance floor. "Go on, you two, get your groove on."

Groove on? Did people still stay that?

Deciding they either danced together or made a scene, Brent took hold of Maia's hand and escorted her to the dance floor. Her slender fingers were soft and warm. He liked how they fit in his.

"What happened to *your* date?" he asked as they navigated the crowd.

"We danced once. He hasn't been back to the table since."

Reaching the edge of the floor, Maia slid into Brent's arms like they'd done this a hundred times before. His hand settled on her back, hers on his shoulder. She was the perfect height, her high heels putting her eyes only a few inches lower than his. They glided and twirled to a pop rendition of "All I Want for Christmas Is You" with Maia easily following his lead.

"Your date doesn't know what he's missing," Brent said, resisting the urge to fold her tight against him.

Maia met his gaze. "Neither does yours."

Oh, brother. He was in big trouble. Maia in his arms felt like a wish being unexpectedly granted. On top of that, he enjoyed her company way too much.

"One dance," he said. "Only to appease my date's mom."

"One dance," Maia agreed, and they circled the floor. When one song merged into the next, they barely noticed. "Are you going to the Christmas tree lighting tomorrow evening?" she asked.

Brent had heard about the annual event at Bear Creek Ranch and seen workers erecting the massive tree in front of the main lodge. Javier and his girlfriend Syndee were planning on being there and had invited Brent to tag along.

"I haven't decided."

"You should come," Maia said. "It's really a lot of fun. The dining hall serves hot chocolate and desserts. There's roasting marshmallows in the outdoor fireplace and a raffle with the proceeds going to the shelter. I'm taking TJ. He's still young, but I think he'll get a kick out of seeing the tree. Fair warning, Dad makes a big deal out of it. He insists the entire family be there. Darla's bringing her husband Garret and the girls."

"I'm not much into celebrating the holidays," Brent hedged.

"Don't be a stick-in-the-mud."

A stick-in-the-mud was all he'd been the last two years. Might be nice to try something different. "I'll consider it."

That appeared to satisfy Maia.

Two dances later, Brent saw that Lizzie and Dillon had disappeared from the corner where they'd been huddling. Maia's date was with yet another new partner "getting his groove on."

"I should go back to my table," she said without much enthusiasm.

"I'll walk you."

Best they quit now before one of their dates complained to Darla, not that they appeared to have a reason. Even so, Brent and Maia were treading on thin ice.

"Hey, you two, come on over." The young woman in charge of the mistletoe photo station hailed to them as they passed. "You have to get your picture taken."

"Ah, no. We shouldn't." Brent looked to Maia for confirmation.

"Yes, you should," the young woman countered and corralled them toward the arch.

Were she and Lizzie's mom in cahoots? Was everybody? Between Lizzie, her mom, Dillon, Maia's date and now this woman, Brent and Maia were being thrown together as if by design.

"One picture," Maia said, relenting.

"Don't just stand there, kiss her." The woman made a hugging gesture once Brent and Maia were standing awkwardly beneath the mistletoe.

Brent doubted one kiss would be enough. He'd want more. Like a dozen.

"You sure about this?" he asked, giving Maia one last chance to decline.

She laughed. "You worry too much."

Hesitating only briefly, he leaned in and pressed his lips to her cheek. If he'd thought her fingers were soft and warm, they were nothing compared to her cheek.

He lingered. She sighed. Her breath tickled his ear, and he resisted the urge to seek her mouth with his.

Dimly, he heard the click of a camera.

"Wooo-hooo!" The woman clapped. "That's going to make a fantastic Christmas card."

Maia was slow leaving the circle of his embrace. When she finally did, the woman passed her the instant photo. She and Brent both stared, watching it gradually develop.

"Thanks," Brent murmured to the woman, and escorted Maia to her chair.

She sat, and he placed the photo in front of her. He couldn't help himself and glanced quickly at the now fully developed picture. The woman had caught them at the exact moment his lips connected with her cheek, the exact moment he'd been contemplating more than a chaste peck.

"You want this?" Maia asked, suddenly shy. Had she also experienced the same incredible connection?

"No. You keep it." How would she react if he asked for a copy?

"Okay." She slipped the photo into her purse.

"About what happened just now."

She gazed up at him, her eyes glittering with expectation.

Brent wavered, unsure what to say. They needed to talk about the kiss. Or should he keep his trap shut? Making a big deal out of it might be worse than pretending nothing had happened.

"We… What happened back there. I don't want you to get the wrong idea."

"I didn't."

He would have liked to say more, only he didn't get the chance. Maia's date chose that moment to return.

"Thanks for keeping her company," the man said, a hint of irritation in his voice. "I ran into some friends."

Brent produced a wan smile. "The pleasure was mine." He nodded at Maia. "Good night."

"Happy holidays," she answered as if they really had only just met.

With that, he returned to his table. Lizzie, he was gleefully informed by her mother, had left with Dillon. Good. Brent hadn't been ready to face her after kissing Maia.

He looked back over to see her once again sitting by herself. Anger at her date gnawed at him. The guy was a first-class jerk. Nonetheless, Brent wouldn't return. He would, however, run into her tomorrow at the Christmas tree lighting.

He'd made up his mind. He was through being a stick-in-the-mud.

CHAPTER SEVEN

MAIA TOOK SUNDAY off work. Wait. Who was she kidding? Day off? Very funny.

Rather than lounging about, she spent the entire morning catching up on housework. While she cleaned, TJ made messes. After lunch, she went grocery shopping. On the way home, she drove through the ATM, the pharmacy pickup window and filled up on gas while TJ napped in his car seat. Lastly, she and TJ ate and then dressed in warm clothes for the Christmas tree lighting at Bear Creek Ranch.

By the time she parked and unloaded the stroller, she was exhausted. TJ, normally growing tired by now, was firing on all six cylinders. They seldom ventured out past dinnertime. The change in routine, coupled with the crowd and activity, had him shouting, "Hi, hi, hi" and banging the stroller bar as Maia pushed him along the dirt path.

She scanned the courtyard in front of the main lodge as they neared, searching for her parents and sister. Right. Another joke. She sought Brent, hoping to spy his cowboy hat and denim jacket among the many dozens gathering on the wrap-around porch or at the fieldstone fireplace. To her great disappointment, he wasn't there.

Had he decided not to come after their close encounter yesterday beneath the mistletoe? He'd seemed worried he'd over-stepped or affected their friendship. In truth, she'd liked the kiss on her cheek and hadn't read more into it than there was. He had no reason for concern. But before she could assure him, her date had appeared at the table, interrupting them.

Should the opportunity present itself tonight, Maia would talk to Brent. If not, she'd find a moment alone tomorrow at work. Or the next day during Snapple's next training session.

"There you are!" Darla hollered to Maia from the porch. She and her husband, Garret, sat on a wooden bench while their girls played nearby with a trio of other children who most likely belonged to guests at the ranch.

Maia gave a holler in return and wheeled the stroller along the winding brick walkway. At the center of the courtyard, opposite the fireplace, stood an enormous Christmas tree, at least twelve feet tall.

As he did every holiday season, Jake Tucker, head of the family that owned Bear Creek Ranch, had obtained a special permit. He and one of the maintenance staff had driven into the woods bright and early yesterday and cut down the tree. They'd hauled it home on a flatbed trailer and then strung endless yards of colored lights. The owner's wife had decorated the tree with unbreakable ornaments resembling crystals that wouldn't shatter if blown off by a strong wind or dislodged by a curious bird.

At seven thirty sharp, Jake Tucker would flip the switch and light the tree. Maia knew from previous years that spectators would be captivated, young and old alike.

"It's chilly tonight." Maia first hugged her sister and then her brother-in-law.

"We're supposed to have record lows this coming week," Garret commented. "And there's a chance of snow tomorrow."

A huge change from last week when the weather had been unseasonably warm. At the wedding where Maia had met Brent, she'd only needed a shawl. Tomorrow, when they were out on the trails, she'd be wearing her all-weather poncho.

Since when had she started contemplating her outerwear choices in relation to Brent?

Since their moment under the mistletoe. No. That was ridiculous. Absurd.

Though, she mused wistfully, the kiss had been nice. Chaste, yes. Even so, she'd experienced an undeniable tingle of awareness. And she'd stared at the photo of them no less than thirty times, always recalling the thrilling sensation of his lips on her cheek.

"Hel-lo! Where'd you go, sis?"

"Hmm? Oh, nowhere." Maia bent to unfasten TJ from his stroller. "I was just thinking about Snapple's next training session."

"Thinking about Snapple or the cowboy helping you with his training?"

Was she that obvious? "Why do you even say that? Brent and I are just friends. We have a strictly platonic relationship."

The instant she set TJ down, he darted off in the direction of his cousins. Maia didn't usually grant him this much freedom, especially outdoors and with so many people. But he was nearby and in close visual range. That, and her oldest niece, while only five, was diligent about watching TJ.

"Okay, okay." Darla held up her hands in surrender. "No reason to bite my head off."

"Did one of our dates complain?"

"No. Why?" Darla's gaze narrowed. "Did you and Brent break any rules?"

"Seriously? You have to ask?" Maia swallowed, mentally crossing her fingers that Darla didn't notice her defensive tone and that she'd deflected rather than answer the question.

"All right." Darla smiled. "Just checking. I trust you."

Maia swallowed again, aware her throat had gone dry. Maybe she wasn't trustworthy. "Where are Mom and Dad?" she asked, attempting to redirect this time.

"They should be here any second." Darla peered over the heads of the crowd.

Maia followed her sister's gaze. Children had gathered in front of the fireplace to roast marshmallows while their parents supervised. Kitchen staff were busily setting up a refreshment table near the front entrance to the lodge. Maia spotted urns for coffee and hot chocolate as well as covered platters holding desserts.

"There they are." Darla raised her hand and waved. "And look who's with them."

Maia's head snapped up. Too late, she realized her mistake. Eagle-eyed Darla noticed.

"Strictly platonic?" Darla narrowed her gaze. "You sticking with that story?"

"What's going on?" Garret asked, not paying attention until now.

"Hello," Maia's mom called to them and waved.

Maia couldn't be more grateful for the disruption. "Hiya, Mom. Dad." She waited a beat. "Brent."

Maia's mom made straight for where her three grandchildren played and proceeded to spoil them rotten with treats and trinkets she produced from her coat pockets.

"Mom," Darla complained. "No candy. Between you and the hot chocolate, the girls will be up all night on a sugar high."

"You should know by now," Maia's dad said, joining her and Maia, "there's no stopping your mom."

"Her or you?" Darla gave him an affectionate hug. "Love you, Pops."

"How are my little girls tonight?"

At twenty-seven and thirty-one respectively, Maia and Darla were hardly little. Still, their dad adored them and they adored him in return.

"Evening," Brent said.

Maia started to say, "You came," only to snap her mouth shut when Darla answered first.

"Hi, Brent."

Maia's face went hot. He'd been addressing Darla. Not her. She'd almost given her sister another reason to complain about her.

"Sorry to impose on your family outing." He cleared his throat. "Again."

"Nonsense," Maia's dad said. "I invited you. And you're always welcome."

Darla raised her brows, her way of asking what was with the chumminess between their dad and Brent.

Maia shook her head. She had no clue.

All right. She suspected her dad of matchmaking. Not that she'd admit as much to Darla. No way.

"Who wants hot chocolate?" her mom asked.

Since everyone did, they all made their way to the refreshment table with Maia's mom running herd on her grandchildren. When TJ spotted Brent, he galloped over to him and grabbed his hand, taking Maia aback. The only man her son had ever voluntarily approached was his grandfather.

TJ's father hadn't seen TJ since he was an infant, and his paternal grandparents were out of the picture. Maia's attempts to include them hadn't been well received, and she'd let the matter drop. If they ever changed their minds, she'd allow them to visit TJ. She wasn't holding her breath, however.

While waiting in line for their hot chocolates, TJ lifted his arms to Brent and cried, "Up, up."

"Hi, buddy." When TJ repeated his demand, Brent turned to Maia, a look of uncertainty on his face.

"He wants you to pick him up."

"Okay."

Brent did, lifting TJ awkwardly into his arms, struggling with how to best hold a wiggly toddler.

TJ immediately grabbed the lapels of Brent's jacket with both his fists and tugged. "Mine."

Maia smiled. "He wants your jacket. See what you've started."

Brent boosted TJ so that they were eye level with each other. "It's a bit cold outside. Maybe later by the fire."

TJ promptly collapsed onto Brent's shoulder, his face nestled in the crook of Brent's neck.

Maia stared, openmouthed. She wasn't alone.

Brent and TJ were adorable together, and she felt a surge of tenderness. It increased when Brent lifted his hand and patted TJ's back.

With their hot chocolates in hand, they found a good spot to wait for the tree lighting. Maia tried to take TJ away from Brent, but her son would have none of it.

"He's getting kind of cozy with the family," Darla whispered in Maia's ear while Jake Tucker made his annual speech. "Don't you think?"

"By family, I'm assuming you mean me."

"You, Dad and apparently TJ."

Jake Tucker finished his speech and, after a round of applause, he flipped the switch—which was actually a plug he inserted into a heavy-duty extension cord. The lights illuminated in a burst of bright colors and to a chorus of oohs and ahhs. Another round of applause erupted, this one louder.

Darla, it seemed, wasn't finished speaking her piece. "Sis, I'm worried you're wading into dangerous waters."

"I told you—there's nothing between us."

"Yet."

"TJ's taking a shine to him. That's all," Maia insisted.

"Only TJ? I've seen how you look at him. And he's looking back."

"All right. You win. I find him attractive. There. Satisfied?"

"He has…" Darla compressed her lips into a thin line. "He's dealing with some stuff."

"He told me."

"He did? What did he say?"

"It's personal. And may be different than what he told you."

Darla harrumphed.

"Not that it matters, as he and I have no intention of becoming involved. We each really need our second jobs and won't jeopardize them."

"As long as we're clear."

At TJ's high-pitched squeal, they both spun to see Brent setting TJ down onto the ground not three feet from them. Shock rippled through Maia. How much of her conversation with Darla had Brent heard? Probably enough, given his next words.

"I have to go. Have a nice evening." He turned on his heel.

"Watch TJ," Maia told Darla and went after him. "Wait, Brent."

He stopped once they were away from the crowd.

"I don't know what you heard—"

He cut her off midsentence. "Your sister's right, Maia. I am dealing with some stuff. And as much as I like TJ, like your whole family, like you, I can't get involved while my life's a mess."

With that, he walked away, retreating behind those emotional barriers of his.

Maia wanted to but didn't go after him. Luke had left her, if not scarred, wary. She wasn't ready to risk her heart, and neither was Brent, as he'd made clear. Better that they give each other a little space before someone wound up hurt.

Brent walked the entire mile and a quarter to the bunkhouse in the dark, the chilly night air sneaking into the collar of his jacket and sending shivers down his arms.

He'd ridden to the tree-lighting event with Javier and hadn't wanted to bother his friend for a lift back. Javier had met up with Syndee, and the last Brent had seen, the two of them were cuddled together on a bench. He'd had no intention of cutting short their time together simply because he chose to leave early.

The quiet stroll gave him plenty of opportunity to reflect on the conversation he'd overhead between Maia and her sister and to talk himself out of disappearing into the dreaded murky place.

Darla wasn't happy about Brent getting close to her family. Maia especially. And while he understood Darla's position, hearing her say as much in plain terms had hit him like a cannonball between the shoulder blades.

Brent could easily explain away Thanksgiving and arriving tonight with Ansel. The older man had invited Brent on both occasions, and Brent had accepted in an attempt to remain on his employer's good side.

Finding moments alone with Maia, dancing together, kissing her, weren't part of the job and had been a mistake. A big one that wouldn't end well for either of them.

A gust of frigid air pelted him in the face, and he embraced the sting. He shouldn't have given in to temptation yesterday at the wedding. Even though it had seemed as if he and Maia had been pushed together by forces beyond their control, he could have—and should have—stopped before they got carried away. Instead, he encouraged something that could never be and caused a problem for Maia and her sister.

What if Darla fired him? Brent had just sent a small payment off to his friend who'd lent him money and included a promise of more to come. He wouldn't be able to keep his promise if Darla let him go.

He needed to be more careful, starting immediately. He'd continue helping Maia train Snapple. Brent was a man of his word, and he'd given his to Maia. But as she'd told Darla, there wasn't anything romantic between them and neither would he encourage it.

A bird suddenly took flight from a branch in one of the tall pines and soared away from Brent, giving him a start. From the size of the bird and *whoop-whoop* of flapping wings, he guessed it to be an owl. He'd seen one the other night roosting atop the bunkhouse roof. In the distance, behind the stand of trees, the creek ran, the splash of water tumbling over rocks mingling with the rustle of mule deer moving through the brush and a coyote howling in the distance.

Brent listened, enjoying the sights and sounds of Bear Creek Ranch. He liked a lot about this place, including his job and the people. He hadn't felt like part of a community since leaving the rodeo world. There, he'd had friends and a respected profession and an ambition that gave him purpose. While he lacked some of those things here at Bear Creek Ranch, he was working steadily, making friends like Rowdy and Javier and, yes, Maia, and had an ambition of sorts—that of paying off his debts. Once he'd accomplished that, maybe he'd find a new purpose.

Too many positives to risk losing them. Tomorrow, he'd reestablish boundaries with Maia—starting with forgetting how much he'd enjoyed dancing with her and the softness of her cheek when he'd kissed her.

Yeah. Not gonna happen. Maia was unforgettable. But he'd try. For both their sakes.

Darla, he was sure, wouldn't fire her. The sisters were too close. Too devoted to each other.

Brent didn't envy Maia's relationship with her family. That would be a waste of energy. But if he ever repaired his broken life and met someone special, he'd be a better husband and father than his own. He'd lacked a good example while growing up and might not know what to do, but he certainly knew what *not* to do.

Around the next bend, the bunkhouse came into view. One lone light shone, indicating the place was empty and that everyone had gone to the main lodge. Brent would have an hour, possibly two, to himself. He could go to bed and bury himself under the covers. After hearing Darla and Maia's conversation, the urge to succumb to the ever-present gloom definitely appealed.

But he'd resisted all week and hated breaking his record. Actually, more than a week. Not since Thanksgiving at the MacKenzies' had he traveled to the dark place. A new record for him.

Once inside the bunkhouse, he made himself a cup of coffee to ward off the chill. He'd been looking forward to hot chocolate with Maia, but that hadn't happened.

"Quit feeling sorry for yourself," he murmured and started the coffee maker. Dwelling on what-ifs and if-onlys served no purpose other than to beckon the gloom.

Sitting at the small dining table with his coffee, the walls started to close in on him. Being alone did that to him. Instead of throwing a personal pity party, he took out his phone and began scrolling through the contacts. His finger stopped on the name and number he'd been thinking about a lot lately: his mom.

After mentally calculating the time difference, he clicked on her number and pressed Connect. She might be startled by a call this time of night, but she'd be glad to hear from him. And she was, given her cheerful greeting.

"Hi, honey." Her tone instantly changed. "Is everything okay?"

"More than okay. I just called to say hi. Been thinking of you lately."

"What's new? How's the job going?"

The smile in her voice caused his own mouth to turn up at the corners. He really should visit more often. At least phone regularly. "All right."

"Just all right?"

She'd wanted him to come home when his rodeo buddy in Tucson suggested Brent had stayed too long on his couch. Brent had declined his mom's plea. She'd pushed, only to back off when he landed the job at Bear Creek Ranch. As much as she wanted to see him, she wanted him gainfully employed even more.

"I'm staying busy," he said, "which I like. The work's not hard but it's honest labor for an honest wage. I get to spend most days in the saddle, live in the middle of the most beautiful mountains in Arizona and meet some interesting people. Could be worse."

He also got to see Maia on a regular basis. Though after that long discussion with himself on the walk home tonight, he didn't include that as a plus.

"What kind of people? Tell me."

His mom listened as he recounted several stories of trail rides, laughing when he imparted a particularly amusing incident. She was full of questions, and when he paused, asked about his side gig with Your Perfect Plus One. Brent told her, omitting the parts that included Maia. His mom would jump to a wrong conclusion.

She hadn't been subtle about her desire for Brent to meet a nice gal and settle down. Like many people, she thought being in a relationship was the answer to his problems, if not everyone's problems. Brent could argue differently. Having a girlfriend at the time hadn't helped him deal with the despair he'd experienced after accepting that a world title was beyond his reach. Then again, they hadn't been serious, and she'd eventually ghosted him.

It hadn't helped his mom, either, in the wake of her divorce from Brent's dad. She'd dated through the years. Once seriously, though they'd split after a couple years. But from what Brent had seen, no man was going to make his mom happy. Not until she learned how to be happy with herself and the person she was.

Discovering that pearl of wisdom differed from accomplishing it. Deep down, Brent wasn't happy and continued to struggle with the hard knocks fate had handed him. Only when he found a dream to replace the one he'd let go of would he also find contentment. The feeling of helplessness, of losing control, was what sent him on those frequent downward trajectories.

He did like his job at Bear Creek Ranch, but he wanted more than to be a wrangler. Not that there was anything wrong with it or it was anything to be embarrassed of. Like he'd told his mom, he was performing an honest job for an honest wage. It could also be a stepping-stone to something more rewarding. Ansel was a business owner. His own boss. Maia had talked once about expanding Mountainside Stables when she took over one day.

If Brent had ambition and an opportunity like those, he'd be happy, too. But he still loved rodeo and competing. He rose each morning wishing he could climb onto the back of a bull or bronc. He always imagined himself standing on the platform in the center of the arena at the National Finals Rodeo and accepting his championship belt buckle. He doubted that would ever stop.

A black cloud entered his peripheral vision. Though entirely in his mind, it was real nonetheless. If he didn't redirect his thoughts and change the subject, that cloud would surround him and then smother him.

"You sound good, honey," his mom said. "Upbeat."

He must be a very accomplished liar. "What are you doing for Christmas?"

"Millie invited me over for dinner. As usual."

Her neighbor. That would be nice. And much better than sitting at home alone, which was likely what Brent would be doing. He didn't expect an invitation from Ansel. And if he got one, he'd graciously decline rather than give Darla another reason to scold Maia.

Maybe he'd volunteer for a wedding date. Darla had mentioned the possibility when she'd hired him. She'd said Christmas weddings were very popular. He'd also heard Cash, the owner of Wishing Well Springs, was getting married on Christmas day.

"Give Millie my best when you see her."

"I will." His mom drew in an audible breath and then paused. "I… There's…"

Brent clenched his jaw. "What's wrong? Did something happen?"

"Oh, I've been wondering if I should tell you or not."

"Tell me."

She released the breath she'd been holding. "Your dad was hurt a few weeks ago. He's fine," she hurriedly added. "Broke his leg. Pretty badly, apparently. He had to have surgery and is still laid up."

"Hurt how?"

"He fell off a ladder. They were painting the house. Elaine Lester happened to mention it the other day. That's really all I know."

The Lesters were old friends of his parents. His mom and Elaine still kept in touch.

Brent began to relax. The news wasn't terrible. "Should I call him?"

"That's your decision. He might appreciate hearing from you."

His mom maintained a neutral role when it came to Brent's relationship with his dad. These days, unlike when he was young. She neither encouraged nor discouraged Brent. Mentioning his dad's fall wasn't expressing an opinion. Rather she was providing information, and Brent could choose for himself how to respond.

"I'll think about it."

With that, the topic was officially closed. They chatted another twenty minutes before winding down the call.

"I've kept you up late," Brent said.

"It's okay. I miss you."

"I miss you, too."

"If you won't come home for a visit, maybe I can come there." She sounded hopeful.

"Maybe." The more he thought about it, the more he warmed to the idea. "Yeah, why not? What about the spring?" That would give him time to get more out of debt and to arrange with Ansel for a couple days off. "I'll call you again on Christmas."

"I love you, honey."

"Love you, too, Mom."

Brent continued sitting at the table, finishing his now lukewarm coffee, long after disconnecting. None of his bunk mates were home yet. He could crawl into bed if he wanted. Except he no longer felt the pull. Talking with his mom tended to boost his spirits.

Would talking with his dad boost them even more? They hadn't spoken for at least seven, no eight, months. No surprise Brent hadn't gotten a call after his dad's fall and surgery.

He checked the time. Was it too late? On impulse, he sent his dad a text saying hi and that he was sorry to hear about his broken leg. He nearly jumped when his phone rang a minute later, a photo of his dad filling the screen.

Brent hesitated a few seconds before answering. "Hey, Dad. Sorry if I woke you."

"You didn't. This darn cast keeps me up. I can't get comfortable."

"Must have been some fall. How are you doing?"

"All right. I assume your mother told you."

Wasn't it just like his dad to be more concerned about how Brent learned of his accident than the fact he'd called to check on him?

"No fun being laid up over the holidays," he said, refusing to rise to the bait.

"No fun at all. I'm driving Raelene and the kids nuts."

The kids. Brent's half siblings. Near strangers to him. Did his dad attempt to control them and Raelene as much as he had Brent and his mom?

After clearing his throat, he asked, "How long until the cast comes off?"

"Another three weeks. If my X-rays go well. Can't come soon enough for me. I hate sitting around the house all day."

"I get that."

"Yeah? I figured you liked loafing around, considering your lifestyle the last couple of years."

Not a very subtle dig. His dad hadn't reacted well to Brent's "retirement" from rodeo. Not an unexpected reaction from someone who'd won three national championships.

"I'm working now, Dad. I got a new job a few weeks ago."

"Doing what?"

"I'm a wrangler for Mountainside Stables at Bear Creek Ranch. It's north of Payson."

"Sounds all right. They raise cattle?"

For a second, Brent considered saying yes. "Bear Creek is a resort. I lead guests on trail rides."

His dad let loose with a barking laugh. "Can't say that's the kind of job I picture for you. But you're gainfully employed, and that's something."

Brent wasn't sure he'd heard correctly. Was it possible his dad's second family had mellowed him? Then next second, his old dad was back.

"Even if a girl could do the job."

A girl, a woman, did. Maia. And she could run circles around his dad on a mountain trail even without his leg in a cast. The image of her besting his dad brought a smile to Brent's lips.

"I like what I'm doing. And I like the people I work with."

"Any chance you're going to get serious and return to rodeo?"

"Not likely."

"Doesn't your old friend Channing Pearce own a rodeo arena in Payson?"

"His family does. Rim Country."

"I'm sure they have some bulls you can practice on."

"I'm not getting back into rodeo, Dad."

"You plan on staying a quitter, then?"

Brent heard the disappointment in his dad's voice. It crawled along his skin, leaving a stain.

He had quit; it was true. And then walked away. At the time, he'd thought it better than publicly humiliating himself with his mounting disqualifications and losses.

The black cloud hovering in Brent's peripheral vision moved closer. He felt its weight bearing down on him as it stole every molecule of oxygen in the air.

Why had he called his dad? Why had he thought this time

would be different? Why did he keep trying to bridge a rift that was impossibly wide?

"It's getting late, Dad. I have an early morning."

"Look son." His dad paused. Inhaled deeply. "I know you think I'm too hard on you. Too demanding. Your grandma was the same with me. The Hayes aren't easy to live with, as your mom can attest to." He inhaled again. "I know what you're capable of, and I was only trying to encourage you."

His dad had a heck of a way of showing it. Impatience. Belittling. Bullying. Punishment. Apparently, he'd never heard of positive reinforcement.

"If you say so, Dad."

"You gave up too soon."

"Gotta go. Good night."

Brent disconnected, the invisible heavy weight bearing down on him.

Had his dad been encouraging him all that time? Brent had always assumed his dad was attempting to turn Brent into a younger clone of himself.

Then again, he'd succeeded. With all his problems, Brent wasn't easy to live with, either.

The rumble of an approaching vehicle reached his ears. Someone was home. Thank goodness they hadn't arrived earlier to hear his conversation with his dad. Brent's hidden shame would remain that: hidden.

He avoided surrendering to his gloom long enough to greet Javier and get the lowdown on the Christmas-tree lighting. After that, he made his excuses, crawled into bed, closed his eyes and dove headfirst into the darkness.

CHAPTER EIGHT

"Where you off to?"

Hearing Ansel call to him, Brent stopped on the way to his truck and pivoted. "To the bunkhouse for a while. Then, I might be heading into Payson."

Rim Country Rodeo Arena had recently purchased a dozen new bucking broncs. Channing had twisted Brent's arm, insisting he come look at the stock and assess them like they had in the old days. He'd also invited Brent to stay on and watch the Friday night bull-riding practice.

Brent had yet to accept. Returning to the all-too-familiar rodeo arena would be hard on him, a glaring reminder of his failed career. He'd needed two full days to crawl out of the murky darkness after his phone call with his dad. To account for his glumness, he'd claimed a pulled hamstring. By the next day his mood had improved and only continued to get better as the week progressed.

This morning, Ansel had at last put Brent in charge of the trail ride. He wasn't keen on backsliding, which facing his past at Rim Country could result in. On the other hand, Brent hadn't seen Channing since arriving in Payson. He owed his friend a visit. And, who knew? Seeing familiar sights might have the opposite effect—heal rather than wound.

"Well, that's fine and dandy," Ansel proclaimed, a mischievous glint in his eyes. "You have time."

"For what?"

"To come with me. I need an extra pair of hands. Got a delivery for the shelter. And seeing as you might be heading to town... You can meet me there," Ansel continued. "Won't take long and then you can be on your way." The shelter—he must mean Payson Rescue Mission.

"Dad recruiting you?" Maia said, coming out of the stables.

Brent hadn't realized she was in there and forced himself to act natural. He'd done well since Sunday's tree lighting at the main lodge, maintaining his distance from her and limiting their conversations. As a result, he had another gig with Your Perfect Plus One tomorrow night. Darla seemed satisfied with him and no longer concerned he was getting too comfortable with her family. Maia especially.

"He is," Brent agreed. "But I don't mind. It's for a good cause."

To his surprise, he truly didn't mind. Not because he'd be winning points with his boss. Brent liked the idea of contributing to worthy causes. That had been a perk of working for the BLM rehabilitating wild mustangs. At times, he regretted his abrupt departure. Then again, that road had led to his job here at Bear Creek Ranch which he liked equally well.

Other than having to avoid the boss's daughter. There was the one drawback.

"Right you are." Ansel beamed. "And this is the season of giving."

Maia had accompanied Brent this morning on the four-hour trail ride. While two shorter rides were scheduled for the afternoon, Rowdy would be taking Brent's place. He'd originally had the entire day off but had switched with Rowdy. The young man was making a secret trip to the jewelry store. Unbeknownst to his girlfriend, she'd be getting a designer watch for Christmas. Brent was happy to contribute to the surprise.

"You still free tomorrow morning for a training session with Snapple?" Maia asked.

"Between rides I am."

They'd been making progress with the big Appaloosa. He was no longer bothered by the sock at the end of a fishing line. Tomorrow, Brent would play the role of a veterinarian, and they'd mimic the pulse and respiration stop Maia would have during a real competition—including listening to Snapple's heart rate with an old stethoscope she'd borrowed.

"Great!" Maia started for the horse pen, a half-dozen halters slung over her arm. "Have fun, you two."

He watched her go, an emptiness in his chest. She hadn't sent Brent a flirty farewell smile like she might have prior to the Christmas tree lighting. They were both on their best behavior. As much as he missed their former exchanges, this was for the best. And he'd just keep telling himself that over and over until it sank in.

A half hour later, he pulled in behind the shelter and parked beside Ansel's pickup. Brent had guessed the multitude of boxes stacked in the pickup's bed contained food, and, it turned out, he was correct.

"These are contributions from the ranch," Ansel explained to Brent while lowering the tailgate. "The owners have been collecting canned goods and nonperishables for the last few months. You probably noticed the donation box at the Christmas tree lighting."

Brent hadn't. His attention had been elsewhere.

"This morning," Ansel continued, "the kitchen added bread and baked goods, a box of potatoes and another of carrots and onions. Gonna really help with Christmas dinner. The shelter will feed upwards of two hundred folks."

"That many?"

"Hunger and cold know no bounds. Valley Fellowship Church put on a sock-and-glove drive. They delivered almost five hundred pairs this week. The elementary schools sold candy canes and raised nearly a thousand dollars."

Brent and Ansel stacked boxes on a handcart which they brought in through the delivery entrance. A pair of cheerful staff members directed them to a large pantry area. Delicious aromas wafted from the kitchen. A crew, Brent suspected, staffed mostly by volunteers like Ansel, worked at the counter or in front of the large stove, prepping and cooking food.

"You mind fetching the rest?" Ansel asked Brent. "I gotta review the food supply for Christmas dinner with Gunther over there." He motioned to a portly man around Ansel's age who, from his authoritative bearing, was clearly in charge.

"No problem." Brent returned to the truck.

On his second trip to the pantry area, he was approached by a rumpled-looking guy in a tattered camo coat and scuffed athletic shoes.

"You need help?" he asked Brent.

"Sure. Thanks."

Together, they brought in and stored the remaining two loads, some in the pantry and the rest in the walk-in cooler. Ansel was still conferring with Gunther, their heads bent over a clipboard. Brent glanced around for a place to sit and cool his heels.

"You want a coffee?" the guy asked. "There's a pot on the counter in the dining room. Free for the taking. Or we got bottled water."

"Coffee would hit the spot."

He accompanied the guy to the coffee station and helped himself to a paper cup of the dark brew. The first sip delivered a serious kick to the belly.

"You a new volunteer?" the guy asked. He appeared to be in no hurry to leave.

"Just giving Ansel a hand."

The guy nodded and fixed a coffee for himself. "I've been staying here the last few days. Name's Pete."

"Pleasure to meet you. I'm Brent."

"Lucky for me they had a bed available," Pete said. "Not sure what I'd have done otherwise. Mighty cold at night on the streets this time of year."

"I bet it is."

Upon closer inspection, Brent realized Pete was younger than he'd first thought. Not much older than him.

"I work for Ansel at Bear Creek Ranch." Brent chose an empty dining table and sat down.

Pete joined him, cradling his coffee as if his hands were chilled, though the inside temperature was comfortable. "I haven't been there. Heard of the place, of course. Everyone in town has, even those of us passing through."

"You leaving soon?"

"Not sure. It depends." He looked down. "Money's a little tight at the moment."

"I understand." Probably better than a lot of people, Brent thought.

"I was a project manager for a tech company until last year," Pete said. "We developed software applications for the manu-facturing industry. I was laid off when the economy tanked."

"Sorry to hear that."

"My house went next. And then my wife." His voice cracked, and he sipped his coffee, swallowing with obvious relief. "Not sure where she is now. Then again, she doesn't know where I am, either."

The statement, made without apology, gave Brent pause. If not for friends like Channing, he could well be this guy. Living on the streets and grateful for a cot in a homeless shelter that came with a once-a-day hot meal. He had a lot to be grateful for.

"Some days are worse than others." Pete offered a wan smile. "True story."

Ansel emerged from the kitchen. "You still here, Brent? I figured you for long gone."

He stood. "Wasn't sure you still needed me."

"We're all set." He smiled at Pete. "Howdy, partner."

"Sir." Pete also stood.

"He helped me carry in the boxes," Brent told Ansel.

"Did you? Appreciate it."

"I like to stay busy," Pete said. "Earn my keep."

"Always plenty of work needing doing around here." Ansel turned to Brent. "You ready to hit the road?"

Brent looked around. "I might be back."

"You're welcome anytime."

Was that Ansel's reason for recruiting Brent today? He hadn't really needed a hand.

"Hope to see you again." Brent reached out his hand to Pete, who hesitated and then shook it, his grip gradually growing stronger.

"Same here."

Ansel walked with Brent to where they'd parked. "Kind of you to indulge Pete. The men here get lonely and like to talk. Particularly with new people."

"He's an interesting fellow. I enjoyed myself."

"They're troubled. You know, emotionally and, well, mentally. Half are addicts or former addicts."

"And some have had a rough go and just need a break. Hopefully, they can get one here."

Ansel studied Brent as if seeing him for the first time. "Not everyone would be that understanding. You're all right, Brent."

"I've been down on my luck. I have you to thank for giving me a break. And Darla."

"Hey, I'm the one who got a skilled wrangler out of the deal. And a pretty accomplished trainer who can help Maia realize her dream of winning the Diamond Cup. I should be thanking you."

Ansel dug in his jacket for his truck keys, which spared Brent from having to answer in what would surely be a gravelly voice.

They went their separate ways after that, with Ansel returning to Bear Creek Ranch and Brent driving to Rim Country Rodeo Arena. He traveled the main road through town, noting the decorated storefronts, garland-wrapped signposts, plastic snowmen and Santas in front yards and a miniature Christmas village outside the antique store. Signs pointed the way to Christmas tree lots or holiday blowout sales.

On a whim, he tuned the radio to a station playing holiday songs. For the first time in a long while, he felt a twinge of... not joy exactly, but optimism. He could pull himself out of this reoccurring funk. Change the course of his life. He still had a long way to go, but he was moving forward. That had to count for something. And who knew? Possibly, in time, he'd have something worthwhile to offer Maia.

Since he had nowhere to be on Christmas Day, he decided he'd volunteer at the shelter. Ansel would be helping with the midday holiday dinner. Brent could hitch a ride with him.

The twinge of optimism grew until it became a bona fide ray of hope.

Wreaths hung from the gateposts at the entrance to Rim Country Rodeo Arena. A sandwich-board sign announcing next week's Cowboy Christmas Jamboree sat just inside the gate. Another larger one appeared at the turnoff to the parking area, advertising a visit from Santa and rides in a pony cart for the kiddies.

Brent wondered if Maia was planning on attending and bringing TJ. She hadn't mentioned it. Then again, they were limiting their conversations to work and Snapple's training.

He refused to let the status of their relationship or reminders of his former rodeo life affect his improved mood. He was about to see an old friend, and the hopeful feeling from earlier continued.

Easing his truck into a free space, Brent stepped out and texted Channing. A moment later Channing replied saying Brent should meet him at the horse pastures. Having been to Rim Country often during his career, Brent required no directions. He strode briskly past the rodeo office, concession stand, the arena with its thirty-five hundred seating capacity, and the livestock pens where several dozen bulls milled about and pawed the ground.

Soon, the animals would be herded through the connecting aisle to the chutes for tonight's bull-riding practice. The participants would gather to assess the bull they'd drawn, along with their competitors' experience level. Their significant others, family and friends would be watching from the bleachers. Some of the competitors would be women. Their participation in the sport of bull riding was constantly growing. Rim Country had begun hosting women's calf roping—both breakaway and tie-down—in addition to barrel racing.

Brent continued walking. The arena had two pastures for their bucking horses. The smaller one housed older, retired stock who lived out the remainder of their days in leisure and comfort. Brent had heard from Channing how he and his fiancée were rehabilitating a few of the more complacent ones.

Brent found the idea intriguing, and he intended to talk to Channing about his techniques. He might learn something useful for Snapple. Taking a bronc bred to buck and training him to be a calm, reliable ranch horse was no easy task. Channing had mentioned that Cash's fiancée even used one of the former broncs in her halftime trick-riding act. Brent was eager to see that.

The larger pasture held the active bucking stock. In addition to supplying bulls and broncs for their own rodeos, Rim Country leased their stock to other arenas. The new horses Channing had purchased were an investment that, if all went well, would eventually pay off. Brent figured his friend was on the right track.

As he neared, he spotted a tall cowboy standing beside Channing at the pasture fence. When Brent got close enough, he recognized Cash Montgomery.

Brent knew Cash, though not as well as Channing did. The rodeo world was a small one, and Brent had regularly crossed paths with Cash during the years he'd competed. Cash had been one of the few who didn't judge or criticize Brent when he quit competing. In fact, rumor was, he'd defended Brent at last year's nationals, saying it took more courage to leave than to stay.

Cash was also co-owner of Wishing Well Springs, the wedding barn where Brent had met Maia his first night in town. What was the saying about six degrees of separation?

It suddenly occurred to Brent that Cash might have had something to do with Darla hiring him. It was possible. Your Perfect Plus One did a lot of business with Wishing Well Springs. He'd ask Cash if the subject came up.

"There you are!" Channing beckoned to Brent.

"Now the gang's all here," Cash added.

The gang? Brent's initial reaction had been to consider himself an outsider. But the sunny smiles as he approached put him as ease and, yes, gave him a sense of inclusion.

Another first-time-in-a-long-time feeling. He'd been having them regularly since coming to Payson and working at Bear Creek Ranch.

A round of handshakes ensued. Channing hooked an arm around Brent's neck.

"'Bout time you showed up, stranger."

"Sorry I didn't get by sooner," Brent said. "Been busy settling into the new jobs."

"Jobs?" Cash asked. "You doing something else besides wrangling for Mountainside Stables?"

Brent chuckled. "I hired on with Your Perfect Plus One. Thought you might have heard from Darla."

"I might have." Cash grinned, confirming Brent's suspicion. "How's that going?"

"Okay. I've met some nice folks, and I can use the extra money. I ran into Maia my first night in town. We were both at your wedding barn. Separately. With different people."

"Small world."

Brent shook his head. "I'm still trying to wrap my brain

around how a former bull rider wound up owning a wedding barn."

"Co-owning," Cash clarified. "My sister and I are business partners. It was her idea to turn our grandparents' old place into Wishing Well Springs."

"He's marrying their wedding coordinator," Channing added. "How's that for keeping the business in the family?"

"I'm a lucky son of a gun. Phoebe's something else." Cash's expression went soft and goofy like a man besotted. "We're getting hitched in a couple of weeks. On Christmas Day."

"I heard," Brent said. "Congrats."

"You should come to the wedding."

"I don't want to impose."

"Are you kidding? We'd love to have you. Unless you've got other plans."

"I might be volunteering with Ansel at the shelter. What time's the wedding?"

"Early afternoon. One thirty. I'll send you the invitation. What's your email address?" They plugged each other's contact info into their phones. "You can come with Channing and his girl."

"Good idea," Channing chimed in.

"You and Kenna don't need a third wheel."

The way things were going with Channing and his fiancée, they were likely the next to walk down the aisle.

"She won't mind," Channing insisted. "She's a people person. The more the merrier is her motto. Besides, a bunch of the guys will be there."

More people who'd borne witness to Brent's downfall. Then again, he couldn't hide forever. He may be down, but he wasn't out.

"Thanks, Cash. I'll let you know."

"What do you say we get to looking at these horses?" Channing said. "Bull-riding practice starts in an hour. Hey, you should stick around, Brent. Take a spin if you've a hankering. Show 'em how a real bull rider does it."

"I'm retired. Haven't been in the arena for over two years now. What I'd show them is how to eat dirt."

"Ain't that the truth," Cash concurred. "I think Channing is the only one of us who still climbs onto a bull or bronc."

"Just for fun. I haven't competed in… I couldn't tell you. Kenna's always lecturing me about being more careful now that I've taken over management of the arena from Dad. Doesn't want me hurt," he said with an air of someone who only pretended to be annoyed. He enjoyed Kenna worrying about him, and it showed.

Love. His two friends were up to their ears in it and couldn't be happier. Brent was glad for them and also a bit envious. His friends weren't competing anymore, and they'd both found new paths to travel that were equally, if not more, fulfilling than rodeo.

Why couldn't he? The new-path part, at least. That had to come before he could consider falling in love. Though, as Maia's face appeared before him, he realized he might not have any say in that matter. The heart didn't always listen to the head.

His emotions tumbled downward and beckoned the black cloud hovering nearby. Before it inched any closer, he forced his attention to the arena and the horses.

"That big sorrel on the left," he said and pointed. "The one with three white socks. He's got a lot of buck in him. Going to be one of your better performers."

"Not that I disagree," Channing said, "but what makes you say that?"

"The look in his eyes. He means business. Have you seen him perform?"

"I've seen all of them perform. Wouldn't have bought them unless they had a lot of buck. But Darth Vader there was one of the best. Any others you'd pick as ones to watch?"

Brent evaluated the herd, paying close attention to the horses' stance, their alertness, demeanor and interaction with their pasture mates. Did they keep to themselves or buddy up? He particularly studied how they held their ears and where they directed their gazes. When they walked, did they move with confidence or wariness?

"The buckskin," he finally announced. "He'll start out slow, lulling his rider into a false sense of security. But then five seconds into the ride, you'd better pay attention. He's going to explode."

Channing looked at Brent with an expression he hadn't seen aimed at him in a while. One of admiration. "You're right. That's exactly how he performs. Anyone ever tell you that you have a sharp eye when it comes to horses?"

"No better than the two of you, I'd bet."

"You have plans the rest of the day?" Channing asked.

"Not really."

"Stick around. I'm serious. Kenna's bringing some sub sandwiches for dinner before the practice. I'll tell her to throw an extra one in for you. You can watch the practice with me in the booth. Give me some more of your opinions on the new stock."

Brent faced Cash. "You staying?"

"I have to get home. Promised Phoebe we'd go Christmas shopping. We won't have any time after this weekend, what with the wedding and out-of-town guests arriving in droves." He shook Brent's hand. "If I don't see you before, I'll see you at the wedding. Remember to RSVP when you get that email invitation. My wedding coordinator is a little OCD about head counts."

Cash left after that. Brent and Channing meandered toward the arena, passing the holding pens where the livestock hands were readying the bulls for transfer to the chutes. At the arena, riders had begun arriving for the practice. Kenna would be here shortly with their sandwiches and, according to Channing, was eager to meet Brent.

At the steps leading to the announcer's booth, Channing's phone went off.

"I've got to take this," he said and lifted the phone to his ear. As he listened to his caller, his brows drew closer and closer together. "Nope. I understand. No need to apologize." He paused. "I'll figure something out. You just take care of yourself. See you later."

He disconnected, exhaling forlornly.

"Problem?" Brent asked.

"That was Grumpy Joe. Our announcer during events."

"I remember him."

"He also fills in as a judge during bull and bronc practices and was supposed to be here tonight. Seems he caught a heck of a cold. Doesn't want to infect anybody before the holidays, which I understand. Except now I'm shorthanded tonight." Channing rubbed a knuckle along his jaw. "It's only practice. Not like we need a real certified judge. Just someone who can spot penalties."

"What about your dad?"

"He and Mom are going to a party tonight for board members of the rescue mission."

Ansel had mentioned something to Brent about it.

Channing's gaze zeroed in on Brent. "What about you?"

"Me judge? No."

"Why not?"

Brent chuckled. "I've never done anything like that."

"It's practice. Not a rodeo. And besides having a sharp eye, you've got the experience. Enough to give the rider a reasonably accurate score."

Brent opened his mouth, fully intending to object. Instead, he said, "Okay. Why not?"

"All right!" Channing grinned.

Brent did, too. He'd been convinced returning to his old

stomping grounds would be difficult. Instead, he was staying and judging the bull-riding practice.

The black cloud fell far behind when Brent followed Channing up the stairs to the booth, a jaunty spring to his step.

CHAPTER NINE

ALMOST SIX O'CLOCK, and TJ showed no signs of slowing down. He'd awoken this morning raring to go, typical for him. And according to Maia's mom, he'd been bouncing off walls all day. Also typical. By this time of the evening, however, Maia would have expected her son's eyelids to begin drooping or for him to nod off in his car seat.

Not happening. This was one of those rare days when TJ operated on some kind of endless energy supply. Swell. There went Maia's plans for a quick supper and hitting the hay early.

Her phone rang, and Darla's name appeared on the SUV's info display. In the back seat, TJ squawked. He'd been doing that lately whenever Maia's phone rang.

"Hey, sis," she said. "Good timing. I'm just on my way home from picking up TJ."

"Well, why don't you turn around and meet me instead?"

"Meet you where?"

"Rim Country. They're having bull-riding practice tonight. Garret signed up."

"Oh. Really."

Darla's husband had never rodeoed in his life. But he'd tried bull riding on a whim a few years ago and *discovered a new passion*—his words. *Middle-aged crazy*—Darla's words. He took lessons and went to practices whenever his schedule allowed. Darla fretted, convinced he'd break his neck. She fretted worse when she stayed home and, as a result, went with him to the lessons and practices. Just in case she needed to ride along in the ambulance.

Maia suspected her sister wanted a hand to hold when Garret blasted out of the chute on some big, angry beast. Any other night, she'd decline. Seven was TJ's regular bath time, and bed followed at seven thirty. But attempting to settle TJ when he was like this would end in a power struggle. Might as well go sit with Darla. Besides, she could always leave when Garret was done.

"Okay," she told Darla. "Meet you there."

"I have snacks and juice boxes if you're hungry."

"Awesome! More sugar." TJ would be impossible. "See you in fifteen."

Pulling straight ahead instead of turning right at the next intersection, Maia tooled through town, mentally reviewing the holiday-related tasks on her list. Shopping was her number-one priority. And mailing those cute photo cards of TJ she'd had printed. She might get a tree this year—TJ would love it. He'd been too young last year to notice and, truthfully, she'd been too exhausted between working and caring for a little baby to bother.

She'd also been down in the dumps, which was most likely a mild bout of postpartum depression piled on top of Luke refusing to acknowledge their child. That was why Maia had related to Brent and his problems. Also why she understood his reluctance to consult a doctor or join a support group. It was hard admitting you suffered from an illness, especially such a misunderstood one as depression.

It made people perceive themselves as weak. Sadly, it often made others see them as lazy. Slovenly. Selfish. Even stupid. They thought those with depression should just be able to pick themselves up and brush themselves off and get back to the business of living.

It wasn't like that. Not in the least. Those with depression hated the way they felt and would give anything to change if only they could. Some, like Brent, became good at hiding their condition. Some struggled and ended up in places like the Payson Rescue Mission. Some lost the battle altogether and, unfortunately, took their lives.

Maia shivered. Brent was strong, she told herself. He would win his battle.

Arriving at the rodeo arena, Maia spotted the sign for the Cowboy Christmas Jamboree next weekend and then a second one at the parking area.

She'd go, of course. Her dad was in charge of the pony-cart rides. In fact, the entire family would be there.

Her thoughts circled back to Luke, where they remained. TJ was young and didn't notice his father's absence. Yet. Before long, he would start wondering why his dad didn't come for visits or live with them like his uncle Garret lived with his cousins.

Maia parked in an empty space. TJ squawked again and swiveled his head from side to side, sensing this wasn't their regular routine. She grabbed her phone off the passenger seat and was about to drop it in her purse when she hesitated.

Should she? What would be the response? A chummy hello? Cool disinterest? A voice mail greeting?

Uncertain, but doing it anyway, she pressed the speed dial number for Luke. Perhaps his heart had softened with Christmas right around the corner.

When the ringing sounded through her vehicle speaker, she quickly transferred the call from Bluetooth to her phone. TJ might not understand what the adults were saying, but he could discern tones and inflections and emotions. If Luke got short with her and lashed out, she'd hate for TJ to hear.

Luke answered on the fourth ring. Had he waited, debating?

"Maia?"

"Yeah. It's, um, me."

"Everything okay?"

Aware of the wobble in her voice, she swallowed and slowed her breathing. "Everything's fine."

"What's up?"

Not one mention of TJ. No *How's he doing?* Or *He's probably walking and talking by now.*

"Is this a bad time?" Maia asked. *Please say yes.* Then she could hang up and not call back unless it was an emergency, her conscience appeased.

"No. I just got home from work. Cheryl has dinner ready but that can wait a minute. This *is* only going to take a minute, yes?"

Cheryl? Maia didn't recognize the name. Must be Luke's latest. There was always a latest.

She swallowed again, grimacing at a bitter taste.

"I was thinking about Christmas," Maia said, mustering her determination. "Wasn't sure if you had any interest in seeing TJ. We could meet you halfway." She wouldn't invite Luke to her house. "Or at Bear Creek Ranch." Neutral territory.

"We're kinda busy." He drew out the response. "I don't know when I could squeeze it in."

Seeing his son was squeezing it in? Maia bit back a retort. Calling had been a stupid idea.

Maintaining a level voice, she said, "Well, if you change your mind, call me." She'd leave the door open as she always did. It was the right thing to do. "Good night, then."

"Maia, wait."

"What?"

"How are you?"

"Don't you want to know how *TJ* is?"

Several seconds of silence passed, a sure sign of Luke's annoyance. "How is he?"

"Fine. Fantastic, in fact. You're missing out on knowing a truly wonderful little boy."

"I told you—I wasn't ready for a family."

"You weren't ready for marriage, either." Before he could

speak, she cut him off. "No reason to rehash this. Sorry I interrupted your dinner. Goodbye."

"Maia—"

She disconnected rather than fan the flames burning inside her and tossed her phone aside.

Looking at TJ in the rearview mirror, she said, "You ready, sweetums?"

She'd take him to watch his uncle Garret ride a bull, let him play with his cousins and forget all about the last ten minutes. Luke wasn't going to ruin her evening. And he sure as heck wasn't going to ruin her and TJ's Christmas.

Once she had TJ in the stroller and the diaper bag shoved in the compartment beneath the seat, she called Darla.

"We're here. Where are you?"

"On the west side. Front row. Section...102."

She imagined her sister glancing around to get her bearings. In the background, she heard her nieces' lively chatter.

"Be there in a sec."

They were easy to spot. Darla wore a bright red jacket and matching knit scarf. The girls were in holiday sweatshirts and stocking caps. They darted to and fro in front of Darla, exhibiting the same boundless energy as TJ. He went nuts the second he spotted them, what Maia called his yapping and clapping.

"Sit." Darla scooted over on the bleachers. "Take a load off."

Maia plopped down on the end seat and parked the stroller next to her.

"What's wrong?" Darla asked, always too astute for her own good.

"I stupidly called Luke to see if he wanted to spend time with TJ over Christmas." Maia leaned over and unbuckled TJ, who made the task almost impossible by flailing his arms and legs in excitement. "He wasn't interested."

"I'm sorry, hon. That must have hurt."

"What it did was make me furious." She set TJ on the ground. "Chill. Seriously. He's not worth it."

"No. He's not." Maia squeezed her eyes shut and inhaled deeply. She opened her eyes a moment later when TJ collided into her legs while evading his cousins in a game of tag. "Hey, there, little man." She patted his head before he ran off. "Be careful."

"In the mood to talk?" Darla asked.

"No." Maia glanced around the arena. "I most definitely am not in the mood to talk." She paused and squinted, her heart-rate involuntarily accelerating. "Is that Brent in the announcer's booth?"

"Took you a whole ten seconds to notice. Bet you'd have seen him in five if you weren't so mad at your ex."

Maia ignored her sister's teasing. "What's he doing in the booth? I had no idea he'd be here tonight. Not that he has to report his whereabouts to me," she added at Darla's sideways glance.

"Garret said he's filling in as judge tonight. Grumpy Joe called in sick or something."

"Brent's judging?"

"Well, he has the experience. And it's only practice."

She sounded like she was repeating back what Garret had told her.

"I suppose."

Maia actually thought Brent judging the bull-riding practice would be good for him. He'd avoided anything to do with rodeo since he'd quit. This, on the other hand, was embracing his past and showed progress or, at least, a willingness to progress. Good for him.

From where she sat, the riders appeared satisfied with Brent's scoring. None of them complained, and Brent frequently came down from the booth to chat with a few of the riders, offering his opinion and advice—or so Garret told them when he came over to chat in between his two rides.

While Maia tried not to stare at Brent, she couldn't stop herself. From the grin on his face and his relaxed manner, he was having fun.

A great time, actually. Maia imagined this was the carefree, confident and happy Brent from days gone by. The current version of him was more serious and more complex and, as a result, intriguing. But a lighthearted Brent also held a lot of appeal.

Despite TJ's energy fading and her brother-in-law finishing his two runs, she stayed. Yes, to watch Brent in his element. Eventually, Garret wandered over, saying he was ready to leave. Maia had no excuse to linger. Too bad. The second she loaded TJ into the stroller, he fell asleep, and they all started toward the parking area.

"My phone!" Maia halted abruptly and rifled through her purse. "It's not here. I must have dropped it back at our seats."

"Want us to watch TJ while you get it?" Darla asked.

"That's okay. You go on ahead. The girls are tired. Garret, too. I'll be right behind you."

"You sure?" Darla stared at Maia, suspicion shining in her eyes. "We can wait."

Her oldest daughter chose that moment to shove her youngest to the ground, which resulted in a firestorm of tears.

"Come on, you troublemakers," Garret said and rounded up the girls.

Darla reluctantly followed, glancing repeatedly over her shoulder.

Maia hurried toward the arena, her heart pounding and the stroller wheels bumping. She'd fibbed to her sister. Her phone was tucked securely in her purse. She wanted to talk to Brent and experience this different version of him up close.

Darla had surmised as much, and Maia would doubtless face the consequences later.

"Well?" Channing sidled up beside Brent and rested his forearms on the arena fence. "What'd you think?"

"The better question is, how did I do?"

"You're hired."

Brent laughed. A real laugh. Not forced. "Very funny."

All but a few of the three-dozen participants had left. A trio of cowboys hung out by the gate, engaged in a heated debate on which of them had the best ride. The lone woman participant slung her canvas equipment bags over her shoulder and joined her boyfriend. She'd scored higher than him, impressing Brent along with everyone else there tonight.

"I'm serious," Channing said. "We can use an extra judge on call. This isn't the first time we've had a last-minute cancellation."

"I'm pretty sure judges have to undergo some kind of training and testing to become certified."

"They do. But certified judges aren't required for practices or non-PRCA and non-PBR events."

Brent glanced toward the holding pens where the livestock hands herded the last of the bulls to the waiting trailer. Once loaded, they'd be returned to their regular pasture on the other side of the arena grounds, across from the horse pastures.

Tired after a night of hard work, the bulls were complacent and ready for a well-deserved rest—in stark contrast to the energy and unruly temperament they'd shown earlier.

"You know your stuff," Channing continued. "And you're fair. In the meantime, while you work on your certification, you can help us out here. It's a win-win."

Brent shook his head, unconvinced. "I had a great time tonight. I did. But I already work two jobs." Not to mention, he spent a portion of his days off with Maia, training Snapple.

"I'd pay you. Not a lot, mind you. Enough to cover your time and trouble." Channing named an amount.

"That's too much."

"It's the going rate."

As much as Brent could use the extra money, he hesitated taking on another commitment. Still, he asked, "How often are we talking about?"

"Once a month. Maybe twice."

He supposed he could manage once or twice a month. And rather than send him hurtling into the dark place, judging the bull-riding practice had left him...heartened, he supposed was an apt description. And who knew? Judging on a regular basis might prove therapeutic.

"Can I think about it?" he asked.

"Take as long as you need. We're not going anywhere. And I hope neither are you."

Brent liked the idea of returning the favor Channing had done him. Maybe he would research the requirements for becoming a professional judge. Just for kicks.

"Lookie there." Channing peered past Brent's shoulder, a grin spreading across his face. "One of us has company, and it's not me."

Brent cranked his head around. At the sight of an approaching figure, his pulse instantly quickened. Maia came toward them, pushing a sleeping TJ in the stroller.

"Evening, Maia." Channing tipped his cowboy hat. "Good to see you. Been a while."

"How've you been, Channing?" She flashed him a small smile, which brightened considerably when she greeted Brent. "Hi."

"I thought you left already."

He'd noticed her from his vantage point in the announcer's booth. And seen her leaving.

"I, ah, dropped my phone and had to come back for it. Then I...spotted you and came over."

"Speaking for the both of us," Channing said, "we're glad you did. Aren't we?" He elbowed Brent.

"Yeah." Very glad.

He and Maia had maintained their strictly platonic relationship this past week. So why was she here?

Channing must have decided three was a crowd for he suddenly made an excuse to leave. "Sorry to run out on you, but

I'm needed at the livestock pens. Merry Christmas, Maia. Give your family my best."

"We'll probably see you next weekend at the Cowboy Christmas Jamboree."

"Tell your dad we appreciate him giving the pony-cart rides. They're a big draw."

"He appreciates Rim Country's sponsorship."

Brent had heard from Ansel that proceeds from the pony-cart rides were going to the rescue shelter. Perhaps he should offer to lend Ansel a hand.

"Later, pal." Channing clapped Brent on the back. "Let me know what you find out about the judging."

"Judging?" Maia asked when she and Brent were alone.

He rubbed the side of his neck, still absorbing his conversation with Channing. "Bull and bronc riding. Channing thinks I did okay and should research what's required to become certified."

"That's a fantastic idea! You absolutely should. Garret was impressed with your advice, and from where I sat, you looked like you were enjoying yourself."

"I was." Her enthusiasm and praise filled some of the empty places inside Brent. "A lot."

"Then do it. What do you have to lose?"

"I might." He would. First thing tomorrow.

Funny, when he'd arrived at the arena this afternoon, his only intention had been to visit a friend and check out the new bucking horses. Now Brent had not one but two people urging him to consider becoming a certified rodeo judge.

Life never ceased to amaze him. It was full of twists, good and bad. Opportunities around unexpected corners. He'd decided in a single moment to walk away from his rodeo career. After a phone call from Channing, Brent had abruptly moved to Payson. Was he due for another big change?

"If I pursue this, and that's a big if," he said, "I promise it won't interfere with Mountainside or your sister's company."

"I'm not worried about that." Maia dismissed his concerns with a wave. "Nobody remains at Mountainside or Your Perfect Plus One for very long. Both are short-term jobs that will hopefully lead to something better."

"Your dad and your sister have been good to me. I won't leave them in a bind."

"You're just researching, not making any decisions."

"True."

They started walking slowly from the booth to the other side of the arena, Maia pushing the stroller.

"What's involved in judging bull and bronc riding, anyway?" she asked. "I know part of the scoring is based on how well the bull bucks. Other than that, I'm clueless. Oh, except that the ride has to last eight seconds."

She was making polite conversation. She couldn't possibly be interested in the nitty-gritty details of rodeo judging. Yet, Brent told her all the same, his excitement growing.

"There are two judges at professional events. We only had one tonight because it was practice, and the scoring is purely a learning tool. And you're right, bulls and broncs, as well as the rider, are scored on their performance. Up to fifty points each for a combined total of one hundred, though anything in the eighties is decent. Like you said, if the rider is thrown before the buzzer goes off, they're disqualified."

"Not too complicated. Buck hard. Stay on."

Brent chuckled. "There's a little more to it—that's why a judge is necessary. If a rider touches either the bull, the rope or himself with his free arm, they're disqualified. That's why you see the rider holding their free arm high over their head."

The arena had completely emptied by now. Still, Brent and Maia stayed and continued talking. He'd been avoiding the subject of rodeo as much as possible these past two years, the reminders of his failures difficult to bear. Talking with Maia was different. He'd forgotten how much he loved the sport even if he'd never compete again or be a world champion.

"You've been a good sport listening to me," he told Maia when their conversation wound down. "You must be bored to tears."

"On the contrary. I was riveted."

Her eyes twinkled with the same merriment he'd noticed during candid moments. When she gazed at her son or bickered with her sister. After Snapple conquered a difficult challenge on the trail. At the wedding reception where she and Brent had danced, and he'd kissed her cheek beneath the mistletoe.

Emotions stirred inside him. Were it not a terrible idea, he'd lean in and claim another kiss from Maia, this time on the lips.

But it *was* a terrible idea, and one that could only get them in trouble. Again. Something neither of them could afford.

CHAPTER TEN

"I'LL WALK YOU to your car," Brent said, needing something—anything—to distract him from thoughts of kissing Maia.

She beamed at him. "Thank you, kind sir."

"You're welcome." He grinned in return, his attempts not to flirt entirely unsuccessful.

They headed in the direction of the parking area where their two vehicles sat a short distance apart. TJ continued to sleep, a plush rabbit clutched tight to his chest.

"Sorry if I talked your ear off," Brent said in the least flirty tone he could muster. But saying the word *ear* caused him to think about nuzzling hers.

"No apologies necessary. You took my mind off my woes, and I needed that."

"Something happen?"

She groaned. "I made the mistake of calling TJ's dad on the way here. I stupidly thought he might want to see TJ over Christmas. But no. He still wants nothing to do with his son."

"That must have hurt."

"It did." She sniffed and blinked her suddenly damp eyes. "A lot."

"TJ's a great kid. I can't understand not wanting to see him."

"He is a great kid. And I shouldn't let his jerk of a father annoy me." She glanced away. "Sorry. I don't usually resort to name-calling."

"I think in this case it's warranted."

She shrugged. "That's my sad story, and now I feel much better because of you."

They reached her SUV and stood, neither of them seeming in a hurry to part ways. If anything, they moved closer together. Maia exuded an attraction impossible for Brent to resist. It didn't matter he had nothing to offer her, that she deserved better than him, and their employment contracts with Your Perfect Plus One prohibited fraternizing. The pull was too strong, fueled by a deep admiration.

Maia had battled the hard knocks dealt her and emerged a better, stronger person. She'd set goals for herself and was determined to achieve them. She was smart and hardworking and immensely talented.

That wasn't all. She had a way of bringing out the best in Brent. She made him want to try when, until meeting her, he'd been content to give up without a fight.

"I should go." If he remained with her any longer, his will to resist would dissolve as it had at the wedding. "And it looks like your partner there is tuckered out."

She glanced tenderly at TJ. "He's had a full day. We both have."

After lifting him from the stroller, she laid him against her shoulder and opened the SUV's rear passenger door.

"Drive careful," Brent said, turning to go. "Lots of traffic from tourists in town for the holidays."

"Wait a second. There's something I forgot to ask you."

He halted, not trusting his waning willpower.

She finished loading TJ in the car seat. He did no more than sigh softly during the entire process. Next, she collapsed the stroller and, with Brent's help, placed it in the SUV's rear compartment. With the press of a button, she lowered the door.

"Okay if I'm a little late for Snapple's training session tomorrow? TJ and I have an appointment at the pediatrician's."

"Sure." Why did he feel like he was agreeing to something more than a training session?

Suddenly, they were at the driver's side door, but he didn't remember getting there.

"Good night, Maia."

"Tell me what you find out about becoming a certified judge."

She inched nearer. A half step more, and she'd be in his arms. Then what? Brent wanted to find out.

Before he surrendered to his impulses, sound judgement prevailed, and he retreated.

He didn't get far. Maia reached up and linked her fingers around his neck. With one tug, he was close enough to see moonlit shadows dance across her face. Or claim that kiss.

His pulse hammered. "Maia."

"Shh," she murmured. "I know what you're going to say. This is a mistake."

"A huge one."

"Right now, I don't care." She raised her face to his. "And I think you don't care, either."

"You're wrong."

"Then why haven't you left yet?"

Good question. Brent tried once more to retreat, but his legs wouldn't cooperate.

"That's what I thought," Maia said and brought her mouth to within a hair's breadth of his.

"Even if we were to… This can't go anywhere."

"Maybe not." She smiled, the twinkle reappearing in her gorgeous brown eyes. "At least we can satisfy our curiosity. You can't tell me you haven't been wondering what it might be like to kiss me. *Really* kiss me."

"I have." Why lie? Maia wasn't stupid and neither was she blind. She could see the truth as if it were stamped on Brent's forehead.

"What if you wake up tomorrow with regrets?" he asked.

"I might." Her voice lowered to a whisper. "But I'd have the memory, too. And that will be so worth it."

Maia's arms were around his neck, and she wanted to kiss him. He need only narrow the tiny distance between them to experience a glimpse of heaven.

Why did she have to make that remark about having the memory? He wanted to create one right now.

"I must be crazy," he murmured and wrapped an arm around her waist.

"Let's be crazy together." She unlinked her fingers and cradled his cheeks with her hands.

Her soft touch was a soothing balm to his wounded soul, and he craved more. "Yes."

One of them moved. He couldn't be sure who. But the next instant, Maia was nestled in his embrace, and her soft lips were pressed firmly against his. He willed time to stand still, for this moment to last an eternity. Too long had passed since he'd held a woman, felt her warmth mingle with his, and never a woman like Maia. Kissing her, there was nothing he couldn't accomplish and no distant star beyond his reach.

For a brief moment, Brent was his old self with a future full of promise and potential. Then, the kiss ended, and the real world with its many disappointments returned.

Maia eased out of his arms and met his gaze unabashedly. Something else he liked about her.

Smiling, she said, "That was worth any trouble we might get into."

He wasn't sure he agreed, but the kiss had been incredible and, perhaps, life altering. For him.

He brushed a stray strand of loose hair from her face. "You're something else."

"Please don't break my heart by telling me this can't happen again. I want to believe things will change one day for us, and we'll be kissing often."

He wouldn't tell her they shouldn't kiss again, but he'd be thinking it.

A tightness gripped his chest making it hard for him to speak. To breathe. He looked about but didn't sense the black cloud anywhere near.

"Good night, Maia."

"See you, Brent."

He'd be seeing her, all right. The way she'd gazed at him, as if he meant the world to her, would stay with him always.

She opened the SUV door and slid in behind the steering wheel. Brent lifted his arm as if to stop her and then let it fall.

The next instant, she was driving away. He fully expected his mood to nose-dive during the drive home. With every soaring flight into the stratosphere came the inevitable plummet back to earth.

It didn't happen this time. When Brent walked into the bunkhouse twenty-five minutes later, he was welcomed by Javier and Rowdy and actually accepted their invitation to play poker.

Maia sat astride Snapple, fuming. Not at the horse but at Brent, who rode behind her on Lone Star. He'd been silent the entire ride. Same for the last however many days. He'd either avoided her or acted like nothing had happened.

Had he not felt the fireworks? Yes, he had. No one kissed like that unless they were into the other person. So why the walls again?

Needing an outlet for her frustration, she urged Snapple to go faster and climb harder. Let Brent keep up with them now. She dared him.

To her great annoyance, he did. How he managed to get speed and power out of an old plug like Lone Star mystified Maia.

Branches slapped Maia's arms and legs as she and Snapple climbed the steep, rocky incline. She leaned forward in the saddle, keeping her head low to avoid injury to her face and eyes. A helmet and sunglasses provided only so much protection. The redistribution of her weight also enabled Snapple to charge up the trail, his front legs churning like massive pistons.

At the top, the ground leveled out. Maia reined Snapple to a stop where the trail widened, then dismounted. Brent came up behind her, Lone Star breathing heavily as if he'd scaled a great height—which he just had. Snapple merely snorted once, his lungs functioning at an amazing capacity, not dissimilar to those of a racehorse.

Brent also dismounted. He left Lone Star to rest and joined Maia. As had become their routine during similar training rides, he assumed the role of a veterinarian at a competition trail ride. He approached Snapple from behind, withdrawing the stethoscope from his jacket pocket. Purposely letting the stethoscope dangle from his hands, he then inserted the ear tips.

When Snapple didn't react, Brent held the stethoscope drum between his thumb and forefinger and pressed it to Snapple's flank behind his left front leg. From his other pocket, Brent removed a stopwatch, which he clicked to start. After a minute had passed, he announced Snapple's heart rate.

"One hundred and thirty."

Maia lifted her shoulders. "Not bad."

This was the first they'd talked since starting the ride an hour ago. Before that, conversation had been minimal. Okay, she got it. Brent's extra caution was hardly a surprise. He'd warned her, after all. But, really, he was taking this keep-things-between-them-professional thing a bit too far. He didn't have to behave like they were strangers.

Or did he? Hadn't they proven—not once but twice—that they had zero willpower? She'd been the one to practically throw herself at him. But, oh, she'd wanted that kiss. And he hadn't disappointed. Best ever. No exaggeration.

"Can he get back down to sixty-five beats per minute in the allotted time?" Brent asked.

"That's why we're doing this, isn't it?" At his raised brows, she cleared her throat and tried again in a nicer tone. "His stats generally return to normal quickly."

Brent busied himself inspecting Snapple's hooves. Maia ground her teeth together. This attitude of his was annoying to say the least.

Granted, kissing had been a mistake, she'd concede to that. But they wouldn't lose control a second time. Darla was depending on them, and they both needed the extra paycheck. Brent more than her. Besides his credit card bills, he had some upcoming expenses.

She'd overheard him talking to her dad about bringing his mom out for a visit. She'd have rather Brent told her himself, except that would have been a *personal* conversation, and those were off-limits.

"Last time he was slow recovering," Brent said, stepping back to evaluate Snapple.

She should be glad at how quickly Brent had picked up on the lingo. "Only by a few minutes. What matters most is that he's not reacting to you and the stethoscope and hasn't for the last three practice rides."

"He's getting used to me." Brent ran a hand along Snapple's scar. "We should try this with someone new. What if we arranged for Javier to meet us at the stables when we return?"

"Does he have any experience with horses?"

"A little. Enough he can hold a stethoscope and pretend to time Snapple's heart rate. Unless you have someone else in mind."

"No." The suggestion was an excellent one, and Maia's irritation waned. "Will he be willing?"

Maia listened while Brent made a call to his bunk mate, gathering from his side of the conversation that Javier was indeed willing and would meet them at the stables.

When Brent disconnected, her impatience won out, and she blurted, "Do you regret kissing me that much?"

He went quiet while pocketing his phone, finally admitting, "I don't regret it. Kissing you was nice."

Where did *nice* land on a scale of one to ten?

"Then why the invisible wall?" she asked.

"Less a wall than a safety zone. My way of resisting temptation."

Wait. Were those slight curves at the corners of his mouth? She squinted her eyes. They *were* slight curves.

"I really like you," she confessed.

"Maia."

"I'm in agreement. We table any romance for the present. But I still want to be friends and go back to the way things were before."

"That's not easy for me. Until I'm better, maintaining some distance between us is easier on me. Fewer ups and downs."

Maia released a long breath. She'd been so preoccupied with her own feelings, she hadn't given any consideration to Brent's. "How's your mood been lately? You don't have to answer if you'd rather not."

"Not bad. Steady. I…did some research last night online."

"Yeah?"

"I joined a support group."

"That's great, Brent." She didn't say more, not wanting to embarrass him.

"I'm just reading posts. I haven't participated yet."

"Reading posts is good. Take your time. You'll participate when you're ready."

"We'll see." The curves at the corners of his mouth deepened. "And, by the way, that was a *stellar* kiss. Off the charts. Knowing I'll never have another one is a definite mood killer."

She took his teasing as a sign of encouragement. "Never say never. Who knows what the future holds?"

Brent reinserted the ear tips. "Time to recheck this horse."

Ouch. His abrupt retreat stung a little.

He put the stethoscope's drum to Snapple's flank. The horse

didn't twitch. Didn't move. Didn't blink. A remarkable difference from two weeks ago. From last week, even.

"You've done an amazing job with him," Maia commented. "A sock attached to a fishing pole. Who'd have guessed?"

"He may blow up with Javier." Brent clicked on the stopwatch and stepped away. "Eighty-seven beats per minute, by the way. His rate is coming down more quickly today."

"You're changing the subject."

"I'm not. We came on this ride to improve Snapple's conditioning for competition."

"Speaking of research, did you start looking into rodeo judging yet?"

"Now you're changing the subject," he accused.

"Am not. We were talking about things between us going back to the way they were and you getting better. Researching a new career falls into both categories."

He groaned. She thought he might refuse to answer her, but then he did.

"I went online but couldn't find a whole lot. I asked Channing yesterday for the names of the judges Rim Country uses and if he'd mind me contacting them."

"And?"

"He'll let me know. He didn't feel right giving me their phone numbers without first obtaining their consent. I also put in a call to the PRCA. The person I need to talk to is on vacation until after the first of the year. I left a message and will follow up if I don't hear back."

"I'm impressed. Even if you decide being a rodeo judge isn't for you, you've taken steps. Big ones."

"It feels good. Positive. I like waking up in the morning with something to look forward to even if it's just a phone call."

Such a small thing most people took for granted. Maia chided herself for being too hard on Brent. "I understand. Looking forward to something positive is what helped me through my own rough times."

He hesitated before responding. "I have a long road ahead of me, Maia."

"Yes. You do."

"No guarantee how long I'll take to reach the end. You shouldn't wait on me. Not when there are plenty of other guys out there whose lives aren't in shambles."

"Who says I'm waiting on you?"

At last, she got a full-blown smile out of him. With a resigned chuckle, he checked Snapple's heart rate again.

"Sixty-seven."

"Great." She reached for the reins and slung them over the saddle horn. "You and Lone Star are doing well. Want to take the lead the rest of the way?"

"No thanks. You and that army tank you call a horse will run us over." He handed her the stethoscope and returned to where he'd left Lone Star tethered. Halfway there he paused. "One good thing about you."

She climbed into the saddle, attempting to ignore the fluttering in her middle. "What's that?"

"I'm motivated again."

"Yeah. Me, too."

"To get my life together. Not...us."

"That's what I was talking about, too. Well, that and winning the Diamond Cup this spring."

Maia glanced away, avoiding Brent's sharp gaze. One look at her, and he'd read the fib in her eyes. She'd totally been talking about them.

Reining Snapple to the right, she trotted him toward the trail. Two miles from the ranch, she literally left Brent and Lone Star in her dust. The veteran trail horse had grown tired and fallen behind as Snapple, sensing they were nearing home, poured on the steam in a late burst of energy.

Brent must have called Javier in advance, for the prep cook was waiting by the hitching post when Maia arrived. She motioned for him to remain where he was and brought Snapple to a stop twenty feet away. She wasn't taking any chances lest the horse spook at the sight of a stranger. But he appeared unbothered by Javier's presence. Then again, he was used to customers milling about the stables.

His calm demeanor could change in a flash, and she debated waiting for Brent. On second thought, Brent would be nowhere near during an actual competition. Today could be a true test of how well Snapple responded to his training.

She hopped down from the horse. "Brent's fifteen or twenty minutes away. Maybe more. You willing to give this a try without him?"

"He told me not to wait on him."

"He did, huh?" Clearly, she and Brent were of like mind. "Okay. But get out of Snapple's way if he makes the slightest move. You hear me?"

"No need to tell me twice." Javier grinned. "I have no desire to be wearing his hoofprint on my forehead."

She led Snapple to the hitching post where she handed over the stethoscope to Javier, relieved the horse continued to pay the prep cook no heed. "Don't worry about actually monitoring his heart rate. Just go through the motions."

"Right." Javier hooked the stethoscope around his neck. Leaning forward, he cautiously placed the drum on Snapple's side.

Maia maintained a firm hold on the reins, watching Javier's every move almost as closely as she watched Snapple's. Other than a flick of his ears and a quick sideways glance at Javier, the horse stood quietly.

"How long you want me to do this?" Javier asked.

"I'll tell you when. We need a full minute." Thirty seconds later, she gave him a nod. "Okay. That's enough."

"Whew." Javier straightened.

"You brave enough to run your hand along his back to his rump?"

"Um, I guess."

Snapple stomped a front hoof at the unfamiliar contact and gave Javier another look.

The prep cook startled and retreated a step. "Whoa there." After a few seconds, he relaxed. "Again?"

"Only if you're comfortable," Maia said.

Snapple resumed ignoring the humans in favor of sniffing the hitching post.

Javier sent Maia a sheepish grin. "Can't have Syndee learning I chickened out."

Ah. His girlfriend. "She won't hear it from me."

Laughing, he ran his hand along Snapple's back, visibly relaxing when the horse failed to react.

"Thanks, Javier. I owe you."

"Anything for Brent. He's a good guy." The prep cook moved away, out of kicking range, showing he was no dummy.

"If you and Syndee want to go on a trail ride one of these days, let me know. Free of charge."

"Seriously? She'd like that."

When Brent rode in on Lone Star a short time later, both rider and horse were moving slowly. Maia had already unsaddled Snapple and walked him around the stables a few times to cool him down.

"Everything went well, I take it," he said, dismounting near the hitching post.

"Javier call you?"

"No. Your smile told me."

"Thanks, Brent. Your training techniques have really paid off."

"Happy to help."

They might have stood there gazing at each other and reconsidering that whole tabling-romance stuff if not for her dad and Rowdy coming down the road with a half-dozen riders. Timing, as the saying went, was everything.

CHAPTER ELEVEN

"EASY DOES IT, BOYS," Ansel called from the back of the horse trailer. "Quit your fussing."

At the side of the trailer, Brent untied Mr. Big Shot's lead rope and tossed it over the speckled gray's neck. He'd done the same a few minutes ago with Boss Man.

"One at a time," Ansel groused as he lowered the gate.

Inside the trailer, the nearly identical pair of ponies shuffled and stomped with their dainty hooves, eager to escape their confinement. Though they'd only been in the trailer for a short five-mile drive, they behaved as if they'd been confined for hours.

Ansel had borrowed Mr. Big Shot and Boss Man from a friend for tonight's Cowboy Christmas Jamboree. He'd then recruited Brent and Pete from the shelter to help. Neither of them minded. Brent was free—he'd attended a wedding last night for Your Perfect Plus One. Pete had told them on the drive from the shelter he was glad for the chance to be useful. And while inexperienced with horses, he'd demonstrated a willingness to perform any grunt work asked of him.

He was also good company. From what Brent had learned, Pete made himself useful at the shelter—something that hadn't gone unnoticed. Ansel had offered to speak to the head of maintenance at Bear Creek Ranch and see if there were any job openings.

Pete was grateful, even getting a little choked up. He didn't care that the job was a far cry from his former occupation of project manager.

Brent knew exactly how the man felt. He'd been similarly grateful when Ansel hired him. If there weren't any open positions in maintenance, he'd ask Javier about a kitchen job for Pete.

"Let's go, boys," Ansel said and stepped back from the rear of the trailer.

Mr. Big Shot and Boss Man twisted in half circles, battling for which of them would be first out. They created a racket as they scrambled down the metal ramp. Once on solid ground, the pair settled, content to stand there and look awesome with their long, silky tails and braided manes intertwined with red-and-gold ribbons.

"All that fuss for nothing," Ansel told the ponies and bent to pat their heads—which came no higher than his waist.

Mr. Big Shot and Boss Man would pull the cart filled with kids in a large circle around the arena grounds. Pete was in charge of selling tickets while Brent would load and unload passengers. The ponies' owner had decorated the cart with shiny garland and battery-operated Christmas lights. The rear seat would hold two to three kids, depending on their sizes.

In addition to pony rides and holiday-themed carnival games, Channing had hired a band to provide Christmas music. The musicians were currently setting up in front of the concession stand. A lighted tree rivaling the one at Bear Creek Ranch stood in the center of the open area. Hundreds of candy canes free for the taking hung from the branches. Inside the arena, a maze of straw bales, sawhorses and barrels had been constructed. Life-size mechanical reindeer trimmed with blinking lights showed the way.

At the end of the maze, Santa awaited on his makeshift

throne. Photos with the jolly old elf cost five dollars each. Like with the pony rides, all proceeds would be donated to the Payson Rescue Mission's holiday food drive.

Brent hadn't noticed any mistletoe, but he remained on the lookout. He'd been serious when he told Maia he was avoiding temptation.

Together, he and Pete unloaded the cart and equipment. While Brent and Ansel harnessed the ponies, Pete parked the truck and trailer out of sight behind the horse barn. He returned on foot just as the sun inched toward the horizon. The jamboree would start promptly at five thirty and end at eight thirty. Between unharnessing the ponies, loading them and the cart into the trailer, returning them home, and, lastly, dropping off Pete at the shelter, it would be a late night for Brent and Ansel.

Again, Brent didn't mind. Though not a purpose exactly, contributing to a worthy cause put him in the Christmas spirit.

He still struggled periodically. There was no instant cure for what ailed him. Three or four times a day a memory had him teetering on the edge of the dark place. His conversation with his dad. A reminder that he and Maia had no future together. The monthly interest hitting his credit card balances. Learning from Rim Country's judges that becoming certified, while possible, required time and money Brent didn't have.

But he told himself, there were plenty of positives to balance out the negatives—something the online support group had been teaching him. He mentally ticked off the list. If all went as planned, his mom would come for a visit in February. Snapple continued to respond well to his training—Maia had entered a local competition next month as a test run for the prestigious Diamond Cup. Brent had sent two payments to his old pal who'd lent him money, which was two more than he'd sent last month. And speaking of friends, he'd counted two new ones in his circle: Javier and Rowdy. Ansel, too, if a boss could be considered a friend.

Maia was also a good friend. She'd listened to him lament and offered good advice even if Brent refused to take it.

"Snap the clamp to the D ring," Ansel instructed Brent. "Pete, make sure the brake's engaged."

Both hurried to do their boss's bidding. They'd decided Ansel would drive the pony cart. Brent was more than able to handle Mr. Big Shot and Boss Man, but he had thirty pounds and four inches on Ansel. The boys, as Ansel called them, could only pull so much weight. Best to conserve their strength.

Ansel climbed onto the cart seat. "I'm going to take the boys for a short spin around the place. Get the kinks out before the first paying customers. You want to come along, Pete?"

The shelter resident's face lit up brighter than any five-year-old's. "You bet."

He climbed in beside Ansel, the two of them squished together in the small seat. Ansel clucked to the ponies, and they took off at a jaunty clip. Having a few minutes to spare, Brent made his way to the concession stand for a bite of dinner. He'd just finished his hamburger and fries when Channing approached.

"Saw the pony cart on the way here," his friend said, sitting down at the picnic table with Brent. "They look great." He wore a Santa cap instead of his usual cowboy hat and had a red woolen scarf around his neck. When he caught Brent staring, he said, "Kenna and my mom's doing. They insisted me and the hands dress the part."

"Wait. I need a picture." Brent opened the camera app on his phone and aimed it at Channing. "To show at your bachelor party. Or better yet, your wedding."

"Ha, ha. Very funny."

Brent snapped a picture.

"Speaking of weddings," Channing said, "where's Maia?"

Brent almost dropped his phone. Had his friend learned about his and Maia's kiss? Kisses. Then he realized Channing was referring to Brent and Maia's shared employer, Your Perfect Plus One.

"She and the rest of the family will be here soon."

At least Darla would be in the vicinity to prevent Brent from repeating past mistakes. He didn't dare kiss Maia, beneath the mistletoe or anywhere, with her sister a few feet away.

"Hey, listen," Channing said. "Are you free January fifteenth? Also, possibly, the twenty-eighth?"

Brent checked his calendar on his phone. "I don't have any weddings scheduled. What's up?"

"We're having an extra bull-riding practice and adding a bronc-riding one to the calendar. Our first in a while. Gonna need a judge."

"Grumpy Joe's not available?"

"He's working the Lucky Eights Rodeo and the Cattle Country Livestock Show."

Brent narrowed his gaze. "For real? You're not just doing me a favor?"

Channing pointed to his cap. "Would Santa's helper lie? I'll shoot you a text with the details."

"I'd feel better if I were qualified. I think your participants would, too."

"You will be soon enough."

"I haven't decided to begin the certification process."

"Okay. Until then, you can judge a few practices."

Brent blew out a breath. "I could use the money."

"A good enough reason for me."

Brent had leveled with his friend about the full extent of his financial predicament. Not, however, what had caused it and his continuing battle with depression. A true friend, Channing would respond with sympathy and compassion—and unintentionally leave what little pride Brent had left in shambles.

"Any chance you can eventually quit Your Perfect Plus One?" Channing asked.

"Not yet. Darla pays too well."

"But you could if you obtained your certification and we hired you as a permanent judge."

"There are just too many costs involved, and paying off my debts comes first."

"What if you had a sponsor?"

"For getting certified? Who would sponsor me and why?"

"Rim Country. And we'd sponsor you to guarantee having a reliable judge on the payroll."

Brent chuckled. "You're crazy, man."

"Think about it."

"What would you want in return? And don't tell me there are no strings attached."

"I haven't decided."

"Let me guess. You just came up with the idea two minutes ago."

"Mmm, more like five minutes ago," Channing admitted with a grin. "We could treat the sponsorship as an advance, if that makes you more comfortable. You'd sign a contract for, say, two years, and we'd take a little off the top of your monthly wages to repay the advance."

"I already have too many loans."

"Not a loan. There's no interest."

Brent crumpled a napkin and tossed it into his empty paper food tray. He needed time to think. He wasn't making any rash decisions that might come back to bite him. "We'll talk after I hear from the PRCA."

"All right. No rush." Channing's grin widened. "But here's something else for you to chew on while you're at it. If you didn't work for Darla, then you and Maia could date."

Brent sat back and studied his friend. "I never said I wanted to date her."

"You didn't have to. It's pretty obvious."

Brent grumbled. He thought he'd done a better job of masking his feelings for Maia. "What I want and what's possible are two different things. I'm in no position to get involved with her or anyone."

"She doesn't care that you aren't rich."

"But she does care that I'm down on my luck and wandering through life with no real direction. Trust me."

"You *were* down on your luck," Channing said. "You're on your way up now."

"I've taken a few steps. Up is still a long way off. Call it ego or self-esteem...whatever...but I need to be in a better place before asking Maia out. She's going places, and I refuse to be an anchor holding her down."

"Okay." Channing nodded in agreement. "I respect that."

"Besides, Darla's counting on me. I made a commitment to her, and one thing I have that's still worth something is my word."

"You don't think she'd be okay with you leaving if it was for a better job with long-term potential and to date her sister, who happens to like you, too?"

"I'm not going to find out," Brent insisted. "And for all I know, Ansel isn't in favor of his employee dating his daughter."

Channing pushed his Santa cap back on his head and contemplated Brent. "When you fall for a gal, you sure don't make it easy on yourself."

"I made poor choices after I quit rodeoing. I won't make another one that drags Maia down with me, no matter how much I like her."

"She may be willing to wait for you. Ask her."

"No!"

"She's a catch. What if some other guy comes along?" Channing asked, his tone serious. "You'd lose your chance."

"Then I lose my chance. Better than her coming to resent me because I'm not the man she thought I was." Brent couldn't live with that.

"Well, speak of the devil." Channing stared at the concession stand entrance. "This is getting to be a habit."

Brent didn't have to turn around. His spidey senses were already tingling. Or should he say Maia senses?

He spun his head around, expecting to see her son and entire family with her. Nope. She'd come alone. Completely alone.

Brent was in trouble. At least Channing was here and able to act as a buffer.

"Whoops. I'm running late." Channing stood and swung a long leg over the picnic table bench. "Evening, Maia. Brent, I'll text you that info."

He sauntered off, leaving Brent and Maia in the very situation he'd hoped to avoid.

Weird. If Maia didn't know better, she'd swear Brent was nervous to see her. Those compelling hazel eyes of his had widened and then glanced away. When she'd offered a bright *Hi there*, he'd responded with a murmured *Hello*.

Not waiting for an invitation, she slipped into the seat across from him that Channing had vacated. "I ran into Dad on the way over. He said you might be here."

"Were you looking for me?"

"No. He just mentioned you were grabbing dinner."

Either her imagination was working overtime or worry tinged Brent's voice. Why? They'd seen little of each other this past week since the practice trail ride when Javier had played the role of vet.

Not because they were avoiding each other. At least, she hadn't been avoiding him. Their hectic schedules were at fault. Maia had been inundated with Christmas-related tasks: shopping, wrapping presents, house decorating, cookie baking and attending get-togethers with friends.

"Actually, I was elected to go on a beverage-and-snack run. Which, in hindsight, doesn't seem fair. I think my brother-in-law, Garret, is a better choice. He has longer arms and can carry more. My nieces call him the gorilla man."

Her efforts to get a laugh out of Brent were wasted.

"Are you mad at me?" she asked.

"No."

"Is something wrong?"

He shook his head.

All right. She could take a hint and stood.

But rather than leave, she tried again. "You mind giving me a hand? I doubt I can handle seven drinks, a large bag of kettle corn and three cinnamon rolls by myself."

"Um, sure." Brent climbed slowly out of the picnic table as if his boots were filled with cement.

This should be interesting. "Thanks."

Maia hadn't been entirely honest with Brent. She'd been dispatched to bring back four drinks and a bag of kettle corn. On impulse, she'd inflated the order. Something was bothering Brent, and she had the distinct impression she was at the root of it. He may not want to talk to her, but she wanted to talk to him.

They chose the shortest of the three lines in front of the concession stand.

"What's new with Channing?" she asked.

Perhaps Brent's worry was actually annoyance and had to do with his friend, not her. He and Channing had been engrossed in conversation right before she'd showed up. That could account for his startled reaction at seeing her.

Another possibility, he was in one of his funks, as he called them. But then, what had triggered it?

"Nothing much," he said.

"You two looked awfully serious."

"He asked me to judge a couple practices in January."

"No fooling! That's fantastic."

Brent didn't reply.

"Isn't it?"

"He's paying me too much money. I'm not worth it."

"You most certainly are. You showed your worth the other night."

"He's doing me a favor."

Maia snorted. "I don't believe that for a second. Channing's a smart businessman. He wouldn't overpay you out of friendship. The practices generate money for the arena, and he needs reliable, expert judges."

"He mentioned Rim Country sponsoring me."

"Wait! What? Are you competing again?"

Brent shook his head. "The sponsorship would cover the costs of me earning my judging certification."

Maia brightened and involuntarily touched his arm. She couldn't help herself. "No kidding!"

"I haven't said yes. There's a lot to consider."

"I suppose," she conceded. "But it's a wonderful opportunity. You won't get another one like it. A sponsor," she repeated with a bit of awe.

"I insisted on paying back the money. I won't take charity."

"I wouldn't call a sponsorship charity, but okay." From what she knew about Brent, he'd want to pay his own way. "I can understand your reasoning, especially if you make a full-time career of judging and work for other arenas."

"Hmm. I haven't thought that far ahead."

"You could be heading for a brand-new career. That's exciting."

"I guess," he hedged.

Was he afraid? Maia doubted it. Hesitant? Sure. Who wouldn't be? The idea of changing careers was intimidating. Risks were involved. Changes necessary. And Brent wasn't coming from a place of strength and security.

"You'd have to travel," she said. "Maybe move." *Please don't move.*

"I would have to travel. But I'd establish a home base."

"Where?" *Say Payson.*

"Around here, I suppose. Seeing as I'd work primarily for Rim Country." He rubbed his chin in thought, only to drop his hand. "I'm getting ahead of myself. I haven't even decided if I'll obtain my certification."

If he was ahead of himself, Maia was in the next county over. She'd already jumped to a future where she and Brent were seriously dating and considering marriage.

Would she be okay with him leaving every week? Maia had always assumed she'd meet a man who wanted to put down roots and stay in one place. TJ already had a father who never saw him, and he deserved more than a part-time stepdad. Not someone who spent a few days out of the week at his *home base*.

Something else occurred to her. Didn't professional cowboys have a reputation for being players? Maia'd had her fill of infidelity with Luke—enough to last a lifetime. She wouldn't tolerate being cheated on again. No way, no how.

Brent didn't impress her as the cheating kind, but, in all honesty, he might have been a different person during his years on the rodeo circuit. He'd never talked about any previous relationships with her. Because he'd been a big-time player? Maybe he still was. Her gut told her no, but she'd been fooled once before and paid the price.

Oh, good grief. What was the matter with her, wasting all this mental energy? Brent wasn't ready to date. He'd told her repeatedly. Indulging in silly fantasies served no purpose other than to make herself miserable.

"I could see myself living here permanently," Brent said as they moved ahead in line.

Swell. Just when she thought reality had returned, here came another silly fantasy.

"Who wouldn't?" she said, trying not to read anything into his statement. "Beautiful scenery. Large town with a small-town feel. Mild winters. Gorgeous summers. Friendly people. The big city is far away but not too far to be inconvenient."

"The scenery is beautiful," he concurred. "Different from Tucson, where I was staying before coming there. Really different from Wichita."

"I bet."

"I spent some time in Colorado," he mused. "The mountains

there are spectacular. It's like living on the edge of heaven, or what I imagine heaven to be."

Colorado? That was a twelve-hour drive. "You have any old friends there?" She gave herself credit for not adding *girl* in front of *friends*.

"One." He didn't elaborate further.

The couple ahead of them moved aside, putting an end to Maia's fishing expedition. She stepped up to the counter and placed her order, wincing slightly when she recited the bogus items. Someone would surely want to eat a piping-hot cinnamon roll that smelled like a dream come true.

Paying with her debit card, she handed the first drink caddy to Brent, along with straws and the bag of kettle corn. She carried the second drink caddy and the cinnamon rolls.

Her family waited by the arena fence, their reactions varied at spotting Brent with Maia. Her mom's face lit up like a beacon, and she hollered, "Yooo-hooo! Over here," as if they were a hundred feet away instead of ten. Garret grinned and asked, "Are those cinnamon rolls?" before being distracted by his two daughters tugging on his arms. Darla produced a polite smile but not fast enough. Maia had glimpsed the initial scowl.

TJ ripped his hand free from his grandmother's grip and galloped toward Maia in that silly gait of toddlers. No, not toward her. Brent was his target.

He collided with Brent who, by some miracle, didn't drop his drink caddy.

"Hey, pal. Whatcha doing?"

TJ reached up and pulled on the hem of Brent's jacket with both fists.

"Sorry. You can't wear my jacket. Not tonight. It's cold out here."

Maia handed off her drink caddy and kettle corn to her mom, who gushed at how impossibly cute TJ and Brent were together.

Darla leaned in close to Maia and hissed, "Why is he here?"

"I needed help carrying everything."

"Right. You are so full of—"

"Maybe we should get in line for the pony-cart rides," Maia announced in a loud voice. "It's getting long."

"We're talking about this later."

"There's nothing to talk about. Brent happened to be at the concession stand when I got there."

"How convenient."

Dividing the food between everyone—Brent didn't want any—they headed en masse over to where a line formed for the pony-cart rides.

"I want a candy cane," Maia's older niece cried when they spotted the Christmas tree.

"Me, too!" chimed her younger sister.

Naturally, they stopped and collected candy canes. Darla had to remind her daughters repeatedly to take only one. The two girls prattled on in their high voices about seeing Santa and the list of toys they planned on requesting. Maia's mom attempted to explain Santa to TJ, who was much more interested in unwrapping his candy cane.

"Have you made any plans for Christmas?" Maia asked Brent while Darla was distracted by her girls.

"I'm volunteering at the shelter."

"Dad twist your arm?"

"I want to."

Not the answer she'd expected. "That's nice of you."

"Getting out of the house on a holiday is good for me. Better than sitting alone by myself."

"Yeah. I remember how hard it was for me that first Christmas after Luke and I split."

Even with her family there, Maia had struggled to stay in the moment and not be consumed by the past. Had he not cheated on her, she'd have been married and celebrating Christmas with her new husband.

Their breakup was for the best. Maia knew that deep in her heart. The knowledge hadn't stopped the memories from stinging or the doubts from surfacing. What might she have done differently? Why wasn't she enough for him? How could she have been so blind? Would she ever meet anyone new and fall in love again?

"I spent the better part of last Christmas holed up in a hotel room," Brent said. "Volunteering at the shelter will be a big improvement."

"You're a good person. Kind. Compassionate."

Luke wouldn't have been caught dead at the shelter, much less volunteering. She should remember that the next time she considered committing to a man. Did he regularly volunteer or donate to worthy causes?

"My reasons are selfish," Brent said. "I'm comfortable there. I relate to the residents."

Maia almost asked Brent if he'd checked out any of the support groups at the shelter, but she decided against it. Last time she mentioned him seeking help and seeing his doctor, he'd become defensive. Plus, he'd joined the online support group. She wanted to ask about that, too, but, beside not being the right time or place, it was too personal of a question. He'd tell her if he wanted. She was just glad he'd taken a step to seek help.

Finally, they were first in line. A few minutes later, Maia's dad drove up with the gaily decorated cart and striking pair of ponies.

Darla appeared beside Maia. "One of us has to go with Dad and the kids."

Maia contemplated before answering. If she insisted Darla go, her sister might suspect Maia of wanting to be alone with Brent. While Darla had nothing to worry about, she might not see it that way. Maia didn't want to add tension to an otherwise lovely evening out with the family.

"I'd love nothing better!" she said.

CHAPTER TWELVE

MAIA HELPED LOAD TJ and his cousins into the back seat of the
pony cart. Though the cart sat low to the ground, Maia's dad
had installed a rope safety harness to prevent little passengers
from falling or climbing out. Maia sat in the front seat with her
dad, the top half of her body twisted sideways to maintain a
watchful eye on the youngsters and, with luck, prevent mishaps.

"Behave." She leveled a finger at her son and nieces. "No
fighting. Santa's watching you."

"Is he?" Her youngest niece's mouth dropped open.

"We'll behave," her older niece promised, serious as only a
five-year-old could be.

"Gud, gud," TJ repeated. He was already attempting to
squirm out of the rope harness.

Maia kept one hand within easy reach to grab a fistful of
coat if necessary. "This is wonderful, Dad," she said when they
started out, the ponies clip-clopping at a brisk pace. "What a
stunning view."

Rim Country Rodeo Arena was situated in the foothills a
half mile above Payson. The lights of the town's many decorated houses and businesses glittered merrily in the distance,
creating the type of charming scene common in sappy holiday movies. For the record, Maia loved sappy holiday movies.

Rather than comment on the view, her dad said, "Glad we have a moment alone to talk."

"About what?" Alarm coursed through her. "Is something wrong with Mom?"

"Whatever gave you that idea?"

"You sounded so serious."

"I am worried, but not about her." He turned the small team left, and they rounded the arena's far side. "You and Brent are getting awful cozy lately."

Darla had used that same word with Maia at Thanksgiving.

"We're friends, Dad. Nothing more."

"You sure about that? I've seen the way you look at him. The way he looks at you."

She and Brent really needed to work on being less obvious.

"We've talked, and you can quit worrying," she said. "We've agreed the timing's not right for us."

"I'm glad to hear that. He's going through a lot. Depression is no cakewalk."

Maia couldn't hide her surprise. "He told you?"

"Not exactly. He hinted, and I know the signs. I've seen a lot of residents at the shelter battling the same demons. Brent's not as bad as some. Or he's more adept at hiding it."

"Some of both, in my opinion. Plus, he's making progress." She glanced at the kids, glad to see they weren't shoving and pushing each other. "When he first told me what he's been going through, I suggested he join a support group at the shelter."

"And?"

"He wasn't receptive to the idea. Not coming from me. He might be more receptive if you were to suggest it."

She didn't mention Brent's online support group to her dad. That was Brent's news to share, not hers.

"Possibly," her dad said. "We'll see. I'd hate to offend him. A proud man like Brent doesn't like admitting he's dealing with mental illness."

"No one does," Maia agreed.

"He was under a lot of pressure to succeed, from his dad and from himself. That took a severe toll on him when he quit rodeo."

"I'm not going to pressure Brent," Maia said, picking up TJ's hand and placing it back inside the cart. "If that's what you're hinting at."

"You have to ask yourself what's best not just for you but Brent, too. If the two of you were to get serious, that is. When the timing's right," he added with a smile.

"I'd be supportive. Not demanding."

"You'd be the most supportive girlfriend ever. I have no doubt. You were to Luke, even when he didn't deserve it. The thing about depression is, while Brent needs support of those around him to get better, he also needs space. As much as you might want to help him, you could be doing him a disservice. He might shut down."

Maia hadn't thought about it like that before. She started to mention Channing's offer for Rim Country to sponsor Brent's judging certification, then changed her mind. That was his business to tell people when he was ready.

"You're right. And like I said, you don't have to worry about Brent and me. We're solidly in the friend zone."

Her dad continued as if not hearing her. "There's TJ to think about, too. Any man you make a part of your life will be a part of his. Brent isn't ready to take on the responsibility of a child, even if he wanted to."

"Got it."

"Sorry, kiddo. Didn't mean to lecture."

"You're not."

Actually, he was lecturing her. A little. But she didn't want to fight. Not tonight. She took his advice in the loving spirit it was given.

They spent the remaining ten minutes until the ride was over talking about gift ideas for her dad to get her mom. As usual, he'd procrastinated until practically the last minute.

"No appliances," Maia warned when he suggested a new blender. "And no slippers. Give her a coupon book instead."

"A coupon book?"

"Make twelve coupons that she can redeem, one for every month of the year. You can include things like a romantic dinner at her favorite restaurant. A foot massage. A shopping trip to the candle store that you hate and she loves. A long afternoon or evening walk. A week when you cook dinner every night and clean the kitchen."

"Have you forgotten how bad my cooking tastes?"

"You can manage for a week, Dad. Order pizza. Pick up a deli chicken and sides at the grocery store."

"I suppose I could," he grumbled and then leaned over to kiss her cheek. "That's a swell idea, sweetie. Thanks."

"I can probably help you with the coupon book."

"I'm counting on it."

They reached the end of the ride. Her dad reined the ponies to a stop at the makeshift depot near the Christmas tree. Even after several trips round the arena, "the boys" weren't the least bit winded. Maia admired their stamina. If bigger, they'd do well in a trail-ride competition.

Two-dozen-plus people waited for their turn in the cart. Brent, Maia observed, wasn't among them. He hadn't left the rodeo grounds, though. He was supposed to help her dad return the ponies to their owner later tonight.

TJ's piercing squawks had her climbing out of the seat. "Hang on a second. Mommy's coming." To her dad, she said, "Thanks. For everything."

"Love you, puddin' pie."

Darla appeared. She and Maia unloaded their children, who wanted to pet the ponies, please, please, please. Maia commended herself for not asking Darla if she'd noticed where Brent had gone off to.

"Hurry," Darla said, shooing the kids away from the ponies. "Time to explore the maze and to see Santa."

Her girls let out a loud cheer. TJ joined in, although he didn't understand what all the excitement was about.

Maia's mom and Garret came over as Maia's dad set off with the next group of passengers for another loop of the arena. When Maia attempted to put TJ in his stroller, he squealed and squirmed and kicked in protest. Eventually, she gave up and let him walk.

"Okay, fine. Have it your way." She feared she'd regret her decision.

They wandered past the concession stand where dancers two-stepped to lively holiday classics. Kids and adults alike carried prizes won at the carnival games. Candy canes were clutched in fists. Heads were adorned with reindeer antlers and elf ears. Bags containing fudge and treats purchased from the food vendors dangled from fingers.

"Enjoy yourself," a teenage girl in a Santa cap and with jingle bells on her boots said as she gestured them into the maze. "Don't get lost."

Darla's girls scurried ahead until she called them back. Maia clasped TJ's hand firmly in hers. If not, he'd have run after his cousins.

"Which way next?" Maia's mom called out, letting her granddaughters choose their path.

Despite the teenager's warning, the maze wasn't very complicated. Maia and the rest of them went along even when the girls chose incorrectly. Twice, TJ stopped and tried to climb one of the mechanical reindeer.

"You have plans Christmas Eve?" Darla asked Maia during a break when the kids were debating whether to take the left or the right fork.

"Hitting the hay by nine. TJ will be up at the crack of dawn, and I figure on arriving early at the folks' to give Mom a hand with breakfast."

Every Christmas, the MacKenzies celebrated by opening gifts together and then having a huge breakfast. That allowed

Maia's dad to spend the rest of the day at the shelter helping with the Christmas dinner. Also for Darla and Garret to take the girls to his parents' house for more celebrating.

Her mom usually went to the shelter to assist with cleanup. Maybe Maia and TJ would tag along. And, no, Brent had nothing to do with her decision.

"If I asked Mom to babysit," Darla said, "would you be interested in working an afternoon wedding for me? I have a special request. Just came in while you were on the pony-cart ride, actually."

Maia pursed her mouth with displeasure. "I wasn't planning on working."

"I know. And, believe me, I wouldn't ask if it weren't an emergency."

"Christmas Eve is six days away. You can't find someone else in that time?"

"Maybe. But that's not the problem. It's the client. Well, the bride is the client."

Maia frowned in puzzlement. "I don't understand."

"She needs a date for her brother. Her younger, nerdy brother who's painfully shy and can't get a date on his own. The bride specifically requested someone who'd be sweet and patient with him. I have no one on staff better suited for that than you."

"Flattery will get you nowhere," Maia scoffed.

"I'm serious. And in a bind."

"How old is he?"

"Twenty-one. A junior in college. Premed. Very intelligent, I'm told."

"Yeesh. I'm too old for him."

"Seven years older. That's nothing these days. Besides, you can pass for twenty-four."

"Again, quit with the flattery. It's not working."

"Please, Maia," Darla pleaded. "The wedding's at Wishing Well Springs. Cash and his sister are very good to me. They've referred dozens of clients. I owe them, and this is a big wedding. A real moneymaker for them. Also, Cash is getting married the next day. This would be like a wedding gift to him and his fiancée."

"Your wedding gift to them, not mine."

"They're good to you, too. You've attended lots of weddings at Wishing Well Springs."

Maia felt herself weakening and tried to remain strong. "I hate leaving TJ. It's Christmas Eve."

"I'll pay extra. Holiday compensation."

"Why does the guy need a date? Would anyone at the wedding really care?"

"It's kind of a sad story. The bride said he was bullied in high school. She claims the experience shaped him and damaged his confidence. She thinks if he attends the wedding with an attractive date, people will notice and that will boost his confidence."

"I see some problems with this plan," Maia argued. "First, it's shallow. People judging him based on the attractiveness of his date? That's terrible. And demeaning to both him and me. Second, I'm sure he needs a lot more than one date to repair years' worth of emotional trauma."

"I agree. But the bride dotes on him and is convinced she's helping. Who am I to argue?" Darla turned puppy-dog eyes on Maia. "She works for the *Payson Tribune*. Your Perfect Plus One could be featured. Imagine what that'll do for business."

"She's bribing you. That's worse."

"No, no. I'm just hoping for a mention in the paper."

"That's almost as bad."

"Maia. I'm in a bind," Darla repeated.

"How does the bride's brother feel about her hiring a wedding date for him? Talk about a blow to one's confidence. She's doing him more damage than good, if you ask me."

"He's going along with it."

Maia studied TJ, who was pestering his grandmother to lift him up onto the mechanical reindeer. He was young. Christmas

Eve was just another night to him. Maia was the one attaching significance to it. The extra money would come in handy, too. After this, she could pay off the custom competition saddle. No more scrimping and saving.

"All right," she relented. "I just hope I don't regret this."

Darla smothered her in a tight hug. "Thank you, thank you."

Santa came into view at the maze's exit. The red-faced man hired to play the part wore the customary red suit, complete with matching cap and long white beard. Four-foot Christmas trees flanked each side of the throne, their lights twinkling in sync to tinny-sounding recorded music. Eager kids and their parents waited on a red carpet leading up to the throne. A man took pictures with a fancy camera while a woman collected money.

Maia was reminded of the wedding where Brent had kissed her cheek beneath the mistletoe, and her heart executed a series of hops and skips. What if he did stay in Payson? They might indeed have a potential future. She wouldn't mind if he traveled for work. She'd be supportive.

And then, suddenly, he was there. He and Channing approached from the other side of the arena, the two of them talking quietly. About the judging-certification sponsorship?

At that same moment, TJ spied Brent and took off stomping through the soft dirt of the arena.

"TJ! Come back." Maia went after him. Sometimes, she swore she spent half her life running after her son.

She wasn't fast enough, and he reached Brent well ahead of her. A string of gibberish followed as TJ hugged Brent's knee.

"What's up, pal? Here to see Santa?" Brent bent down and lifted TJ into his arms without a trace of the awkwardness from the night of the Christmas tree lighting at Bear Creek Ranch.

Maia came to a standstill and stared as TJ put his face nose to nose with Brent's and said, "Be doo doo."

"Be doo doo to you, too. Whatever that means."

TJ hugged Brent around the neck.

Maia's heart dissolved into a puddle. This was the kind of man she'd hope to find. One who delighted in seeing TJ, not considered him an irritating and unwanted responsibility.

She closed the distance between her and Brent. Channing seemed to disappear, for he was suddenly nowhere around.

"Let me take him," she said to Brent.

TJ was having none of it and gripped Brent tighter.

Brent smiled. "He's no trouble."

Why hadn't some woman nabbed this guy already? Had he been too focused on his career and then too down in the dumps after losing it?

She glanced over her shoulder at the line of people waiting to see Santa. Darla watched Maia and Brent intently from her place near the back. She wasn't the only one. Maia's mom watched her and Brent, too, her delighted expression in stark contrast to Darla's annoyance.

"I should…go." Maia hitched a thumb at the line.

"Yeah." Brent hefted a complaining TJ from his arms to Maia's. "We don't want to upset the boss."

Ah. He'd also spotted Darla.

"She can't get too mad at me. I just agreed to do her a big favor and work a wedding Christmas Eve at Wishing Well Springs."

Brent's brow furrowed. "You did? She asked me last week if I'd work the same wedding."

He and Maia stared at each other. Then, in unison, they turned to stare at Darla.

What had happened to her sister's insistence on Maia and Brent keeping their distance? What about their own similar commitment?

"We can do this," Brent said.

"Yeah. We can," Maia agreed.

One wedding. A large, crowded wedding. Surely they could manage to avoid each other for a few hours.

* * *

Brent stared at himself in the bunkhouse bathroom mirror and adjusted his bolo tie. Freshly shaved and showered, in his recently dry-cleaned Western suit, he supposed he'd meet his wedding date's expectations.

Since the night of the Cowboy Christmas Jamboree, he and Maia had avoided discussing the Christmas Eve wedding they were both attending. An easy feat as they hadn't seen much of each other. From what Ansel had told Brent, she'd been busy. As a result, Brent had led almost every trail ride.

His hard work appeared to be paying off. Ansel had mentioned Brent was doing well and fitting in. Several clients had left positive feedback about Brent on the Bear Creek Ranch web page.

Did fitting in refer to Mountainside Stables, Bear Creek Ranch or the community in general? Whichever, Brent had taken the praise to heart. As a result, he'd had a good week. The black cloud continued to follow him wherever he went, but it lagged well behind.

This past Sunday, he'd attended a holiday open house at Channing's parents' home. Brent had initially gone out of a sense of duty—a sense of duty he'd forgotten all about soon after arriving with a box of candy for his hosts. Channing's parents were warm and friendly and made everyone feel like a long-lost relative. Brent knew several other people there, either from the rodeo world or from having met them at the bull-riding practice the other night. For once, he hadn't felt like a stranger.

One plus of attending, he'd gotten to know Channing's dad, Burle Pearce, on a more personal level. Burle had mentioned the judging certification sponsorship when he and Brent had a moment alone and assured Brent that Rim Country would gain as much from the arrangement as Brent. His argument was convincing, and Brent was leaning toward accepting.

Javier and Rowdy had been doing their part adding to Brent's sense of inclusion. They'd dragged him on their outings whenever Brent was free and insisted he eat breakfast with them every morning at the kitchen. Brent was certainly less lonely than he had been the previous two Christmases—less lonely and more like his old self.

He'd even begun interacting with the members of his online support group. Not a lot. A response here and there to someone's post. He'd even asked a question about medication and which were the best. If he did wind up going to a doctor, he wanted to be prepared.

Could he be on the road to recovery or was this a temporary reprieve? Brent was a realist and knew his emotional state remained tenuous at best. He was, and might always be, an elephant walking a tightrope. One misstep, one distraction, one shift in balance, and he'd fall crashing to the ground. But if he concentrated, kept his eye trained on the platform at the end of the tightrope, he just might make it all the way across.

Where did he go from here? Remain at Mountainside Stables in a job with little advancement potential but was steady employment and a place he felt safe? Or did he pursue a judging certification? A move not without risks, but one that could lead to a whole new career.

He'd failed at his last one. Miserably. He could fail again. What if Brent wasn't good enough? Talented enough? Dedicated enough? Lucky enough? He could hear his dad's voice berating him.

You don't have what it takes. No son of mine is a quitter.

Brent squared his shoulders and continued to study his reflection in the mirror. With sudden clarity, he realized he wanted to stay in Payson regardless of which path he chose. He'd been afraid to admit as much for fear of having his hopes dashed again. If that happened, his depression would return worse than before.

Or not. The last month had changed him, given him courage and motivation to, as the saying went, get back in the saddle. No reason he couldn't continue working at Mountainside

Stables and judging practices at Rim Country while obtaining his certification. And, if he chose, go on the periodic gig for Your Perfect Plus One.

It was a lot. He'd be busy. But Brent wasn't afraid of hard work. In a few months, he'd be able to pay down a good chunk of his debts and have enough money to purchase his mom's plane ticket to Arizona.

His life could, might, *would* come together. He just needed to stay on the tightrope and not lose his balance. That included maintaining the status quo with Maia. For now. He wanted more, dreamed of more, but he'd have to wait. And if she found someone else in the meantime, then they clearly weren't meant to be.

He quickly shoved that last very unpleasant thought aside before it affected his mood. Stay in the moment, he told himself, repeating something he heard a lot in his online group.

Running a comb through his hair one last time, he collected his shaving bag and headed out of the bathroom to the bunkhouse's main room.

Whistles and catcalls greeted him from his four bunk mates.

"Aren't you pretty," Javier joked.

Brent glared at him, hiding his amusement. "Don't you have someplace to be?"

The dining hall had closed early today so that the employees could have Christmas Eve off. Guests at the ranch were either driving to town or eating in their cabins. The staff would return early tomorrow morning for breakfast and lunch services, then be released after cleanup to spend the rest of Christmas with family and friends.

Mountainside Stables was closed and wouldn't reopen until the twenty-sixth, giving Brent the entire day off and allowing him to attend Cash's wedding at Wishing Well Springs. He hadn't accepted the invitation until the open house at Channing's parents' where Cash and his lovely fiancée had refused to take no for an answer. Yet another feeling of inclusion.

"I'm heading to Syndee's in an hour," Javier said. "Her best friend from high school is in town for Christmas."

"Ah! Getting the best friend's approval." Brent slipped his heavy coat on over his suit jacket and plunked his cowboy hat onto his head.

Javier groaned. "I swear, the two of them are like this." He crossed his first and second fingers. "If I don't pass muster, Syndee will kick me to the curb."

"If that happens," Jimmy Roy, the bunkhouse's oldest resident said, "give her my number, will you?"

"No way, amigo. She's too good for you."

They all laughed at that.

"Don't wait up for me, guys." Brent swung open the bunkhouse door and stepped out onto the stoop.

A blast of cold air hit him square in the face. Tilting his head back, he stared up at the late-afternoon sky, a dense blanket of gunmetal gray. Tiny snowflakes drifted downward to land on his face where they melted on contact. If the light dusting gained momentum and morphed into a snowstorm, it was possible they'd wake up tomorrow to a white Christmas.

He met his date at their prearranged place outside a bookstore in a small strip mall. They shook hands and introduced themselves. Olive was an attractive fortysomething HR director at the *Payson Gazette*.

"I work with the bride," she told Brent. "I'm her supervisor."

He smiled. "I read that in your bio."

She blushed. "Yes. I forgot. This is all new to me."

"You'll do fine." He gestured toward her car, marveling that he was the experienced one attempting to make a client comfortable. "Shall we?" They'd previously agreed she'd drive to Wishing Well Springs.

"I suppose you think it's silly, me requesting a younger man for a wedding date," Olive said once they were on the road.

"Not in the least." He'd learned during his employment at

Your Perfect Plus One that clients had all sorts of reasons for their date choices.

He took her elbow on the walk from the parking area to the wedding barn. Strings of white lights climbed tree trunks to weave among the branches above, glittering like stars in the light snowfall. While creating a beautiful picture, there would be no outdoor receiving line or dining tonight. Even giant space heaters would be useless against the frigid air.

Inside the barn, they entered a Christmas wedding wonderland. A majestic tree stood to their left. Beside it sat a table decorated with curling ribbons and holding the guest book. Olive stopped to sign their names. More red ribbons adorned the pews and poinsettia plants had been placed throughout the room. Piped-in holiday music floated on the air along with a hint of pine.

Brent escorted Olive up the aisle. She chose a pew midway on the bride's side, and they excused themselves as they squeezed past an elderly couple on their way to the vacant seats in the middle.

"Is this all right?" Olive asked.

"Fine."

Brent immediately glanced about for Maia and saw no sign of her. Was she not coming? Then he remembered her date was the bride's younger brother. The family often entered last, shortly before the bride made her appearance. Maia was likely with the bride's brother and due any moment.

A set of parents and their young daughter entered Brent and Olive's pew from the far side, the adults smiling as they sat.

"We're friends of Shelby's," the woman said, referring to the bride.

"Olive and Brad." Olive pointed to herself and Brent.

"Nice to meet you," Brent said, responding to his fake name.

As Olive shared a story about working with the bride, Brent leafed through the paper program. Like before, the reception was being held at the Joshua Tree Inn next door. The same place as that first wedding where Brent had met Maia. The similarities between then and tonight were adding up.

Except back then he'd seen her merely as an attractive wedding guest. Now she was someone he knew, liked, admired and respected. Someone he could care for a lot if things were different.

Olive barely paused to breathe as she talked about her teenage son—she worried he spent too much time playing video games—and her sister, who'd apparently married a perfect ten. Brent sensed a slight trace of jealousy between Olive and her sister. Was that the reason she'd wanted to appear in the wedding photos with a younger man?

Inside his suit jacket pocket, his phone buzzed once, alerting him of a text message. He checked it only when Olive said, "Go on—I don't mind."

The message was from his mom, wishing him a merry Christmas and sending her love. He fired off a quick reply, returning the sentiment and saying he'd call tomorrow.

Should he text his dad, too? Brent returned his phone to his suit pocket. His dad would probably say something upsetting, and Brent was feeling too good to take any chances.

Several elegantly dressed individuals appeared and walked down the aisle, before sitting in the front pews on the groom's side.

"Looks like the family's arriving," Olive whispered in Brent's ear.

More people strolled past, their expressions ranging from serious to beaming. Brent forced himself to appear mildly interested and not waiting in eager anticipation for Maia.

"Here comes the bride's brother," Olive said. "Wow, his date is really pretty."

Brent couldn't help himself and turned to stare. Maia wore the same outfit she had to the wedding where they'd first met. Another similarity.

One big difference today was his heart raced. No, that was

incorrect. His heart soared at the sight of her—a vison in shimmering gold, her silky brown hair tumbling past her shoulders to gather in soft, touchable waves.

She glided up the aisle alongside her date as if in slow motion. When she passed Brent, their gazes locked and lingered until continuing to do so was impossible.

"Do you know her?" Olive asked.

"No." Brent shook his head.

The single word was all he could manage, his throat having gone completely dry upon seeing Maia.

He hadn't fallen for a woman in a very long time. But not so long that he'd forgotten the sensation. Rather than deny or resist, as he should, he closed his eyes and embraced the heady rush.

CHAPTER THIRTEEN

"DO YOU KNOW HIM?" Maia's date, Simon, asked once they were seated in the front pew on the bride's side.

"Um…" Should she lie? Hard to explain her prolonged staring session with Brent other than with the truth. "Yes. We've met before. At work. My day job. I wasn't sure at first it was him."

A version of the truth. Thankfully, Simon seemed satisfied and didn't question her further.

He really was a nice young man. Insecure and shy—Darla hadn't exaggerated. Every time he spoke to Maia, he swallowed first as if gathering his courage, his Adam's apple bobbing.

"Does that happen a lot?" He swallowed. "Running into people you know?"

"Not usually," Maia said. "I mostly attend weddings for out-of-town couples."

"We're not from out of town."

She didn't admit this date had been a bit of an emergency and instead offered a vague response. "It all depends."

Maia spoke low so as not to be overheard. As it turned out, the people in their immediate vicinity weren't paying attention. They fidgeted in anticipation and chatted excitedly, waiting on the start of the wedding.

"Cool" was all Simon said, then he tugged at his tie.

Maia suspected he rarely wore a suit and felt uncomfortable. The complete opposite of Brent, who carried off formal wear with the same ease he did jeans, boots and a denim jacket.

He may have suffered from depression, but that hadn't affected other aspects of his personality. The confidence he'd gained from years of competing professionally had stayed with him on some level and was evident in how well he handled himself in new situations. Maia took that as a sign he possessed the strength and determination to conquer his problem, even if he didn't realize it himself. Yet.

Her and Simon's pew filled up with his family—his grandmother and grandfather, a cousin and the cousin's husband.

The parents came next. The groom's mother wore a flattering dress of deep Christmas green adorned with a red rose corsage. An usher escorted the bride's mother. Her dress was of a similar color but trimmed with gold. Once the parents were seated, the groom, his best man and two groomsmen emerged from behind a corner to stand at the altar.

The groom smiled nervously, as most grooms do, and exchanged words with the minister. His best man—a brother, given their strong resemblance—put an arm around his shoulders.

All at once, the piped-in music faded to silence, and the air filled with excited tension. A gray-haired guitarist sitting on a stool to the left of the altar began playing a short melody of traditional Christmas songs with flourishing strokes of his fingers, ending with "Here Comes the Bride."

Everyone stood, and then the bride materialized at the end of the aisle, a Christmas angel in a snow-white wedding dress adorned with matching fake-fur collar. A sheer veil like liquid ice hung from a crown of lilies on her head to well past her waist.

Gasps of delight filled the wedding barn, and Maia pressed a hand to her mouth, struck by the stunning vision strolling elegantly down the aisle on the arm of a middle-aged man. Maia and Luke had talked about a spring wedding. In hindsight, *she'd* talked about weddings. Luke had simply gone along. She should have realized something was amiss with them, but she'd believed herself in love and been blinded by her desire to marry and start a family. In Luke's defense—no, in her defense—he'd treated her well and been attentive. Until he didn't and wasn't.

She tamped down the twinge of sadness that surfaced at the memory of her former fiancé. It quickly vanished. Maia had learned the hard way not to dwell on the past.

Was this how Brent felt when he struggled with his moods? Only, he couldn't shake off his negative emotions as easily as Maia did hers. Even during her most difficult periods, she'd been able to keep moving forward.

She'd had TJ to focus on and worry about and care for. He'd been—he was—her reason for overcoming her struggles. Brent didn't have that same motivation, none that he'd told her about. There was no special woman in his life, he was estranged from his dad and half siblings and he lived halfway across the country from his mom. According to him, he'd burned bridges these past two years with all his friends save Channing. And while employed, he had no solid plans further ahead than tomorrow.

Despite his difficulties, he showed up every day for work—two jobs and soon to be three—plus helped her with Snapple's training. That spoke highly of him and his drive to get better.

Was it any wonder she admired him? More than admired him, though she wasn't ready to put a name to the emotions growing inside her.

"Your sister is beautiful," she whispered to Simon. The bride had reached the altar and smiled radiantly at her soon-to-be husband.

"Yeah. I guess." After a moment, he said, "Mom wanted me in the wedding."

"I'm not surprised."

From Maia's experience, a lot of grooms asked their future brother-in-law to be a groomsman or an usher. Then again, this groom could have several brothers and best friends. Or his parents had applied pressure.

"I didn't want to," Simon mumbled.

His shyness. Of course. That made sense.

Maia was quiet after that, watching the beautiful wedding unfold. She couldn't help imagining herself in the bride's place, gazing into the eyes of the man she loved and reciting her vows.

A soft, warm feeling filled her chest. Despite all she'd been through, the disappointment and betrayal that might have soured her on love forever, she still believed in happy endings and finding her soul mate.

The touching ceremony came to a close with the newlyweds sharing a happy kiss. Cheers and applause rose from the guests. Once the couple and the wedding party had walked back down the aisle, the first pews began to empty. The parents went first, followed by the rest of the family. Maia and Simon were among the last.

Near the entrance, he was swept up by his mother who, giving Maia a friendly but brief hello, guided him over to the wedding party. Maia had expected this—the newlyweds and their families were forming the receiving line. She wouldn't be part of that, naturally, having just met Simon.

Instead, she moved away to a secluded place along the wall where she could watch. After checking her phone, for no reason other than she was standing there doing nothing, she dropped it back into her clutch and looked up—to catch Brent's gaze across the large entryway. She went still, watching until he and his date entered the receiving line.

Maia shouldn't have cared; she *didn't* care, she told herself, but studied his date, nonetheless. The very attractive woman was probably fifteen years older than Brent. Funny, they were both on dates with people either much younger or older than them. Then again, Maia had noticed all manner of age combinations at the many weddings she'd attended.

He gestured for his date to precede him through the line. At the end, they blended in with the other guests, and Maia lost track of Brent.

Just as well, she assured herself. They'd promised Darla to be on their best behavior.

"Aren't you Simon's date?" a woman beside her queried.

"Yes." Maia produced a smile.

"I'm his neighbor. My husband and I have lived next door to his parents since Simon was just a tiny tyke."

"Oh. That's great." They shook hands. "A pleasure."

"Don't take this wrong, but you're a little older than the women he usually dates. Not that he dates a lot from what I hear, or ever has."

"Age is merely a number." Maia amplified her smile. She wasn't "going there" with this woman. "Personality matters more, and Simon is a sweet guy."

"Yes. He is." The woman appeared disappointed and cut her conversation with Maia short. "My husband is waiting for me. See you at the reception."

"Looking forward to it."

The woman had no sooner disappeared than Maia felt a presence behind her, one her senses instantly recognized. Brent.

She turned to find him not a foot from her. "You shouldn't be here," she said in a murmur.

"My date forgot her mittens." He held them up.

"Ah."

"You handled that well."

"The neighbor? Hmm." Maia rolled her eyes. "She was fishing for some juicy gossip. I didn't bite."

Brent nodded at the receiving line. "Looks like the last of the guests have gone through. You're back on the clock."

"This hasn't been my worst date by any means. I was telling the truth when I said he's a sweet guy."

"I'd better get these mittens to my date."

"You'd better."

Brent hesitated. For a moment, Maia thought he might reach for her cheek. But he didn't and melted away.

She sighed. They shouldn't have spoken; their dates might have noticed. And if they were caught, no good could come of it.

Eventually, Simon meandered over, his gait lanky and loose-jointed. He was joined by his sister Shelby.

"I just wanted to meet you," she gushed and took both of Maia's hands in hers. "Darla spoke so highly of you."

"Congratulations on your wedding," Maia said. "Your dress is stunning, and the ceremony was lovely."

"Thank you."

"Simon." The bride turned to her brother. "Go ask Dad to bring the car around, would you?"

"Okay," he grumbled and shuffled off.

Maia pegged Shelby to be about ten years older than Simon. She was probably used to bossing him around, and he was used to doing her bidding.

Once Simon was out of earshot, Shelby leaned in close to Maia and said, "I appreciate you being so nice to him."

"I've enjoyed getting to know him."

Shelby glanced over at Simon talking with their dad. When she faced Maia again, her expression had become serious. "He has a tiny crush on you."

"Really? I had no idea. We only just met."

"Yes, but I can tell. Simon's easy to read. So, please be careful. He's very sensitive."

"I will. You have nothing to worry about." Seeing Simon return, she flashed him a smile. "Hi, there."

"Thanks." The bride winked at her, mussed her brother's hair, which elicited a groan, and then danced away in a swirl of white satin.

"Ready?" Maia took hold of his arm.

Simon's eyes went wide, and he grinned like he'd won first prize at the science fair.

Mission accomplished, thought Maia. She'd be careful not to encourage Simon, but she was also glad she could help boost his confidence.

At the reception, Maia and Simon sat with both sets of his grandparents, his uncle and great-aunt. Normally, the date of the bride's brother would be someone well-known to the family, or at least not a complete stranger. As a result, Maia found herself the subject of much curiosity and was put on the spot more than once. Forced to improvise, she received little assistance from Simon.

"How do you feel about dating a younger man? What do your parents think of it?"

"You know Simon's premed at college. He won't be ready to have children for years."

"You say you met at a sci-fi convention? Were you wearing one of those costumes?"

Maia answered those questions she could and dodged the rest. She ignored the many raised eyebrows and whispers behind the shield of hands. No one had ill intentions, rather they cared about Simon. They probably worried she'd break his heart and were only looking out for him.

Maia wished she could offer reassurances. She'd be out of his life in a matter of hours and soon after that a distant memory. People would point at the few candid wedding pictures in which she appeared and ponder, "Who was that woman with Simon? Did they ever go out again?" Eventually, she'd become a random guest with no identity.

Following a delicious dinner, cake was served and toasts made. Simon reluctantly participated in a hilarious Christmas-themed skit—something he'd agreed to only to appease his sister and their parents.

As the guests laughed and played along, Maia allowed her gaze to roam the room. She wasn't searching for Brent. No.

Absolutely not. And if you believed that, she had some ocean front property in Arizona for sale.

There he was! At a table near the far wall, chatting amiably with his date while they watched the skit. He abruptly stopped when he spotted Maia staring. Her face went hot, and she glanced away. Fortunately for her, the skit ended at that moment. None of the applauding and laughing guests paid her the slightest attention. Or so she'd thought.

"Are you all right, my dear?" Simon's great-aunt asked. "You look a little flushed."

"I'm fine." Hardly.

"A bit too much champagne?"

"Maybe." She'd had only one glass.

"Wasn't the wedding lovely? Christmas Eve. Who'd have guessed?"

"It was very lovely. And the best way I can think of to spend Christmas Eve."

A large group of merrymakers pulled Simon aside, so Maia continued engaging his delightful great-aunt in conversation.

"I had a June wedding." The elderly woman sighed wistfully. "We were married outdoors in my parents' garden. The roses were in full bloom. My mother made my bouquet."

"Sounds wonderful."

"We had a four-piece band and danced the night away." She sighed again. "I so miss dancing. My Joseph died three years ago. That man could trip the light fantastic."

"Tell me about him."

Maia listened, enjoying every moment of Simon's great-aunt's stories, until he returned and quenched his thirst—or perhaps hid his embarrassment—with a long drink of water.

While his great-aunt was chatting with another guest at the table, he leaned in and whispered to Maia, "Aunt Edna is a talker. I hope you don't mind."

"Are you kidding? She's a treasure." Maia suddenly missed her late grandmother.

"Yeah. She's cool in her way."

Maia smiled at him. He may be young and unworldly, but he clearly adored his great-aunt. That made him a-okay in her book.

"You're an all right guy, Simon."

He swallowed and blushed and looked away. When, after a moment, he returned his gaze to her, his expression was filled with childlike earnestness. "I don't suppose…"

"What?"

"That, um…" He grinned sheepishly. "That we could go out sometime? For real."

"Oh, Simon." She reached over and patted his hand. Thank goodness his sister had warned Maia of Simon's tiny crush. Otherwise, she'd have been flummoxed and ill prepared. "Under any other circumstances, I'd say yes. But it's against company policy."

Actually, she'd stretched the truth. Darla's employment contracts contained a clause prohibiting employees seeing clients, but only for the first ninety days post wedding date. This was Maia's way of letting Simon down gently.

His features crumpled. "Okay. I get it."

"You're going to meet an amazing girl one of these days," she said. "Trust me. She'll see the real you and fall head over heels."

He chuckled mirthlessly. "Right."

Maia patted his hand again. "You'll see."

At that moment, the DJ announced the father/bride dance. The sentimental pop song he played was a special request by the bride's father. Midway through the song, the bride's new husband cut in to claim her. Applause followed. Maia, along with several others nearby, wiped away a tear.

"Would you like to dance?" Simon asked Maia three songs later.

"I'd love to."

She rose from her seat. Simon's great-aunt Edna had turned her chair around in order to watch the dancers and tapped her toe in time to the music. Maybe he'd ask her to dance next when he and Maia returned. She hoped so.

On the dance floor, she slipped into Simon's arms. He wasn't the most skilled dancer, but he managed not to stomp on her feet. A far cry from when she and Brent had danced, and he'd guided her across the floor with a confidence that almost had her swooning.

Perhaps Simon would loosen up when the DJ played more lively party numbers.

"Excuse me," he said when he inadvertently propelled Maia into another dancer.

Maia spun. When Brent's face appeared inches from hers, she gasped.

"My fault," he said and smiled at her.

She took a wrong step, and her knee buckled. It was Brent who caught her by the arm, not Simon.

"You okay?"

"Y-yes. Thanks." Aware that people on the dance floor were watching, Maia returned to Simon's arms and, assuming the lead, danced them away from Brent and his date to the opposite side of the dance floor.

"That's the guy you know," Simon said. "Isn't it?"

"Yes." She tilted her head to the side. "Sorry about that. The dance floor's crowded."

"My mom saw you talking to him earlier."

She had? Darn it. Maia and Brent should have been more careful. "Um, yes. We said hello."

When the song ended, Simon escorted Maia to their table. She was more than a little relieved when he didn't suggest a second dance. The close encounter with Brent had left her unsteady.

Ridiculous. Absurd. She wasn't a teenager pining over a heartthrob.

Yeah, tell that to the butterflies playing soccer in her stomach.

The bride appeared at their table. "Come on, Simon. The

photographer wants some pictures of the family in the court-yard outside with all the Christmas lights. You don't mind, do you?" she asked Maia.

"Absolutely not. Go. Have fun."

Simon groaned but went along with his sister and their grand-parents. Maia expected the bride to ask Great-Aunt Edna as well, but she didn't. Maia suffered a pang of sympathy when the elderly woman stared after them, intense longing on her face. The next moment, she resumed watching the dancers, no doubt remembering her late husband.

A few minutes passed, and Maia spotted Brent striding pur-posely toward her. She gripped the edge of the table. What in heaven's name was he doing?

He stopped at the table, a gentle smile on his face that had her wishing they were alone and not in the middle of a crowded room.

"Would you care to dance?" He held out his hand.

Not to her. Rather, to Great-Aunt Edna. Maia blinked in sur-prise, then smiled when she realized that had been his inten-tion the entire time.

"Me?" the elderly woman twittered.

"I saw you tapping your toe and thought *that lady needs a partner.*"

"Surely, a handsome fellow like yourself is here with some-one. Your wife?"

"A date. But she doesn't mind. She said she wanted to sit this one out."

"Then I accept." Giggling, Simon's great-aunt took Brent's hand, and he helped her to her feet. "My name's Edna, by the way."

"Brad."

They started toward the dance floor, but not before Brent, a.k.a. Brad, sent Maia a wink.

She stared after them, her heart melting into a warm puddle. Out of everyone here, Brent had noticed Great-Aunt Edna longingly watching the dancers and tapping her toe. Out of everyone here, only he'd asked her to dance. Such a small gesture that required little effort. And, yet it meant a great deal.

He was kind and compassionate. He acted in ways that truly counted. He cared. He also owned his mistakes. Granted, he'd gotten himself in serious debt, but he was diligently eliminating that debt by working three jobs. He wasn't shirking his responsibilities or looking for a free ride.

He acknowledged he had a problem, and, she believed, he was on the verge of seeking professional help. He'd joined that online group, had finally sought information about the men's group at the shelter and reached out to residents like Pete—the last two according to her dad. Brent had also opened up to her and Channing, which was a big step for someone as private as Brent.

If Maia let herself, she'd fall head over heels for him.

Who was she kidding? She'd already fallen a little.

No, he wasn't perfect. Neither was she. Minor flaws aside, Brent had all the important qualities Maia wanted in the man she married. The qualities she'd once thought her former fiancé had until she'd learned different. Luke wouldn't have asked an elderly woman to dance, not unless Maia had nagged him. He'd cheated on her. Twice.

Don't let Brent get away.

The thought came from nowhere. Wait, not nowhere. It came from the place inside Maia where she hid her deepest secrets.

Tell him how you feel before it's too late.

She should. He'd say he wasn't right for her and not in a good place. Maia didn't care. She had everything that mattered in life. A happy, healthy son, her family, a small but comfortable home, a job she loved and the chance to follow her dreams.

He'd say their employment contracts prohibited them from dating. Maia would dismiss his concerns. She'd have her saddle paid off soon and could quit Your Perfect Plus One. They'd be free to explore what the future held for them.

They just needed to be patient a while longer and stay the course. Easy-peasy.

Tell him, the voice repeated.

Should she? Maia had no doubts Brent harbored similar feelings for her.

Tomorrow. She'd find the right moment to talk with him. Or tonight. After the wedding.

Seeing him and Great-Aunt Edna approaching, she broke into a wide, happy grin that must have conveyed the entire contents of her heart because Brent responded with a broad, happy grin of his own.

Why wait until tomorrow?

He helped Great-Aunt Edna into her seat.

"Thank you so much, young man. You made my evening."

"My pleasure. Merry Christmas, ma'am."

His glance met Maia's, and she saw in his eyes he wanted to ask her to dance. He wouldn't, though. He'd resist.

Not Maia. Unable to hold back the flood of emotions surging inside her, she popped out of her chair and snatched her clutch off the table.

"Brent, do you have a minute? There's something I need to tell you."

He hesitated. Rules were rules.

She was the rebel between the two of them. "It's important."

"Okay."

"Do you two know each other?" Great-Aunt Edna asked.

Maia didn't reply. Neither did she look behind her to confirm that Brent was following or to question her actions. Walking on air, she wove a path through the tables to the dining room exit, confident her and Brent's lives were about to change.

CHAPTER FOURTEEN

BRENT WAS CRAZY. He had no business following Maia out of the wedding reception. They'd agreed to avoid each other tonight, and he'd already broken that vow once by seeking her out earlier at Wishing Well Springs. Then again when he'd asked Edna to dance—something Olive had actually suggested when they'd seen the elderly lady tapping her foot.

But the second Maia's dark brown eyes lit up at the sight of him, his brain had short-circuited. He'd barely noticed returning Edna to her chair. He'd seen only Maia. When she'd said she had something to tell him, he'd followed, his misfiring brain sending go-go-go signals to his legs.

What did that say about the intensity of his feelings for her?

He taken the long way around the room so as not to draw attention to themselves and then met up with her outside in the hall.

She led him past the hostess podium outside the dining room entrance, and around a corner. Once hidden from view, she pivoted to face him, their faces close, their lips a millimeter away from kissing. Brent tried not to think about that.

"What's up?" he asked.

"I, um…" She faltered, a blush coloring her cheeks. "I thought I knew what I was going to say."

"Are you okay?" Perhaps he'd misunderstood. "Is it your date? Did he say or do something inappropriate?"

"What? No. He's sweet. This has nothing to do with him." She drew in a long breath. "You made Edna's night. Probably her entire week."

"This is about her?" Now Brent was confused.

"You're a nice person, Brent. You saw she wanted to dance and asked her when no one else did."

"Actually, Olive suggested it. But I could relate to Edna. I know what it's like to sit on the outside looking in. I've been doing a lot of that the past two years."

"Not so much lately." Maia placed a hand on his arm.

"No, not so much."

"Brent." She paused again. "Seeing you with Edna got me to thinking. I realize the time's not right for us, and the last thing I want to do is pressure you."

"Where is this leading, Maia?"

"You're...you're the kind of man I've been hoping to find. I realized that tonight. And I wanted you to know I'm willing to wait. For however long it takes."

"You are."

He took a moment to let what she'd said sink in. They'd discussed their mutual attraction and that the timing couldn't be worse. He'd told her she deserved someone with their life together, not in shambles.

Yet, she stood here with him, bearing her heart and saying she'd wait no matter how long.

"I'm still broken, Maia."

"You're making progress."

"I may not be that man you've been waiting for when I come out on the other side."

"I don't believe for one second you aren't the same man you were two years ago before you walked away from rodeo or the man you'll be two in two years' time. Plus or minus a couple of tweaks. People don't change that drastically."

He stared into her eyes. She was the kind of woman he'd been hoping to find, too. Regardless, he held back.

"Call it ego," he said, "or pride, but I need to have a good job before we get serious."

"You're working on that."

"I'd rather be further along in the process and not buried in credit card bills."

"Like I said, I'm willing to wait. I just needed to tell you before I lost my nerve."

His chest filled with a range of emotions he hadn't experienced in a long, long time. Joy. Gratitude. Optimism. Hope. Anticipation for the future.

"You have no idea what it means for me to hear you say that."

"You're wrong." She stood on tiptoes. "I do have an idea."

"I don't deserve you."

"You're wrong about that, too."

And then, her lips were on his, pliant and tender and giving. Brent abandoned resisting and wrapped his arms around her. This was the magic he'd been chasing his entire life. Not a world-championship title.

For the first time since quitting rodeo, Brent wasn't just wanting to change, he was ready. He had a reason to fight. A future to run toward rather than shy away from. Because of Maia.

The kiss came to an end, but they didn't break apart.

"I'm going to join a men's group at the shelter," he said, his lips finding and nuzzling her ear.

"You are?"

"I suddenly have good reason."

"Me?" Her eyes twinkled.

"You. And Rim Country Rodeo Arena."

"You accepted the judging sponsorship!"

"I planned on telling Channing Monday." He traced the curve of her cheek with his fingertips. "I may not wait now."

"Oh, Brent. I'm so happy for you."

"Yeah, well, I've got my work cut out for me. Professionally and personally."

"You can do this. I have complete faith in you." She kissed him hard.

Faith. He couldn't recall his father ever speaking the word. His mother, yes, during the early days of his career. Not recently. Only Maia.

"Sweetheart." He brushed his lips across hers. "There's something more I want to tell you."

Should he? Was it too soon? How would she react?

"What?" she breathed, her face aglow with expectation.

"I—"

"Mindy!" A squeaky male voice cut him off.

Mindy?

Maia pulled away from Brent and looked past him, her eyes growing wide with horror and dismay. "Simon. I'm... Oh, God." She gasped.

Simon? Brent turned, momentarily confused at the figure staring at them accusingly. The confusion faded quickly. Clarity dawned with a vengeance, and he froze.

Maia's wedding date had rounded the corner and stood facing them, his expression a combination of shock and anguish. "Mindy," he repeated, this time on a whine.

"Simon, I am so, so sorry. I didn't mean..." She squeezed past Brent. "I can explain. Let's go back to the reception."

"You ditched me," he said in the same whiney voice. "I waited for you and waited for you and when you didn't show I came searching. I thought you'd left."

"Again," Maia pleaded. "I'm sorry." She reached out a hand to him. He glared at it as if she held a snake and retreated a step. "Please, Simon. I didn't ditch you. I..." She bit back a sob.

Brent wanted to kick himself. Or worse. What had they done? How could he have let this happen? Uncertain of what he'd say and consumed by guilt, he started forward. Maia shook her head and mouthed, "Don't."

"You're supposed to be my date," Simon accused, his demeanor visibly changing to anger.

"Hey, pal," Brent said, attempting a congenial tone. No way would he let Maia take the blame for what happened or the brunt of her date's wrath. "This was my fault. Don't be mad at her."

"Who are you?"

"My question exactly." Another voice entered the fray. "And what the heck are you doing hiding behind the corner with my brother's date?"

Just when things couldn't get worse, the bride had joined them, a white whirlpool of indignation. Her keen gaze instantly assessed the scene, and she obviously reached a conclusion not far off the mark for she fired a full arsenal of invisible daggers at Brent and Maia.

Brent placed a palm on the small of Maia's back and propelled her out from behind the corner. Staying where they were made them look like a pair of petty criminals—which maybe they were no better than.

Darla would agree. She'd be furious and with good cause. Why hadn't Brent told Maia no when she asked to speak with him? Then none of this would have happened, and they'd all be in the reception, dancing and celebrating.

There was only one choice. One course of action. Brent had to fix this and fix it now. And, in the process, spare Maia from any repercussions.

"I'm Brent." He stepped forward. "Brent Hayes. I work with Maia at Mountainside Stables. And Your Perfect Plus One," he added.

"Who's Maia?" the bride and her brother asked at the same time.

"Me," Maia said. "I… Mindy is the name I use for…weddings."

The bride clamped a hand to her forehead "This is completely unacceptable. You can bet I'm going to call the owner."

"I understand."

"Don't blame her," Brent said. "I'm the one responsible."

Maia faced him. "No, you aren't. It was me." She swung back to the bride. "I asked him out here to talk."

"You were doing a lot more than talking," Simon accused.

The bride fired a second round of invisible daggers at Brent and Maia. "Guess you aren't just coworkers."

Maia answered before Brent could. "I'll see that Darla issues you a full refund."

"Darn right I'll get a full refund." The bride put an arm around her brother's shoulders. "Poor Simon's mortified."

He stiffened with annoyance, whether from his sister's show of sympathy or at being the center of attention. Brent wasn't sure which and hated himself for the part he'd played.

"I'll speak to Darla," he said. "Make this right."

"Speak to Darla about what?" a voice asked.

Everyone whirled in unison to see the newest member of their gathering: Brent's date, Olive.

Swell. Could this fiasco get any worse?

"Brian?" Confusion clouded her eyes.

"Olive." He cleared his throat. "This is Maia. She's my coworker. And my friend."

"*Girl*friend," the bride answered sharply.

Olive blinked. "I thought she was your brother's date?"

"She is. His hired date. And I'm guessing Brian or Brent is yours."

"He is." Olive went quiet.

Brent couldn't feel more like a heel if he tried. "Olive, I'm sorry."

"*Is* she your girlfriend?"

Brent shared a glance with Maia. They hadn't gotten that far in their conversation. "We're involved."

"They were kissing," Simon said, still miffed.

A man appeared. The groom. "Honey? Is there a problem?"

Brent's spirits sank. Where was a hole in the floor when you needed one?

"Maybe we could all return to the dining room," Maia suggested, "and let you get back to your reception."

"You're kidding, of course." The bride glared at her. "I think what should happen is you and he leave. Now would be good."

"Wait a minute," Olive objected. She turned to the bride. "I know you're upset."

"Upset? I'm going to have them fired. And get my money back."

Olive reached up and straightened the bride's tiara like she was dressing a small child. "You just got married." She sent the groom an appreciative glance. "To an incredible guy, I might add, whom you're madly in love with." The smile turned sad. "Some of us aren't that lucky. We, and I'm talking about me, not just Simon, hire dates because we can't stand the idea of people thinking we're losers."

"No one thinks you're a loser, Olive."

"Brian is a great guy."

"His name is Brent."

"Whatever his name, he made me feel special. On Christmas Eve, a night I expected to be alone and miserable because that's how I spent last Christmas Eve. And I'm sure, until a few minutes ago, Simon felt special, too."

The young man stared at the floor, neither agreeing nor disagreeing with Olive.

"I forgot Brian... Brent...whoever...was my hired date," Olive continued. "I bet it was the same for Simon. What these two people do—" she indicated Brent and Maia "—is pretty incredible, if you ask me. They make people's lives better, just for a little while, and change our entire outlook. I looked forward to tonight when a few weeks ago I was dreading it. I danced and toasted and laughed rather than sitting in a corner. Brent cared. He was attentive and considerate. I'm sure Maia treated

Simon similarly." She visibly struggled for composure. "With so much love to give, is it any surprise they found each other?"

"Olive." The bride's features collapsed. "I had no idea you dreaded coming to my wedding."

"I would have come no matter what. Wild horses couldn't have kept me away. But with Brent as my date, I truly enjoyed myself."

"I wanted to come alone," Simon grumbled and kicked the carpet with the toe of his dress shoe.

The bride pulled him close. "I shouldn't have insisted. I love you, and I meant well. Please forgive me."

He extracted himself with aw-shucks awkwardness. "It's okay, sis. But I can take care of myself."

"I know you can." She brushed the hair away from his eyes. "I messed up. I'm sorry."

"Don't be hard on Brent and Maia," Olive said. "I agree they shouldn't have disappeared together. But they're in love. You of all people should understand."

"We're not. We—" Maia faltered.

Brent didn't correct her. He'd been seconds away from confessing his feelings for her before Simon appeared. This wasn't the time or place to complete that comfession.

"I suppose you're right." The bride stepped around Olive and addressed Brent and Maia. "I admit, I possibly overreacted."

"You didn't," Maia insisted. "We were wrong."

"Yes. But I won't get you fired. Olive has a point." She reached for her husband's hand. "Besides, it's my wedding day."

"Thank you," Maia answered humbly.

"I do want my money back."

"We'll see to it," Brent said. "We promise."

The bride lifted her chin with an air of satisfaction. "It's up to Simon and Olive if you're invited back to the reception. I'm leaving the decision to them."

"Whatever," Simon grumbled. He hadn't looked at either Maia or Brent since his sister showed.

"Tell you what," Olive said, linking arms with him. "Why don't we let Brent and Maia leave, and you be my date for the remainder of the reception?"

"Me!" He gulped and gawked at her. "You're joking."

"I've never been more serious." She tweaked his lapel. "A good-looking young man like you? I'd be flattered. All the single women here are going to be sooooo jealous of me."

"Um, okay. Sure. Yeah." The beginnings of a goofy grin pulled at the corners of his mouth.

"Well, come on then." Olive tugged Simon along with her. Not before sending a mischievous smile at Brent that he interpreted as, *You're welcome*.

"Let's go," the bride said to her husband. "I'm ready for another glass of champagne."

"Your wish is my command."

"You say that now. What about twenty years from now?"

"Darling, I'll be saying that fifty years from now."

Grabbing the sides of her voluminous dress, the bride made a grand exit in the wake of Olive and her brother. The groom accompanied her, their murmured voices carrying across the widening distance. Brent and Maia had given them a lot to talk about.

"I suppose things could have gone worse," he said to Maia. There would be some explaining to do. The good news was Maia wouldn't lose her job.

She evidently didn't share his opinion.

Heading down the hall toward the inn's main entrance, she said, "We need to call Darla and implement damage control."

There was that. Brent's mood threatened to plummet with each step he took.

By some miracle, he remained steadfast. This wasn't the time for him to dive into the darkness. Maia was depending on him.

CHAPTER FIFTEEN

MAIA HADN'T PLANNED on standing outside at night in near-freezing temperatures. Thank goodness the snow, such as it was, had ceased falling an hour ago.

"Where's your truck?" she asked Brent, hugging herself to ward off the chill.

"Not here. My date drove."

"Mine, too." She groaned and rubbed her upper arms.

Stranded. No less than they deserved. She discarded the idea of returning to the dining room for her coat, preferring not to encounter Simon or his sister again.

"I'll get us a ride service." Brent reached into his pocket for his phone.

"Okay," Maia said, her teeth chattering.

Brent shrugged off his suit jacket. "Here. Take this."

"I'm f-fine."

"You're freezing."

She relented. Brent had worn a lined vest over his cotton dress shirt. Warmer than the thin fabric of her outfit.

They could huddle. Conserve body heat.

Probably not wise under the circumstances. Huddling was what had gotten them in trouble.

"We screwed up tonight," she said.

"Yeah." He opened the app on his phone and began tapping on the screen.

She slid her arms into the jacket sleeves, anxiety sparking like a live electric wire. "Darla's going to mad, and it's all my fault."

"No, it's mine."

"I invited you to talk," Maia insisted.

"And I should have said no. I knew better."

"I *really* knew better. Darla and I've had multiple discussions about this." Maia let out a long groan. "I know you think my sister can be difficult and demanding. But the company rules are in place for good reason. To prevent disasters like tonight."

"I don't think she's difficult."

"She's poured her heart and soul into Your Perfect Plus One. Her family depends on the income."

"We'll get through this," Brent assured her and finished requesting their ride. "The driver will be here in eight minutes. I expected longer on Christmas Eve."

"Yeah. Christmas Eve." She grimaced at the reminder. "I don't want to think about what it'll be like tomorrow at my folks'. Darla will tell them, of course. They'll be disappointed in me." Maia closed her eyes and saw her parents' faces. "I've ruined Christmas for the whole family."

"Do you want me to go with you? For moral support?"

"No! Absolutely not." At the injured look in his eyes, she added, "Thanks for the offer. But I think you being there would only make the situation worse. Darla may become defensive if it appears we're siding together against her."

He nodded. "I'll call her tomorrow. When's a good time? I don't want to interrupt her holiday."

"We need to call her right now." Maia removed her phone from her clutch. "The sooner the better. The only chance we have of salvaging things is to tell her what happened before the bride or Olive does. Otherwise, we're doomed."

"We're doomed anyway."

Maia prayed for strength and pressed the speed dial for her sister. Darla had likely put the girls to bed already. She and Garret were either wrapping last-minute gifts from Santa or spending a quiet evening together. They may have even fallen asleep from sheer exhaustion. In which case, Maia would wake up Darla. She didn't like being woken up.

Darla answered on the third ring with a very alert "What's wrong?"

Maia didn't call when she was on a date unless she had a problem. "I'm here with Brent at the inn. There's been a...a... complication."

"Tell me."

Maia could hear her sister's voice echoing as she walked from room to room through the house. She must be getting out of earshot from Garret and the girls if they were awake. One tiny positive, Maia had reached Darla before either the bride or Olive.

"Brent and I left the reception."

"Why?"

"We meant to leave for only a few minutes. To talk. Out in the hall."

"You went out in the hall to talk," Darla repeated, her voice level.

"Then..." Oh, gosh. This was so hard. Brent must have sensed Maia's anguish for he placed a hand on her shoulder. She steeled her resolve and continued. "We kind of kissed."

"Kind of?"

"We kissed. Then my date came out and found us. He was upset." That was putting it mildly. "After that, um..." Maia faltered. "The bride came out."

"The. Bride."

"She was upset, too."

"What about Brent's date? Where was she during all this? Please don't tell me she came out, too." When Maia didn't respond, Darla sucked in a breath. "Who else?"

"The groom."

Darla muttered a word she'd scold her daughters for saying. "I'm sorry."

A lengthy silence followed during which Maia considered and then discarded a dozen different excuses and explanations.

Darla finally murmured, "Continue."

Relaying only the relevant details—Darla wouldn't be moved by Maia and Brent's conversation about their potential future together and their feelings for one another, not right now, anyway—Maia spilled the entire awful tale.

"Brent's date gave this nice speech about wedding dates," Maia said, "and the bride was fine with everything."

"I highly doubt that."

"She wants her money back, naturally. Which you can take out of my pay."

"My pay," Brent insisted.

"Brent's pay, too," Maia told Darla.

"I'm giving Brent's date a refund, too."

"That's more than fair."

"Is he with you?" Darla asked, her tone hard to read.

"Yes."

"Put me on speaker."

Maia did as her sister requested and held the phone out so that both she and Brent could hear and be heard. "Go ahead."

"Brent?" Darla asked.

"Yes?"

"You're fired. I understand you care for my sister, but my duty is to my clients. They have a right to expect their wedding date isn't going to leave with someone else."

"I understand." To his credit, he didn't miss a beat.

Unlike Maia, who squeaked out, "Darla, no."

"I love you, Maia. I want nothing more than to help you with your dream of winning the Diamond Cup. But you're fired, too. For the same reasons as Brent."

A pitiful sound escaped Maia's lips. She should have seen this coming and yet she hadn't, and the pain cut like a knife.

She and Brent deserved reprimands, for sure. But fired? Without a chance to plead their case and make amends? Without Darla talking to the bride and Olive? They hadn't been angry. Yes, at first. The bride. Not Olive. They'd been understanding. Even appreciative, in a way.

Maia instantly realized her error. She and Brent hadn't just breached their employment contracts, she'd hurt Darla. Deeply. Perhaps irreparably.

"Okay," Maia managed, her voice fracturing. "Can we talk later?"

"We'll all three talk. On Monday. I'm not going to let this spoil Christmas. Plus, I need a day to process."

"Right. I'll see you tomorrow?"

"You'll see me. Good night."

Compared to the chill in Darla's voice, the winter night air now felt like a tropical breeze. The family gathering tomorrow would be far from jovial. Thank goodness the kids were young. The adults would put on a good show for them, and they'd be none the wiser.

Maia returned her phone to her clutch, her mind in a jumble. She didn't care about her job. She cared about Darla and Your Perfect Plus One's reputation and repairing the damage she'd caused.

"Where's our driver?" she asked.

Brent looked at his phone. "Two more minutes."

She slapped her arms again, as much to get her blood circulating as to ward off the cold. "I don't know what I was thinking."

"We weren't. That's the problem."

"I'm not like that. Impulsive. Thoughtless. Selfish."

"We were caught up in a moment," Brent said.

"That's no reason. My family's always been good to me. They've supported me unconditionally at every step—when Luke cheated on me, when he turned his back on me after I found out I was pregnant. Mom babysits TJ so I can work and train. Dad lets me set my own hours at the stables. Darla gave me a part-time job to earn extra money. And look how I repay them." Maia covered her face with her hands. "I'm a terrible daughter and sister."

"You're not."

"What if this damages Darla's business?"

"I doubt that will happen."

Brent's lack of concern suddenly irritated Maia. Did he really have no clue? Did he possibly not care?

"Our dates could post terrible reviews that discourage potential clients. They could tell their friends and family about their awful experience. Darla relies heavily on word-of-mouth advertising."

"Your sister's going to refund their money. They might be annoyed, but they can't say she refused to make things right. And you heard Olive. She won't post a bad review."

Maia stared. "You're missing the point."

"I'm not. We made a mistake, and it's going to have serious ramifications. But us being fired, or your dad letting me go isn't the worst. It's that you lost Darla's trust and may not earn it back."

All right. He wasn't missing the point.

"I betrayed her."

"Not intentionally."

"That may not make a difference."

"Possibly," he agreed. "I'm not taking any bets."

She heard the despondency in his tone. The hints of hopelessness and despair. "Dad won't fire you," she said.

"He'd have good reason."

"He can't fire you because you screwed up at a different job. That's not fair."

"His opinion of me will change when he hears what happened."

Maia hadn't considered that. "I won't let him fire you," she insisted.

"He may not have a choice if Darla insists."

"She won't." *Would she?*

Maia wanted to break down and cry. The ripple effect from their mistake just kept increasing and increasing. All because of a single kiss.

One minute, she'd been soaring among the clouds, in Brent's arms and talking about their future together. The next, she'd dropped to the ground, hitting like a ton of bricks.

Darla wouldn't be mad at Maia forever. They'd make up eventually. Particularly if no bad reviews surfaced. But they might not return to where they had been for a long, long time.

"Here's our ride," Brent said.

Another new ripple appeared and hit Maia like a tidal wave. She and Brent wouldn't survive this disaster unscathed. They might not return to where they had been before, either, for a long, long time. Maybe never.

Brent waved to the approaching red Honda. When the driver reached the curb, Brent opened the door for Maia, and she gratefully climbed inside. He was glad the driver—a middle-aged woman wearing a hat resembling a Christmas tree, complete with a star on top—had cranked up the heat. Maia shook from head to toe. His suit jacket was worthless in thirty-two degree temperatures.

"Merry Christmas, ya'll," their driver chirped.

"Same to you," Brent mumbled, not feeling the least bit merry. How had the night gone from fantastic to disaster in the blink of an eye?

"Let's see—" the driver said, tapping the phone mounted on her dash "—129 North Cypress Road? That's right?"

"Yeah."

He and Maia buckled their seat belts. She leaned back, closed her eyes and sighed, appearing to luxuriate in the warm air gusting from the heater. Suddenly, she sat up.

"Where did she say?"

"Books Galore. That's where my truck's parked. Where I met Olive."

"Hmmm." She nodded.

"I'll drive you to your car."

The reminder of their evening quieted them both. Their driver must have sensed her passengers weren't in the mood to chitchat, for she turned up the radio. Christmas music filled the car's interior, allowing Brent and Maia to talk softly without being overheard.

"I'm sorry, Maia."

"Me, too. About a lot of things."

How many apologies in total would be uttered before this was over and done with?

"I shouldn't have gotten involved with you," he said. *Not kissed you, not held you, not let myself imagine a future together.* "I should have put a stop to it when I had the chance. Instead, I encouraged you."

"We need to quit playing the blame game."

She was right. They'd both made mistakes, were both responsible. Brent attempting to assume the lion's share was his way of appeasing his guilty conscience. What he deserved was to drown in it.

"If your dad fires me, I'm going to leave Payson. I may anyway, even if he doesn't."

"Leave?" She twisted to confront him. "Where did that come from? And like I said before, he won't fire you."

"Me staying will make things difficult for you. I'll be a constant reminder." And *she'd* be a constant temptation. Brent had already demonstrated the magnitude of his weaknesses where Maia was concerned.

"What about Channing and your plans to become a rodeo judge?"

Brent had yet to think that far ahead. In fact, thinking was getting harder and harder by the minute. The black cloud had zoomed in from where it had been hiding these recent weeks and hovered directly over his head. The air inside the car grew heavy, and the familiar weight bore down on him.

He resisted. Pushed back. But the cloud would win eventually. He was fighting a losing battle.

"I'll talk to Channing," he said. "Explain what happened. Turn down the sponsorship."

"So, you're running away."

"I'm not."

He was. Running hard and fast. As usual. Some part of him reasoned if he changed locations, then perhaps he could somehow change and repair his broken self.

What was the old saying about the definition of insanity? Doing the same thing over and over and expecting a different result? Brent was living proof. Except this time the result was not the same. He'd hurt others besides himself. People he cared about and who mattered to him.

"With me out of the picture," he continued, "you can mend your relationship with Darla. She'll hire you back."

"Ahhh. You're leaving for my benefit. Not yours. How noble of you."

He didn't flinch at the snap in her voice. "I don't want to cause more strife between you and Darla."

"Whatever. Leave. Just stop making yourself the villain in a bid for pity."

Okay, that stung. "You're mad at me. Nothing less than I deserve."

"For Pete's sake, Brent. I'm not mad at you." She pushed ruthlessly at her hair as if it were responsible for her annoyance. "I'm mad at myself and at life in general. We're two nice people, two deserving people, who happened to meet at the wrong time. That stinks, frankly."

"I agree. Life is seldom fair."

"But here's the problem. Rather than accept our circumstances or wait until the time was right, we threw a stick of dynamite into a crowd."

She groaned.

"We're not kids or ignorant or stupid," he continued. "We knew the risks when we left that reception. Shame on us."

Brent could see that his remarks hit home. He would have liked to reach for Maia's hand. He didn't. That would send the wrong message, give her hope when there wasn't any.

"We were wrong," she said. "But is that reason enough to destroy all possibility for potential happiness? For you to up and leave behind everything you'd built here? Throw away the progress you've made? When are you going to stop punishing yourself for walking away from rodeo?"

Was that what he'd been doing? Punishing himself?

"I wish I'd met you two years ago," he said. "Then I might not have left rodeo or at least had an exit plan before I did."

She touched *him* then. Taking his chin in her fingers, she turned his face toward her. "Don't leave. Not yet. Let's see what happens first. Tomorrow's Christmas. You're not working. Take the morning to think. Make an appearance at Cash's wedding in the afternoon. You don't have to stay for the reception. Then spend the rest of the day mentally regrouping. We can talk later, if you want. I'll be home by six."

Her advice was good. Sensible. Thoughtful. Brent rejected it anyway.

"I won't leave right away," he said.

"Promise?"

"I told your dad I'd feed the horses and clean the corral in the morning so he and Rowdy could have the day off."

"That's nice of you."

He could tell by her expression, she'd misinterpreted his remark and assumed he wasn't leaving until they'd had a chance to talk. Brent didn't correct her. He figured he could be on the road by noon at the latest.

"Dad said you were volunteering at the shelter tomorrow before Cash's wedding."

He'd forgotten. His plan had been to take his suit with him

to the shelter and change there. "I doubt your dad will want to see me."

"Are you canceling?"

"Yeah."

"Brent—"

"I'm not going."

She hunkered down in her seat. "Fine. I won't push. A little time apart might not be a bad idea."

He'd be skipping Cash's wedding, as well. No big deal. He wouldn't be missed.

"Let's meet on Monday. You, me, Dad and Darla. We'll explain our side."

He'd be long gone by then. "We don't have a side."

"We'll express our regret. Make amends. Maybe we should say we've decided not to see each other for a while. Dad will come around. And Darla. When you think about it, this could wind up being for the best."

"You're kidding."

"You'll have more time to judge the bull-riding practices at Rim Country and obtain your certification. Three months from now, no one will remember."

The black cloud had affected Brent's ability to think clearly. In an effort to clear the fog, he put what Maia had said into bullet points.

Express regrets. Make amends.

Brent had that down. He'd been doing nothing else for the last two years. Expressing regrets, anyway. Not so much making amends. He'd only started that after coming to Payson and working for the MacKenzies.

Ansel would come around. Darla, too.

In three months? Nope. Maia was fooling herself. And if Brent ever screwed up again, this disaster would be dragged out and paraded around as evidence he hadn't deserved a second chance.

I'd have more time to judge bull-riding practice and obtain my judging certification.

A whole lot more time. Brent would be out of a job again. If Ansel had a lick of sense, he'd fire Brent like Darla had.

What was that last one?

"Maybe we should say we've decided not to see each other for a while."

"Temporarily," Maia said. "Take a step back until this blows over."

Brent hadn't realized he'd spoken out loud. "No." He shook his head. "Not temporary. Permanent."

"You can't mean that."

"We're here!" their driver announced.

Her voice sounded the like a snowy owl's screech. That happened when Brent started his descent into the darkness. Sounds were amplified and distorted. Retreating into himself was the only way to muffle them.

The small Honda rocked as they went over a speed bump at the entrance to the strip mall parking lot. Brent's truck sat in front of the bookstore. Blinking lights from the store's window reflecting in the windshield created a surreal effect that matched his mental state.

"There," he said. "The Ford pickup."

"You got it!" Their driver pulled up behind Brent's truck. "Merry Christmas, you two. And happy New Year. Stay safe."

"I'll tip you in the app," Brent said and opened his door. It weighed a ton.

"Thanks! And cheers."

A moment later, he was opening his truck's passenger door for Maia. She hadn't spoken since he'd refuted her statement about a temporary separation.

He hoped she wouldn't resume their conversation. Fate, for once, accommodated him. Silence hung between them the entire drive to where she'd left her SUV. She unbuckled her seat belt before Brent had come to a complete stop and opened the door the instant he shifted into Park. To his surprise, she hesitated rather than jumping out.

"We can get through this, Brent."

"Define *get through*."

"Everything's going to be all right. For us. For Darla. For Your Perfect Plus One."

"People don't easily recover from screwups like this."

"But they do recover."

"Your dad and Darla gave me a chance, and I repaid them by breaching my employee contract and causing a scene."

"I have faith."

That word again. Brent was starting to wonder how Maia could be so naive. She'd had her share of hard knocks and in some ways was still coping with them.

"There's a difference between having faith and sticking your head in the sand."

Maia bristled. "Is that what you think I'm doing?"

"You focus on the positive and ignore the negative."

"Is that so wrong?"

"It's unrealistic. You're setting yourself up for hurt and grief."

"Why are you acting like this?" She stared at him in puzzlement.

"Like what?"

"A pessimist."

"Pessimism and depression go hand in hand. Let's be honest—the world is a pretty bleak place. You and I—" he chuckled dryly "—we don't stand a chance. Even if we get through this, as you say, nothing will go back to the way it was before. Don't believe me? I have some scars to show you."

Her eyes flashed with pain.

Brent wished he wasn't the cause of her anguish, but he refused to mislead her with false optimism. Remaining in Payson and continuing to see Maia every day at work would intensify her anguish. Him leaving was the only sensible solution.

"Better a clean break now," he said, "than a messy and miserable break later when we're more invested in each other and have more to lose."

"Are you sure that's what you want?"

"Don't do that, Maia."

"Do what?"

"Keep fanning a dying fire. Your family comes first. And your sister's business comes next. You and I are at the very bottom. We're the most expendable."

She shivered despite the warmth. "I could love you if you let me. If you were willing to try. Give us a chance."

Her admission was no doubt intended to soothe. It had the opposite effect. Brent felt like a first-class heel. He was abandoning her. Same as her ex.

"That's what happens when you love someone who doesn't love themself. They disappoint you. They can't help themselves."

"You can," Maia said, her tone a blend of anger and sorrow. "You just won't."

For a moment, Brent was hurled back in time to a conversation with his dad. He'd said the same thing to Brent, nearly verbatim.

"You're right."

She flung open the door. After stepping out into the cold, she hurried to her SUV. Brent waited until he was certain her vehicle had started without problem and then followed her down the road for the next mile where she turned left, and he continued out of town to Bear Creek Ranch.

He arrived at the bunkhouse without remembering how he got there. That happened sometimes. He drove on automatic pilot, as if in a hypnotic state. Actually, he went through entire days on automatic pilot without remembering anything.

His bunk mates weren't home, either spending the holiday evening with their family, friends or girlfriends. Brent had the place to himself.

Wasting no time, he removed his boots and belt and clothes,

trading them for sweatpants and a T-shirt—his favorite outfit for sinking into the murky depths. Under the bedcovers, the blackness opened its jagged arms, welcoming him like an old friend.

I've missed you.

Why had he taken the jobs with Mountainside and Your Perfect Plus One? Forget about himself. He'd caused a rift between Maia and her sister. Possibly between her and her dad. Gotten her fired from a lucrative part-time job. Potentially damaged her sister's business. He wasn't just making himself the villain or attempting to appease his guilty conscience. He was a wrecking ball demolishing everything in his path.

The darkness pulsed and throbbed as it sang its siren's song. Brent stopped thinking about Maia and listened, letting his mind go blank.

CHAPTER SIXTEEN

"TJ, SWEETIE. Come back here."

Maia had spent the last ten minutes chasing her son from one end of the house to the other. She'd mistakenly thought it might be fun letting him open a present or two from Santa here before they went to her parents' house where there'd be more gifts and a big family brunch.

Because she hadn't had a bag large enough to hold the plush stick pony that made "realistic" galloping and whinnying sounds, she'd simply taped a giant red bow on the pony's neck and laid it beneath the tree. TJ had gone wild with excitement the second he laid eyes on the pony. He'd ignored the rest of his gifts and played only with Windy, the name printed on the side of the halter, riding him up and down imaginary mountains while mimicking the sounds the pony emitted.

Giving up, Maia let TJ play a while longer. She was in no frame of mind this morning to engage in a battle of wills.

Bits and pieces of scenes from last night had been returning at frequent intervals. Was Brent all right? He'd been upset when they parted, which could trigger one of his funks. Should she call or text him?

Given a second chance, there were at least ten things she'd say or do differently. She tried telling herself her worry was a waste of time and energy. He was attending Cash's wedding later today, and then on Monday, they'd meet with her dad and Darla, who'd have calmed down by then.

Except Maia couldn't quite remember Brent agreeing to the meeting.

She'd call tonight if she hadn't heard from him by…six. Six thirty. No, seven.

With that conundrum settled, she readied her food contribution to brunch—a tangy fruit salad and banana-nut bread—and tried desperately to get some food into TJ.

"Sweetie," she coaxed on his next gallop past her. "Have some milk and a cookie."

Not a cookie, an oatmeal bar. More a snack than breakfast. She reasoned he wouldn't starve before they got to her parents and had a real meal.

TJ stopped long enough to grab the sippy cup and oatmeal bar and give her a quick kiss. Then he set off, eating and drinking as he rode Windy from room to room.

Maia sighed and then smiled. Seeing her son having fun eased some of her worry. For a total of ten seconds.

Perhaps Brent had been such a pessimist because he didn't care for her as much as she cared for him. She'd maybe read too much into his declarations at the reception because that was what she'd wanted to hear.

Maia's stomach knotted. He hadn't purposefully deceived her. If anything, he'd been excruciatingly honest, insisting more than once he wasn't ready for a relationship.

With a sinking feeling, she forced herself to admit the truth. She'd unfairly pressured Brent, disregarding her many claims to the contrary. Why? She wasn't a needy or insecure person.

This answer hit her like a knock to the knees. Luke. His cheating on her, his abandonment when she revealed her pregnancy and his turning his back on TJ, had left a crack in her strong, independent woman armor. Without her realizing it, insecurities had snuck in and affected her relationship with Brent.

If only she'd waited a few weeks to talk to Brent and reveal her feelings for him. A few days. Heck, a few hours. One snap decision. One wrong step. One little mistake, and a future with Brent had gone from promising to bleak.

"Whee, heee, heee," TJ shouted as he rode his stick pony down the hall—his version of whinnying. Next came the galloping. "Gum, gum, gum, gum."

Finished with her food prep, Maia resumed chasing after him. "Sweetie, we've got to get ready to go to Grandma and Grandpa's."

Was she seriously attempting to reason with a sixteen-month-old?

At last, she cornered him in the kitchen and then wrangled him into the bathroom. Of course, he refused to go in the tub without the stick pony. They compromised, and Maia propped the pony's head over the side of the tub. After his bath, riding imaginary mountains resumed while she dressed.

Loading the food cooler, gifts and, of course, the stick pony, into the SUV, they left for Maia's parents' home. TJ neighed and galloped during the entire drive. The constant noise didn't distract Maia from her continued ruminations about her and Brent. Had he called her dad about canceling his volunteer shift at the shelter today? When did Darla plan on telling their parents about what had happened at the wedding? Before or after brunch?

By the time Maia and TJ swung into the driveway, she was physically and mentally exhausted. Seeing her sister's car there launched a fresh wave of anxiety. Maia had wanted to arrive first and run a little interference with her parents. So much for that idea.

After removing TJ from his car seat, Maia set him on the ground. "Here, sweetie. Help Mommy. Take this, okay?" She handed him the diaper bag.

He whinnied and pointed a pudgy finger at the car.

The pony. How could she forget?

Carrying the stick pony in one hand, he dragged the diaper bag across the ground to the front door with his other hand. Maia tried not to cringe, envisioning the scuffs and scratches. She grabbed the food cooler and the large plastic bag of gifts for her family and started for the house. TJ had already rung the doorbell. And rung it and rung it.

"Hello! Look who's here," Maia's mom gushed when she answered the door, not at all perturbed at her grandson's annoying antics. "And what's that? Did Santa bring you a present?" She tweaked the stick pony's ear.

"Puh!" TJ shouted and held up his prize.

"Such a beautiful horse." She straightened and enfolded Maia in a hug. "Where's Brent?"

"Brent?" Maia's heart faltered.

"I thought he was coming with you."

Impatient, TJ galloped into the house.

"Why would you think that?" Maia asked, covering her disconcertion by shifting her load. Darla must not have told their parents yet.

"Well, I guess I assumed. Your dad mentioned Brent was going with him to the shelter today and I..." She relieved her of the food cooler and stepped back. "I thought you two were getting close. Am I wrong?"

"Yes!"

"You're not wrong, Mom," Darla said, joining them in the living room, a dish towel tucked into the waistband of her pants. "Maia and Brent *are* getting close. Maybe little too close."

Maia sent her sister a look and waited for Darla to say more, only she didn't. Was she granting Maia a reprieve?

Her mom's glance traveled from one daughter to the other. "I don't understand."

"Let's head to the kitchen," Maia said, changing the subject. "This fruit salad needs to chill."

Her mom didn't fall for the ploy. "Are you two squabbling again? Honestly, it's Christmas."

"We're aren't squabbling," Darla answered.

"Then what?"

"We're having a disagreement. About work."

"Can this wait until Monday?" Maia asked as they walked past the family room to the kitchen. "I know you're angry, and you have every right to be..."

Darla glanced away, but not before Maia saw the pain in her sister's eyes. Her heart sank. Her broken promise and impulsive actions had hurt her sister. If Darla was put out, she had good reason.

Maia tried again, her voice soft. "Brent and I are planning on talking to you and Dad then."

"Talk about what?" her mom asked. When no one answered, she insisted, "Girls. Please. What's going on?"

"We might as well tell her," Darla said with a resigned sigh. "She won't quit pestering us until we do."

"You're right, I won't."

Maia really didn't want to have this conversation. If only she could find an excuse to stall.

"Honey," Darla called to Garret. "Can you please watch the girls for a while. TJ, too. Maia, Mom and I are going to be busy."

His head popped up from where he knelt in front of the fireplace, stuffing balls of crumpled newspaper into the spaces between logs in preparation for lighting a fire.

"Okay." He searched the room as if conducting a silent head count. Satisfied, he returned to the fireplace. "Will do."

Had Darla told her husband about what happened? Maia assumed yes, and her cheeks warmed from embarrassment.

"Where's Dad?" Darla asked their mom.

"He's in the bedroom. He'll be out any second."

Maia supposed she should be thankful for that. She wouldn't have to see the expressions of disappointment on both her parents' faces, just her mom's.

* * *

"Maia and Brent were at the same wedding last night," Darla said once she, Maia and their mom were standing at the kitchen island.

"Together or with different dates?" their mom asked.

"Different."

"Don't you usually avoid sending coworkers to the same wedding?"

"I do," Darla said. "This was an emergency."

Suddenly, Maia's dad burst into the kitchen. Maia couldn't recall ever being happier to see him, though she knew her reprieve was short-lived.

"Brent just called." He held out his phone as if to support his announcement.

Maia glanced away. Brent was calling to inform her dad he wouldn't be at the shelter today. This was her fault, too.

"Did you invite him to dinner?" her mom asked.

"I didn't get the chance. He quit!"

"Quit?" Maia squeaked.

"Quit?" her mom echoed. "Why on Earth would he do that?"

"Just said the job wasn't for him." Maia's dad shoved his fingers through his silver hair, leaving tufts standing up in places. "I was sure he liked working for us. The men all speak highly of him."

"I think I know why he quit," Darla said.

"You don't know," Maia countered.

"All right. Then tell us."

She hesitated.

"Maia?" her dad pressed.

"He thought you'd fire him. I guess he was beating you to the punch."

"Why would I do that?"

"Because of what happened last night." She met her sister's gaze.

"Somebody needs to tell me what in blue thunder is going on," her dad demanded.

"Yes," her mom seconded.

In the background, TJ whinnied and galloped back and forth in front of the Christmas tree. Maia's nieces whispered and giggled as they examined the many wrapped presents. Garret succeeded in lighting the fire. He closed the screen and stood to inspect his handiwork.

"Well," Darla started.

"While Brent and I were at the wedding last night," Maia said, "we left the reception briefly, to talk outside in the hall. My date discovered us, and the situation got a little messy after that."

"Why would he care that you and Brent were talking?" her dad asked.

"Because they weren't just talking," Darla said and filled their parents in on all the gory, ugly details.

When she finished, Maia's dad speared her with a look—the same one he'd used when she and Darla were young and pushing the boundaries.

"I like Brent," he said, "don't get me wrong. But you shouldn't have abandoned your dates like that. Not at a wedding when you were there as representatives of your sister's company."

"I know, Dad." Maia stared at the floor. Her shame and regret had been hard to bear before her parents were involved. Now it was unendurable.

"Don't be so hard on her," Maia's mom interjected. "She and Brent have feelings for each other."

"They also had an obligation to Darla. She's not wrong for being upset."

"But they're sisters."

"Maia is also Darla's employee." Her dad put an arm around her shoulders. "I love you, sweetheart. However, I'm going to support Darla on this." He nodded at his oldest daughter.

"And you should support her." Maia barely held back her tears.

"I get that you think I'm the wicked witch of the west," Darla said.

"I don't."

"I am sorry that I was gruff last night. I was surprised. And shocked. And upset, yes. Very upset."

"I'm sorry," Maia said, still fighting for control. "We were wrong. Really wrong."

"What are you going to do about it?" her dad asked.

"Darla's refunding the two clients' fees and taking the money out of my and Brent's pay. I'll issue a written apology, although neither of the clients was that mad in the end."

"Not them. What are you going to do about Brent? Now that he's quit, he's likely to leave town. Frankly, I don't want him to go. You don't want him to go, either, or you wouldn't have gone out into the hall to do more than talk."

"We agreed we aren't going to see each other."

She'd said temporarily. Brent, permanently. The bits and pieces of that scene returned to Maia, hitting her like tiny daggers. She must have been in denial, refusing to accept that another man would choose to walk away from her, and had put the memory from her mind.

"He needs this job," her dad said. "It's giving him a purpose."

"I'm sure he'll find another job," Darla said. "I've read his résumé. He's landed on his feet before."

Maia's dad looked at her with concern. "Have you told him how you feel?"

"Yes," she murmured.

"And he doesn't return your feelings?"

"Yes. He said he does. But he argued that staying would make things awkward for me and cause a rift between me and Darla."

"Will it?"

All eyes turned to Maia's sister.

"We're going to make up, sis. We always do. I am going to need a day or two to process. Put things in perspective."

"Fair enough," Maia's dad announced.

"Not to be a Debbie Downer," Darla continued, "but I have to ask. Is Brent staying what's best for everyone, him included? The fact is, he has some issues. Mental-health issues. That's no secret. He told me when I interviewed him. He didn't come right out and say depression, but I got the gist."

"Which is why he needs a job and a purpose," Maia's dad said. "Those are crucial for healing what ails his soul."

"He needs professional help, too," Darla said. "I'm not sure he's ready to accept that. Or ready for the commitment holding a steady job requires. People with depression often struggle with fulfilling their responsibilities. They can be unreliable. Irresponsible."

"That's pretty judgmental of you," Maia snapped. "It's not like Brent's a criminal or a liar or a degenerate. He has a common illness a lot of people suffer from. He deserves our compassion and our understanding."

"He *did* lie," Darla said sadly. "He promised to avoid you at the wedding, and then he didn't."

"Because I asked him to talk."

She stood straighter. "I'm looking out for us. For the family. Brent is very likable and charming. He has a ton of good qualities. He's kind. Nice. Polite. That's the reason I hired him. And he may, someday, once he's better, be the guy of your dreams. Before then, he has to deal with his issues. This wasn't the first time he ran into difficulties at work. And not the first time he was fired."

"You *fired* him!" Maia's mom asked.

"Yes, I did."

"She fired me, too," Maia said. "All right, deservedly, though I wish you'd given us a chance to explain first."

Her mom gasped. "You fired your sister?"

"Mom." Darla visibly struggled for composure. "She signed an employment contract. No fraternizing between coworkers. What happened last night is exactly the reason I have those clauses in the contract. If I let her slide, I have to let other employees slide or I risk being sued."

"She needs that money to pay for her saddle."

"Don't give Darla any grief," Maia's dad told her mom. "She a business owner, and sometimes business owners have to make difficult decisions."

"It was a mistake. People make mistakes. And family should get more breaks than other employees."

Maia wasn't sure about that.

"Fine," Darla pushed her fingers through her hair. "Maia, you can have your job back. But not Brent."

"I don't want it back. The saddle's mostly paid for, anyway."

"In all honesty, maybe that's for the best."

Maia's nieces and TJ chose that moment to burst into the kitchen.

"We're hungry," Darla's oldest exclaimed.

"Wanna open presents," her youngest demanded.

"Let's talk more about this later," Maia's dad said. "These young'uns are expecting a happy Christmas morning, and I for one want them to have it. Darla, I know you and Garret are leaving for his parents' after brunch. Why don't we all get together tomorrow and pick up where we left off?"

Maia and Darla both nodded, Maia glumly. They opened the gifts after that, the children in a chaotic frenzy. TJ abandoned his stick pony for the toddler push tricycle his grandparents had bought him. He then tried to ride the tricycle while balancing the stick pony across the handlebars. The girls squealed with delight at the identical baby dolls with matching wardrobes from Aunt Maia.

She tried to muster enthusiasm over the cashmere sweater from Darla and ruby earrings from her parents. Her heart just wasn't in it.

She had to find a way to talk to Brent. Later today. Tonight. In the morning. He may have quit Mountainside Stables, but he hadn't left town yet and might not for a few days. There was his final paycheck to process. Plus, he was attending Cash's wedding this afternoon.

What if she showed up at the bunkhouse? Or waited outside Wishing Well Springs after the wedding for him to appear. How would he react? Surely she could reason with him. Assure him that her dad wanted Brent to stay on and convince him to remain.

Maia picked at her food rather than eat, her appetite having abandoned her. Darla wasn't eating much, either, though the food was delicious. Their mom was pouring a second round of coffee when Darla's phone rang.

She stared in bafflement at the display before answering. "This could be work. I forwarded the office phone to my cell." She placed the phone to her ear. "Your Perfect Plus One. Darla speaking." As she listened, the creases in her brow deepened. "No. I understand. Take care of your son. He comes first. I'll call the client. Let me know how it goes." Frowning, she disconnected.

"Problem?" her mom asked.

"It's Lindsey. She has to cancel. Her son fell off his new skateboard and, she thinks, broke his arm. She's taking him to the emergency room. Now I have to inform the client his date is a no-show."

"Don't you have someone else available?"

"Normally, I would. But it's Christmas Day. And the wedding's in a few hours." Darla buried her forehead in her hand. "Just what I need on top of everything else."

Maia sat up, excitement coursing through her. She believed in signs, and this had all the makings of one.

"I'll do it," she blurted. "I'll be his date. If Mom's willing to watch TJ."

"No." Darla shook her head. "This is for Cash's wedding. Brent will be there."

"I won't talk to him. He'll be invisible to me. I swear."

"Absolutely not."

"I owe you. Big time. Let me make it up to you by covering for Lindsey."

"Give her a chance," their mom pleaded. "This could be an opportunity to mend the rift between you."

Darla looked to Garret who shrugged. She closed her eyes and moaned. "I must be out of my ever-loving mind."

"Is that a yes?" Maia sprang to her feet.

"Yes. But don't make me regret my decision."

Maia hugged her sister's neck. "I won't. Scout's honor. I'll be the best wedding date ever."

"Talk to Brent," her mom said as Maia was leaving a couple hours later, her cheek sticky from TJ's kisses.

She had every intention of talking to Brent. After the wedding. Long after. If he avoided her, which he might, she'd track him down at the bunkhouse.

Brent had been ready to give up on them without a fight. Well, Maia had enough fight in her for the two of them and the determination to go after what she wanted.

CHAPTER SEVENTEEN

AT HOME, MAIA CHANGED as fast as she could into one of her standard wedding outfits. Freshening her hair and makeup, she read the bio for her role and their fictional backstory on her phone. Sam was a former calf roper. Maia styled her hair and chose her outfit accordingly, wearing her flashiest Western boots and a striking turquoise necklace.

No sooner was she in her SUV and on the road to the pre-arranged meeting place when Darla phoned. Maia hit the Answer button on her car's display.

"You have your work cut out for you," her sister said. "The client is less than thrilled about the last-minute change."

"Understandable. I'll be all smiles and win him over with my wit and sunny personality."

Sam had once competed professionally with Cash and Channing back in the day. Did Brent know him, too? Possibly. Sam's longtime girlfriend had recently dumped him. According to the notes Maia had read, he didn't want to arrive at the wedding single and stand out like a sore thumb from his cohorts who were there with their gals.

Maia sincerely doubted his friends would think poorly him. But Sam was nursing a broken heart and was entitled to feel sorry for himself.

"Don't blow it," Darla told her.

"I won't."

"Check in with me the first chance you get."

"Want me to text you a picture?"

"This isn't funny."

"I'll call," Maia promised. "And Darla? Thanks."

She sighed. "Talk to you later. After I get a glowing report from Sam," she added with a hint of warning.

Once Maia hung up, she wondered if she should warn Brent she'd be there? That way, he wouldn't mistake her for a regular wedding guest and attempt to talk with her. She decided yes and, pulling into an empty bus stop, fired off a text ending with Sorry about last night. Hope you're doing okay.

Brent didn't respond. In fact, he still hadn't responded by the time Maia was in her date's car and on their way to Wishing Well Springs. Was he busy getting dressed? Was he out of cell range? She decided he must already be at the wedding and had shut off his phone to prevent it from going off during the ceremony.

She did her best to concentrate on her date. Sam seemed like a nice guy, other than he rambled on endlessly about his ex-girlfriend during the twenty-minute drive. Maia was no relationship expert, but she'd bet money he was still hung up on this gal and that their breakup had been nasty.

Honestly, she felt bad for him. More so, perhaps, because of what she and Brent recently went through.

"Crummy way to spend Christmas," Sam commented while parking the truck. "Not that I had any other plans. I did until a couple weeks ago when Ellie decided I wasn't paying her enough attention. One missed anniversary." He snorted. "Who keeps track of the day they met, anyway?"

"I'm sure Cash appreciates you coming today and giving up your holiday plans. He's a great guy. His fiancée, too. I've met her a couple of times."

"Ellie likes her. They met at a barbecue last summer."

Once again, Sam had brought the conversation back to his ex-girlfriend. Definitely hung up on her, she decided, noting his hound-dog expression.

Wishing Well Springs was decorated much the same as it had been last night. The Christmas tree greeted them when they entered. The giant wreath hanging from the wall waved at them with its long gold ribbons. On closer inspection, Maia noticed a billowy, fibrous material resembling snow covered the floor at the altar and silver fairy lights adorned the arch. The effect was lovely and very festive.

She started searching for Brent the second she and Sam sat in a pew near the back. Brent was nowhere in sight, and she tried not to let Sam notice her disappointment. She needn't have bothered as he completely ignored her.

The reason became obvious when he said, "There's Ellie," and glowered at a pretty auburn-haired woman two rows ahead and six seats over.

"She's here?"

"Yes." His stare intensified.

"Did you know she was coming?"

"Yes," he repeated.

Maia forgot about Brent and observed Ellie. The young woman sat with an attractive cowboy and flashed him what Maia considered an exaggerated smile. All of a sudden, she flicked a glance back at Maia and Sam. Then, dialing up her smile another notch, she returned her attention to her date.

Okay, thought Maia. Here's why Sam hadn't wanted to attend the wedding solo. He'd known Ellie would be here with another man.

She supposed she could help the poor guy out. The next time Ellie glanced back at them, Maia made sure to gaze attentively at Sam.

He didn't notice, but Ellie did, and her brightly lipsticked mouth flattened.

More guests arrived, filling the remaining pews. None of the people squeezing into the last vacant seats was Brent. Maia's anxiety increased, and she discreetly checked her phone. No reply to her text. No missed call from him.

Where was he? She sent a second text, this one a GIF of a penguin waving hello.

He could be with Channing and Cash, lending moral support to the best man and groom. Though Brent and Cash were only casually acquainted, Brent and Channing were good friends.

Yes, that made sense. In which case Brent would be the last one seated before the start of the wedding. It would also explain why he'd turned off his phone.

Maia remained optimistic right up until the first bridesmaid walked up the aisle, resplendent in her vibrant maroon dress. On her heels came four more bridesmaids, a flower girl and then the ring bearer. No sign of Brent. He wasn't here and, evidently, not coming.

Sam remained fixated on Ellie. Maia was able to sneak in several quick peeks at her phone with him being none the wiser or appearing to even care what she did.

The ceremony felt like the longest one in the history of weddings. When it finally ended, Maia had to prevent herself from shoving her way out of the pew and hurrying to—where? The entrance, she supposed, where she could call Brent.

Except she couldn't, shouldn't, do that. One, she owed Sam her full attention. Two, she'd promised her sister she wouldn't screw up again. Maia had no choice but to wait.

An image of Brent loading his truck sprang to her mind and sent a surge of alarm coursing through her. Her breath quickened.

What if he'd been packing when he called her dad this morning and quit? Why hadn't she tried to reach him earlier instead of waiting? She'd been so sure he would be here, take one look at her and realize the two of them belonged together.

There had to be another reason he wasn't answering her texts and had missed the wedding. A dead battery, in either his phone or his truck. He was embarrassed he didn't have enough money for a gift. He'd forgotten. He'd confided what happened last night to Channing, who then told Brent to stay away.

By some minor miracle, she survived the next fifteen minutes without having a meltdown. As the wedding party gathered to form a receiving line, she spied Channing nearby speaking with his parents.

"Excuse me just a minute, will you?" she said to Sam.

He grunted a reply, his attention riveted on Ellie and her cowboy companion twenty feet away.

Maia rushed over to Channing.

"Channing. Hi. I'm so sorry for interrupting." She acknowledged his parents. "I won't keep you, but have you seen or heard from Brent?"

"No. He was supposed to be here, but he didn't show."

"I've tried texting him, and he's not answering."

"Did you call?"

"No. Not yet. I'm here with a date. A Your Perfect Plus One date," she clarified.

"Are you worried? Did something happen?"

Maia considered before answering. "We had a fight." A simplification but true. "He called my dad and quit this morning. What if he left town?"

Channing exhaled a long breath. "He wouldn't leave without calling me."

"Then where is he? Why isn't he answering me?"

"I'm sure he's okay. Probably hiding out. That's what he does when he's having a rough time."

"Maybe you're right." She glanced back at Sam. "I have to go. Let me know if you hear from Brent."

"You do the same."

She hurried back to Sam, aware she'd pushed the boundaries. They entered the receiving line, and when their turn came, expressed their congratulations to the newlyweds.

Just like last night's wedding, the reception was being held at Joshua Tree Inn next door. It would be quite the affair as the bride's parents were rumored to have pulled out all the stops.

Outside the wedding barn, Maia and Sam waited for…well, she wasn't sure what. She suspected he was hoping to run into Ellie.

A nearby family of four with two teenage boys engaged Maia in congenial conversation while Sam pouted. She knew the instant Ellie exited the barn, for he stiffened, and his brow furrowed.

"Are you from Payson?" the wife asked Maia.

"I am. Born and raised."

Sam muttered something unintelligible and took off before Maia could reply.

"Is he okay?" the woman asked while their dad admonished the bored and restless teenagers to quit picking on each other.

"I think he spotted someone he knows."

Between Sam's behavior and her anxiety over Brent, Maia had trouble concentrating. She didn't immediately realize the raised voices were people arguing and not celebrating. Or that one of the two voices belonged to Sam.

"Look!" the younger teenager said and pointed. "That dude who was here is yelling at some lady."

"Oh, no." Maia watched in horror as the argument between Sam and Ellie escalated.

People literally stepped away, leaving the pair in the center of an open circle. Where were Cash and his bride? All Maia could think of was how awful to have a scene like this at a wedding.

"Should you, maybe, go over and say something?" the wife asked Maia.

Sam and Ellie fired curses and insults at each other like cannon shots, some Maia wouldn't dare repeat. Sam's face burned a bright red. Ellie gestured wildly, her hands slicing the air.

Maia caught sight of Ellie's date off to the side. Like everyone there, he stared in confusion and annoyance. He didn't much like his companion causing a scene. No one did.

"I'm not sure I want to get in the middle of that," Maia told the wife.

What would she say, anyway? She hardly knew Sam.

Luckily, one of his rodeo buddies intervened. He pulled Sam aside and spoke to him in a low voice. Ellie spun around. Spotting her cowboy friend, she went over to him, straightening her coat, which had become disarrayed during the intense exchange.

He backed up at her approach, raised his hand and shook his head. Maia didn't blame him. She didn't want to get near her date, either. But she supposed she had no choice.

"Enjoy the reception," she mumbled to the family and checked her phone again as she walked away. Nothing from Brent or Channing. Darn it.

Sam's rodeo buddy whisked him away to a secluded spot by one of the tall pine trees. When the buddy spotted Maia, he mouthed, "Give us a minute." She was more than happy to comply.

Waiting, she sensed the stares of everyone gathered outside or strolling to the parking area. They probably felt sorry for her, thinking her date had made a fool of himself. They'd be wrong. Maia couldn't care less. She'd not met the vast majority of people here today and would likely never see them again.

At last, Sam and his buddy separated. Maia readied herself, assuming Sam would meander over, shamefaced, and offer her an apology. A quick survey of the gathering outside the wedding barn revealed Ellie and her date had left. Presumably together. Maybe not.

Instead of coming toward her, Sam changed direction and made a beeline for the parking area. No *See you around* or *Are you okay*?

What? Seriously?

His buddy came over. "Hey, sorry about this. Sam left."

"So, I see."

"I think he may have forgotten you were here."

"Apparently."

Maia watched Sam weave back and forth between vehicles. A few seconds later, the headlights on his truck flashed.

"Bye-bye," she murmured.

"Can I give you a ride to the reception?" the pal asked.

"No. Thank you, though." She smiled.

"You sure?"

"Very. I have somewhere else to be. Merry Christmas." Maia hurried down the walkway to the edge of the parking area where she phoned Darla and relayed the details of Sam's abrupt departure.

"He's gone?"

"He hightailed it out of here five minutes ago. Call him if you don't believe me."

"What kind of jerk does that?" Darla groused. "Argues in public with his ex and then deserts his date? Yeesh."

"He's in love with this gal and went a little nuts when he saw her with another man."

"I'm really sorry you had to suffer the likes of him."

"Is it okay if I leave?"

"Sure. Unless you want to go to the reception. You can. You were invited."

"No. I'd rather not, if you don't mind." *I have to find Brent.*

"I'll pay you the full amount. You've earned it."

"That's not necessary." Money was the least of Maia's concerns at the moment.

"Hey, sis." Darla paused. "Thanks. A lot."

"Well, I owed you."

"About this morning. The argument…"

"I'm really sorry," Maia said.

"Let's talk later, okay?"

Relief washed over her. She and Darla would be okay. "Sounds good. I love you."

"Love you, too."

The instant she hung up, Maia opened the ride service app on her phone and ordered a car to take her to where she'd left her

SUV. The driver arrived fairly promptly. Twenty minutes later, she was in her own vehicle and on her way to Bear Creek Ranch.

She phoned her mom to check on TJ. He was napping soundly on the carpet near the Christmas tree, his stick pony and tricycle beside him. Maia's mom hadn't had the heart to move him and had just put a pillow beneath his head and an afghan over him.

"You're the best, Mom. I won't be too long. Five, six at the latest."

"Take all the time you need, honey. My fingers are crossed you and Brent work this out."

Maia drove as fast as the legal limit allowed. Once at Bear Creek Ranch, she headed straight for the bunkhouse, saying a silent prayer that she'd find Brent.

"Yes," she whispered when she spotted his truck behind the bunkhouse. "Thank you, thank you, thank you."

She didn't stop to consider what she'd find. Jumping out of the SUV, she ran to the bunkhouse door.

An insistent banging penetrated the dense layer of cotton batting surrounding Brent. Was someone hammering outside his window? That made no sense. A woodpecker on the roof? Fireworks?

He tried ignoring the noise to no avail. Each sharp report caused an excruciating pain inside his head like a series of small explosions. He cracked open an eye and encountered a dull blackness.

What time was it? What day? Where was he?

The banging continued. Brent rolled over onto his other side and covered his head with his pillow.

"Brent! Hello. I know you're in there."

Someone was at his door. He lifted the pillow and squinted at the wall as if that would provide an answer.

"Brent. Come on. Answer the door."

Maia? He covered his eyes with the blanket and willed the wheels of his muddled brain to start turning.

Bear Creek Ranch. He hadn't left yet. The day of the week and the time continued to elude him. Last he recalled, it had been Christmas morning. Who knew now? Brent had slept away entire days before, at his lowest points.

Christmas Eve had been one of those low points. When the memory of Maia's anguished eyes floated to the forefront of his consciousness, he shoved it back to the recesses where it belonged.

Bang, bang, bang.

For crying out loud. When would that infernal racket stop? How was a body supposed to get any sleep?

He burrowed farther beneath the covers, pulling the blanket past his ears. If he concentrated, he could block out the noise and the disappointments and regrets.

"Brent! Please. If you don't answer the door right now, I'm coming in."

Maia again. Brent was certain he'd locked the door. He always did before he sank into the murky depths.

"I have a key."

A wave of déjà vu poured over him like cascading water. He'd been here before. No, not here. In this same situation. Him trying to shut out the world and someone trying to push through his defenses. His mom? Channing?

"Brent!"

Maia wasn't taking the hint. Hmmm. There probably was a hidden spare key, and she'd use it.

Slowly, one inch at a time, he peeled back the bedcovers. His arm felt like a dead weight and functioned only marginally. Cold air penetrated the fabric of his T-shirt, causing his muscles to contract. As if rising from a coma, he sat up. His head spun. Wavy lines appeared before his eyes. His stomach lurched.

"I'm not leaving," Maia called and jiggled the doorknob.

"Okay, okay. Cool your jets," Brent said, his voice hoarse and unrecognizable.

With tremendous effort, he swung his legs over the side of

the bed. The icy floor sent a jolt through the soles of his bare feet. By now, his eyes had adjusted to the darkness. None of the other beds were occupied, which meant he was alone. It must still be Christmas Day. Or it was the day after Christmas, and his bunk mates were at work.

"Brent?"

"Give me a minute", he said, his voice louder and stronger.

Spying his discarded socks on the floor, he donned them with fumbling fingers. Reaching for the old hoodie lying at the foot of his bed, he shoved his arms through the sleeves. The zipper defied him, and he abandoned the effort.

Standing wasn't for the faint of heart. His knees wobbled like they had the first time he'd ridden a bull at thirteen. Then, his unsteadiness had been the product of exhilaration and adrenaline flooding his veins.

Not now. Must be hunger and dehydration. Brent hadn't eaten or drunk any water in a while.

One step. Two steps. Three. He ran his fingers through his hair on the way to the door and scrubbed the last remnants of sleep from his bristled face before letting Maia inside.

"My God, Brent." She gaped at him, her brown eyes wide with shock. "Are you all right?"

He must look pretty awful. "I was sleeping."

"I've been knocking on the door for almost ten minutes. I thought something had happened to you."

"No such luck."

"Don't say that." She reached for him, but he sidestepped her. "I'm okay. A little out of it is all."

He went over to the refrigerator and removed a bottled water and downed the entire contents in six swallows. The cool liquid jump-started his system. His knees were already steadier. Seeing the plate of Christmas cookies Syndee had baked for the guys, Brent fished one out from under the plastic wrapping and ate it in three bites. The sugar infusion hit him instantly.

What would caffeine do? He eyed the coffee maker on the

counter. Naw, too much effort. He settled for a second cookie and closed the refrigerator door.

"I thought you'd left town," Maia said.

"What day is it?"

"Saturday. Christmas. You called Dad this morning and told him you quit."

Brent dug through the cotton batting and found the memory. "What time is it?"

"Around four thirty."

He'd slept for almost sixteen hours, except for the ten minutes this morning when he'd woken long enough to call Ansel and resign. "Why is it so dark outside?"

"The sky's overcast. It's supposed to snow again." She glanced around the bunkhouse. "And you have the curtains drawn."

Brent wiped his mouth with a paper napkin and considered this information.

"I was expecting to see you at Cash's wedding," Maia said.

"I didn't go."

"I texted you. Channing did, too. We were concerned when you didn't answer."

Brent cast about for his phone. Must be in his pants pocket among the pile of clothes on the floor. "I was sleeping soundly."

She studied him with cautious uncertainty. The way people reacted to someone gravely sick or—go on, say it—someone with a mental illness.

Face facts. Normal healthy people didn't sleep for sixteen hours straight. Brent suffered from depression. Not a funk. Not a black cloud. Not *issues*. He had an illness that, if left untreated, could destroy his life and drive away every person who cared about him. He could deny it all he wanted, pretend he was fine, hide his condition and hope no one noticed, but he'd never improve without treatment.

Difficult to get that treatment when he didn't have a job and a place to live. Might as well get used to living out of his truck or on the streets. Pete and the others at the shelter could give him tips.

"Brent?"

"Yeah." He shook his head. "I was just thinking."

"Me, too," Maia said.

"About what a mistake it was getting involved with me?"

"No. The opposite, actually."

He almost laughed.

"Darla and I told Dad what happened last night."

"Bet that went over big."

"He doesn't want you to quit. He wants you to stay and keep working for Mountainside." She paused, her demeanor tender now. "I want you to stay, too."

"Are you two gluttons for punishment? Look at me. I'm a mess. A walking disaster. Darla's the only one of you who has any sense. She isn't offering to rehire me, is she?"

Maia shook her head.

"Smart woman."

"She hired me back. I filled in today at Cash's wedding when another employee had to cancel at the last minute."

"That's good. I'm glad." Brent sat at the kitchen table, his energy level not yet restored.

Maia dropped into the chair beside him and repeated, "Stay, Brent."

"There's no chance for us."

"You need a job and professional help and a support system. You can get all that here."

She was right. And without gainful employment, Brent wouldn't be able to continue paying off his credit card debt and the loan to his friend.

In hindsight, calling Ansel this morning had been a rash response to guilt and remorse. He'd decided he wasn't worthy of a good job and a fair shot from his boss.

"You've made so much progress this past month," Maia continued. "Your job at Mountainside. Judging the bull riding.

The online support group. The shelter. Don't throw it all away. Which you would if you left."

She reached for his hand. The gesture took him by surprise. How could she look at him, touch him, in his current disheveled and emotionally weak state? He must disgust her.

He'd seen it before on the face of his friend from Tucson who'd booted Brent out right before he came to Payson. On the face of his former supervisor at the BLM. On his dad's face.

"Why are you really here?" he asked Maia.

"I told you. To convince you to stay."

"Is that all?"

She gazed at him with heart-tugging sincerity. "And to convince you that what we have, could have, is worth fighting for. But that can come second. Your mental health is more important."

He didn't flinch when she said the words *mental health*, as he had when others spoke them. Was that because of the progress he'd made recently or because of Maia?

"I think my mental health and what we have, what we *could* have, are related. You've been my motivation, Maia. Losing you could cause me to backslide."

"Then why did you end things so abruptly?" she asked.

He let out a long sigh. "That's what I do. What I've done these past two years. I leave before I'm kicked to the curb."

"I would never do that."

"Maybe. I have a way of wearing thin."

"You can change." Maia's fingers tightened on Brent's. "Break the pattern, if you want."

"Why are you wasting your time with a guy like me? You have everything going for you. A family who would move Heaven and Earth for you. A terrific son. A job you love. A successful business you'll take over one day from your dad. A dream that drives you."

"Why not a guy like you?"

"I have nothing to offer you. Zero. Zilch."

"First of all, I don't need you to offer me anything more than your commitment, your loyalty, your help, your time and—okay, I'll say it—your love."

"Maia." Did she have any idea what she was saying?

Her gaze remained steady, and sincerity shone in her eyes. "I think I'm falling in love with you, Brent Hayes, and I'm pretty sure you're falling in love with me. Tell me I'm wrong."

Love. Just hearing her give voice to his growing feelings caused the dam inside his heart to burst. He'd been heading toward love since the moment he'd laid eyes on Maia at that first wedding.

"Besides," she added, still staring at him with that incredible sincerity. "You have a lot going for you, too, when you think about it. A job you love. Not working for Mountainside. Judging rodeo. And can't that also be your dream?"

Brent sat back in the chair and closed his eyes. Climbing out of the murky depths was a slow process. But he was climbing out. Out and toward a goal. Toward Maia.

"Being with me won't be easy," he said. "Not initially. Maybe not ever. Mental illness is something I'll be managing for the rest of my life."

"Nothing worthwhile is easy."

"That's not true."

"Stay," she whispered. "We can do this. Together. I'm here for you."

Brent couldn't believe his ears. No one had ever said that before. He was used to hearing *You're more trouble that you're worth* or *Man, you are one messed-up guy.*

"I need to see a doctor. Talking to Pete at the shelter and the people in the online support group has helped me finally accept that I can't get better on my own."

"That's a really big step. I'm glad for you."

"Will you come with me?" he asked, expecting her to say no.

"Of course. Whatever you need."

Brent swallowed the huge lump that had formed in his throat.

Maia was sitting there, offering him everything in the world he could possibly want. Still, he hesitated.

"I'll have setbacks. Mood swings. I'll disappoint and frustrate you. What if I shout at TJ because I stepped on one of his toys?"

"You'd be human. And we'll talk about it. Learn coping techniques. For both of us."

"You say that now. Just wait."

"I have my own baggage. A toddler son who's ten kinds of trouble. A pushy, meddling family—Darla, especially. I guarantee you they will be constantly sticking their noses in our business."

Maia wasn't going away, Brent realized, or kicking him to the curb. She truly wanted him to stay.

"You're crazy, you know," he said. "And I'd be crazy to agree. This could end badly. It will end badly. I'm unreliable. At loose ends. Rock bottom."

"Then we have nowhere else to go but up." She smiled, her entire face radiating joy. "And it won't end badly if we're patient and considerate of each other and willing to put in the work." She squeezed his hand again. "Are you, Brent? Willing to put in the work?"

Here it was. One of those defining moments like in a movie or that people wrote about in their memoirs. He either walked through the door Maia held open or he packed his bags and left town, relegating her to the role of someone in his past. There was no in between. No hanging in limbo. In for a penny, in for a pound.

Was Brent in? For better or worse?

"I'm a catch." Maia pretended to preen. "You'd be a fool to turn me down."

Brent released her hand and pushed to his feet. "I'm a lot of things, Maia, including a fool. On more than one occasion."

The joy drained from her.

"But not today. If you're willing to take a chance on us, then so am I."

Leaping up from her chair, she then skirted the table, threw herself into his open arms and found his mouth with hers.

"I am falling in love with you," she said, her lips brushing his, the sunshine returning to her face. "Make no mistake."

"I'm going to get better, Maia. I promise."

They kissed and kissed again. An optimism Brent hadn't experienced in too many years lifted him from the depths and into the light. He had a long way to go. With Maia beside him, the journey would be an adventure.

Several minutes passed before they broke apart. Brent lost track.

Maia cradled his cheeks with her palms. "Let's spend the rest of Christmas with TJ. If you want to and are up for it. He's had a big day and will be impossible. Fair warning."

"I need to shower first."

"I'll wait. Maybe fix us some coffee."

"That'll hit the spot. And give me a boost. I'll need one before talking to your dad about getting my job back."

"No worries. He likes you."

"Will he like me as the man dating his youngest daughter? Dads can be funny about that."

"He'll approve. Mom, too."

"What about Darla? She hates me."

"She doesn't. She is overprotective," Maia conceded. "But all she really wants is for me to be happy. And I am. Very happy."

Brent pulled Maia close. "Me, too. More than I thought was possible."

When they stepped outside a while later, it was to a robust snowfall.

"A little late," Maia said, "but we're having a white Christmas."

"How about that."

She punched him teasingly in the arm. "You're not even looking."

He'd been staring at her, unable to tear his gaze away.

"We should make a wish," she said and closed her eyes.

Brent did, too. But his Christmas wish had already come true, and she was standing right beside him.

One Year Later

EPILOGUE

"WANNA SEE SANTA!" TJ announced from the back seat of Maia's SUV in what was definitely not his inside voice.

"We will, sweetie. Soon."

His vocabulary over the past year had increased at a remarkable rate. Of course, she credited his above-average intelligence. In reality, it was the result of his outgoing personality, an active social life and the village of people who helped raise him.

Besides Maia, there were his grandparents, his aunt and uncle and cousins—Maia's nieces loved teaching TJ new words—his teacher and playmates at Little Tykes Learn and Grow, and his best buddy Brent.

Maia loved watching the two of them together. Not only did Brent have an abundance of patience, he was one of the few people who talked to TJ. Really talked to him. And TJ responded by listening. *Really* listening.

"You excited?" Brent asked Maia.

He reached across the SUV's console to straighten her crooked stocking cap. They were all three decked out in holiday garb, though Brent's only concession was a red-and-white woolen scarf. He did look dashing in it.

A burst of warmth filled her, and she took her eyes off the

road for only a second to offer him a smile. "I am excited. I love the Cowboy Christmas Jamboree."

"You seemed a little tired at dinner."

"Well, I did work from six to three and then went *s-h-o-p-p-i-n-g*," she spelled out the word, "with Mom and Darla."

Her extremely bright son would ask what she'd purchased if he realized she'd been to the store. Maia was having enough trouble as it was keeping Santa's stash of goodies hidden from him.

They were meeting Maia's family at the event for an evening of holiday fun and entertainment. As usual, the highlight would be a visit with Santa. TJ had learned, mostly from his older cousins and playmates at class, what Santa was all about. He couldn't wait to meet him in person to recite his wish list. A big change from last year when he'd cried and then wanted down from Santa's lap.

"I thought you were going to get another practice session in today," Brent said, as they turned onto the road that would take them to Rim Country Rodeo Arena.

"Didn't happen. Too busy. I was thinking Saturday morning if you're available."

"I don't have a rodeo until mid-January, so all my free time is yours until then."

"All?"

"Every second." He grinned.

He'd recently returned from the National Finals Rodeo in Las Vegas where he'd once competed for a championship title. This time, his purpose had been to watch and learn and shadow a seasoned bull-riding judge.

Brent had earned his certification this past August and had landed several judging jobs at small rodeos in addition to Rim Country. He worked most weekends. Weekdays, when his schedule allowed, he led trail rides for Mountainside Stables and helped Maia's dad with horse care and maintenance.

He no longer resided in the bunkhouse. Once he'd started rodeo judging, and Rowdy hired on with the forest service, the two of them moved into a cabin belonging to Channing's family.

Javier and Syndee remained a couple. Sadly, Rowdy's romance with his girlfriend had run its course. He'd been ready for a change when Brent mentioned the cabin was newly available to rent, and having a roommate kept Brent on track. Both he and Rowdy volunteered at the shelter regularly. Brent attended a weekly men's support group and private counseling sessions with a therapist.

Getting the help he'd needed and finding his passion had made all the difference. Brent flourished, professionally and personally. His mom had visited not once, but twice this past year. She and Brent talked regularly, and he often included Maia and TJ in the video calls. Maia liked his mom very much. How could she not? The woman loved and supported Brent one-hundred-percent. Plus, she adored TJ.

Six months ago, Brent had reached out to his dad and half-siblings. He'd felt he couldn't move forward until he resolved his past. With his therapist's coaching, Brent was able to better understand his dad, how his strict upbringing had shaped him, and choose the right words to say when they conversed. He and his dad weren't the best of friend, but they were making progress. Brent had recently mentioned a possible trip to see his dad and half-siblings.

Maia snuck another peek at Brent, and her heart filled to bursting. The person she'd glimpsed deep down had fully emerged, and she'd fallen more in love, if that was possible. Every day she discovered something new about him and herself, too, because she was also flourishing.

Darla often teased Maia, saying she wore rose-colored glasses. She didn't care. A little positivity never hurt anyone. And while Maia was ready to take her and Brent's relationship to the next level—to start discussing a lifetime commitment—she was content to wait until he was ready.

"I'm glad you're free," she said, "because Snapple's been acting a little temperamental lately."

"His scar again?"

"Not that. He's developed a stubborn streak. We're having constant arguments about who's in charge."

Problems of this nature frequently arose with highly athletic, strong-willed horses like Snapple. Along with the good qualities that made him an outstanding competitive trail horse came a few bad ones: stubbornness and skittishness, for instance.

Maia hadn't won the Diamond Cup in April, but she'd finished twelfth. Not too terrible. There was always this coming April, and she had her sights on placing in the top three. Snapple had the ability, as the numerous ribbons and trophies in less-prestigious competitions had demonstrated. If Maia could just correct this recent crop of pesky little quirks.

"We need your expert training," she said. "Again."

"Might cost you this time," Brent teased.

"Oh? What did you have in mind?"

"You and TJ come with me to the Gila Bend Rodeo in January."

"Hmm. You drive a hard bargain, Mr. Hayes."

He didn't drive a hard bargain at all. Maia had been wanting to see Brent occupying the judges' booth at a rodeo other than Rim Country. Now she'd have her chance.

"Wanna go," TJ shouted from the back, apparently understanding the part of the conversation that involved a road trip.

"We will," Maia said, though she was answering Brent and not TJ.

Arriving at Rim Country, they parked and walked toward the entrance, Brent holding TJ's hand. Maia phoned her mom for an update. The rest of the family was already there and waiting by the concession stand.

Maia's dad had decided out of the blue three days ago he wasn't giving the pony-cart rides. Instead, Rowdy would be in charge with Pete's help. The change in plans had surprised Maia. When she'd questioned her dad, he'd vaguely alluded to spending the evening with his family.

Okay, she supposed. His choice.

"Santa this way," TJ said. "Hurry."

"Don't you want some hot chocolate first?" his grandma asked.

"See Santa first."

"We want to see Santa, too," his cousins echoed.

"TJ," Maia cajoled. "Don't be bossy."

"I not bossy," he argued back and tugged hard on Brent's hand.

Brent gave her a wink. "Let's see Santa. It'll be fun."

Maia's dad led the way, which seemed kind of funny to her. He usually lagged behind, letting the grandkids charge ahead. "Lois, do you have your phone?" he asked. "We need to get some pictures."

"Let Darla. She's better at it."

On cue, Darla plucked her phone from her purse. Well, she was the designated family photographer.

She and Brent had become good friends since the Your Perfect Plus One fiasco last Christmas Eve. It wasn't just that Brent treated her little sister right. Darla also respected Brent for his valiant effort battling his depression and for obtaining his judging certification. Both had required hard work and dedication. Two qualities Darla valued as a successful business owner.

"Hurry," TJ urged.

Brent laughed. Maia groaned. They and the family followed TJ to the arena where the maze had been set up. Once again, animated reindeer pointed the way and, once again, TJ begged to ride them.

Maia noticed Brent becoming quieter and quieter as they

traversed the maze, and she tried not to worry. His last episode had been seven months ago and mild compared to others.

"I know TJ and the family are overwhelming," she said. "You coming tonight means a lot to me."

He reached for her hand and brought it to his lips. "Nowhere else I'd rather be."

There. The smile she adored bloomed on his face. Maia did more than relax; she lost herself in his eyes and reveled in the incredible way he made her feel. This was surely another Christmas in what would be a lifetime of Christmases together.

Waiting to see Santa was no easy task for three rambunctious and excited children. TJ and his cousins jumped up and down, twirled, squabbled and tugged eagerly on the coat sleeves of the nearest adult. As they neared the front of the line, Maia's dad paid the donation for photos of each child with Santa, sitting atop his makeshift throne.

Darla readied her phone. Maia, too. She wanted a few of her own shots.

The girls went first, much to TJ's consternation. Maia's efforts to quiet him were in vain. "Manners, TJ."

"My turn, my turn," he protested.

At long last, Santa finished with his cousins. TJ bolted forward, only to stop short in front of Santa, abruptly shy.

"Go on," Maia coaxed.

TJ shook his head.

"Come on, young man." Santa beckoned. To be correct, Channing beckoned. That was him beneath the long white beard and hair. His new wife Kenna played the role of elf helper and photographer.

TJ spun and ran to Brent, hugging his leg. Brent knelt and took TJ by the shoulders. She missed hearing what Brent said, her attention distracted by the pony cart pulling up to the arena fence and stopping. Rowdy and Pete waved, grinning from ear to ear.

"What are they doing here?" Maia asked her dad.

"Just watching your young'un."

Whatever Brent said to TJ must have worked because her son slowly approached the throne and let Brent lift him onto Santa's lap.

They all watched, and Maia snapped pictures while TJ shyly whispered his list in Santa's ear. His elf helper took the photo. Darla videoed the entire exchange.

Maia laughed, expecting her son to jump off Santa's lap. Except that didn't happen. Instead, Santa reached into his coat pocket and pulled out a small gift bag. Odd, he hadn't done that with the other kids. He then put the bag in TJ's hands, pointed to Maia and said something to TJ she couldn't hear.

With an exaggerated nod, TJ clambered down and scurried over to Maia, holding out the gift bag. "For you, Mommy."

"What's this?" She automatically accepted the gift bag, exchanging glances with Brent.

He shrugged. "Open it and find out."

"Open it," TJ parroted.

Darla, Maia noticed, continued to video. The remainder of her family had moved closer as if jockeying for a glimpse of what was in the bag. They were certainly acting strange. Brent, too.

"We're waiting," her mom encouraged.

Maia stuck a hand into the gift bag and felt a small jewelry box nestled in the tissue. Her heart beat faster. Her breath quickened. Her nerves tingled.

Slowly, because she wanted this moment to last forever, she lifted the box from the bag.

"Brent?" She swallowed. "Is this from you?"

"Maybe." He gazed at her with both expectation and trepidation. "That depends on your answer."

The gift bag fell from her fingers to the ground.

"Mommy." TJ bent down to retrieve it. "You dropped this."

"Hold on to it for me, okay?"

She ran her fingers along the top of the velvet box. Could it be…? She cracked the lid, just enough to peek inside. Her world came to a standstill.

"Maia MacKenzie."

Brent was suddenly standing before her. He took the velvet box from her trembling fingers and opened it all the way. A gorgeous diamond-and-emerald ring twinkled in the moonlight.

"You're like no one I've ever met," he said, a catch in his voice. "You pulled me out of a dark place and into the light. You encouraged me to repair bridges I'd thought burned and taught me the importance of family and forgiveness. You gave me a dream and supported me every step of the way while I achieved it. You had faith in me when others didn't."

He cleared his throat, and she noticed his eyes had gone a little misty. How sweet. Her own eyes filled with tears as well. Then, he removed the ring from the box and held it out to her.

"Will you marry me, Maia? I'll always be a work in progress, but I promise to do my best to make you happy and be a good father to TJ—"

"Yes." She didn't let him finish. "Yes, yes, yes."

"Yes, yes," TJ repeated and raised his arms in the air.

Maia watched, a lump in her throat, as Brent slipped the ring on her finger. "It fits!" she exclaimed.

Cheers erupted, and Maia looked around to see the faces of her family and friends filled with joy for her and Brent. They'd known all along, of course. How could she have seen the clues and not put them together? Her dad taking the lead on the walk here. Darla continuing to video. Rowdy and Pete in the pony cart. Brent's silence, which was likely a case of nerves.

As if he had anything to be nervous about. There wasn't a chance she'd have turned him down.

"I love you, Maia."

She flung her arms around his neck and kissed him on the cheeks and his lips and even his forehead. "I love you, too. We are so going to have the best life ever."

She barely heard the hoots and hollers and congratulations. Maia had eyes only for Brent.

"Wishes do come true," she murmured and claimed another kiss. Especially Christmas wishes.

* * * * *

Keep reading for an excerpt of
From Christmas To Forever?
by Marion Lennox.
Find it in the
A Christmas Gift anthology,
out now!

CHAPTER ONE

CHRISTMAS IN THE middle of nowhere. Wombat Valley. *Hooray!*

Dr Pollyanna Hargreaves—Polly to everyone but her mother—beefed up the radio as she turned off the main road. Bing Crosby's 'White Christmas' wasn't exactly appropriate for Christmas deep in the Australian bush, but it didn't stop her singing along. She might be a long way from snow, but she was happy.

The country around her was wild and mountainous. The twisting road meant this last section of the journey could take a while, but the further she went, the further she got from the whole over-the-top celebration that was her parents' idea of Christmas.

'You can't be serious!' She could still hear her mother's appalled words when she'd broken the news that she wouldn't be spending Christmas with them. 'We've planned one of the most wonderful Christmases ever. We've hired the most prestigious restaurant on Sydney Harbour. All our closest friends are coming, and the head chef himself has promised to oversee a diabetic menu. Pollyanna, everyone expects you.'

Expectation was the whole problem, Polly thought, as she turned through the next curve with care. This road was little more than a logging route, and recent rain had gouged gutters along the unsealed verge. The whole of New South Wales had been inundated with weeks of subtropical downpours, and it looked as if Wombat Valley had borne the brunt of them. She was down to a snail's pace.

But she wasn't worried. She wasn't in Sydney. Or in Monaco, where she'd been last Christmas. Or in Aspen, where she'd been the Christmas before that.

Cute little Pollyanna had finally cut and run.

'And I'm not going back,' she told the road ahead. Enough. She felt as if she'd been her parents' plaything since birth, saddled with a preposterous name, with nannies to take care of every whim and loaded with the expectation that she be the perfect daughter.

For Polly was the only child of Olivia and Charles Hargreaves. Heiress to the Hargreaves millions. She was courted and fussed over, wrapped in cotton wool and expected to be...

'Perfect.' She abandoned Bing and said the word aloud, thinking of the tears, the recriminations, the gentle but incessant blackmail.

'Polly, you'll break your mother's heart.' That was what her father had said when Polly had decided, aged seven, that she liked chocolate ice cream, eating a family tub behind her nanny's back and putting her blood sugars through the roof. And ever since... 'You know we worry. Don't you care?'

And then, when she'd decided she wanted to be a doctor...

'Pollyanna, how can you stress your body with a demanding career like medicine? Plus you have your inheritance to consider. If you need to work—which you don't—then at least take a position in the family company. You could be our PR assistant; that's safe. Medicine! Polly, you'll break our hearts.'

And now this. Breaking up with the boy they wanted her to marry, followed by Not Coming Home For Christmas. Not being there to be fussed over, prettied, shown off to their friends. This was heartbreak upon heartbreak upon heartbreak.

'But I'm over it,' she said out loud. 'I'm over families—over,

over, over. I'm an independent career woman so it's time I started acting like one. This is a good start. I'm five hours' drive from Sydney, in the middle of nowhere. I'm contracted to act as locum for two weeks. I can't get further away than this.'

And it was exciting. She'd trained and worked in city hospitals. She didn't have a clue about bush medicine, but the doctor she was relieving—Dr Hugo Denver—had told her things would be straightforward.

'We're usually busy,' he'd said in their phone interview. 'The valley could use two doctors or more, but over Christmas half the population seems to depart for Sydney or the coast. We run a ten-bed hospital but anything major gets helicoptered out. Mostly we deal with minor stuff where it's not worth the expense of sending for the Air Ambulance, or long-termers, or locals who choose to die in the Valley rather than in acute city hospitals.'

'You provide palliative care?' she'd asked, astonished.

'Via home visits, mostly,' he'd told her. 'Most of our oldies only go to the city under duress, and it's an honour to look after them at home. I also deal with trauma, but the logging industry closes down for three weeks over Christmas and the place is quiet. I doubt if you'll have much excitement.'

'But I wouldn't mind a bit of excitement,' she said aloud as she manoeuvred her little sports car around the next bend. 'Just enough to keep me occupied.'

And then, as if in answer to her prayers, she rounded the next bend—and got more excitement than she'd bargained for.

Dr Hugo Denver was well over excitement. Hugo was cramped inside a truck balanced almost vertically over the side of a cliff. He was trying to stop Horace Fry from bleeding out. He was also trying not to think that Ruby was totally dependent on him, and his life seemed to be balanced on one very unstable, very young tree.

The call had come in twenty minutes ago. Margaret Fry, wife

of the said Horace, had managed to crawl out of the crashed truck and ring him.

'Doc, you gotta come fast.' She'd sobbed into the phone. 'Horace's bleeding like a stuck pig and there's no one here but me.'

'He's still in the truck?'

'Steering wheel jabbed him. Blood's making him feel faint.'

'Bleeding from where?'

'Shoulder, I think.'

'Can you put pressure on it?'

'Doc, I can't.' It was a wail. 'You know blood makes me throw up and I'm not getting back in that truck. Doc, come, fast!'

What choice did he have? What choice did he ever have? If there was trauma in Wombat Valley, Hugo was it.

'Ring the police,' he snapped. 'I'm on my way.'

Lois, his housekeeper, had been preparing lunch. She'd been humming Christmas carols, almost vibrating with excitement. As was Ruby. As soon as the locum arrived they were off, Lois to her son's place in Melbourne, Hugo and Ruby to their long-awaited two-week holiday.

Christmas at the beach… This was what his sister had promised Ruby last year, but last year's Christmas had become a blur of shock and sorrow. A car crash the week before. A single car accident. Suicide?

Hugo's life had changed immeasurably in that moment, as had Ruby's.

Twelve months on, they were doing their best. He was doing his best. He'd moved back to Wombat Valley so Ruby could stay in her home, and he fully intended to give her the longed-for beach Christmas.

But commitment meant committing not only to Ruby but to the community he lived in. The locals cared for Ruby. He cared for the locals. That was the deal.

Lois had been putting cold meat and salad on the table. She'd looked at him as he disconnected, and sighed and put his lunch in the fridge.

'Ring Donald,' he'd told her. Donald was a retired farmer who also owned a tow truck. It was a very small tow truck but the logging company with all its equipment was officially on holidays since yesterday. Donald's truck would be all the valley had. 'Tell him Horace Fry's truck's crashed at Blinder's Bend. Ring Joe at the hospital and tell him to expect casualties. Tell him I'll ring him as soon as I know details, and ask him to check that the police know. I need to go.'

'Aren't you expecting the new doctor?' Lois had practically glowered. She wanted to get away, too.

'If she arrives before I get back, you can give her my lunch,' he'd said dryly. 'I'll eat at the hospital.'

'Should I send her out to Blinder's? She could start straight away.'

'I can hardly throw her in at the deep end,' he'd told her. 'Hopefully, this will be the last casualty, though, and she'll have a nice quiet Christmas.' He'd dropped a kiss on his small niece's head. 'See you later, Ruby. Back soon.'

But now...

A quiet Christmas was just what he wanted, he thought grimly as he pushed hard on the gaping wound on Horace's shoulder. The steering wheel seemed to have snapped right off, and the steering column had jabbed into Horace's chest.

And he'd bled. Hugo had stared in dismay into the truck's cab, he'd looked at the angle the truck was leaning over the cliff, he'd looked at the amount of blood in the cabin and he'd made a call.

The truck was balanced on the edge of the cliff. The ground was sodden from recent rain but it had still looked stable enough to hold. He'd hoped...

He shouldn't have hoped. He should have waited for Donald with his tow truck, and for the police.

It didn't matter what he should have done. Margaret had been having hysterics, useless for help. Hopefully, Donald and his tow truck were on their way but he'd take a while. The police had to come from Willaura on the coast, and he hadn't been able to wait.

And then, as he'd bent into the cab, Horace had grasped his wrist with his good arm and tried to heave himself over to the passenger seat. He was a big man and he'd jerked with fear, shifting his weight to the middle of the cabin...

Hugo had felt the truck lurch and lurch again. He'd heard Margaret scream as the whole verge gave way and they were falling...

And then, blessedly, the truck seemed to catch on something. From this angle, all he could see holding them up was one twiggy sapling. His life depended on that sapling. There was still a drop under them that was long enough to give him nightmares.

But he didn't have time for nightmares. He'd been thrown around but somehow he was still applying pressure to Horace's arm. Somehow he'd pushed Horace back into the driver's seat, even if it was at a crazy angle.

'You move again and we'll both fall to the bottom of the cliff,' he told Horace and Horace subsided.

To say his life was flashing before his eyes would be an understatement.

Ruby. Seven years old.

He was all she had.

But he couldn't think of Ruby now. He needed to get back up to the road. Horace had lost too much blood. He needed fluids. He needed electrolytes. He needed the equipment to set up a drip...

Hugo moved a smidgen and the truck swayed again. He glanced out of the back window and saw they were ten feet down the cliff.

Trapped.

'Margaret?' he yelled. 'Margaret!'

There was no reply except sobbing.

His phone... Where the hell was his phone?

And then he remembered. He'd done a cursory check on Margaret. She'd been sobbing and shaking when he'd arrived. She was suffering from shock, he'd decided. It had been an instant diagnosis but it was all he'd had time for, so he'd put his jacket across her shoulders and run to the truck.

His phone was still in his jacket pocket.

'Margaret!' he yelled again, and the truck rocked again, and from up on the cliff Margaret's sobs grew louder.

Was she blocking her husband's need with her cries? Maybe she was. People had different ways of protecting themselves, and coming near a truck ten feet down a cliff, when the truck was threatening to fall another thirty, was possibly a bad idea.

Probably.

Definitely?

'That hurt!' Horace was groaning in pain.

'Sorry, mate, I need to push hard.'

'Not my shoulder, Doc—my eardrum.'

Great. All this and he'd be sued for perforating Horace's eardrum?

'Can you yell for Margaret? We need her help.'

'She won't answer,' Horace muttered. 'If she's having hysterics the only thing that'll stop her is ice water.'

Right.

'Then we need to sit really still until help arrives,' he told him, trying not to notice Horace's pallor, deciding not to check his blood pressure because there wasn't a thing he could do about it. 'The truck's unstable. We need to sit still until Donald arrives with his tow truck.'

'Then we'll be waiting a while,' Horace said without humour. 'Donald and his missus have gone to their daughter's for Christmas. Dunno who's got a tow truck round here. It'll have to be a tractor.'

'Can you get Margaret to ring someone?'

'Like I said, Doc, she's useless.'

There was an SUV parked right where she wanted to drive.

It was serviceable, dirty white, a four-wheel drive wagon with a neat red sign across the side. The sign said: 'Wombat Valley Medical Service'.

It blocked the road completely.

She put her foot on the brake and her car came to a well-behaved standstill.

The road curved behind the SUV, and as her car stopped she saw the collapse of the verge. And as she saw more, she gasped in horror.

There was a truck below the collapse. Over the cliff!

A few hundred yards back she'd passed a sign declaring this area to be Wombat Valley Gap. The Gap looked to be a magnificent wilderness area, stretching beneath the road as far as the eye could see.

The road was hewn into the side of the mountain. The edge was a steep drop. Very steep. Straight down.

The truck looked as if it had rounded the curve too fast. The skid marks suggested it had hit the cliff and spun across to the edge. The roadside looked as if it had given way.

The truck had slipped right over and was now balanced precariously about ten feet down the cliff, pointing downward. There were a couple of saplings holding it. Just.

A woman was crouched on the verge, weeping, and Polly herself almost wept in relief at the sight of her. She'd escaped from the truck then?

But then she thought… SUV blocking the road. Wombat Valley Medical Service… Two vehicles.

Where was the paramedic?

Was someone else in the truck? Was this dramas, plural? *Help!*

She was a city doctor, she thought frantically. She'd never been near the bush in her life. She'd never had to cope with a road accident. Yes, she'd cared for accident victims, but that had been in the organised efficiency of a city hospital Emergency Room.

All of a sudden she wanted to be back in Sydney. Preferably off-duty.

'You wanted to be a doctor,' she told herself, still taking time to assess the whole scene. Her lecturers in Emergency Medicine had drilled that into her, and somehow her training was coming back now. *'Don't jump in before you've checked the whole situation. Check fast but always check. You don't want to become work for another doctor. Work out priorities and keep yourself safe.'*

Keeping herself safe had never been a problem in the ER.

'You wanted to see medicine at its most basic,' she reminded herself as she figured out what must have happened. 'Here's your chance. Get out of the car and help.'

My, that truck looked unstable.

Keep yourself safe.

The woman was wailing.

Who was in the truck?

Deep breath.

She climbed out of her car, thinking a flouncy dress covered in red and white polka dots wasn't what she should be wearing right now. She was also wearing crimson sandals with kitten heels.

She hardly had time to change. She was a doctor and she was needed. Disregarding her entirely inappropriate wardrobe, she headed across to the crying woman. She was big-boned, buxom, wearing a crinoline frock and an electric-blue perm. She had a man's jacket over her shoulders. Her face was swollen from weeping and she had a scratch above one eye.

'Can you tell me what's happened?' Polly knelt beside her, and the woman stared at her and wailed louder. A lot louder.

But hysterics was something Pollyanna Hargreaves could deal with. Hysterics was Polly's mother's weapon of last resort and Polly had stopped responding to it from the age of six.

She knelt so her face was six inches from the woman's. She

was forcing her to look at her and, as soon as she did, she got serious.

'Stop the noise or I'll slap you,' she said, loud and firm and cold as ice. Doctor threatening patient with physical violence... *Good one*, Polly thought. *That's the way to endear you to the locals*. But it couldn't matter. Were there people in that upside down truck?

'Who's in the truck?' she demanded. 'Take two deep breaths and talk.'

'I...my husband. And Doc...'

'Doc?'

'Doc Denver.'

'The doctor's in the truck?'

'He was trying to help Horace.' Somehow she was managing to speak. 'Horace was bleeding. But then the ground gave way and the truck slid and it's still wobbling and it's going to fall all the way down.'

The woman subsided as Polly once again took a moment to assess. The truck was definitely...wobbling. The saplings seemed to be the only thing holding it up. If even one of them gave way...

'Have you called for help?' she asked. The woman was clutching her phone.

'I called Doc...'

'The doctor who's here now?'

'Doc Denver, yes.'

'Good for you. How about the police? A tow truck?'

The woman shook her head, put her hands to her face and started loud, rapid breathing. Holly took a fast pulse check and diagnosed panic. There were other things she should exclude before a definitive diagnosis but, for now, triage said she needed to focus on the truck.

'I need you to concentrate on breathing,' she told the woman. 'Count. One, two, three, four—in. One, two, three, four—out. Slow your breathing down. Will you do that?'

'I…yes…'

'Good woman.' But Polly had moved on. Truck. Cliff. Fall.

She edged forward, trying to see down the cliff, wary of the crumbling edge.

What was wrong with Christmas in Sydney? All at once she would have given her very best shoes to be there.